HONORÉ DE BALZAC was born in Tours in 1799, the son of a civil servant. He spent nearly six years as a boarder in a Vendôme school, then went to live in Paris, working as a lawyer's clerk then as a hack-writer. Between 1820 and 1824 he wrote a number of novels under various pseudonyms, many of them in collaboration, after which he unsuccessfully tried his luck at publishing, printing and typefounding. At the age of thirty, heavily in debt, he returned to literature with a dedicated fury and wrote the first novel to appear under his own name, *The Chouans*. During the next twenty years he wrote about ninety novels and shorter stories, among them many masterpieces, to which he gave the comprehensive title *The Human Comedy*. He died in 1850, a few months after his marriage to Eveline Hanska, the Polish countess with whom he had maintained amorous relations for eighteen years.

MARION AYTON CRAWFORD taught English Language and Literature in the Technical College at Limavady, Northern Ireland. She translated five volumes of Balzac for the Penguin Classics: *Cousin Bette, Domestic Peace and Other Stories, Eugénie Grandet, Old Goriot,* and *The Chouans*. She died in 1973.

Honoré de Balzac

THE CHOUANS

TRANSLATED
WITH AN INTRODUCTION BY
MARION AYTON CRAWFORD

PENGUIN BOOKS

Penguin Books Ltd, Harmondsworth, Middlesex, England
Penguin Books, 40 West 23rd Street, New York, New York 10010, U.S.A.
Penguin Books Australia Ltd, Ringwood, Victoria, Australia
Penguin Books Canada Ltd, 2801 John Street, Markham, Ontario, Canada L3R 1B4
Penguin Books (N.Z.) Ltd, 182–190 Wairau Road, Auckland 10, New Zealand

—

This translation first published 1972
Reprinted 1978, 1984

—

Made and printed in Great Britain by
Hazell Watson & Viney Limited,
Member of the BPCC Group,
Aylesbury, Bucks
Set in Monotype Garamond

Contents

Translator's Introduction

As an enthralling tale of passion and adventure, for its depiction of an episode of civil war in Revolutionary times, in 1799, as close to the times when Balzac was writing as the 1939–1945 War is to our own, and for its evocation of the ancient and less distant past, and the beauty of a part of France – Brittany and the confines of Normandy – whose spell is felt by the increasing number of tourists who haunt it year by year, *Les Chouans* cries out for retranslation.

For those interested in the history of literature and the life and art of Balzac, it is a document of the first importance. *The Chouans* was the first volume of Balzac's life-work, *The Human Comedy*, one enormous historical novel which was to be the history in all its aspects of the three or four generations spanned by his own life, and was to initiate a way of looking at human beings and of writing their story that belongs to the modern world. The novel, not greatly esteemed as a literary form when Balzac wrote, was to become the characteristic genre of the nineteenth century, and he was one of the pioneers and the giant.

Balzac, aged thirty in 1829 when *The Chouans* appeared, had been writing to earn his bread ever since at the age of eighteen he had turned down the lawyer's career for which he had been destined and opted for literature. He had spent a year in a Paris garret on a starvation allowance provided by his parents to prove his talents, and had turned out an unreadable classical tragedy entitled *Cromwell*. In the intervening years he had written a mass of work, of which the six novels whose publication in 1836–7 he authorized as *Works of Youth* are only a small part. It was designed frankly to hit the market, written often in collaboration and published under strange pseudonyms, but regarded by Balzac as training in his art, for

7

he remained always conscious of his genius and sure of his high destiny as a writer.

His public was the growing and increasingly bourgeois one of post-Napoleonic times, when great social changes were accompanied by a ferment in literature, and France was wide open to influences from abroad and the new interests and materials of the Romantic Movement. A wave of translations, chiefly from English and German, swept the country. Following the fashion for sentimental romance and tales of 'Gothic' horror like those of Ann Radcliffe, 'Monk' Lewis and their French imitators, as well as, on a different level, Ossian, Byron and Shakespeare, there was a vogue in the 1820s for history and historical fiction. *Waverley* had appeared in 1814 and been rapidly followed by the best of Sir Walter Scott's other novels. Scott was a best-seller. There were many writers in France anxious to be 'the French Walter Scott' and many imitations, including a weak parody of *Ivanhoe* from Balzac in his early days. But most of the historical novels were mere escapist costume dramas set in the past against exotic backgrounds. They were written in single unrelated volumes whose authors took no note of the historical continuity of Scott's books, or of his immense interest in the surroundings and circumstances of everyday life not simply as background but as an expression of character and nature.

To Balzac's great credit and advantage he had grasped the true originality of Scott's novels. Scott had shown that society was not static as the eighteenth century had imagined and demonstrated its violent movement and change. He showed that beyond the great events of history what matters is their effect socially and economically on the lives of ordinary people. He presented characters typical of the trades, classes and varieties of men, with their characteristic clothing and accoutrement, and showed the same human material shaped by different circumstances of place and time.

Balzac early conceived the idea of doing the same thing for France. As Scott had brooded over the Jacobite rebellions, the Scottish Reformation, the struggles of the Covenanters against the Stuart kings, Balzac brooded over turbulent periods in the history of France: strife and civil war in the fifteenth century between Armagnacs and Burgundians, in the sixteenth between Valois monarchs and the Guises, and in the immediate past between the revolutionaries and the supporters of the Bourbons. When his financially disastrous business ventures between 1825 and 1828 into publishing, printing and typefounding came to an end he took the idea up again. We see him in the Preliminary Announcement for *The Gars* envisaging a vast task. He announces to begin with two volumes as a pair depicting civil war in Paris and the provinces: *The Captain of the Firebrands* set in the fifteenth century, and *The Gars* on the theme of Royalist uprisings in Revolutionary times. *The Captain of the Firebrands* was never written – we have only fragments of plans for it; but *The Gars* over a long period of expansion, revision and rewriting, in manuscript, proof and printed edition, was to become in turn *The Last Chouan or Brittany in 1800*, the title under which it was published in March, 1829; *The Chouans or Brittany in 1799* in the edition of 1834; and finally *The Chouans*, in the thirteenth volume of *The Human Comedy* among *Scenes of Military Life*, in 1845.

In the different stages through which the novel evolved, in the Preliminary Announcement for *The Gars*, the first edition of 1829 with its introduction, and the most carefully revised edition of 1834, the student is afforded a unique opportunity to watch Balzac searching for what he meant by the historical novel, acquiring methods of documentation and construction that he was to use in future novels, assimilating and transmuting elements from his omnivorous reading, developing the key ideas and principles of *The Human Comedy*.

The history of Balzac's whole life is the history of his realization, sometimes gradual, sometimes in blinding flashes of illumination, of what his *Human Comedy* (as it was eventually called), was to be and how he was to create it. With this novel he knew he had begun the achievement of his high aims as a writer, and he signed it, the only work he had ever so signed, Honoré Balzac, for he had not yet adopted the style of Honoré de Balzac.

9

It was a natural choice for Balzac to start his history not with the fifteenth-century work he had planned but with his father's generation in Revolutionary times. A series of sporadic counter-Revolutionary movements had started in 1792 in the West, and spread from the Vendée to the borders of Brittany and Normandy. They were led at first by the dispossessed minor clergy who refused to swear the required oath of allegiance to the Revolutionary civil powers, and later by noblemen relying on the Count of Artois who had promised to land in the West himself to lead a Royalist army, and on support from England and the Continent. Balzac had been familiar since boyhood with stories about the insurrectionists. His father had been living in Brest in 1795, as a civilian in charge of Army supplies. The accounts for the army under Hoche fighting the Royalists in the Vendée were in his care in Tours when his son Honoré was born there in 1799 – the year to be chosen for the events of the novel, the year when Napoleon seized power. There were many eye-witness accounts, journals and biographies of times still vivid in everyone's memory, written by people who could be questioned.

Balzac had read the Irish tales of Maria Edgeworth, whose descriptions of characters of different classes and of customs in an adjacent but strange-seeming country had had some influence on Scott. In a province where ancient Celtic antagonisms still held sway, in tradition and atmosphere farther from Paris than Northern Ireland is from London today, he found a setting ultimately affected as everything had been by the convulsions and searing catastrophes of Revolution and Terror, but sufficiently removed in place and time for detachment to be possible, and for the clash of interests and ideas in the swiftly changing world to be examined in isolation yet as part of the larger struggle.

A valuable family friend in this connection was a retired General, the Baron de Pommereul, who before fighting with Napoleon at Austerlitz, Eylau and Wagram had taken part in the campaign against the Chouans. He owned property in and near Fougères, which had been a centre of Chouannerie, and was living there. Balzac invited himself to stay, and remained several weeks during September and October 1828.

He charmed his host and was mothered by his hostess and her house-keeper, who so fattened him up that he had not lost his 'newly-acquired *embonpoint* and fresh colour' even some weeks after his return to Paris. His room with a small green table to work at looked out over the Couësnon Valley towards the Pellerine Mountain where the Vendéan leader General Lescure had died in a famous ambuscade in 1793. He spent much time in the Baron's well-furnished library, and more out of doors, talking to the local people, exploring the town with its ancient ramparts, the winding Nançon at their foot surrounding the feudal fortress, absorbing topographical detail and responsive to the characteristic beauty of the misty autumn landscape, with its streams and rivers, enclosing mountains and forest, oddly fortified fields and narrow hollow ways.

He was told tales of the risings which had occurred in the district and in Fougères itself between 1793 and 1800. His host owned a mansion in the country five or six miles to the north-east, the Marigny Castle, which earlier, under the ownership of the Comte de Marigny, had been a Royalist centre and head-quarters of the Comte de Puisaye. Balzac knew of Puisaye as one of the leaders at the disaster of Quiberon. A force of ten thousand French exiles had landed from British ships anchored off Quiberon in June 1795 and were joined by Chouans under Cadoudal, but they were routed by General Hoche and prevented by a heavy swell from re-embarking. The Convention refused to pardon them. Some were shot at Quiberon and the rest later taken to Auray and Vannes and shot there. Marigny, removed to a situation off the Mayenne-Fougères road, was to serve Balzac as model for La Vivetière. Marie de Verneuil, 'struck by a sudden memory', refers to one of Montauran's collaborators as being involved in the Quiberon affair and playing a dubious part in it. Cadoudal, known as 'the last Chouan', escaped and carried on the struggle. He was offered and refused a pardon and the rank of general by Napoleon. In 1804, he went to Paris to kidnap Napoleon and was captured and sentenced to death.

Balzac was also told stories of La Rouerie's anti-Revolutionary conspiracy of 1792 which ended with the execution of thirteen citizens of Fougères; of the attempt of insurgent peasants to carry the town in March 1793 and its capture in November of the same year by the Vendéan army; and of the tragic death of the Royalist leader Boishardy near Lamballe in 1795. General de Pommereul had known many of these heroes well.

In the Introduction to the first edition Balzac speaks of Montauran as a composite figure, and of 'a veteran well-informed about these events' to whom he is indebted for many facts. General de Pommereul is obviously also the person referred to in the note that ends the story in the later editions and relates it to later novels and to Balzac's own day, who had watched Marche-à-terre placidly driving a cow in Fougères market many years later.

Although General de Pommereul had served finally under Louis XVIII, it is said that he remained a Bonapartist at heart. To Balzac too by early sympathies and upbringing Napoleon was a hero. He has been accused of anti-legitimist feeling in *The Chouans* because of the unfavourable light in which he places the self-seeking and squabbling Royalist gentry and the Princes themselves, whom Montauran serves only as symbols of the monarchy, the cause whose righteousness he has never doubted. It is certain that in 1828 partisan feeling still ran strong in Fougères, and that Balzac heard of these events in the town's recent history from all points of view. It was noted there as recently as 1936 that political opponents still had the habit of denouncing one another as 'Chouan' or 'Blue'.

There were naturally many stories of the clergy, in particular of two fanatical priests, Abbé Bernier and Abbé Duval. Balzac does not flatter the *recteurs* in the person of Gudin as a type of the non-juring clergy in the West; and he does more than hint in the Introduction to the first edition that he is suppressing much worse things than Gudin's unscrupulous use of the religious fanaticism and superstitious awe of his flock as a political instrument.

However impressive the scene of dedication in the forest, reminiscent of the gatherings of Scott's Covenanters, Gudin is certainly not comparable to the disputatious divines of Scotland. We have only to think of the psychological complexity of Balfour in *Old Mortality*, for example, and Macbriar's profoundly moral self-forgetting fanaticism, to see how lacking in subtlety the portrait of Gudin is, and what an ignoble character he is made to appear. He is one with his parishioners in their greed and opportunist indifference to the larger issues of the war, and perhaps it is this oneness that Balzac is concerned to emphasize.

The *recteur* who marries Montauran and Marie is brought in too late to redress the balance, as a type of the clergy with no personal ambition who heroically resisted the State's attempt at secularization and did their duty as laid down by the Church. He is not individualized. His bland assurance to Marie that God will hear her prayer (for Montauran's safety) is echoed ironically (whether Balzac so meant it or not) by Marie's dying cry that God has indeed heard her, a too neatly contrived reminder that her prayer had been for a day with no morrow.

And what are we to think of the clergyman who took the Oath, d'Orgemont's brother, dead and plastered up in d'Orgemont's secret hiding-place? He is there partly to show Gudin's relentless ferocity against a man who has betrayed the cause, and partly to add horror to Marie's visit to the place.

In a letter to the Baron dated March, 1829, announcing that he would be sending a copy of his book five or six days later, Balzac said, 'Everything is yours, to the author's heart and pen and memories. Everything, from the song "Time to go, my lovely!" to the Mélusine Tower, grew out of our talks . . . I hope Madame de Pommereul will be amused by some of the details I have included – the *pichés*, resin candles, the marriage ceremonies [in the forest], the *haies*, the *échaliers*, and the difficulties of getting to the ball . . . I have not forgotten your charming wife's dislike of the title *The Gars*, and this has been changed . . .' He changed it at this stage to *The Chouans in Brittany Thirty Years Ago*, and then before publication to *The Last Chouan or Brittany in 1800*.

All this new material Balzac added to what he had previously learned about the Republican soldiery in conversation with his father. He had also talked about the manoeuvring of formally trained troops against guerrilla bands in guerrilla country with a group of instructors at the Military Academy of Saint-Cyr. He may have learned something too from the father of Horace Raisson, one of the literary tradesmen for whom he had worked, who had served in the police under Fouché and Desmarets. Balzac's problem now was one of construction, revision of episodes already written, alteration and addition of characters and scenes in intensive concentrated work that continued while the book was being set up by the printer. The book was not well-received in this edition by critics or public.

One of the strongest unifying forces in the mass of material is the increasing momentum of the narrative that brings with it an increasing involvement of the reader. Whether Balzac was unjust or not (in the Preliminary Announcement for *The Gars*) in calling Scott a worker in mosaic and marquetry (elsewhere he praises his *weaver's* art), the system of construction he evolves here and was to use consistently in the future owes a good deal to Scott. The Scottish novelist is accustomed in a leisurely way to acquaint the reader in great detail with scene and characters and apparently only casually related circumstances, and then he sets them all moving together in a closer contact with one another at an ever increasing pace. Balzac in *The Chouans* uses a much tighter composition from the beginning. Though the book moves off at the laggard pace of the unwilling Breton conscripts escorted by Hulot's column across the hills and valleys towards Maine, description and digression are continually interrupted by exciting incident. But the first episode is similarly an exposition, and by the end of it we have absorbed an enormous amount of information of all kinds, including the national military and political circumstances and the local situation, and absorbed it in an atmosphere of military tension and expectation.

With the love intrigue and the spy plot introduced and all the chief characters together in the Alençon inn, with currents of attraction and antagonism sparked off between Montauran, Marie, Madame du Gua and Corentin, Hulot involved in spite of himself, a Republican escort and Chouans all around, the second episode opens electrically, and tension increases steadily to the climactic events at La Vivetière.

The third episode is no anticlimax. The long description of Fougères with which it starts, a set piece in the style of Chateaubriand, involves much more than the merely picturesque. It integrates country with event and roots strange happenings firmly in reality. It is important for the reader too for relief and change of focus. But we are quickly made aware that nothing is concluded in the drama of the relations between Marie and Montauran; and from Madame du Gua's wild shot across the Nançon to the end we become more and more mesmerically held by the swift-moving series of sequences.

In the Preliminary Notice for *The Gars* Balzac speaks of his aim to 'represent peoples by certain figures pre-eminently typifying the common spirit' and also to show opposing ideas and forces in conflict. These key ideas of *The Human Comedy* he begins to work out in *The Chouans*. They are among the means by which, using a not unmanageably great number of characters, he presents a province, a civil war, a psychological drama, a spy plot and a tale of Chouans; and was later to present a whole society.

From the beginning Brittany is set against France in the persons of the military intruders – Hulot, his officers and men. Marche-à-terre at his first appearance is a symbolic figure – 'the spirit of Brittany risen from a three-year sleep' – dramatically confronting Hulot and slapping down the butt of his whip at the boundary of Brittany beyond which the conscripts will not go. With his voice like the horn the peasants use to call their beasts, his ox-like head and goatskin-covered body, he is indeed scarcely human but rather the soil of Brittany made flesh, and closely linked with the animal creation. Later he is to represent the Breton peasants in a quite different fashion, all too human in his unquestioning obedience to the narrow rules of conduct of his group when he comes with Pille-miche through the mist to execute grim justice on Galope-chopine for the treachery of which he was not in fact guilty.

In the first episode we meet every type of Breton except the gentry: the carefully described mixed band of conscripts, most of whom flee to join Marche-à-terre and the attacking Chouans, leaving a small group loyal to the Republican escort – including the younger Gudin (representative of the intelligent townsman, who as he tells his uncle, might have joined the Royalists 'if only the King had returned himself to lead his army'); and the travellers by the robbed post-chaise – Gudin the *recteur*, the banker (who is the wealthy and cunning kind of Breton who dares not take sides but buys up confiscated property), Pille-miche and the driver, a new Chouan recruited by the way. There are also the Republican Bretons in the National Guard from Fougères, who with their families and fellow-townsmen are to be in evidence throughout the book.

As there are Royalists and Republicans among the Bretons, so there are among the strangers, all intruders in Brittany, who meet at the inn in Alençon. Montauran, the Royalist leader, is as alien to the Bretons as Hulot, the Republican Commandant. He represents the aristocratic *émigrés*, not the Chouans or the provincial gentry. Marie de Verneuil, daughter of a Duke and brought up at the Court of Louis XVI, is only by life's accidents on the Republican side. With the Royalist Madame du Gua, what she represents is the whole class of aristocratic women set adrift and blown to one side or the other by the Revolutionary storm. She is a bridge between Royalist and Republican, and through her eyes we look at the Chouan and Vendéan leaders assembled at La Vivetière as Montauran identifies them for her, and at the dinner-table immediately afterwards note the contrast between them and the Republican officers, Merle and Gérard. They are all symbolic of the ideas they fight for. ' "Oh, they stand for the Nation and Liberty," she said to herself, and then, glancing at the Royalists; "and those men stand for one man, a King and Privilege." ' Merle and Gérard are also representative types of young men torn from their studies by the country's need. 'What do you think of the magistrates, surgeons and lawyers who are in charge of the Republic's affairs?' Montauran asks the Royalists round the dinner-table when Gérard has walked with dignity to his death, and Merle has taken the offered safe-conduct only to defy the Gars and swear to have his head. In addition they are representative types of Republican soldier. Merle – 'This gay soldier was so admirably typical of the French fighting man as one imagines him, whistling a tune amid flying bullets and always ready with some droll jest about an unlucky comrade.' Gérard – 'Serious and coolly self-possessed, he looked a true Republican in mind and heart, one of those men of whom at that period there was a host in the French armies, to which the noble devotion of obscure men lent a driving force unknown until then'. These two men, then, represent a political idea, and the professional classes who have taken up arms for the Republic as opposed to the Vendéan and Breton gentry, and they are also typical soldiers of France – members of the disciplined regular forces of the Blues as opposed to the Breton guerrilla bands.

Madame du Gua, for whom our sympathies are enlisted at the beginning, becomes in opposition to Marie a type of injured and revengeful woman, in places almost a symbolic figure of hatred, a classical tragic mask, as when Francine, observing her in horror and foreboding, sees a spirit from hell look out from this woman's face. She is a fore-runner of Cousin Bette.

Francine, like Marie, is a link between Brittany and France, a Breton unspoiled by the hothouse atmosphere of Paris just as Marie is a Parisian who cherishes memories of a Breton childhood. The essential Breton is unchanged, as Marie finds when, an alien surrounded by fanatical worshippers of a primitive religion, she turns to Francine for sympathy and finds that she is as completely convinced by the *recteur's* miracles as Galope-chopine. To a certain extent she is a symbolic figure representing Marie's conscience, as when she

17

urges Marie not to revenge herself on Montauran. 'If there were no joy in a hopeless love what would become of us poor women? God, Marie, . . . will recompense us for having fulfilled our vocation on earth, to love and endure!' It is the voice of many wives and mothers in *The Human Comedy* who by love and uncomplaining suffering raise themselves nearer to God, and the voice of one of Balzac's early religious convictions. Francine's love-affair with Marche-à-terre is one of the bonds tying the different kinds of character and fundamentally different kinds of story in *The Chouans* together.

Corentin stands apart, odious to the others, the serpent in what might be paradise to the lovers, ridiculous to Merle in his fashionable Parisian *Incroyable* garb, taken more seriously by Gérard, the laughing-stock of the Fougères National Guardsmen. He belongs to Paris and Fouché's web of intrigue, and links the aliens in Brittany with high political and police activity as Hulot links them with the Government, and with French armies and the surrounding enemies. He stands for power by cunning and diplomacy as Hulot and the men he commands are power by military force. He is set in opposition to the bluff Commandant, but Montauran is his quarry. It is amusing to note how the instinctive antipathy between this green-eyed serpent and the charming Montauran at their first meeting, and Montauran's affectation of ingenuous folly and carefully curled blond hair, make them the ancestors of antagonists in so much Revolution and police fiction, of innumerable intriguing villains and apparently inane, foppish, but brilliant fair-haired blue-eyed aristocratic heroes from the Scarlet Pimpernel to Lord Peter Wimsey.

Another dimension is given to the characters, and authenticity and vividness to the history, by the constant evocation of the past, especially through their memories of it. The remote and less distant past of Brittany surrounds and has moulded them in its man-raised stones from the megaliths and dolmens, the ancient stones of Fougères, its castle, ramparts and churches, to the traditional dwellings in faubourgs and little towns and rural cottages. It obstinately survives too in unpractical methods of farming and customs and such relics as

18

the broad-brimmed peasant's hat once worn only by the feudal seigneurs. It is the spirit of ancient feuds and wars that brings National Guardsmen of Fougères out against the Chouans. The personal histories of the characters are so many leads into the immediate history of their times. The four typical veterans picked out as scouts by Hulot had fought the Chouans before with him under Hoche. Most of Hulot's demi-brigade had fought in Italy under Napoleon, and survived the seige of Mayence. Marie de Verneuil hearing the shout of the Breton peasants in the forest 'Long live the King' cannot restrain her tears as she thinks of the murdered royal family and the scenes of her youth at Court. Her first intimate conversation with Montauran evokes the atmosphere of post-Terror Paris. Her Directoire dress at the ball, her hair dressed fashionably in the 'Grecian' style, show up the powdered provincial ladies in their silks and satins as the outmoded representatives of a bygone way of life, utterly changed by the Revolution, which to them seems a passing political disturbance. Her girlhood among the representatives of sceptical eighteenth century society that surrounded her father reminds us of a more distant past. Balzac's sense of the past alive in the present, and of the currents and stagnant pools in time, makes this book organically part of *The Human Comedy* and was to inspire Proust.

The brilliant skill displayed in the spinning together of the different strands of the plot, with its sensation and romance and military campaign, historical persons and events, psychological analysis, and typical characters is matched in the integration of very diverse elements in surroundings and atmosphere. One of these elements Balzac owed to Fenimore Cooper, the first three of whose *Leatherstocking Tales* of Red Indian life in the forests and wilderness had appeared and been translated by 1826. The Redskins' ability to become part of the landscape, their acute senses and their skill in reading clues had fascinated Balzac, and he gave some of these characteristics to his Chouans. Of more importance was his absorption of Cooper's feeling for a country's atmosphere and the inhabitants as part and manifestations of it.

The actual Breton countryside in autumn is pervasively present as the experience of all the characters, perpetually on the move about it, by day or night, riding ass or horse, by carriage or on foot, with its long vistas from high points and claustrophobic enclosed roads and fields, its effects of moonlight on water, the autumn sunshine and the pungent smell of dying leaves; and of this scene the Chouans are visually part. But there is as well a sense of supernatural participation, which the Chouans with their superstitious fears increase, and of the elements themselves being involved. The mountains incline their heads in solemn Wordsworthian conclave about Marie, alone on the St Sulpice Heights but surrounded by Chouans who flee from her in superstitious horror, as she flees from them. Gloom and croaking ravens prelude the grim Udolpho-like ruin of La Vivetière when the first shadow has been cast on the lovers. Marie, waiting for Montauran in Galope-chopine's cottage feels the snow-laden sky add nature's sadness to her own – 'There was misfortune in the air'. And finally mist closes in on the last act of the drama, preventing Marie from seeing Montauran's signal, allowing Montauran to enter Fougères unseen, affecting Corentin and Hulot – 'Mist and darkness wrapped the theatre in grim shadow where the drama plotted by this man was to be played out. . . . A deep solemnity had fallen on man and Nature'. In the marrying of the poetry of nature with what is supernaturally or elementally strange but dramatically true to the characters' emotions one is reminded of Coleridge's and Wordsworth's aims in *Lyrical Ballads*.

Balzac called his book 'a tragi-comic history'. The comedy sparkles throughout in the cut and thrust of wit, in brilliantly revelatory conversation, in the spirit and grim gaiety of people in tight corners or droll predicaments. The tragedy, although imposed by the romantic pattern, is like the tragedy of later novels in illustrating the ineluctable working of destiny. Hero and heroine are star-crossed lovers, whose fate is brought about by the forces of the times acting on their own internal weaknesses: the complex and ambivalent impulses of Marie's nature which she analyses for Montauran with a frank directness that misleads him; Montauran's light-mindedness and susceptibility to women. From these spring Marie's need to test Montauran's sincerity up to the hilt, and the urgent questions perpetually posed in new situations – will Marie betray the Gars, the genuineness of whose love she has sensational reason to doubt? – will the ever-deepening passion of the Gars lead him to risk his life yet again in still more dangerous circumstances? – which reach their climax and are answered in the final betrayal and final proof of love. Characters and situation are Balzac's demonstration that he is not himself guilty of what he calls Scott's inability to paint love other than as a static condition. Marie's self-analysis and criticism of Montauran's ideas, and Balzac's own comment, reflect a great deal of thought on Balzac's part about the relations between the sexes, and in particular about the psychological and social situation of women in marriage and out of it, a matter that profoundly interested him and was to be a major theme of *The Human Comedy*. One remembers that he had read Stendhal's treatise *On Love*, published in 1822, and that he had himself already sketched a light and flippant *Physiology of Marriage*, later to be rewritten, not in a serious tone but with serious consideration and diagnosis of the ills of marriage and understanding of feminine frustrations. This second version was to be published in December, 1829, later in the year of *The Chouans*.

Balzac's personal life had focused his attention on such matters early. Of his father, Balzac's sister, Laure Surville, wrote 'he had something of Montaigne, Rabelais and Uncle Toby in his philosophy'; and Balzac was accustomed to free and frank discussion of all matters in his own home. His father was fifty-three when this son was born, and his mother thirty-two years younger. He himself since the age of twenty-three had been involved in the love-affair with Madame Louise-Antoinette-Laure de Berny, then aged forty-five, that was a major influence in his life. Madame de Berny owed her first two names to Louis XVI and Marie-Antoinette, her godparents. Her mother had been Woman of the Bedchamber to the Queen, and she had grown up at Court. During the

Terror she had been married (at barely sixteen) to provide her with protection, and had lived apart from her husband from 1800–1805 with a Corsican to whom she had borne a daughter. It was natural that Marie de Verneuil in the first edition of *The Chouans* should be modelled on Laure de Berny.

The character was one over which he continued to take great pains. For the edition of 1834 his revisions made the character more subtle and complex, and he curbed some of the freedoms of expression in order to make it more pleasing to Countess Evelina Hanska, whom he was eventually to marry in March, 1850, less than six months before his death. 'If you only knew how much there is of you in every altered phrase of *Chouans*!' he wrote to her in 1834.

Though Montauran in spite of his heroic role has fundamental weaknesses, his loyalty to his cause is never in doubt. In all his meetings with leaders, however, Balzac is concerned to suggest the unreliability of their support and the inevitable failure of his mission. The collapse of the insurrection is prepared before the tragedy of the lovers, and Montauran's arranged flight with Marie to England is not a flight like Antony's from his military responsibilities. The end of the love story is irrelevant to history. The forces of reaction in the west will not affect Revolutionary change. Napoleon, in his desire for the fusion of old and new, is to uphold the principles of the Revolution, allow *émigrés* to return and Catholics to practise their religion in peace.

In the vast series of inter-related works on contemporary history that Balzac envisaged in 1833 to take the place of the series of historical novels extending over centuries that he had formerly planned, *The Chouans* became almost the first chronologically of the new series instead of the last of the old. He planned that it should be one of a number of *Scenes of Military Life*, announced in the Preface to his *Philosophical Studies* in 1834. In the short Preface to the third edition of 1845, translated below, he mentions that of the *Scenes of Military Life* in preparation *The Chouans* is the only one completed, that it represents one aspect of civil war – guerrilla warfare – at the turn of the century, and that the other aspect

– open warfare – is to be the subject of another novel, *The Vendéans*. That novel, dealing with the earlier war of insurrection in the West, is often spoken of in Balzac's plans, its publication is even announced for 1837, it is listed in the Catalogue of 1832, and in 1844 he speaks of going to the West 'to do *The Vendéans*', but it was never to be written.

Balzac had meant to cover the entire story of the French Army's wanderings through Europe during the Napoleonic era, including at least one full-scale battle (Wagram) conceived as early as 1830. But of the four volumes planned for his *Scenes of Military Life* in the edition of *The Human Comedy* whose sixteen volumes were published between 1842 and 1846 only one was written, of which *The Chouans* remained the most important piece.

Threads from *The Chouans*, however, are woven into other works of *The Human Comedy* in various references and through the reappearance of a number of characters. In *A Murky Business* (*Une Ténébreuse Affaire*), published in 1841, an older Corentin reappears, still a cold subtle serpent, still a dandy, and still an agent of Fouché's. The story of it Balzac's parents had heard from the elder General de Pommereul, father of Balzac's host at Fougères, and the book has something of the atmosphere of *The Chouans*. There is also a memorable description of the meeting of the heroine with Napoleon on the eve of the battle of Jena.

Montauran is alluded to in many other novels. Hulot is seen again in *The Provincial Muse* (1843), in Madrid, still a Colonel, with Beau-pied, now a Captain, still under his command. He is made General and Comte de Forzheim by the Emperor, and is seen in *Cousin Bette* (1846) in retirement, full of years and honours, a Marshal and Peer of France, with Beau-pied as his factotum. When he dies the funeral of the old Republican is followed by Montauran's younger brother, 'brother of the Comte de Montauran who had been Hulot's ill-fated adversary in 1799'. This character appears in other novels. Montauran's dying wish for this brother Balzac wrote into *The Chouans* when he revised it for the collected edition, and he also altered the names of a few minor characters to those of characters appearing elsewhere, added the picture of Marche-à-terre in Fougères market-place and dated the novel, first Paris, January 1828, and then Fougères, August 1827. In the final lines he alluded to 'the famous trial involving Rifoël, Bryond and La Chanterie, and the Chouan Pille-miche whose real name was Jean Cibot'. This was a trial for participation in a Royalist plot of 1808, and links the novel with others.

While he was revising *The Chouans* in 1843 Balzac wrote this to Madame Hanska: 'There's no doubt about it – it is a magnificent poem. I had never really *read* it before. It's now ten years since I revised it for a second edition. I've now had the pleasure of reading my work critically and considering its merits. It's full of Cooper and Walter Scott, with in addition a passion and *verve* due to neither of them. The passion is sublime, and I now understand why you have cherished a special devotion to this book. The country and the war are portrayed in it with a truth and felicity that surprised me. All in all, I am very pleased with it'.

There are few of his readers who will not concur in Balzac's verdict.

The text translated in this edition is the final one prepared by Balzac just before his death, with the division he then made into three parts; the chapter divisions of the first two editions which he had had to eliminate for reasons of economy have been restored. The alterations made by Balzac between the first two editions may be easily studied in the Garnier edition prepared by M. Maurice Regard. A translation is appended of parts of the Preliminary Announcement for *The Gars*, the Introduction to the first edition (which served with only very minor cuts and alterations for the second), and the Preface to the third edition.

My thanks are due to Mr Raymond Wright and pupils of Limavady Technical College for plans of Fougères and the country where the action of the novel took place, and for typing the translation.

M.A.C.

Extracts from the Preliminary Announcement for

The Gars

THIS fragment at the beginning of the manuscript of *The Last Chouan* purports to be written by the editor of the forthcoming work (*The Gars*) on behalf of the fictitious author, Victor Morillon. It mingles autobiographical truth about Balzac with fiction in its description of Morillon as a simple peasant who had studied 'under the rod' of a former Oratorian hidden during the Revolution by his parents (as Balzac had studied at the Jesuit Collège de Vendôme), reading his master's books, and for long years living a hermit's life, but among his fields and under the thatched roof of his cottage experiencing a phantasmagoric life of the imagination, taking on the identity and living in the circumstances of the persons he read about with an intensity and reality that made their experience his own. Parts of this were to be expanded later in the more or less autobiographical work *Louis Lambert*, published 1832.

Sometimes Morillon speaks directly to the editor in a letter, with Balzac's voice. In answer to a letter pointing out the danger of writing a novel in the style of Walter Scott:

I do not believe in a nation so unjust as to reject as plagiarist a man who venturing to take his country's life and history as his subject tries to portray them in a recently approved form. I am not aware that the German critics stopped M. de Goethe from writing by objecting that he would be aping Shakespeare. *La Métromanie, Les Plaideurs, Le Joueur,** I think, are not less masterpieces for being composed in the style of Molière's comedies. Was the poet who composed the second quatrain or the second eclogue felled by the crushing argument that he was walking in another man's footprints? If one does not combine with the creator's instinct that of the man who finds a new accepted form to mould his creations in, termed system, manner, school, does it follow that one must abstain from creation? Is there a *school* of those who wish to paint

* Comedies by Piron, 1738; Racine, 1683; Regnard, 1696.

landscapes, and real men wearing actual clothes? Because Teniers depicted Dutch people smoking tobacco and drinking beer, may a painter not depict Neapolitans celebrating the grape harvest? Finally, in what way does open-hearted France going gaily to war resemble crafty and prosaic England? One might as well say that a cock is the same creature as a fox.

As for me, gentlemen, I do not mean in any way to denigrate Sir Walter Scott. I regard him as a man of genius. He knows the human heart, and if on his lyre the strings are missing that can sing of love (for he presents it ready-made, never springing up, never developing) his brushes make history domestic. When one has read him one understands a century better, he evokes its spirit and in a single scene can express its essential genius and physiognomy.

However as the creator of a genre – I think of certain remarks of Champfort's, some pages by Pigault-Lebrun (who has not received adequate recognition), Ann Radcliffe's descriptions, of Cervantes and Beaumarchais, of Vandyck's portrait of Charles I, and imagine that the Scottish cabinet-maker's thought and skilful fingers by selection and arrangement have made a splendid piece of Marquetry. His style is a successful mosaic. In him the painter is superior to the workman and he has given us admirable paintings. The colours are there for everyone, for after all one can only use nature herself and what makes a man of genius is his ability to solve the problem of making a better setting for her than others . . .

The writer speaks of himself as

a man whose conscientious endeavour it is to place his country's history in the hands of the man in the street, make it popular by the interesting arrangement, awaken the taste for historical study by books which will above all satisfy the growing need to feed the mind created by our present-day civilization . . . a man who is trying to supply hunger with more substantial dishes, attempting to present scenes from ordinary life, that paint the national history by means of the little-known facts of our manners and usages for imaginations weary of wickedness; to illuminate and make the ordinary mind realize the repercussions that entire populations feel of royal discord, feudal dissension and popular uprising; to show the consequences of setting up legal institutions to serve particular interests, requirements of the moment or the conflicting aims of kings or feudal lords; to configure kings through their peoples, and peoples by certain figures most eminently typifying the common spirit; a man who endeavours to portray the immense variety and detail of life down the centuries, give an idea of the vibrations of the forces set up by intense religious fanaticism; in sum, to put an end to the making a charnel-house of history, a gazette, an official register of the nation, a chronological skeleton. Such a man must continue long on his way without heeding outcry and clamour before he is understood. He will halt if he realizes through the voices of faithful friends that the task is beyond his strength. If he has had the courage to undertake it, he will have the courage to understand that a great conception and a powerful will do not always provide the talent for execution.

The tragi-comic history he has undertaken is sufficiently vast to command respect, has sufficiently noble aims not to suffer defamation. It has lessons to teach as impressive as those of the classic Muse of history, and less tedious, perhaps even more deeply discerning. His work has as much claim to public esteem as that of the courageous young historians who find their way through a thousand impediments to study the spirit of the darkest eras of our history, endeavouring to bring to light again the truth concealed by the priesthood, mutilated by the aristocracy, and so opening the road to those who come with a more daring imagination to chisel and decorate the monument whose first stones they have laid . . .

In any case, I shall soon learn by the publication of *The Gars* and *The Captain of the Firebrands* whether I am only a village fiddler or an artist worthy of your concert performances. There is just one consideration that even if I fail will win me respect. The village fiddler must learn the same elements of his art as Lafont, Baillot and Jarnovick,* and in this case the foundation is history with its thousands of conflicting volumes, the elements are men and things, dress in its most fleeting fashions, the language with the neologisms added by every new event, furniture and architecture, changes in the law, customs. Even for a mediocre work one must have read prodigiously, studied and reflected . . .

The so-called editor writing the Preliminary Announcement declares that he chose *The Gars* from two works offered: *The Captain of the Firebrands* set in the turbulent period of the fifteenth century and the contemporary history of *The Gars* – which present contrasting pictures of civil war in different eras, one set in the provinces, the other in the heart of Paris.

* Three famous violinists: Lafont, 1781–1839; Baillot, 1771–1841; Jarnovick, 1745–1804.

Introduction to the First Edition, 1829

IN taking as the subject of his work a very important part of contemporary history which is at the present time a very delicate matter, the author finds it necessary to declare solemnly that it has never been his intention to hold opinions or persons up to ridicule or contempt. He respects convictions; and the majority of the persons are unknown to him. It will not be his fault if events speak for themselves and in no uncertain voice. He has neither created nor discovered them. His imagination has not been called on to supply any part of all he has transferred to this scene, the only kind of work in which a writer may feel free to set forth a drama in its whole truth. In this book the country is the real country, the men the true men, and the words are the words they used. The facts have not been contradicted by the Memoirs published during the various phases of the Restoration nor by the French Republic. Only the Empire's dark censorship suppressed them; and to say that this work would not have seen the light during Napoleon's reign is to do honour to public opinion which has won us liberty.

The author has tried to relate the events of one of those sadly instructive incidents in which the French Revolution was so prolific.

The existence of certain interested persons has made it necessary for him to be strictly exact in his delineation, and to use only such licence as is permitted to a painter in his endeavour to present a good portrait: to set the subject in a natural light and make him convincingly alive. But one must define the word 'exact'. The author has not felt himself obliged to lay the facts out tediously one by one and demonstrate how far history may be reduced to the state of a skeleton with carefully listed bones. Today it is requisite that the great lessons written in history's pages should be popularized and made available to everyone. Accordingly, following the practice in recent years of certain talented men, the author has tried to reproduce the spirit of an age in this book and bring historical events to life. He prefers to present living speech rather than documentary evidence, the battle in progress rather than an official report, dramatic action rather than chronicle. So none of the results of this national strife, however minor, have been omitted, and none of the dreadful events that shed blood over so many now peaceful fields. The persons concerned will find themselves there, full face or in profile, in full light or in shadow, and even the least decisive misfortunes are shown as they occurred or in the causes that led to them.

However, respect for a number of persons of high social standing, whom it would serve no purpose to name and who have miraculously reappeared on the political scene, has led the author to dilute the horror of a great many circumstances. He has singularly omitted, for example, any demonstration of the part played by the clergy in these calamitous and futile outbreaks of violence. His hesitation is the result of his reading of the official reports of certain Revolutionary trials in the West, full of sworn evidence that even in the dry official form could not be brought into the light of day without considerable odium. In the case of many families, of course, certain trials bear glorious testimony to devotion and have become rightly famous.

In the person of the *Last Chouan* the author pays homage and lays a wreath. That character testifies to the author's whole-hearted respect for convictions. If some fact-pinning persons should seek to know which of the noble victims of Republican bullets he is, they must choose among several noblemen who fell while leading the insurrections of 1799. The personal qualities possessed by a young aristocrat and information given by a veteran well-informed about these events may have served to complete and polish the *Last Chouan*, but the author finds himself obliged to confess that the hero of this book is not an exact portrait of the real leader. In thus indicating the fictitious parts of the work he hopes to assist the reader to recognize the truth of what is factual.

Politic considerations of the kind mentioned above have induced the author to set his name to the book, although a very understandable diffidence about a first work might have counselled him to suppress it. From the literary point of view, he reflected that it is perhaps more modest to sign a book, since there are so many who have made anonymity a proud advertisement.

As for the book's story, he does not present it as new, as one may see by the epigraphy*, but it is deplorably true to the facts, with the exception that events which take four or five days in the narrative actually happened in forty-eight hours. The horror of the speed with which the actual catastrophe was precipitated might perhaps have been mitigated even further. The facts are atrocious, and for what he has done the author finds his excuse in human nature.

As at the moment of writing he is ignorant of the fate of a number of actors in his drama, he has altered several names; and his feelings of delicacy also extend to place-names.

The Fougères *district* will not be so unfriendly as to reproach him with having made it the theatre of events that took place several leagues away. Was it not natural to choose one of the cradles of Chouannerie, and perhaps the most picturesquely situated place in these lovely regions, to represent *Brittany in 1800*?

Many persons of taste and leaders of feminine fashion will no doubt regret that the author has not given them Chouans and Republican soldiers as little like the real thing in costume and speech as the savages in the tragedy *Alzire*† or the comic-opera *Azemia*‡; but he had more important problems to solve than that of putting a pretty dress on Truth.

May this work help to realize the prayers of all the pro-

---

* From the Book of *Judith*:

'She was marvellously beautiful . . .

'And Judith said, "Who am I to refuse my lord? Surely whatever pleases him I will do at once, and it will be a joy to me until the day of my death! . . ."

'And she struck his neck twice with all her might, and severed his neck from his body.'

† By Voltaire.   ‡ By Soisson de la Chaboussière.

vince's friends for the betterment, materially and in civilized attitudes, of Brittany! Civil war came to an end there almost thirty years ago, but not ignorance. Agriculture, education, commerce, have not advanced one step in half a century. The poverty of the countryside is worthy of feudal times and superstition takes the place of Christ's teaching.

One of the most powerful obstacles to the undertaking of very generous projects lies in the obduracy of the Breton character. The question of Brittany's prosperity is no new one. It was fundamentally the cause of the lawsuit between La Chalotais and the Duc d'Aiguillon.*

The upheaval in men's minds in the rapid onset of the Revolution has until now prevented the re-examination of this celebrated lawsuit; but when an upholder of truth comes to throw some light upon this clash, the historically accepted faces of oppressor and oppressed will show a different aspect to that given by contemporary opinion. The national patriotism of a man who perhaps sought only to do what was best for the Treasury and the Kingdom met the narrow provincial patriotism that is so harmful to the progress of civilization. The Minister was in the right, but oppressive; the victim wrong, but in chains; and in France regard for liberality stifles even justice. Oppression is as odious for the sake of right as in justifying wrong.

Monsieur d'Aiguillon had tried to have Brittany's embanked hedges razed, to give Brittany bread by introducing the cultivation of barley, build roads and canals, make French the spoken language, improve commerce and agriculture; in sum, to sow the seed that would bring comfortable conditions

* In his attempt to modernize Brittany, the Duc d'Aiguillon, Governor of Brittany, clashed with the Breton Parliament over the imposition of new taxes. Later, in 1761, a new subject of dispute arose in the attempt by the Jansenist Breton lawyers to have the Jesuit Colleges, very powerful in Brittany, closed. La Chalotais, the Public Prosecutor, by his Report induced the Breton Parliament to vote the dissolution of the Order. When the Councillors refused the Governor's request to reconsider its decision, Louis XV summoned them to Paris, sent three into exile, and the rest resigned. In Paris, the Paris Parliament supported the Rennes Parliament.

to the majority and enlightenment to all. Such were the long-term aims of the measures whose framing gave rise to this impassioned dispute. There was hope for a fertile and prosperous future for the country.

People of sincere good-will may well be astonished to learn that the victim defended the abuses, the ignorance, the feudal system and the aristocracy, and called for tolerance only for the sake of perpetuating his country's wrongs! There were two men in that man: the Frenchman whose liberal voice in important matters of the national interest proclaimed the most beneficent principles, and the Breton to whom ancient prejudices were so dear that, like Cervantes' hero, he talked the utmost nonsense with great determination and eloquence as soon as the question arose of removing Brittany's disabilities. The Breton La Chalotais has found successors recently who have declared themselves guardians of the ignorance of this unhappy land. On the other hand, Monsieur Kératry has depicted the other La Chalotais in a way that does him honour,* so that it takes the two extreme wings of the Chamber to piece this illustrious Breton together.

Today, in 1829, a newspaper remarks that a Breton regiment of the French Army has arrived back in Nantes after travelling across France and being garrisoned in Spain, without a single man having learned a word of French or Spanish. It was Brittany on the move, traversing France like a Gallic tribe.

That is one of the results of Monsieur de La Chalotais's victory over the Duc d'Aiguillon.

The author will say no more on this subject. It could not be appropriately treated in the book, and its ramifications are too many for an introduction.

If some practical considerations may have a place after all in these political and literary credos, the author here warns the reader that he has tried to import the little typographical con-

---

* In a controversy which two newspapers, *Le Courrier* and *L'Etoile*, were conducting in 1826, Kératry, a Breton and liberal Deputy, defended La Chalotais.

vention by which English novelists indicate the gestures of persons engaged in conversation . . .*

* There follows a paragraph on the English use of the dash to show interruptions of the dialogue for a shrug or a nod. In French the dash introduces direct speech. The first edition of *The Chouans* contains a great many dashes, which disappear in subsequent editions.

Preface to the Third Edition, 1845

THIS work is my first, and its success was tardy. I could not promote its acceptance in any way, occupied as I was, and still am, by the vast undertaking of which it is such a small part. Today, I have just two remarks to make.

Brittany knows the actual events on which this drama is based; but related events of some months in fact took place in twenty-four hours. Apart from this poetic licence used with regard to time, even the most minor incidents of the book are completely true, and the descriptions are authentic to the last detail.

The style, originally involved and extremely faulty, has now the relative perfection which permits a writer to present a work with which he is not too displeased.

Among the *Scenes of Military Life* which I am preparing, it is the only completed work. It presents one of the facets of civil war in the nineteenth century – guerrilla warfare; the other – organized military civil war – will be the subject of *The Vendéans*.

Paris
January 1845

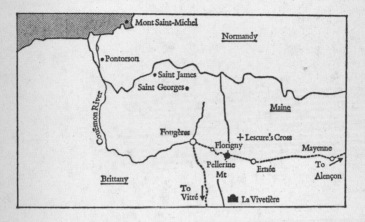

General Map of Fougères and Surroundings

PART ONE – THE AMBUSCADE

Chapter 1

IN the New Year of the year VIII, one day at the beginning of the month of Vendémiaire, or towards the end of September 1799 in the present calendar, a crowd of about a hundred peasants together with a large number of townsmen were climbing the Pellerine Mountain. They had left Fougères that morning to march to Mayenne; the Pellerine lies about half-way between Fougères and the little town of Ernée which is a usual halting-place for travellers. The dress of the groups large and small that made up this party was such a bizarre mixture, and the persons themselves seemed such a mixed collection from different places and different occupations, that a description may be useful, and serve to add to this story the bright colours that people prize so highly nowadays, although in the view of some critics they stand in the way of the portrayal of human emotion.

Some of the peasants, the majority indeed, went barefoot and were clad each only in a great goatskin, which reached from neck to knees, and breeches of very coarse white cloth, whose rough badly-trimmed yarn was evidence of the region's lack of interest in industrial skills. Their long lank locks seemed part and parcel of the hair of their goatskins and hid their downcast faces so completely that at a first glance it was easy to imagine the goatskins to be their own pelt, and confuse these wretches with the animals that clothed them. One soon saw their eyes shining through this hair like dewdrops in thick verdure; but the human intelligence they revealed was no pleasant surprise, but terrifying rather. On his head each wore a dirty red woollen cap, like the Phrygian cap that the Republic was adopting at that time as the emblem of Liberty, and each carried a heavy gnarled oak stick across his shoulders with a not very well-filled long cloth bag hanging at the end of it.

A clumsy wide-brimmed felt hat was worn over the cap by a different group, with a vari-coloured woollen chenille cord for trimming round the crown. The clothes of these were made of the same material as the breeches and bags of the others, and there was little in their costume to show a connection with modern civilization. Their long hair fell over the collars of round jackets, with narrow, vertical, cuffed pockets, which barely covered their hips, garments characteristic of the peasants of the West. Under the open jacket a large-buttoned waistcoat of the same stuff was visible. Some of them wore sabots, while others carried their foot-gear economically in their hands.

The dress of this second group, though soiled by long use and discoloured by sweat and dust, was less eccentric than that of those first described and so had the merit, historically speaking, of serving as transition to the comparatively sumptuous attire of a few men here and there among the throng who shone like flowers. It is no exaggeration to say that the blue cloth breeches of these men and their red or yellow waistcoats, adorned with two parallel rows of copper buttons and close-fitting like a cuirass, stood out as strikingly against the white clothes and goatskins of their companions as cornflowers and poppies in a cornfield. A few wore the kind of sabot Breton peasants make themselves but most of them had heavy nailed shoes, and coats of very coarse cloth cut in the old French style still religiously preserved by our peasants. Their shirt collars were fastened with heart- or anchor-shaped silver buttons. Finally, their bags seemed better furnished than those of their companions, and several of them were equipped for the road with a flask, no doubt filled with brandy, hanging by a string round their necks.

A number of townsmen were to be seen among these half-barbarous men, as if to mark civilization's farthest boundaries in these regions. They wore round or cocked hats or peaked caps and top-boots or shoes held by gaiters, and their costume, like the peasants', divided them into groups showing notable differences. About ten of them wore the Republican jacket known as the *carmagnole*. Others, no doubt prosperous artisans, were clad from head to foot in cloth of the same colour. The smartest were distinguished by dress coats or riding coats of more or less threadbare blue or green cloth. These last were veritable personages. They wore boots of various kinds and flaunted heavy walking-sticks with the air of men courageously making the best of a very bad business. A few carefully powdered heads and passably well-dressed queues showed the studied elegance of those who are beginning to rise in the world, through improved fortunes or education.

Anyone looking at this apparently haphazard collection of men quite surprised to find themselves in each other's company might have thought that a fire had driven a town's population from their homes; but the nature of the times and the place gave a very special interest to this gathering.

Almost all the members of the band had been fighting against the Republic four years before. It would have been easy for an observer aware of the internal discords then agitating France to pick out the few citizens on whose loyalty the Republic might depend, for one final very striking difference between the individuals in this mass of men left the division between their political sympathies in no doubt. Only the partisans of the Republic marched almost gaily. As for the others, they might wear a wide variety of dress but their expressions and attitudes had the uniformity misfortune imposes. Peasants or townsmen, profound melancholy marked them all. Their silence was fiercely sullen. Their spirits seemed weighed down by the same heavy thought, which though it was undoubtedly grim could only be guessed at, for their faces were quite impenetrable. Only the extraordinary slowness of their march might seem to give away some secret calculation. A few among them, distinguished by the rosary worn round their necks in spite of the risk involved in preserving this evidence of a religion which had been suppressed but by no means destroyed, from time to time shook back their locks and raised their heads cautiously. They then stealthily scanned the woods, paths and great rocks that closed in on the way, like a dog putting his nose to the wind trying to scent game; but hearing only the monotonous tramp of their silent companions, lowered their heads again and resumed their despairing expressions, like criminals being led to the hulks to live or die there as they might.

The march of this column towards Mayenne, its heterogeneous character and the different loyalties it professed were explained naturally enough by the presence of another party forming the vanguard. About a hundred and fifty soldiers were marching at the head with arms and baggage, under the command of a Demi-brigade Commandant. This appellation at that time replaced the proscribed rank of Colonel, which had sounded too aristocratic to patriots' ears, as those who were not involved in the drama of the Revolution may need to be told. The soldiers belonged to an infantry demi-brigade stationed at Mayenne. In these times of civil strife the natives of the West nicknamed all Republican soldiers the *Blues*, because of their first blue and red uniforms which are still well enough remembered to make description unnecessary.

The detachment of Blues, then, was acting as escort to a collection of men nearly all rebellious at being sent to Mayenne, where the military discipline was calculated to make short work of giving them the corporate feeling and uniformity of dress and behaviour and marching pace so noticeably lacking at the moment. The column was the unwillingly drafted contingent from the Fougères district due in accordance with a decree of the Directory Government of the French Republic made law on the preceding 10 Messidor.

The Government had called for ten million francs and a hundred thousand men in order to send immediate aid to the armies at that time defeated by the Austrians in Italy and the Prussians in Germany, and threatened in Switzerland by the

Russians, whom Suvorov had led to hope for the conquest of France. The Departments of the West known as the Vendée and Brittany and part of the confines of Normandy, which had been pacified by General Hoche in 1796 after a four-year civil war, appeared to have seized this opportune moment to start the struggle again.

Assailed on so many sides, the Republic had rediscovered its pristine vigour. It had first provided for the defence of the endangered Departments by delegating the responsibility to the inhabitants who had remained loyal, by one of the articles of the Messidor law. The Government had neither men nor money available for use internally so it got round the difficulty by a piece of Gascon sleight of hand – with nothing to send to the insurgent Departments it bestowed its trust upon them. Perhaps there was also some hope that by arming the citizens against one another this measure would cut down the insurrection at its source. The article, destined to have disastrous repercussions, was framed in these terms: *Citizen Companies shall be raised in the Departments of the West for military service.*

This impolitic act excited such hostility in the West that from the very beginning the Directory had no hope of overcoming it. Accordingly, a few days later, the Assemblies were asked to approve special measures for the small contingents due in respect of the article authorizing Citizen Companies. A new law, then, promulgated some days before the beginning of this story and made effective on the third complementary day of the year VII, decreed the organization into Legions of these small bodies of conscripted men. The Legions were to bear the names of the Departments of Sarthe, Orne, Mayenne, Ille-et-Vilaine, Morbihan, Loire-Inférieure and Maine-et-Loire. *These Legions,* so the law declared, *whose special mission is to fight the Chouans shall not under any circumstances be moved beyond the frontiers.*

These details, tedious perhaps but not generally known, show the weakness of the Directory and explain the movement of this troop of men led by the Blues. It is perhaps not superfluous to add that these fine and patriotic resolutions of the Directory were entered in the Statute Book but never executed. The Decrees of the Republic were no longer backed by grand idealistic conceptions, patriotism or the Terror, which formerly had made them effective, and they raised vast sums of money and forces of men on paper, none of which the Treasury or the Army ever saw. The impetus of the Revolution had been dissipated in unskilful hands, and circumstances decided how laws should be applied instead of being controlled by them.

The Departments of Mayenne and Ille-et-Vilaine were at this time under the command of an experienced officer who took expediency as his guide and was anxious to extract Brittany's contingents from her and withdraw them particularly from Fougères, one of the hot-beds of Chouan revolt. He hoped in this way to weaken the districts that offered a threat. This loyal soldier took advantage of the airy provisions of the law to announce that he would equip and arm the *requisitionary soldiers* at once, and have available a month's pay at the rate the Government had promised for these exceptional levies.

The Bretons at this time were refusing to have any truck with any kind of military service, but on the strength of these promises the operation was successful from the start, so successful that the officer became uneasy. He was a wary old war-dog, hard to catch out, and as he saw a large part of the required contingents flock to the district he smelt a rat. His guess that they were coming in so eagerly only in order to obtain arms was probably correct. Without waiting for laggards he prepared to try to effect his withdrawal to Alençon nearer more settled country, although the fact that the insurrection was spreading in these regions made the success of the plan very doubtful. He had followed instructions in breathing no word of our armies' misfortunes or the unreassuring news from the Vendée.

So it was that on the morning when this story begins this officer was attempting to reach Mayenne by a forced march, and once there he had every intention of executing the law according to his own ideas and replenishing the ranks of his demi-brigade with his Breton *conscripts*. This word *conscript,* later to become so well-known, had just for the first time replaced in the laws the name *requisitionary soldiers* originally given to Republican recruits. Before leaving Fougères the Commandant had issued ammunition to his soldiers and rations for the whole body of men in secret, in order to avoid calling the attention of the conscripts to the length of the march they were to make; and he had no mind to make a halt at Ernée, where the new recruits as they recovered from their shock might very well join hands with the Chouans of whom there were no doubt a great many in the surrounding country.

The glum silence of the crowd of men whom the old Republican's manoeuvre had taken by surprise and their snail's pace over this mountain had kept the Commandant, called Hulot, on the alert. He was keenly interested by the striking features of the contingent which have been noted above. And he walked in silence, surrounded by five young officers who were silent too out of respect for their chief's abstraction. But as Hulot reached the summit of the Pellerine and instinctively turned his head suddenly to inspect the uneasy faces of the requisitionary men he broke into forthright speech, for the increasing slowness of these Bretons had put a gap of some two hundred paces between their escort and them. Hulot's face puckered in a characteristic grimace.

'What the devil's holding up these Royalist dandies?' he exclaimed in a deep resonant voice. 'Our conscripts need to stir their stumps; they're closing their compass legs instead of opening them, I think!'

As he spoke his escorting officers turned involuntarily as if suddenly waking with a start. The sergeants and corporals followed their example, and the detachment came to a standstill without having heard the longed-for word 'Halt!'.

The officers may have glanced at first at the contingent winding like a long slug up the mountain, but they were so struck by the view that met their eyes that they made no answer to the remark, on a fact whose importance in any case they did not know. These were intelligent young men, torn like so many others from their studies to defend their country, and war had not yet blunted their aesthetic sensibility. They were travelling from Fougères where they might see the same panorama, but they could not help admiring it once more from a different view-point, like musical *dilettanti* whose enjoyment of a piece of music is increased by knowing it better in detail.

From the top of the Pellerine the great valley of the Couësnon lies spread out to the traveller's view, with the town of Fougères rising as one of the most prominent focal points on the horizon. Its castle from its rocky height dominates three or four important roads, a position which formerly made it one of the keys to Brittany. From their point of vantage the officers could see the whole expanse of this extremely fertile valley with its notable variety of scenery.

Mountains of schist rise on all sides to form an amphitheatre whose warmly-coloured slopes are clad with oak forests and have fresh little vales sheltering in their sides. These heights surround what looks like a vast circular enclosure with a floor of soft rolling grassland landscaped like an English garden. Innumerable growing hedges surrounding each owner's irregularly grouped fields, which are all planted with clumps of trees, give this wide plain a carpet of verdure rare in French scenery; and the immense scale makes the rich contrasts and variety of its beauty striking enough to impress the least impressionable.

At this moment the scene was lighted by the fugitive brilliance with which it sometimes pleases nature to enhance her imperishable creations. While the detachment was crossing the valley the rising sun had slowly dissipated the pale mists that float over plains on September mornings, and just as the soldiers turned the valley was disclosed, as though an invisible hand had drawn aside the last of the veils of fine vapour which had previously wrapped it, like the diaphanous tissue through which jewels sparkle mysteriously. In the whole vast expanse of sky as the officers gazed to the far horizon there was not the smallest cloud to show by its silvery reflection that the immense blue vault was the firmament. It looked more like a silken canopy supported at varying heights by the mountain summits, and hung in the air to protect the magnificent composition of fields, meadows, streams and groves.

The officers gazed absorbed at the wealth of natural beauty set in the spacious landscape, and after long consideration dwelt on the aspect that pleased them best. The eyes of some lingered on the astonishing variety and number of groups of trees, splashed in places harshly with the rich bronze tints of autumn colouring and standing out strikingly against the emerald green of those meadows which were still uncut. Others were held by the warmly-coloured fields, in some of which sheaves of harvested buckwheat were stacked in conical piles like soldiers' guns at a bivouac, while among them, separating them and setting them off by contrast, other fields were gilded by the stubble of reaped barley. Here and there the dark slate of scattered roof-tops with white smoke rising from their chimneys, and the bright silver dividing lines of the Couësnon's meandering streams, beguiled and held the eye in the kind of fascination that leads the soul to wander in a vague dream one does not know why.

The scented freshness of the autumn breezes and the pervasive aroma from the woodlands rose headily like a cloud of incense to the men who stood contemplating this lovely country, enchanted by its unknown flowers, luxuriant growth and verdure like that of its neighbour Britain, whose name it shares. Scattered flocks and herds animated the already dramatic scene. Birds sang and filled the valley with a liquid murmur of music that thrilled the air.

Imagination does its best to recapture the full beauty of the rich accidental play of light and shade, the hazy mountain-filled horizons, the fantastic vistas opened by treeless expanses and stretches of water and the seductive windings of streams into the distance, and memory may appear to colour a scene which was as fleeting as the moment when it was noted. And yet persons who find such sketches not without merit have been given only an imperfect painting of the enchanting spectacle which took the still impressionable souls of the young officers as it were by storm.

Reflecting now that these poor people were sadly leaving

47

their own land and cherished customs perhaps to die on alien soil, the officers understood and impulsively excused their lagging march; and with the natural kindness of soldiers disguised their perhaps patronizing tolerance by affecting an interest in the military possibilities of this lovely country. However, Hulot, who must be called the Commandant to avoid the uneuphonious title of *Chef de Demi-brigade*, was not the kind of soldier to let himself be captivated by the charms of a landscape, even an earthly paradise, in the face of impending danger. He shook his head and knitted the heavy black eyebrows that lent his face a severe and frowning look.

'Why the devil do they not come on?' he asked again, in a voice that the rigours of war had made thunderous. 'Is there some fine virgin in the village that they're busy shaking hands with?'

'Do you ask why?' came an answer.

Hearing a voice that seemed to issue from the horn the peasants of these valleys use to gather their cattle together, the Commandant turned sharply as if a sword had pricked him and saw a person two paces away who looked even stranger than any of those being taken to Mayenne to serve the Republic.

He saw a thickset man, broad-shouldered, with a head almost as heavy as an ox's, which it resembled in more than one respect. Wide nostrils made the man's nose appear even shorter than it actually was. His thick lips which did not close over the snow-white teeth, great round black eyes with overhanging eyebrows, large pendulous ears and rufous hair seemed more appropriate to some animal of the genus Herbivora than to a member of our handsome Caucasian race, and there seemed nothing at all in his other characteristics to mark a civilized man.

The only visible part of this strange individual was his face, tanned by the sun, with angular contours that suggested the granite outcrops of these regions. He was wrapped to the neck in a garment like a smock-frock, a kind of tunic of rusty red cloth even coarser than the breeches of the least well-off conscripts. This *sarrau*, to use the French word, in which the antiquary would have recognized the *saye* (*saga*) or *sayon* of the Gauls, covered him to the hips where two goatskin sheaths were fastened by roughly shaped pieces of wood, some still with the bark on. The 'nannyskins', as the Bretons call them, that furnished his legs and thighs disguised their human shape. Enormous sabots concealed his feet. He wore no hat and his long lustrous hair, very like that of his goatskins, fell on each side of his face in the fashion of the medieval statues we see in ancient cathedrals. In place of the gnarled stick that the conscripts bore over their shoulders he carried a great whip across his chest as if it were a gun, and its skilfully plaited lash seemed twice as long as that of normal whips.

It seemed easy enough to explain the sudden appearance of this odd person, and at first sight some of the officers supposed him to be a requisitioned man or conscript (still interchangeable terms) who was falling back on the column as he saw it halted. The Commandant however was inexplicably surprised by his arrival. He did not appear disconcerted, but his brow darkened; and after eyeing the stranger from head to foot he repeated automatically as if his mind were busy with gloomy speculation. 'Yes, what's keeping them? Do you know?'

'It's because,' his grimly sullen interlocutor replied with a pronunciation that showed some difficulty with the French language, 'because there,' and he stretched out his great uncouth hand in the direction of Ernée, 'there that's Maine, and here's the end of Brittany.' And he grounded the heavy butt of his whip with a resounding thwack at the Commandant's feet.

To the spectators of the scene the stranger's laconic speech sounded like a tomtom beaten while an orchestra was playing. The word 'speech' does not convey the hatred, the longing for revenge, implicit in the haughty gesture, the abrupt words, and the countenance stamped with a cold savage vigour. The rough uncouthness of this man who seemed to have been carved from the block with a hatchet, his gnarled rind, the stupid ignorance graven on his features made him look like a kind of barbarous demi-god. He stood there in a prophet's pose, an apparition like the very genius of Brittany risen from a three-years' sleep to recommence the kind of war where victory can bring nothing but mourning to both sides.

'Here's a pretty rascal,' Hulot said to himself. 'He looks to me like a messenger from people getting ready to start their conversation with bullets.'

He muttered these words between his teeth, and then turned from staring at the man to scan the countryside, looked from the countryside to the detachment, from the detachment to the steep slopes of the road, their ridges overgrown with the tall-growing furze of Brittany; then he abruptly turned his gaze again on the stranger in a silent interrogation which he concluded with the brusque question, 'Where do you come from?'

His acute intensely-searching eye tried to get at what lay behind the impenetrable face, which during this pause had taken on the vacant torpid look an inactive peasant assumes.

'From the *Gars's* country,' the man replied with no appearance of uneasiness.

'And your name?'

'*Marche-à-terre.*'

'Why do you use your Chouan nickname, against the law?'

Marche-à-terre, since that was what he called himself, looked at the Commandant with such unquestionable downright imbecility that that soldier thought he had not been understood.

'Are you one of the men requisitioned from Fougères?'

To this question Marche-à-terre replied with the maddening kind of 'I don't know' whose obtuseness puts an end to any attempt at communication. He sat down tranquilly by the roadside and pulling a few pieces of flat black buckwheat cake – that uninviting national delicacy only Bretons can relish – from his tunic, he began to eat with a placidly stupid indifference. It seemed obvious that he was completely devoid of any spark of intelligence, and the officers as they looked at him remarked to one another that he was like one of the animals browsing over the rich valley pastures, or an American redskin, or some savage from the Cape of Good

Hope. The Commandant himself was deceived and about to dismiss his suspicions, when, casting a last wary look at the man who he had thought might be the herald of an impending carnage, he noticed that his hair, tunic and goatskins were covered with thorns, fallen leaves, bits of twig and brushwood, as though this Chouan had travelled a long way through the thickets. He gave his adjutant, Gérard, who happened to be at his side, a significant look, grasped his hand and in a low voice said, 'We came here to shear sheep and are likely to go away shorn.'

The astonished officers looked at one another in silence.

Chapter 2

A DIGRESSION is in place here to explain Commandant Hulot's fears to certain Doubting Thomases accustomed to question everything because they live between four walls and never see anything, who are capable of denying Marche-à-terre's existence and the sublime behaviour at that time of the peasants of the West.

The word *gars*, pronounced *ga*, is a relic of the Celtic tongue. It passed from the Breton dialect into French, and in the modern language has more echoes of the past than any other word. The *gais* was the principal weapon of the Gaels or Gauls; *gaisde* meant armed, *gais* – gallantry, *gas* – strength.

Comparison proves the kinship of the word *gars* with these expressions from the tongue our forebears spoke. The word is analogous to the Latin *vir* – man, from which comes *virtus* – strength, courage.

This discourse may be excused by its patriotic interest; and perhaps too it will serve to rehabilitate, for some people at least, the words *gars*, *garçon*, *garçonnette*, *garce*, *garcette*, which are considered vulgar and not permissible in conversation but which have such a martial origin. They will turn up now and then in the course of this story. 'She's a famous *garce*!' is a little-understood commendation Madame de Staël won when she was staying in a little place near Vendôme for some days of exile.

Gaulish ways and manners have left a deeper imprint in Brittany than anywhere else in France. Where the untrammelled way of life and superstitious spirit of our rude forefathers hit one in the eye, if one may so express it, to this day in certain regions of the province, people speak of '*Gars* country'. When a number of savages like the one who has just made an appearance in this Scene live in a certain canton, the people thereabouts speak of 'the *Gars* of such and such parish', and the classic name seems an acknowledgement of their fidelity to the Gaelic language and customs and effort to preserve them. Vestiges of ancient beliefs and pagan practices are to be found profoundly influencing their present way of life. They still honour feudal customs there. Archaeologists find Druidic stones still standing; and the spirit of modern civilization hesitates to cross vast primordial forests.

The inhabitants are incredibly ferocious and brutishly stubborn, but their sworn word is to be trusted absolutely. They do not recognize our law, manners, dress, our new money or our language, but live with patriarchal simplicity and practise the heroic virtues. That paints the portrait of a people more intellectually backward and less subtle even than the Mohicans and redskins of North America, but just as noble, as full of guile, and just as tough.

Brittany's geographical position in Europe makes it seem a much stranger place than Canada. The surrounding bright lights do not warm or illuminate it, and it remains as unnoticed and dark as a frozen coal in the middle of a fire blazing on the hearth. Some public-spirited individuals, as well as the Government, have made attempts to win this lovely corner of France, with its wealth of little-known treasures, for social integration and prosperity; but they all founder against the obdurate immovability of a population dedicated to doing what it has always done since time immemorial.

The topography of the country partly explains this sad state of affairs, because the land is divided by ravines, torrential streams, lakes and marshes; each field is like a citadel, surrounded by hedged banks like earthwork bastions; and there are few proper roads and no canals. It is also due to the spirit of an ignorant population which will have nothing to do with our modern agriculture, and is led by strongly held opinions and ideas whose dangers the incidents of this story will make evident.

The natural features of this country, picturesque though they may be, and the superstitions of its inhabitants, make concentration of the population and the benefits obtained by comparing impressions and exchanging ideas impossible.

There are no villages here. The ramshackle structures that are called houses are scattered across the countryside. Each family lives as if alone in a desert. The only social events are the brief gatherings for public worship on Sundays and Church holidays. These silent reunions, controlled and dominated by the *Recteur* – the only person with authority over these rough uncivilized spirits, last a few hours. After listening to his priest's awesome voice the peasant returns to his insalubrious dwelling for another week; he leaves it for work, he returns to it to sleep. If a visitor comes to it, it is the *Recteur*. He is the country's soul. It was at the word of the *Recteurs* that thousands of men rose against the Republic, and hosts of soldiers from these parts of Brittany supplied the first Chouan bands five years before this story begins.

The Cottereau brothers, the daring smugglers who gave their name to this war, carried on their hazardous profession from Laval to Fougères. The insurrection in these parts, how-ever, had nothing noble about it, and it may be said without qualification that if the Vendée turned highway robbery into a war, Brittany turned war into highway robbery. The proscription of the Princes, the destruction of religion, were no more to the Chouans than pretexts for plundering, and this intestine struggle was conducted to some extent with the harsh savagery characteristic of the manners of these regions. When whole-hearted defenders of the Monarchy came to recruit soldiers from these ignorant bellicose peasants, they tried to lend a certain idealism under the Royalist white flag to the forays that had made the name of Chouan odious, but vainly. The Chouans have remained a notable example of the danger of stirring up the barely civilized masses of a country.

The scenic beauty of the first valley in Brittany to meet travellers' eyes, and the men composing the column of requisitionary recruits, and the *gars* who appeared on the summit of the Pellerine, as they have been described, together present a small-scale but faithful picture of the province and its inhabitants at this time. Knowing these a practised im-agination can re-create the theatre and the instruments of the war, for these were the elements. The hedges of these lovely valleys with all their flowers were hiding invisible enemies. Each field was a stronghold and behind every tree lurked an ambush, and some murderous booby-trap was set in every hollow old willow stump. The battlefield was all around. Guns waited at road corners for laughing girls to entice Blues within their range, and the girls had no thought that they were treacherous – they used to go with their fathers and brothers to visit shrines in order to ask the worm-eaten wooden Virgins to grant them not only absolution but fresh ways to decoy and dupe. The religion or rather fetishism of these ignorant creatures stripped murder of the need for qualms of conscience and remorse.

Once war had begun everything in the country became dangerous: silence was as deadly as noise; what was frightening was no more to be feared than kindness; the domestic hearth held as many threats as the open road. The treachery was inspired by righteous conviction. These were savages serving God and the King in the fashion of Mohicans on the war-path. But to complete an exact and faithful picture the historian must add that as soon as Hoche's peace treaty was signed this was a smiling friendly land once more, and families whose members had been at one another's throats took their supper in perfect safety under the same roof next day.

As soon as Hulot realized that what Marche-à-terre's goatskin gave away was a treacherous plot, he was certain that the happy interlude of peace that Hoche's skill had contrived was ended and its further maintenance impossible. There was no doubt that war more terrible than ever after its three years' lull was to be unleashed again. The Revolution, which had followed a gentler course since the 9 Thermidor,* was perhaps now about to resume the terror that had made it hateful to all right-thinking men. As usual, English gold must have been used to fan the flame of French discord. Without the young Bonaparte who seemed to be its tutelary genius the

* 27 July 1794, when Robespierre was overthrown and the Terror in Paris ended. – *Trans.*

Republic appeared incapable of resisting so many enemies, and the latest was not the least cruel of them. The civil war foreshadowed by numerous small and minor risings became a much more serious affair if the Chouans planned to attack such a strong escort. These in brief were the reflections that passed through Hulot's mind when in Marche-à-terre's sudden appearance he believed he saw a warning of a skilfully laid ambuscade. He was the only one at this time to know the danger.

In the silence that followed his prediction to Gérard that terminated the last scene Hulot recovered his sang-froid. The old soldier had almost wavered. He could not hide or shake off his grim thoughts as he saw himself already plunged into the horrors of a civil war even cannibals might think savage and atrocious. Captain Merle and the adjutant Gérard, his two friends, tried to find a clue to the apprehension they saw so strangely on their chief's face, and studied Marche-à-terre eating his buckwheat cakes at the roadside, unable to find any possible connection between this almost animal creature and the uneasiness of their intrepid commanding officer. But Hulot's face soon cleared. The Republic's misfortunes might appal him, but it was a matter for congratulation that he was to fight for her; and he joyfully assured himself that he would not let the Chouans dupe him, and would turn the mysterious and cunning man that they had done him the honour of using against him inside out.

Before taking any decision he set himself to examine the position where his enemies were planning to surprise him. Observing that the road which he was obliged to follow led into a kind of gorge, not very deep indeed but flanked by woods and with several paths leading into it, he frowned, knitting his heavy black eyebrows, and said in a muted and deeply concerned tone, 'We are in a fine hornet's nest.'

'What in the world are you afraid of?' Gérard asked.

'Afraid? . . .' the Commandant took him up. 'Yes, I'm afraid. I've always been afraid of being shot at a turning in a wood like a dog, without so much as a shout of "Who goes there?"'

'Bah!' said Merle laughing. 'There's not much joy in "Who goes there?"'

'Are we really in danger then?' asked Gérard, as surprised to see Hulot's present coolness as he had been by his moment of alarm.

'Tut!' said the Commandant. 'We're in the wolf's throat. It's as dark as the inside of an oven, and we'll have to light a candle. It's lucky that we're on the upper side of this . . . slope!' He qualified it with a robust epithet, and added, 'I'll see my way perhaps in the end.'

He motioned his two officers to follow him and they closed in on Marche-à-terre. The *gars* made a show of thinking that he was in their way and promptly rose.

'Stay where you are, you ruffian!' Hulot roared and thrust him down on the bank where he had been sitting. From then on the Commandant constantly watched the Breton, who was quite unconcerned.

'My friends,' he said then in a low voice to the two officers, 'it's time I told you that the whole show is in a mess over there. There's been a great to-do in the Assembly and the Directory has done some clearing out and sweeping clean. The pentarchy of Directors, or five puppets on a string* – that's better French, have just lost a good fighter: Bernadotte has given up.'

'Who is to replace him?' Gérard asked quickly.

'Milet-Mureau, an old fossil. They've chosen a pretty poor time to put blockheads in charge! There are the English letting off their fireworks off the coasts, and now all these hare-brained Vendéans and Chouans are in a fizz. The people behind these cats-paws know how to seize their opportunity at a time when we're practically sunk.'

'What!' said Merle.

'Our armies are defeated in all quarters,' Hulot said, lowering his voice still more as he went on. 'The Chouans have intercepted the mail twice already, and I had my despatches and the latest orders only by an express messenger

* There is a pun here in the French. – *Trans.*

57

Bernadotte sent just before he left the Ministry. Luckily friends wrote to me confidentially about this turn-up. Fouché has discovered that the tyrant Louis XVIII was given the word by traitors in Paris to send a leader to his pigeons in the country districts. It is thought that Barras is playing a double game. To cut a long story short, Pitt and the Princes have sent a *ci-devant* here, a live wire, very able, and he thinks he can make the Republic lower its colours or take off its bonnet by combining what they're doing in the Vendée with the Chouans' efforts. This fellow landed somewhere in Morbihan. I had the news first and told the smart boys in Paris – the *Gars* he calls himself. All these brutes,' and he indicated Marche-à-terre, 'are fitted out with names that would give an honest patriot colic.

'Now our man is in this part of the world. This Chouan's turning up,' he nodded again towards Marche-à-terre, 'makes it plain to me that he's on our heels. But an old monkey doesn't have to be taught to pull faces, and you are going to help me cage my song-birds and *faster than that*! A fine noddy I should be if I let this *ci-devant* coming from London with the idea of giving our headgear a dusting lime me like a rook!'

The two officers, knowing their Commandant was never alarmed without good cause, took this critical secret news with the seriousness of tough soldiers beset by danger when they are men accustomed to looking beyond the immediate moment. Gérard, whose rank, which has now been done away with, made him close to his chief was anxious to ask for all the political news, for part of it had obviously been passed over, but a sign from Hulot silenced him, and all three turned to look at Marche-à-terre. The Chouan did not appear in the least disturbed at finding himself an object of study by these formidable men, not only physically formidable but in their intelligence too. The two officers, new to this kind of warfare, thought of it as the beginning of an almost romantic adventure and were keenly excited and curious and ready to treat it frivolously; but at the first word Hulot looked at them gravely and said, 'By God's thunder, Citizens, let's not smoke on the powder-keg! Courage at the wrong moment is just about as useful as carting water in a basket. – Gérard,' he went on, bending to his adjutant's ear, 'go nearer this brigand without making a fuss about it, but at the slightest suspicious movement be ready to run your sword through him. As for me, I'm off to take measures to keep the conversation going if it pleases our friends to begin it.'

Gérard nodded and turned to survey the valley, whose aspects may now have become familiar, as if wanting to make a close study from different points of view. He walked about casually and quite naturally, but one may be sure that the landscape was the last thing he was studying. On his side Marche-à-terre showed no understanding that the officer's manoeuvre might threaten his safety; he was making casts, with his whip-lash as fishing-line, into the ditch.

While Gérard was looking for a tactical position near the Chouan the Commandant said in a low voice to Merle, 'Take ten picked men with a sergeant and post them yourself above us, at the place on this side of the summit where the road widens into a flat expanse; from there you can see a good slice of the road to Ernée. Choose an open place, clear of trees, to allow the sergeant a wide view over the countryside. Call La-clef-des-coeurs – he's a sharp fellow. This is no laughing matter. If we don't make the most of the odds in our favour I don't give a farthing for our skins.'

While Captain Merle carried out this order post-haste, realizing the importance of speed, the Commandant with a gesture of his right hand enjoined complete silence on the soldiers talking and amusing themselves all round him and then silently brought them to attention. When all was in order he scanned both sides of the road one after the other, listening with anxious concentration as if hoping to surprise some muffled noise, some sounds of arms or steps giving warning of the expected attack. His dark and piercing eye seemed to search the woods to extraordinary depths; but finding no sign there he studied the gravel surface of the road, as savages do, to try to discover some traces of the enemies beyond his vision whose audacity he well knew. Then giving up hope of finding anything there to justify his fears, he moved to the slopes overlooking the road, climbing the hillocks with some difficulty and walking slowly along their ridges. But then suddenly remembering how vital for the safety of his soldiers his experience was he climbed down, with a sombre grimace, for in those times leaders always hated not being able to keep the most dangerous task for themselves.

The other officers and the soldiers watching this commanding officer whom they liked and whose valour was well-known had noticed his preoccupation, and now thought that his intent scrutiny must indeed mean danger, but they could not guess how serious it was and stayed motionless and almost held their breath just by instinct. These soldiers looked like hunting-dogs working with a skilled hunter, alert to divine his intentions and obey his command on the instant however incomprehensible, as they scanned the Couësnon valley, the woods by the road and the Commandant's stern face, trying to read what lay in store. They exchanged glances and more than once a smile spread from face to face.

When Hulot screwed up his face Beau-pied, a young sergeant who was considered the company wit, said in an undertone, 'What the devil fix can we have got ourselves into to make our old war-horse put on such a sulky face at us? – He looks like a court-martial judge!'

He earned a stern look from Hulot which at once produced the silence required of troops under arms. Amid this solemn silence the conscripts' lagging march, with the gravel crunching dully under their feet, made a regular tramp that added an obscure emotion to the already charged atmosphere, an indefinable feeling that will only be understood by people who at some time have been waiting in torturing anxiety, and in the night silence heard their heavily thudding hearts echoed by some monotonously repeated sound, that drop by drop seemed to drip terror.

As he returned to the middle of the road the Commandant was beginning to ask himself, 'Can I be wrong?'. He stared with intense anger flashing in his eyes at the obtuse placid Marche-à-terre, but the barbarian derision he could read behind the Chouan's lack-lustre regard convinced him that he should not relax his precautions. Just then, having carried out Hulot's orders, Captain Merle rejoined him. The silent actors in this scene, one of a thousand scenes like it that made this kind of warfare the most dramatic of all, waited impatiently for new sensations, eager to learn of fresh moves that would enlighten them about the obscure points of their military situation.

'We were right, Captain, to let the few patriots we have among the conscripts bring up the rear of the column,' the Commandant said. 'Take another dozen stout fellows, put Sublieutenant Lebrun in charge and march them fast to the rear. They are to support the patriots there, and push on the whole collection of those cage-birds and smartly too, so that we can get them together up on the height with the comrades double-quick. Then come back to me.'

The Captain disappeared among the soldiers. The Commandant picked out with his eye four fearless men whose agility and craft he knew. He pointed to each in turn and silently brought them to him with a beckoning forefinger raised to his nose in a friendly gesture.

'You served with me under Hoche,' he said, 'when we made these brigands who call themselves *Chasseurs du Roi* see reason, so you know how they used to take cover to snipe at the Blues.'

At this tribute to their nous and experience the four soldiers nodded, screwing their faces up knowingly. Their faces were of a heroically pugnacious cast, and their expressions, at once resigned and carefree, made it clear that they had had no thought beyond their cartridge-pouch behind them and their bayonet in front since the struggle between France and Europe began. With their mouths pursed like well-tied bags, they stared at their Commandant with alert curiosity.

'Well,' went on Hulot, who could speak their own picturesque language like one of themselves, 'old campaigners like us can't let Chouans push us around, and there are some here or my name isn't Hulot. You four go and beat both sides of this road. The detachment will take it easy meantime. Your job is to keep your noses on the scent, try not to get picked off and let me know what's there without dragging your feet!' And he pointed to the dangerous heights overlooking the road.

Each man, by way of thanks, touched the back of his hand to his old tricorne hat with its high rain-battered age-softened brim curling back over the crown. One of them, a corporal known to Hulot named Larose, said with a rattle of his gun, 'We'll sound a sweet tune in their ears with this clarinet, Sir.'

Off they went, two to the right, two to the left; and it was not without some secret misgivings that the detachment watched them disappear on each side of the road. Their anxiety was shared by the Commandant for he believed he was sending them to certain death, and he shivered involuntarily when the high peaks of their hats passed beyond his view. Officers and men, they listened to the gradually diminishing rustle of footsteps among the dry leaves with an emotion all the sharper because it lay so deeply concealed. It happens sometimes in a war that four men at risk arouse more dismay than the thousands of dead laid low at Jemmapes.

The expressions on these military types of face are so varied and so quickly gone that writers depicting them can only appeal to soldiers' memories, and leave those who are not fighters to study these dramatic figures for themselves; for it would not be possible to describe these scenes of storm in all their rich diversity of detail properly without tedious prolixity.

At the moment when the last flash from the four soldiers' bayonets had gone, Captain Merle returned after carrying out the Commandant's orders at lightning speed. With two or three words of command Hulot drew up the rest of his band in battle formation in the middle of the road. Then he gave the order to march on to the summit of the Pellerine where his little advance guard was posted. He himself walked last, with his face turned to the valley in order to observe the slightest movement at any point in this scene that nature had made so ravishing and man was now making so grim.

He had reached the spot where Gérard was guarding Marche-à-terre, who had followed all the Commandant's manoeuvres with an apparently indifferent eye but then watched the two soldiers beating the woods to the right of the road with an intelligence hard to believe, when the Chouan suddenly whistled the owl's clear penetrating hoot three or four times.

The three famous smugglers, the Cottereau brothers, whose name has already been mentioned, were accustomed to use certain modulations of that cry at night to warn one another of ambushes, dangers or whatever might concern them. From that had come the nickname *Chuin*, which means screech-owl or barn-owl in the local patois. A corruption of this word was used to designate those who copied the ways and signals of the three brothers in the first rising.

When he heard this suspicious cry the Commandant stopped and stared at Marche-à-terre; but wanting to keep him at hand as a kind of barometer for forecasting the enemy's movements, he feigned to be taken in by the Chouan's simpleton pose, and stayed Gérard's hand as he was about to despatch him. Then he placed two soldiers a few paces from the spy and in a loud clear voice ordered them to shoot him if he made the slightest sign. In spite of the knife-edge on which his life hung Marche-à-terre showed no trace of emotion, and the Commandant, studying him, took note of this insensibility.

'The fellow doesn't know much!' he said to Gérard. 'Aha! It's not easy to read a Chouan's face, but this one has betrayed himself by wanting to show his fearlessness. D'you see, Gérard, if he had acted terrified I should have taken him for an imbecile. He and I would have made a pair. I had come to the end of my rope. Oh, we're going to be attacked all right! But let them come now, I'm ready!'

Having said this triumphantly, in an undertone, the old soldier rubbed his hands and looked at Marche-à-terre in mocking satisfaction; then, standing in the middle of the road with his two favourite officers on either side, he crossed his arms on his chest and awaited the result of the steps he had taken. Certain of battle now, he calmly surveyed his soldiers.

'Oh, there's going to be a scrimmage!' Beau-pied said under his breath. 'Did you see the Commandant rub his hands?'

Chapter 3

WHEN life is literally at stake as in the critical situation facing Commandant Hulot and his men, it is esteemed a point of honour by men of mettle to show complete coolness and composure. By that men are judged in the last resort. And so the Commandant, better informed about the danger than his two officers, made it a matter of pride to appear the least concerned. It was not without some anguish of mind that he waited, his eyes dwelling in turn upon Marche-à-terre, the road and the woods, for the alarm volley from the Chouans whom he believed to be hiding like alien and derisive spirits around him; but his face was impassive. At the moment when all the soldiers' eyes were fixed on his, his brown pock-marked cheeks creased slightly, the right side of his mouth twitched and his eyes screwed up in the grimace his soldiers always took for a smile. Then he tapped Gérard on the shoulder, saying, 'Now we have some peace. What was it you wanted to say just now?'

'What new crisis has come up, Sir?'

'It's not new,' he replied in a low voice. 'Europe is all against us, and this time she has the game in her hands. While the Directors are fighting one another like horses left in a stable without oats, and their whole government falls to pieces, they leave the armies without support. We are overwhelmed in Italy! Yes, my friends, Mantua has been evacuated after the disasters at the Trebbia, and the battle at Novi has been lost by Joubert. I hope Masséna will be able to hold the Swiss passes for Suvorov has overrun Switzerland. We're done for on the Rhine. The Directory has sent Moreau there. Will that fellow hold the line? . . . I hope he may; but it looks as if the Coalition is going to crush us, and by bad luck the only General who could save us is leagues away in Egypt. There's no way he could come back either – England is mistress of the sea.'

'I'm not worried by Bonaparte's absence, Commandant,' said the young adjutant, Gérard, who had been carefully educated and attained some maturity of mind. 'But is our Revolution to come to a full stop? Ah! We're not only required to defend French territory – we have a double mission. We're responsible, aren't we, for preserving the country's soul as well, the noble principles of liberty and independence, the sense of human justice our Assemblies kindled, that will prevail everywhere by degrees, I hope. France is like a traveller entrusted with a light: she guards it with one hand and defends herself with the other. If your news is true, we have never in the past ten years been surrounded by so many people trying to blow it out. Everything – political doctrine and country both – is in danger of perishing!'

'It's only too true,' said Commandant Hulot with a sigh. 'Those buffoons in the Directory have managed to quarrel with all the men who had the ability to steer the ship. Everyone has left us: Bernadotte, Carnot, even Citizen Talleyrand. There's only one good patriot left, in short – friend Fouché, who controls everything through the police. Now, there's a man! Indeed it was he who warned me in time about this rising. And yet here we are caught, I'm quite certain, in some vermin trap.'

'Oh, if the Army doesn't bear a hand in governing us the lawyers will leave us worse off than we were before the Revolution,' said Gérard. 'Do you think those weasels know how to govern?'

'I'm always afraid of getting news that they are negotiating with the Bourbons,' said Hulot. 'God's thunder! If they reached an agreement, just imagine the fix we should find ourselves in here!'

'No, no, Commandant, we'll not let things come to that pass,' said Gérard. 'The Army, as you say, will raise its voice, and so long as it doesn't borrow Pichegru's* language and

* A French General who conspired with Cadoudal, the Vendéan leader. – *Trans.*

turn traitor, we'll be all right. I should hope we will not have been holding the line and standing to be hacked at for ten years only in order to watch others harvest our flax and spin our thread for themselves at the end of the day.'

'Oh, yes indeed!' exclaimed the Commandant. 'We've paid a heavy enough price for changing the colour of our uniforms.'

'Well,' said Captain Merle, 'we can only go on being good patriots here, and try to prevent our Chouans from communicating with the Vendée; for if they link hands and England joins in, I would not answer this time to the Republic one and indivisible for the safety of its Phrygian bonnet.'

The owl's cry sounding from some distance broke in on the conversation. The Commandant, once more uneasy, turned to examine Marche-à-terre yet again; but that expressionless face gave no sign, one may almost say of life. The conscripts, rounded up by an officer, were gathered like a herd of cattle in the middle of the road, about thirty paces from the drawn up detachment. Then behind them, at ten paces, were the soldiers and patriots commanded by Sublieutenant Lebrun. The Commandant surveyed this battle order and looked finally again at the picket posted on the road ahead. Satisfied with his dispositions, he was turning to give the command to march when he observed the tricolour cockades of two soldiers returning after searching the woods on the left, and paused to await them, not seeing the two on the right reappear.

'It may be from there that the bombshell will be thrown,' he said to his two officers, nodding towards the wood where his two lost children seemed to have been swallowed up.

While the two scouts were making a hasty report, Hulot took his eyes off Marche-à-terre. The Chouan then began to hoot piercingly in such a way as to make his cry carry a prodigious distance. Then before either of his guardians could even take aim he lashed out violently with his whip and knocked them down into the ditch at the road edge. Immediately yells, or rather wild howls, electrified the Republicans. A withering volley from the wood above the slope where the

Chouan had been sitting brought down seven or eight soldiers. Marche-à-terre, followed ineffectually by shots from five or six men, disappeared into the wood after climbing the slope at wildcat speed. His sabots rolled down into the ditch, and it was easy to see then the heavy nailed shoes on his feet that the Chasseurs du Roi habitually wore. At the Chouans' first yells all the conscripts had leapt into the woods on the right, like a flight of birds taking wing at a traveller's approach.

'Shoot those curs!' shouted the Commandant.

The soldiers fired, but the conscripts had all managed to take cover from this volley behind tree-trunks, and had disappeared before it was possible to reload.

'So much for creating conscript companies from the Departments by decree!' Hulot said to Gérard. 'Only a Directory could be so idiotic as to count on levies raised in this part of the world. It would be a much better thing if only the Assemblies would stop voting us so much clothing and money and munitions and would hand them over.'

'Those toads would rather jump for their buckwheat cakes than stay for our ration bread,' said Beau-pied, the company wit.

This quip was followed by booing and jeering laughter from the Republican troops, mocking the deserters, but silence fell suddenly. The soldiers saw painfully climbing down the slope the two scouts whom the Commandant had sent to comb the woods on the right. The less severely wounded of the two supported his comrade, who was streaming with blood. The two poor soldiers had covered half the way when Marche-à-terre's hideous face appeared. His aim was so accurate that he killed both Blues with a right and left shot and they rolled heavily into the ditch. His great head had hardly been glimpsed before thirty gun-barrels were raised, but he was gone like a phantasmagoric figure behind the deadly clumps of furze. These events, which take so many words to relate, took only a moment to happen; then, almost immediately the patriots and soldiers of the rearguard rejoined the rest of the escort.

'Forward march!' shouted Hulot.

The party advanced swiftly to the high open place where the outpost had been stationed. There the Commandant drew them up in battle order; but he saw no hostile show of force on the part of the Chouans, and thought that the freeing of the conscripts might have been the only object of the ambush.

'I can judge by their shouts that there are not many of them,' he said to his two friends. 'We may go on at a faster pace and perhaps reach Ernée without having them about our ears.'

This remark was overheard by a patriot conscript, who left the ranks and presented himself before Hulot.

'General,' he said, 'I have fought in this war before as a Counter-Chouan. May I have a word with you, Sir?'

'He's a lawyer; they always think they're still in Court,' said the Commandant in an undertone to Merle. 'Well, go on, plead your cause,' he answered the young citizen from Fougères.

'Sir, the Chouans have no doubt brought arms for the men they have just recruited. If we try to show them our heels now they will go on and wait for us at every turning in the woods, and kill us to the last man before we can reach Ernée. As you say, we must plead our cause, but with bullets. While the affray is going on, and it will last longer than you think, one of my comrades can go and fetch the National Guard and Volunteers from Fougères. We may be only conscripts, but you'll see then if it's ink that flows in our veins.'

'So you think there's a large number of Chouans?'

'Judge for yourself, Citizen Commandant!'

He took Hulot to a level place on the height where the gravel had been disturbed as if it had been raked; then, having pointed this out, he led him for some distance along a path where they saw traces of the passing of a large number of men. The leaves were stamped into the trampled earth.

'Those are the *gars* from Vitré,' the young man said. 'They have gone to join the men from Basse-Normandy.'

'What is your name, Citizen?' asked Hulot.

'Gudin, Sir.'

'Well, Gudin, I appoint you Corporal over your fellow

townsmen. You look to me like a reliable man. I give you the duty of choosing which one of your comrades should be sent to Fougères. You, stay near me. But first go with your fellows to our poor comrades that those brigands laid low on the road and take their guns, cartridge pouches and coats. You shall not stay here to put up with bullets without a chance to return them.'

The daring conscripts from Fougères went to fetch the dead soldiers' equipment, which they succeeded in doing without the loss of a single man thanks to the fire with which the whole company blanketed the woods.

'These Bretons will make capital soldiers,' Hulot said to Gérard, 'if they ever get to like the mess-tin.'

The messenger chosen by Gudin set off at a trot through the woods on the left by a roundabout path. The soldiers were busy seeing to their arms in preparation for combat. The Commandant inspected them, smiled on them, and went forward to post himself a few paces in advance with his two favourite officers, and there resolutely awaited the Chouan attack. Silence reigned again for the moment, but did not last long.

Three hundred Chouans dressed exactly like the requisitioned men issued from the woods on the right, running in no sort of order and uttering fearful howls, and filled the whole road in front of the Blues' small band. The Commandant formed up his soldiers in two equal parties each with a front of ten men. He placed his twelve requisitionary recruits, hastily equipped, between these two, and himself at their head. This little army was protected by two wings, each of twenty-five men, under the command of Gérard and Merle, which would manoeuvre on each side of the road. The two officers were to take the Chouans in flank at the right moment and prevent them from carrying out the manoeuvre called *s'égailler*. This word from the patois of these regions signifies withdrawing and scattering so that each peasant could place himself in the best position to fire on the Blues without danger. In such circumstances the Republican troops were at a loss to know how to get at their enemies.

These dispositions made by the Commandant with the speed necessary in the situation communicated his confidence to the soldiers, and they all marched in silence against the Chouans. After a few minutes while the two opposing parties advanced against each other, a volley was exchanged at point-blank range which scattered death through the two bodies of men. At this moment the two Republican wings, having met no effective resistance from the Chouans, arrived on the Chouan flanks, and with a rapid continuous discharge sowed death and disorder among their enemies. This manoeuvre made the two parties almost equal in number. But in intrepidity and steadfastness the Chouans were of a stuff proof against anything. They did not give way; their losses did not shake them; they closed up and tried to envelop the dark, correctly dressed lines of the Blues' little band, which seemed to occupy so little space in comparison that it was like a queen bee surrounded by the swarm.

The action that was then engaged was of that horrible kind in which the crackle of musketry is heard only now and then and is replaced by the clash and rattle of hand-to-hand fighting; and with courage equal on both sides it is by weight of numbers that victory is won. The Chouans would have carried the day at once had not the two wings commanded by Merle and Gérard succeeded in getting in two or three volleys which caught them in the rear obliquely. The Blues of these two wings ought to have held their position and gone on effectively dealing with their terrible enemies in this way; but electrified by the sight of the perilous situation of the heroic main band, then completely surrounded by the Chasseurs du Roi, they rushed on to the road in a mad bayonet charge, and for a few minutes made the contest less unequal. The two bands were then locked in desperate battle, their violence fed by all the fierce intransigent bitterness of partisan feeling which made this war exceptional. Each man, heedful of his peril, fell silent. The scene was sombre and chill as death. In this silence, through the clash of arms and the grating of gravel underfoot one heard only the dull heavy groans of the grievously wounded or dying men as they fell to the ground. In the middle of the Republican band, the twelve requisitionary men showed such courage in their defence of the Commandant, hard at work with a host of decisions and commands, that more than once two or three soldiers cried, 'Bravo, the recruits!'

Hulot, unmoved, with an eye for everything, presently remarked a man among the Chouans surrounded like himself by a picked band, who must be the leader. It seemed to him essential to take careful note of this officer; but the attempts he made to see his features were frustrated again and again by the red Republican caps and broad-brimmed hats between them which repeatedly cut off his view. He did indeed notice Marche-à-terre, who, at his General's side, repeated his orders in a raucous voice, and whose gun was ceaselessly active. The Commandant grew impatient at this unending obstruction. He took his sword in his hand, urged on his requisitionary guard, and charged the Chouan centre with such fury that he penetrated their mass and was able to catch a glimpse of their chief, whose face unfortunately was completely hidden by a large felt hat with a white cockade. But the mysterious leader, surprised by such an audacious attack, made a movement backwards, raising his hat abruptly; and then Hulot was able hastily to note the appearance of this personage.

The young man, whom Hulot judged to be not more than twenty-five years old, wore a green cloth hunting jacket. His white sash held pistols. His heavy shoes were hobnailed like those of the Chouans. Hunters' gaiters to the knee over breeches of very coarse duck completed this costume, which was worn by a man of only medium height, but slender and well-proportioned. Furious at seeing the Blues attain his very person, he pulled down his hat and advanced towards them; but he was promptly surrounded by Marche-à-terre and a number of alarmed Chouans. Between the heads which crowded round the young man, Hulot fancied he saw the broad red ribbon of a decoration on a wide-lapelled coat-breast. The Commandant's eyes, first attracted to the royal decoration, the Cross of St Louis, at that time completely fallen into oblivion, were quickly raised to the young man's face, but it was soon lost to view as he was forced by the chances of the affray to look to the safety and manoeuvring of his little band. And so he had barely a glimpse of sparkling eyes whose colour he did not determine, fair hair and rather delicate features, tanned by the sun. He was struck by the whiteness of a bare throat, set off by a carelessly-knotted loose black cravat. The young leader's impetuous ardent attitude was soldierly in the spirit of those who look for a certain traditional romance in a fight. His well-gloved hand brandished a sword that flashed in the sun. Both elegance and strength were in the lines of his face. His rapturous emotion in the execution of his duty, enhanced in its appeal by the charm of youth and his distinguished bearing, made of this *émigré* a gracious representative of the French nobility. He formed a vivid contrast to Hulot, four paces from him, who for his part seemed a living symbol of the vigorous Republic for which the old soldier was fighting, with his stern face, blue uniform with worn red facings, tarnished epaulettes dragged back behind the shoulders, which so well revealed his hard circumstances and his character.

The young man's graceful bearing and expression were not lost on Hulot, who shouted as he tried to reach him. 'Come on, you're not dancing at the Opéra now! Come here and let me pulverize you!'

The Royalist leader, incensed at being taken at a momentary disadvantage, pushed forward desperately; but immediately his men saw him so imperil himself they all flung themselves against the Blues. Suddenly a sweet clear voice rang out above the noise of combat, 'Here the Saint of Poitou, General de Lescure,* was slain! Will you not avenge him?'

At these inspiring words the Chouans formidably increased their effort, and the Republican soldiers held the orderly ranks of their little formation only with the greatest difficulty.

'If he were not a young man,' Hulot said to himself, giving way step by step, 'we should not have been attacked. Have Chouans ever been known to give battle? But all the better, they won't have a chance of killing us like dogs along the

* Vendéan General, mortally wounded in 1793. – *Trans.*

73

way.' Then, in a voice that made the woods resound, 'Come on, my boys, put your backs into it! Are we going to let ourselves be *pushed around* by brigands?'

We use only a milk and water substitute for the expression employed by the gallant Commandant; but veterans will be able to supply the real one, which to a soldier certainly sounds spicier.

'Gérard, Merle, recall your men,' the Commandant said. 'Form them up and take up your position again in the enemy's rear. Shoot the dogs and let's have done with them.'

Hulot's order was difficult to carry out; for at the sound of his adversary's voice the young leader cried, 'By Saint Anne of Auray, don't let them get away! Spread out, *égaillez-vous*, my *gars*!'

When the two wings commanded by Merle and Gérard withdrew from the thick of the fray, each little formation was accordingly dogged by Chouans, persistent and superior in number. These experienced *nannyskins* swarmed round the soldiers with renewed yells that had the sinister ululation of wolves' howling.

'Less noise, *gentlemen*, one can't hear oneself kill!' cried Beau-pied.

This piece of wit put fresh fire into the Blues. Now, instead of fighting at one single place, the Republicans were defending themselves at three different points on the Pellerine plateau, and the noise of gunfire awoke all the echoes in these valleys which had been so peaceful such a short time before.

Chapter 4

VICTORY might have eluded the grasp of either party for hours yet, or the struggle ended for want of surviving combatants, for Blues and Chouans seemed equal in valour. On all sides the battle was raging ever more furiously, when in the distance the faint beat of a drum was heard. From its direction the body of men it heralded must be approaching by the Couësnon valley.

'It's the Fougères National Guard!' yelled Gudin at the top of his voice. 'Vannier must have met them.'

As this shout reached the ears of the young Chouan Chief and his ferocious aide-de-camp, the Royalists gave way in a backward surge swiftly halted by an animal cry from Marche-à-terre. Upon two or three commands given in a low voice by the leader and passed on by Marche-à-terre in Breton patois to the Chouans, they executed their retreat with a skill that disconcerted the Republicans and surprised even their Commandant.

At the first order the most able-bodied of the Chouans formed a line, presenting a sufficiently formidable front behind which the wounded and the rest of their force retired to reload. Then suddenly the wounded, moving with the swift agility which Marche-à-terre had already demonstrated, scrambled up the height flanking the road on the right, and were followed by half the Chouans who climbed swiftly to occupy the summit, showing only their heads in energetic movement to the Blues. There they used trees as a defensive wall and turned their guns to cover what was left of the escort, who, following a succession of orders from Hulot, had quickly formed up in line to oppose the Chouans on the road on an equal front. The Chouans retreated slowly, defending the ground they held while wheeling to bring themselves under the protection of their comrades' fire. When they reached the ditch at the roadside, they climbed in their turn the hill occupied by a line of their fellows and joined them, bravely enduring the Republicans' fire, which was accurate enough to heap the ditch with corpses. The men holding the summit answered with a fire no less murderous.

At this point the Fougères National Guard reached the scene at the double, and its presence brought the action to an end. The Guardsmen and a few hotheads among the soldiers had already climbed over the road drainage channel and were making for the woods; but the Commandant shouted in his stentorian voice, 'Do you want to be cut to pieces in there?'

They returned then to rejoin the Republican force, victors on the field though not without heavy losses. All the old hats were draped on bayonet points, the guns raised high in the air, and there was a unanimous shout twice repeated from the soldiers, 'Long live the Republic!' Even the wounded sitting by the roadside shared in the enthusiasm, and Hulot grasped Gérard's hand saying, 'Well, these are something like brave fellows!'

Merle was given the task of burying the dead in a gully off the road. Other soldiers set about the business of transporting the wounded. Horses and carts were requisitioned from neighbouring farms and as quickly as possible they laid their suffering comrades in them on the clothing taken from the dead. Before leaving, the Fougères National Guard handed over a seriously wounded Chouan to Hulot. They had picked him up at the bottom of the slope the escaping Chouans had climbed, where he had rolled as his strength failed.

'Thank you for your help, Citizens,' said the Commandant. 'God's thunder, without you we might have had a very rough quarter of an hour. Look out for yourselves – the war has begun! Good-bye, stout fellows.'

Then Hulot turned to the prisoner. 'What is your General's name?' he said.

'The Gars.'

'Who? March-à-terre?'

'No, the Gars.'

'Where did the Gars come from?'

To this question the Chasseur, whose fierce and rugged face was drawn with pain, returned no answer. He pulled out his rosary and began to recite prayers.

'The Gars is the young *ci-devant* with the black cravat, I suppose? He's been sent by the tyrant and his allies, Pitt and Cobourg.'

At these words the Chouan, who had not known so much, proudly raised his head. 'Sent by God and the King!' he said, with a vigour that took all that remained of his strength.

The Commandant saw that it was hard to question a dying man every line of whose face expressed a fanaticism past comprehension, and turned his head away, frowning. Two soldiers, friends of those whom Marche-à-terre had so brutally despatched by the roadside with his whip, for they were dead, drew back several paces, took careful aim at the Chouan, whose fixed eyes were not lowered before the gun barrels levelled at him, fired point-blank, and he fell. When the soldiers approached to strip the dead man, he cried loudly once more, 'Long live the King!'

'Yes, yes, off with you, old fox. Go and eat your buckwheat pancake with your blessed Virgin,' said La-clef-des-coeurs. 'He's a deep one. Look at him shouting "Long live the tyrant" in our faces when we thought him dead and done for!'

'Look, Sir,' said Beau-pied. 'Here are the brigand's papers.'

'Oho!' cried La-clef-des-coeurs. 'Come and see this soldier of God's who wears his flag on his stomach!'

Hulot and a number of the soldiers gathered round the Chouan's stripped body, and saw a representation of a heart surrounded by flames tattooed in bluish colour on his chest. It was the emblem and rallying-sign of the Brotherhood of the Sacred Heart. Above this Hulot made out *Marie Lambrequin*, no doubt the Chouan's name.

'You see how it is, La-clef-des-coeurs!' said Beau-pied. 'Well, you would never guess in a thousand years what this piece of equipment is for.'

'How should I know the Pope's uniforms!' replied La-clef-des-coeurs.

'Idiot footslogger, don't you ever try to improve your education?' returned Beau-pied. 'Don't you see this chap has been promised that he'll come to life again and he's painted his gizzard so as to be recognized?'

Hulot himself could not help joining in the general hilarity at this flight, which indeed had some foundation in fact.

Merle had now completed the business of burying the dead, and the wounded had been settled as comfortably as possible in the two wagons by their comrades. The other soldiers formed up of their own accord in two files alongside these improvised ambulances, and they moved on down the opposite slope of the mountain, which looks towards Maine and from which one can see the lovely Pellerine valley, which is almost as beautiful as the valley of the Couësnon. Hulot, in company with his two friends Merle and Gérard, slowly followed his soldiers, hoping that they might reach Ernée, where the wounded should find medical attention, without mishap.

This skirmish, which passed almost unnoticed amidst the great events then preparing in France, took the name of the place where it was fought. In the West indeed it attracted some attention, and there the inhabitants who were concerned about this second rising noted a change of spirit in the way the Chouans had started the war again. Formerly these people would not have attacked such a large contingent.

Hulot conjectured that the young Royalist he had seen must be the Gars, a new leader sent to France by the Princes, who was following the custom of the Royalist chiefs in concealing his title and name under the kind of nickname known as a *nom-de-guerre*. This thought had the effect of making the Commandant as uneasy after winning his joyless victory as he had been when he first suspected the ambuscade. He turned several times to contemplate the Pellerine heights that he was leaving behind him, from which from time to time the muffled beating of the National Guards' drums could be heard as they marched down into the Couësnon valley at the same time as the Blues were entering the valley dominated by the Pellerine in the opposite direction.

'Is there one of you', he said abruptly to his two friends, 'who can guess the motive for the Chouan attack? Fighting is a way of doing business to them, and I still can't see what they had to gain this time. They must have lost at least a hundred men. And on our side,' he added, his right cheek creasing and his eyes crinkling in a smile, 'we haven't lost sixty. God's thunder! I don't understand why they were taking a risk. They could easily have done without attacking us, we should have gone by like letters in the post; and what good it did them to put bullet-holes through our men I don't know.' He waved sadly towards the two wagons full of wounded. 'Perhaps they just wanted to give us a greeting,' he added.

'But, Sir, they have won our hundred and fifty cage-birds back,' said Merle.

'If the requisitioned men had jumped into the woods like frogs we would not have gone after them to fish them out, especially after having a volley fired at us,' Hulot answered. 'No, no, there's something more behind it.' He looked back again towards the Pellerine. 'Look!' he exclaimed. 'Do you see?'

Although the three officers were by now at some distance from the ill-omened flat expanse at the top, their practised eyes easily distinguished March-à-terre and other Chouans again in occupation of it.

'Quick march!' shouted Hulot to his band. 'Put some length into your step, open your compass legs and make your horses move *faster than that!* Are their legs frozen? Can these animals be Pitts and Cobourgs too?'*

These words set the little band moving at a more rapid pace.

'As for the riddle I find hard to read,' he said to the two officers, 'God grant, my friends, that we're not given an answer by gunshots at Ernée. I'm very much afraid we may find our road to Mayenne cut by the King's subjects again.'

* i.e. followers of Pitt and General Frédéric de Saxe-Cobourg. At the time of the Revolution anyone suspected of being a counter-Revolutionary or Royalist was so called. – *Trans.*

79

The question of the Chouans' enigmatic tactics which was making Commandant Hulot's moustaches bristle was causing just as much concern at this moment to the persons he had seen at the top of the Pellerine. As soon as the drum-beat of the Fougères National Guard had died away, and when Marche-à-terre saw the Blues reach the foot of the long slope they had marched down, he uttered a spirited owl's hoot and the Chouans reappeared, although there were fewer of them. Many of them had no doubt gone to take the wounded to Pellerine village, on the side of the mountain looking down on the Couësnon valley. Two or three Chasseurs du Roi leaders walked over to Marche-à-terre. The young aristocrat was sitting on a granite block a few paces from them, apparently absorbed in consideration of the many difficulties his campaign was already presenting. Marche-à-terre shaded his eyes from the brilliant light with his hand and dejectedly studied the route the Republicans were taking along the Pellerine valley. His small black piercing eyes tried to discern what was happening on the farther slope, on the skyline beyond the valley.

'The Blues are going to intercept the mail-coach,' said the nearest chief grimly to Marche-à-terre.

'By Saint Anne of Auray!' chimed in another. 'Why did you make us fight? Was it to save your skin?'

Marche-à-terre cast a venomous look at the questioner and slammed the butt of his heavy gun on the ground.

'Am I chief or am I not?' he demanded. Then, after a pause, 'If you had all fought like me none of the Blues would have escaped;' he gestured in the direction of Hulot's diminished band. 'And then the mail-coach would have reached us perhaps.'

'Do you think that it would have entered their heads to give it an escort or hold it if we had let them pass undisturbed?' said a third. 'What you wanted was to save your own cur's hide, just because you wouldn't believe the Blues were on the way. He has shed our blood to keep his snout clean,' the speaker added, turning to the others, 'and we're going to lose a solid twenty thousand gold francs into the bargain . . .'

'Look out for your own snout!' snarled Marche-à-terre, moving three paces backwards and aiming his gun at his assailant. 'You don't hate the Blues, it's gold you care about. All right, damned soul, you'll die without confession, and you haven't received Holy Communion this year!'

This insult was enough to make the Chouan turn pale, and growling deep in his chest he stood back to take aim at Marche-à-terre. The young leader hastily strode between them and knocked the guns from their hands with his own gun-barrel. Then he demanded an explanation of the dispute, for the conversation had been held in Breton patois, whose idiom he was not very familiar with.

'It's all the worse of them to bear me a grudge, Monsieur le Marquis,' said Marche-à-terre, concluding his explanation, 'because I left Pille-miche behind and he'll perhaps be able to save the post-chaise from the thieves' clutches.' And he gestured towards the distant Blues, who in the eyes of these faithful servants of the Church and Crown were all murderers of Louis XVI and highway robbers.

'What's this you say!' the young man exclaimed angrily. 'So you're hanging about here to hold up a coach, a fit job for a cowardly crew that couldn't win my first battle in the field! But you hadn't much hope of winning if that was all that was in your mind! So God's defenders and the King's are nothing but highway robbers. By Saint Anne of Auray, it's a war against the Republic we're fighting, not against stage-coaches! Men responsible for such disgraceful attacks in future shall not receive absolution nor enjoy the favours reserved for the gallant servants of the King.'

A deep muttering rose from the midst of the band. It was easy to see that the new leader's authority, so difficult to establish over an undisciplined mob, was about to be challenged. The rebellious reaction was not lost on the young man and he was already searching for some way of preserving his honour as leader when the clop of a trotting horse broke the silence. All heads turned in the direction from which the newcomer was about to appear. It was a young woman, riding side-saddle on a small Breton horse, that she forced into a gallop to reach the Chouan band as fast as possible as soon as she saw the young man.

'What's the matter?' she asked, looking from the Chouans to their leader.

'Would you believe, Madame, that they are waiting here for the Mayenne to Fougères post-chaise and planning to rob it, just after we've had a fight to set our Fougères *gars* free and lost a lot of men without succeeding in wiping out the Blues!'

'Well, where's the harm in that?' asked the lady, taking in the situation and acting with natural feminine tact. 'You've lost men but we'll never be short of men. The post-chaise is bringing money, and we'll always be short of that! We'll bury our men and they'll go straight to heaven, and we'll take the money and let it go into the pockets of all these brave men. What's wrong with that?'

Smiles from the Chouans unanimously approved this speech.

'You don't see anything there to make you blush?' the young man asked in a low voice. 'Do you need money so badly that you have to take it on the roads?'

'I have such a thirst for it, Marquis, that I would put my heart in pawn for it, I believe, if it weren't already taken,' she said, smiling at him coquettishly. 'But where can you come from if you imagine that you can make use of Chouans without letting them rob a few Blues here and there? Don't you know the saying *as big a thief as an owl*? And isn't that what Chouans are? Besides,' she added, raising her voice, 'isn't it justice? Haven't the Blues taken all the Church property and ours?'

These words were applauded by another murmur from the Chouans, very different from the growl with which they had answered the Marquis. The young man, with a darkening face, drew the lady aside with an aristocrat's quickness to take offence, and said, 'Are those gentlemen going to come to La Vivetière on the day arranged?'

'Yes,' she answered, 'all of them: L'Intimé, Grand-Jacques and perhaps Ferdinand.'

'Excuse me if I go back there then. I can't condone highway robbery like this by staying here. Yes, Madame, highway robbery I said. There's a certain nobility in being robbed, but . . .'

'Well, then,' she interrupted, 'I'll have your share, and thank you for leaving it to me. The extra share will be very welcome. My mother is so dilatory in sending me money that I really don't know what to do.'

'Good-bye,' exclaimed the Marquis, and he strode off. But the young woman rode quickly after him.

'Why don't you stay with me?' she asked, with the half-commanding, half-caressing look women can use so skilfully to convey their wishes to a man who owes some deference to them.

'But are you not going to rob the mail?'

'Rob?' she said. 'What an odd word! Let me explain . . .'

'Explain nothing,' he said, taking her hands and kissing them with a courtier's formal gallantry. 'You must understand,' he went on after a pause; 'if I stayed here while they captured this post-chaise our men would kill me, because I would . . .'

'You would not kill them,' she retorted quickly; 'they would tie your hands with all proper respect for your rank; and then after they had levied a tax on the Republicans for the money they need for their equipment, subsistence and gunpowder they would obey you blindly.'

'And you want me to command an army here? The cause I fight for may demand my life, but allow me to preserve my honour as leader. By withdrawing I can remain in ignorance of this despicable thing. I shall return to escort you.' And he strode rapidly away.

The lady listened to his departing footsteps with considerable displeasure. When the rustling of dry leaves underfoot had grown fainter and ceased, she remained a moment longer as if at a loss, then turned back quickly to the group of Chouans. She gave vent to her feelings in an abrupt disdainful gesture, and said to Marche-à-terre as he helped her to dismount, 'That young man would like to wage war against the

Republic exactly according to all the rules! . . . Ah, well! In a few more days he'll alter his views. – What a way to treat me!' she said to herself presently.

She sat down on the rock which had been the Marquis's seat and waited in silence for the arrival of the chaise.

The involvement of young ladies of noble birth like her in this war monarchies were fighting against the spirit of the age was a phenomenon of the times and not one of the least remarkable. Violent passions had brought her here and fanatical enthusiasm driven her to actions to which, if one may so express it, she was not a consenting party. Like a great many others she had been swept along by a current of exalted emotion, which in many cases led to great achievements. Many women like her played a heroic part or one open to censure in the turmoil of events, and such women were among the most dedicated and active agents of the Royalist cause. None of the heroines on the Royalist side who were led involuntarily, through devotion to their cause, into slips of conduct or deviations which are not forgiven to their sex paid more dearly than she did when, sitting on a granite boulder by the roadside in this moment of despair, she was unable to withhold her admiration for the young leader's lofty contempt and integrity. Insensibly she fell into a profound reverie. She looked back through bitter memories and wished she could turn back again to the innocence of her early years. She regretted that she had not been a victim of that Revolution whose now victorious march could not be arrested by such feeble hands as hers.

Chapter 5

THE vehicle which was connected in some way with the Chouan attack had left the little town of Ernée some minutes before the skirmish. Nothing reveals a country better than the condition of the working stock of its public services, and in this respect the post-chaise deserves an honourable mention. The Revolution itself had not the power to destroy it; the same vehicle is still on the road in our own day. When the monopoly of transporting travellers throughout the realm, granted to a company under Louis XIV, was redeemed by Turgot in 1775 and the network of stage-coaches nicknamed the *turgotines* set up, the old carriages owned by Monsieur Vougcs, Monsieur Chanteclair and the Widow Lacombe were washed up on the provincial roads; and it was one of those wretched vehicles that served the connection between Mayenne and Fougères. It had been christened the *turgotine* ironically long before by certain obstreperous fellows in mockery of Paris or as a sneer at a Minister who attempted innovations.

This turgotine was a sorry vehicle with two very large wheels, so compressed at the back that two persons of the slightest corpulence could barely have found room. As the frail contraption held so little of any bulk or weight and the boot, which formed the coachman's box, was reserved for the mail, travellers were obliged to keep any baggage they had between their legs, which were already cramped and suffering tortures in the bottom of the minute body shaped rather like a bellows. The original colour of the paint on chassis and wheels was any traveller's guess. Two leather curtains, far from pliable in spite of long service, were intended as protection against cold and rain. The driver, on a seat like those of the most lamentable Paris *coucous*, shared perforce in the conversation because of the way he was set between his biped and quadruped victims. The vehicle was fantastically like one of those decrepit old men who have survived any number of rheums and apoplexies and seem to be given a wide berth by death. It whined and complained as it went and at times groaned aloud. It lurched backwards and forwards alternately like a traveller heavily asleep, as if it were trying to resist the violent tugging of the two little Breton horses dragging it over a rather bumpy road. This monument to another age contained three passengers who as they left Ernée, where they had changed horses, continued a conversation with the driver begun before the relay.

'How could the Chouans possibly have been seen around here?' the coachman was saying. 'They've just told me in Ernée that Commandant Hulot has not left Fougerès yet.'

'That's all right for you, friend!' replied a traveller rather younger than the others. 'All you risk is your carcase! If you had three hundred crowns on you like me, and were known as a good patriot, you would not be so easy.'

'You have a very easy tongue, at any rate,' the coachman answered, shaking his head.

'It's the counted lambs the wolf devours,' added another passenger.

This last, a man of about forty, dressed in black, was probably some *Recteur* of the district. His chin rested on a double roll of fat and his florid complexion seemed to belong to the ecclesiastical order. Although fat and short, he showed a certain agility whenever they had to climb down from the vehicle or get in again.

'If you turned out to be Chouans,' exclaimed the owner of three hundred crowns, who wore a goatskin worth a good deal of money over breeches of good cloth and a very respectable jacket and who must be some prosperous farmer, 'by Saint Robespierre's soul I can guarantee you would get a hot reception.' And he let his grey eyes wander significantly from the coachman to the other traveller as he showed them a pair of pistols at his belt.

'Those don't frighten Bretons,' the Recteur said scornfully.

'Besides, do we look as though we had designs on your money?'

Whenever the word *money* was mentioned the coachman always became uncommunicative, and the Recteur had just sufficient acuteness to doubt whether the patriot possessed many crowns and suspect that their whip might have some.

'Are you carrying much today, Coupiau?' the Abbé asked.

'Oh, Monsieur Gudin, I've practically what you might call nothing!'

As the coachman answered, the Abbé Gudin, studying his and the patriot's faces found them equally expressionless.

'All the better for you,' returned the patriot. 'So I am free to take my own measures to protect my property if there's any trouble.'

This high-handed assertion of rights affronted Coupiau, and he answered fiercely, 'I am in charge of this chaise, and so long as I drive you . . .'

'Are you a patriot or are you a Chouan?' the other broke in hotly.

'Neither,' answered Coupiau. 'I'm a coachman, and what's more, a Breton; and it follows from that I'm not afraid of the Blues nor the noblemen neither.'

'You mean the noble robbers,' the patriot retorted sarcastically.

'They're only taking back what was taken from them,' said the Abbé sharply.

The two travellers looked each other in the face, probing, if the colloquial expression may be permitted, the very bull's-eye of each other's eyes.

At the back of the vehicle there was a third traveller, who in all this discussion going on about him had preserved complete silence. The driver, the patriot and even Gudin paid no attention to this mute person. He was indeed one of those awkward unsociable fellows who travel like a dumbly submissive calf being taken with its feet tied together to the nearest market. They begin by occupying every inch of their legitimate space and end up sleeping without any human consideration for their fellows on their neighbours' shoulders. So the patriot. Gudin and the driver had left him to himself in acceptance of his slumber, once they had seen that it was useless to talk to a man who, according to his stiffly expressionless face, spent his life measuring yards of linen cloth and concerned his mind with nothing beyond selling it for more than it cost. This fat little man huddled in his corner had opened his small china-blue eyes from time to time, and during the dispute turned them on each speaker in succession with an expression of alarm, doubt and mistrust. But he appeared to be afraid only of his travelling companions and worry little about Chouans. When he looked at the driver one would have said they were two freemasons. Just then the exchange of shots began on the Pellerine. Coupiau, in some perturbation, brought his vehicle to a stop.

'Oh, oh!' said the clergyman, who seemed to know what he was talking about. 'It's a serious action, there's a large number engaged.'

'The worrying thing, Monsieur Gudin, is to know who's going to win,' exclaimed Coupiau.

Now all the faces wore the same anxious expression.

'Let's take the carriage into that inn-yard,' said the patriot; 'and we can hide it there while we wait to see what happens.'

This seemed such good advice that Coupiau took it. The patriot helped the driver to conceal the vehicle from any casual eye behind a heap of faggots. The Recteur, as he seemed to be, seized an opportunity to whisper to Coupiau, 'Has he really any money?'

'Hey, Monsieur Gudin, if Your Reverence had all his money in your pockets, you wouldn't find them too heavy.'

The Republicans, hurrying to reach Ernée, passed the inn without stopping. At the tramp of their quick march Gudin and the innkeeper, moved by curiosity, walked to the inn-yard gate to see them pass. Suddenly the fat cleric ran to a soldier, who paused a moment.

'What's this, Gudin!' he exclaimed. 'Obstinate fellow, are you really going with the Blues? My child, can you think of that?'

'Yes, Uncle,' the corporal replied. 'I have sworn to defend France.'

'Ah, wretched man, it's your soul you're risking!' the uncle said, trying to stir his nephew's religious feeling, which is so strong in Breton hearts.

'Well, Uncle, if the King had put himself at the head of his armies, I don't say but what . . .'

'Idiot! Who's talking about the King? Does your Republic give benefices? It has overturned everything. Where do you want to get to in life? Stay with us; we'll win sooner or later, and you'll become Judge of some High Court.'

'Courts? . . .' said Gudin derisively. 'Good-bye, Uncle.'

'You shan't get three louis from me to call your own,' said his uncle furiously. 'I cut you off with nothing!'

'Thank you,' said the Republican. And they parted.

The fumes of the cider the patriot had treated Coupiau to while the little band of soldiers passed by had been having their effect on the coachman's head; but he woke up to rejoice when the innkeeper, who had inquired the result of the action, announced that the Blues had won. Coupiau then set his vehicle on the road once more, and it was soon to be seen travelling along the floor of the Pellerine valley, where it was easily visible from the heights of both Maine and Brittany, looking like wreckage floating on the waves after a storm.

As he reached the top of a slope the Blues were climbing, from which one could still observe the Pellerine in the distance, Hulot turned to see if the Chouans were still there. The sun shining on their gun-barrels picked them out for him as brilliant points. As he cast a last look at the valley he was leaving to descend into the Ernée valley, he thought he could descry Coupiau's vehicle on the main road.

'Isn't that the post-chaise from Mayenne?' he inquired of his two friends.

The two officers followed the direction of his gaze and had no difficulty in recognizing the old turgotine.

'Well,' said Hulot, 'how is it that we didn't meet it?'

They looked at one another in silence.

'Is this another riddle?' exclaimed the Commandant. 'I begin to have an inkling of the truth, all the same.'

At this moment, Marche-à-terre, who also recognized the turgotine, was pointing it out to his comrades, and the general outburst of noisy delight woke the lady from her thoughts. She walked forward and saw the vehicle making its way with fatal speed towards them up the Pellerine. The hapless turgotine soon reached the level summit. The Chouans, who had concealed themselves again, pounced avidly upon their prey. The silent traveller let himself slip to the bottom of the vehicle and immediately crouched down, endeavouring to look like a package.

'Well!' exclaimed Coupiau from his box seat, pointing to the peasant. 'You must have smelt the patriot here, for he's got money, a sackful of it!'

The Chouans greeted these words with a general roar of laughter and shouts of 'Pille-miche! Pille-miche! Pille-miche!'

Amid this laughter, in which Pille-miche himself joined like an echo, Coupiau climbed down, much disconcerted, from his seat. But when the well-known Cibot, nicknamed Pille-miche, helped his neighbour down, a respectful murmur arose.

'It's the Abbé Gudin!' cried several men.

At this respected name all hats were snatched off. The Chouans knelt before the priest and asked his blessing, and the Abbé gravely bestowed it on them.

'He would fool Saint Peter and steal the keys of Heaven,' said the Recteur, clapping Pille-miche on the shoulder. 'If it had not been for him the Blues would have met us on the way.' Then, seeing the lady, the Abbé Gudin went to talk to her, a few paces off. Marche-à-terre swiftly opened the chaise boot, and with a savage delight held up a bag whose shape suggested rolls of coins. It did not take him long to divide up the contents. Each Chouan received his share, allotted with such impartial justice that there was no occasion for the mildest dispute. Then Marche-à-terre walked over to the lady and the priest and offered them about six thousand francs.

'Can I accept this with a good conscience, Monsieur Gudin?' she asked, feeling a need for someone's approbation.

'By all means, Madame. The Church in former times approved the confiscation of Protestant property. How much more justification is there then for taking the property of Revolutionaries who deny God, destroy chapels and persecute religion.' The Abbé added example to precept by accepting the new form of tithe offered him by March-à-terre without hesitation. 'In any case,' he added, 'I am now free to consecrate all I possess to the defence of God and the King, for my nephew has gone off with the Blues!'

Coupiau bewailed his bad luck and declared mournfully that he was ruined.

'Come with us,' said Marche-à-terre. 'You shall have your share.'

'But they'll believe I let myself be robbed on purpose, if I go back without any signs of violence.'

'Is that all that's worrying you? . . .' said Marche-à-terre. He gave a signal, and a volley of shots riddled the turgotine. At this unexpected attack the old vehicle uttered such a lamentable cry that the Chouans, superstitious by nature, recoiled in fear; but Marche-à-terre had seen something start up and fall back again into a corner of the chaise – the pale face of the taciturn traveller.

'You have another fowl in your hen-coop,' he said under his breath to Coupiau.

Pille-miche winked knowingly.

'Yes,' the driver answered; 'but if I join up with your crowd, you will have to let me take this worthy man safe and sound to Fougères. I have sworn by Saint Anne of Auray to do it.'

'Who is it?' asked Pille-miche.

'I mustn't tell you,' Coupiau answered.

'Let him be!' and Marche-à-terre nudged Pille-miche. 'He has sworn by Saint Anne of Auray. He'll have to keep his promises. But', went on the Chouan, 'don't go down the mountain too fast. We'll overtake you. And for why? I want to see the cut of your passenger's jib; and we'll give him a safe-conduct.'

As he spoke they heard a galloping horse rapidly approaching, and soon the young leader appeared. The lady promptly concealed the bag she was holding in her hand.

'You need have no scruples about keeping that money,' said the young man, with a hand under the arm she was holding behind her back. 'Here is a letter for you I found among those waiting for me at La Vivetière; it is from your mother.' With a look first at the Chouans making their way back to the woods, and then at the post-chaise making its way down into the Couësnon valley, he added, 'I came as fast as I could but I see I have come too late. Let's hope I'm wrong in what I suspect!'

'It's my poor mother's money!' exclaimed the lady, when she had unsealed the letter and read the first lines.

Some stifled guffaws were heard from behind the bushes. Even the young man could not help smiling as he looked at the lady with the bag in her hand holding her share of her own stolen money. She began to laugh herself.

'Well, Marquis. Thanks be to Heaven, this time I've come out of the affair quite blameless!' she said.

'You treat everything frivolously, don't you? Even regret and remorse . . .' said the young man.

She blushed, and looked at the Marquis with such sincere contrition that he was disarmed. The Abbé politely returned the tithe he had just accepted, but with a rather equivocal expression; then he followed the young leader, who was moving off towards the unfrequented road he had come by. Before joining them, the lady beckoned Marche-à-terre.

'You will go off and take up a position barring the way to Mortagne,' she said in a low voice. 'I know that the Blues must keep sending large sums in cash to Alençon to pay for the preparations they're making for the war. If I let your comrades keep today's takings it's on condition that they'll be able to make it up to me. But make sure the Gars knows nothing of the purpose of the expedition, he might object to it. If anything goes wrong, though, I'll pacify him.'

'Madame,' said the Marquis, when she had mounted to ride pillion behind him after giving up her own horse to the Abbé, 'our friends in Paris write warning me to beware. The Republic intends to try fighting us by ruse and treachery.'

'That's not at all a bad idea,' she replied. 'Those folk manage to think up quite good plans! In that case I'll be able to do my share in the war and find foes I can fight.'

'I've no doubt of it,' the Marquis agreed. 'Pichegru urges me to be scrupulously careful and circumspect in any kind of friendship. The Republic does me the honour of thinking me more dangerous than all the Vendée insurgents put together, and counts on using weaknesses of the flesh to catch me.'

'Would you suspect me?' she said, using the hand she was holding on to him with to tap his heart lightly.

'Would you be here if I did? . . . Madame,' he said, turning his face down towards her, and she kissed his forehead.

'So,' the Abbé pursued the subject, 'they think Fouché's police more dangerous to us than the mobile battalions and the Counter-Chouans?'

'Just so.'

'Ha!' cried the lady. 'So Fouché's sending women against you? . . . I'll be ready for them,' she added after a moment's pause, in a voice from the heart.

At a distance of three or four gunshots from the lonely height which the leaders were leaving, a scene was taking place of a kind which was to be frequent enough for some time yet on the main roads. At the exit from the little village of Pellerine, Pille-miche and Marche-à-terre had stopped the turgotine again in a hollow. Coupiau was brought down from his box after a show of resistance. The taciturn traveller, winkled from his hiding-place by the two Chouans, found himself kneeling in a gorse-bush.

'Who are you?' Marche-à-terre demanded in an ominous voice.

The traveller still kept silent, until Pille-miche repeated the question with a blow from the butt of his gun.

'I am Jacques Pinaud,' he said then, casting a look at Coupiau, 'a poor shopkeeper, a linen-draper.'

Coupiau shook his head, not thinking this a breach of his promises. Pille-miche found the gesture illuminating and took aim, while Marche-à-terre bluntly presented this explicit and terrible ultimatum: 'You are too fat to be a poor person with poor people's worries! If you make us ask you your real name again, my friend Pille-miche here is ready to win your heirs' esteem and gratitude by just one shot.' And then, after a pause, 'Who are you?' he said.

'I am d'Orgemont of Fougères.'

'Aha!' exclaimed the two Chouans.

'It wasn't me who gave your name, Monsieur d'Orgement,' said Coupiau. 'The Holy Virgin is my witness that I defended you well.'

'As you are Monsieur d'Orgemont of Fougères,' said Marche-à-terre with mocking respect, 'we'll let you go safe and sound. But you're not a good Chouan nor a real Blue neither though you did buy the monastery of Juvigny's lands, so you shall pay us ...' he appeared to be reckoning the number of his associates '... three hundred six-franc crowns for your ransom. Neutrality is well worth that.'

'Three hundred six-franc crowns!' repeated the hapless banker, Pille-miche and Coupiau in chorus, but in very different tones of voice.

'My dear sir, I'm sorry to say I'm a ruined man,' d'Orgemont went on. 'The hundred million *forced loan* that this devil's own Republic is raising has cost me an enormous sum and cleaned me out completely.'

'How much does your Republic want from you, then?'

'A thousand crowns, my dear sir,' the banker said piteously, thinking he might get some rebate.

'If your Republic squeezes such big forced loans out of you, you see you've everything to gain by being in with us – our government costs less. Three hundred crowns, is that too much for your skin?'

'Where am I to get it?'

'From your cash-box,' said Pille-miche. 'And see that your crowns have not been clipped, or we'll clip your claws in the fire.'

'Where can I pay it?' d'Orgemont asked.

'Your country house at Fougères is not far from the Gibarry farm, where my cousin Galope-chopine, formerly known as Big Cibot, lives. You'll hand the money over to him.'

'It's quite irregular.'

'What's that to us?' said Marche-à-terre. 'Just turn over in your head that if it's not handed over to Galope-chopine within a fortnight we'll pay you a little visit that will cure you of the gout, supposing your feet are troubled with it. As for you, Coupiau,' the Chouan chief went on, 'your name from now on is *Mène-à-bien*.'

With this the two Chouans went off. The traveller climbed into the turgotine again, and by the exercise of Coupiau's whip was whirled rapidly towards Fougères.

'If you had been armed,' Coupiau said, 'we might have defended ourselves a bit better.'

'Idiot! I have ten thousand francs in here,' rejoined d'Orgemont, displaying his heavy shoes. 'How can a man defend himself with such a lot of money on him?'

Mène-à-bien scratched his ear and turned to look behind him, but his new comrades had vanished.

Chapter 6

HULOT and his soldiers stopped at Ernée to set down the wounded soldiers at the little town's hospital; then, with no untoward incident to interrupt their march, the Republican troops reached Mayenne. There next morning the Commandant was able to resolve his perplexities, for by next day the whole town knew how the post-chaise had been plundered. A few days later, the authorities drafted sufficient patriot conscripts to Mayenne for Hulot to complete the complement of his Demi-brigade there.

Soon very unreassuring rumours began to come in about the insurrection. The rising was general at all points where the Chouans and Vendéans had established the chief centres of insurrection during the earlier war. In Brittany, the Royalists had taken possession of Pontorson in order to be within reach of communication by sea. They had taken the little town of Saint-James, between Pontorson and Fougères, and appeared to intend to make it temporarily their strong-hold, the centre for their stores and operations. From there they could communicate with Normandy and Morbihan without danger. The junior leaders were on the move everywhere throughout the three regions, stirring up the Monarchy's supporters and trying to achieve a measure of coordination in their operations.

At the same time news from the Vendée showed a similar ferment of intrigue and plot there, with four celebrated leaders as the prime movers: the Abbé Vernal, the Comte de Fontaine, Monsieur de Chatillon and Monsieur Suzannet. Their opposite numbers in the Department of Orne were said to be the Chevalier de Valois, the Marquis d'Esgrignon and the Troisville brothers. At the head, in effect, of the vast plan of operations, now unfolding slowly but formidably, was the Gars – that was the name given by the Chouans to Monsieur le Marquis de Montauran at the time of his landing. The information Hulot had sent to the Ministers was proved correct in every point.

The authority of this General sent from outside had been immediately recognized. The Marquis was even achieving sufficient hold over the Chouans to make them see the true purpose of the war and persuade them that the excesses for which they were being held responsible dishonoured the noble cause they had embraced. The bold assurance of the young aristocrat, his dash, coolness and ability, were awakening the hopes of the Republic's enemies, and appealed so strongly to the sombrely fanatical spirit of the insurgent regions that the least zealous were working together to prepare the ground for events that might prove decisive in favour of the defeated Monarchy.

Hulot was receiving no answer to repeated requests and reports sent to Paris. This astonishing silence must portend some new revolutionary crisis.

'Is it possible,' the veteran Commandant said to his friends, 'that they now write *refused* against requests for instructions as well as requests for money?'

But the news of General Bonaparte's magical return and of the events of the 18 Brumaire* was not long in spreading. The military commanders in the West then understood the reason for the Ministers' silence; but this made them all the more impatient to be relieved of their heavy responsibility, and they became increasingly anxious to know what measures the new Government was going to take.

When they learned that General Bonaparte had been appointed First Consul of the Republic, military men were delighted: the soldiers saw one of their own kind set in control of the handling of affairs for the first time. France, which had made an idol of this young general, was vibrant with hope. The nation took on new vigour. The capital, weary of gloom, gave itself up to the festivities and pleasures of which it had been so long deprived. The Consulate's first acts

* 9 November 1799, when Bonaparte overthrew the Directory. – *Trans.*

did nothing to diminish hope, and no shock was given to Liberty.

The First Consul issued a Proclamation to the people of the West. Such eloquent addresses to the masses, which Bonaparte had, so to speak, invented, produced a prodigious effect in those times of ardent patriotism and evident miracles. His voice resounded through the world like the voice of a prophet, for none of his Proclamations had ever yet failed to be stamped and sealed by victory.

COUNTRYMEN,

A fratricidal war is setting the Departments of the West ablaze for the second time.

The agents of these troubles are traitors sold to England or brigands fishing in troubled waters, seeking in these civil clashes only the conditions in which their crimes can flourish and go unpunished.

To such men the Government owes nothing: it need not spare them nor declare its principles to them.

But there are citizens dear to the country who have been seduced by their intrigues; and to these citizens we owe enlightenment and the truth.

Unjust laws have been promulgated and executed; arbitrary acts have threatened the security of citizens and the liberty of consciences; the entering of names on lists of *emigrés* without proper authentication has put citizens in danger. In sum, great principles of social order have been violated.

The Consuls affirm that since religious liberty is guaranteed by the Constitution, the law of the Eleventh Prairial of the year Three, which gives citizens the use of buildings intended for religious worship, shall be carried into effect.

The Government declares an amnesty: it will grant a free pardon to those who repent; mercy shall be unconditional and absolute. But it will strike whoever after this Declaration dare still resist the sovereignty of the nation.

'Well,' said Hulot after the public reading of this Consular address, 'what do you think of that for a fatherly attitude? But not a Royalist brigand will change his views for all that, you'll see.'

The Commandant was right. The only effect of this Proclamation was to confirm the members of each party in their allegiance.

A few days later Hulot and his colleagues received reinforcements. The new Minister of War informed them that General Brune had been apppointed to take command of the Army in the west of France. Hulot, who was known as an experienced officer, was meantime acting commander in the Departments of Orne and Mayenne. A new drive soon began to make itself felt in every department of government. A memorandum from the War Office, signed also by the Minister responsible for Police, announced that vigorous measures, to be put into effect by the military commanders, had been decided upon to stamp out the insurrection *at its source*. The Chouans and Vendéans had already taken advantage of the Republican inaction, however, to raise the countryside and take complete possession of it. In these circumstances a new Consular Proclamation was made, the General this time speaking to the troops.

SOLDIERS,

In the West there now remain only brigands, *émigrés*, hirelings of England.

The Army has more than sixty thousand brave men. Let me soon have news that the rebel leaders are no more. Glory is only won by toil in the field. If it could be obtained by staying at headquarters in the large towns, would we not all be glorious? . . .

Soldiers, whatever rank you may hold in the Army, the nation's gratitude is yours for the winning. To deserve it you must brave the inclemency of the elements, ice, snow, extreme cold by night; you must surprise your enemies at dawn, and exterminate those miserable wretches who dishonour the name of Frenchmen.

Let yours be a short effective campaign. Be merciless to the bandits, but observe strict discipline.

National Guardsmen, add the might of your arms to those of the troops of the line.

If you are aware of partisans of the bandits among you, seize them! Let them find refuge nowhere against the pursuing soldier; and if there be traitors who dare shelter and defend them, let them perish with them!

'What a comrade!' exclaimed Hulot. 'He's just the same as he was with the Army in Italy – he rings the bell and says mass too. How's that for straight speaking, eh?'

'Yes, but he speaks for himself alone and in his own name,' said Gérard, who was beginning to feel some alarm about the consequences of the 18 Brumaire.

'Ho, bless my soul, what's wrong with that, since he's a soldier?' cried Merle.

A few paces away, a group of soldiers had crowded in front of the Proclamation posted on the wall. But as not one of them could read they were studying it, casually or curiously, while two or three of them were trying to pick out a citizen who looked like a learned man from the passers-by.

'See here, La-clef-des-coeurs, tell us what's this scrap of paper here,' Beau-pied said slyly to his comrade.

'It's very easy to guess,' replied La-clef-des-coeurs, who like his friend was always ready to pick up a cue.

Hearing this, everyone turned to look at the pair.

'Look at that,' went on La-clef-des-coeurs, pointing to the crude engraving at the head of the Proclamation, in which by a recent change a pair of compasses had replaced the spirit-level of 1793, 'That means that us footsloggers have to put our best foot forward! They've put compasses with their legs open, that's what they call a symbolic emblem.'

'My boy, it doesn't suit you to act the scholar, that's called a problem,' said Beau-pied. 'I served in the Artillery to begin with, and my officers lived on nothing else.'

'It's a symbolic emblem.'

'It's a problem.'

'What will you bet?'

'What do you say?'

'Your German pipe.'

'Done!'

'With respect, Sir, isn't it true that that's a symbol not a problem?' La-clef-des-coeurs asked Gérard who, deep in thought, was following Hulot and Merle.

'It's both,' he answered gravely.

'The Adjutant was having us on,' pronounced Beau-pied. 'That paper means that our Italian General has had a raise to Consul, and that's a first-rate promotion, and we're going to get great-coats and shoes.'

PART TWO – AN IDEA OF FOUCHÉ'S

ONE day towards the end of the month of Brumaire,* while Hulot was spending the morning on manoeuvres with his Demi-brigade, which was now by official orders concentrated in Mayenne, an express messenger from Alençon brought despatches; and as he read them an expression of extreme annoyance overspread Hulot's countenance.

'Well then, we must be off!' he exclaimed testily, stuffing the papers into his hat. 'Two companies are to march with me towards Mortagne. The Chouans are there. You will come with me,' he said to Merle and Gérard. 'May they make an aristo of me if I understand a word of my despatches. It may be that I'm nothing but a blockhead. Never mind. On our way! There's no time to lose.'

'Sir, is there something so abominable in this game-bag?' Merle said, touching the envelope with the Ministerial seal with the toe of his boot.

'Jove's thunder! It's nothing, except that they're *pushing us around.*'

Whenever the Commandant used the military expression which we water down here, as we did once before, by a euphemism, it was a sure sign of a storm in the wind. To the Demi-brigade the different intonations of this phrase were so many degrees precisely graduated on the thermometer of their Chief's patience; and the old soldier's openness made recognition so easy that the most heedless drummer soon knew his Hulot by heart, just by observing the variations in

* In duration from 23 October to 21 November. – *Trans.*

the little grimace which creased the Commandant's cheek and made his eyes seem to wink. On this occasion, the tone of smouldering anger with which the expression was uttered reduced the two friends to silence and circumspection. The very smallpox scars that pitted the old warrior's face seemed deeper and his colour more weather-beaten than usual. His wide queue, braided at the sides, had swung over one epaulette when he put his tricorne hat on again, and Hulot tossed it back with such fury that the locks were disarranged. However, as he stood there motionless, his fists clenched, his arms folded stiffly across his chest, his moustache bristling, Gérard ventured to ask, 'Do we leave at once?'

'Yes, if the cartridge pouches are replenished,' he growled.

'They are, Sir,'

'Shoulder arms! Left ... wheel! Forward ... march!' cried Gérard, in obedience to a gesture from his Chief.

And the drummers took their place at the head of the two Companies detailed by Gérard. At the sound of the drum the Commandant, still lost in deep reflection, appeared to rouse himself, and he marched from the town escorted by his two friends, to whom he did not address one word. Merle and Gérard several times silently exchanged glances as if asking 'How long is he going to hold out on us?' And they cast sidelong looks at him as they marched and watched him stealthily as he went on muttering vague syllables between his teeth. Several times it sounded to the soldiers' ears as if he were swearing, but not one of them dared breathe a word; for when the occasion demanded it they all knew how to observe the strict discipline which soldiers formerly commanded in Italy by Bonaparte had grown inured to. Most of them were, like Hulot, survivors of the famous battalions which were given the honours of war when they capitulated at Mayence,* with the condition that they would not be em-

* In 1793 the French had sustained a famous siege at Mayence against the Prussians and the *émigré* forces, and were given the honours of war when it ended, but it was agreed that these troops should not be used in the line again against the Coalition, which was why they were now employed in the West. – *Trans.*

ployed again beyond the frontiers; and the Army had nick-named them the *Mayençais*. It would be hard to find soldiers and leaders who understood one another better.

Chapter 7

ON the morning after their departure, Hulot and his two
friends were to be seen very early on the road from Mortagne
to Alençon about a league from the town, a part of the road
that runs beside the stretches of grassland watered by the
Sarthe. One picturesque aspect of the grassy plains after
another comes into view on the left, while on the right thick
woods which are an outlying part of the great forest of Menil-
Broust act as a foil, if one may borrow the artists' term, to
set off the enchanting windings of the river. The roads are
embanked and lined with ditches kept clear of earth, which is
thrown up on the fields, producing high banks crowned with
whins, the name given throughout the West to the broom
bush. This shrub, which spreads in dense masses, furnishes
excellent winter fodder for horses and cattle. However, while
it remained unharvested it harboured Chouans at this time
behind its dark green clumps, so that the banks and the broom
that tell the traveller he is approaching Brittany made this
part of the road as dangerous as it is beautiful.

The hazards of the journey from Mortagne to Alençon
and from Alençon to Mayenne were the reason for Hulot's
expedition; and at this point he at last gave vent to his wrath
and revealed its cause. At the moment he was escorting an
old mail-coach pulled by post-horses that his tired soldiers
had obliged to adopt a walking pace. The companies of Blues
attached to the garrison at Mortagne had accompanied this
wretched conveyance to the limit of their stage and were now
to be seen returning to Mortagne as black dots in the distance,
while Hulot had replaced them in this duty which the soldiers
with good reason called a patriotic *sickener*. One of the old
Republican's two companies marched a few paces ahead of
the vehicle and the other followed it. Hulot, marching between

the advance detachment and the coach, with Merle and Gérard on either side, suddenly broke silence.

'Thunder and lightning! Would you believe that the General despatched us from Mayenne just to escort the two petticoats in the old waggon!'

'But, Sir, when we took up our position just now by the citizenesses,' said Gérard, 'you saluted them in no ungallant fashion.'

'Ho! that's what's so galling. Those Paris fops require us to treat their damned women with the utmost deference! How can they shame good honest patriots like us by making us trail after a skirt! I'm a man who goes straight on his own road and I don't like other people's zigzags. When I saw Danton with his mistresses and Barras with his mistresses I said to them, "Citizens, when the Republic called you to govern it it was not authorizing you to adopt the old régime's ways of amusing itself." You'll tell me that women? . . . Oh, yes, one has women! That's right enough. Good lads of course must have women, and good women too. But in times of danger, enough of that. What good would it be to have got rid of the old régime's abuses if the patriots start them up again? Look at the First Consul: there's a man for you – no women, always on the job. I'll bet my left moustache he has no finger in the idiotic task they've given us here.'

'Faith, Commandant,' Merle replied, laughing, 'I had a glimpse of the nosetip of the young lady tucked away in the coach, and I swear it wouldn't shame anyone to feel as strongly inclined as I do to take a turn round the coach and have a little chat with the travellers.'

'Beware, Merle,' said Gérard. 'The two jennies in bonnets have a citizen with them who's wily enough to serve you up on toast.'

'Who – the beau who's for ever sliding his little eyes from one side of the road to the other as if he were seeing Chouans? The dandy with the legs you can barely see who looks like a duck with its head sticking out of a pâté when his horse's legs are hidden behind the coach? If you imagine that booby can ever keep me from caressing his pretty warbler . . .'

'Duck, warbler! Oh, my poor Merle, you're off among the feathered tribes with a vengeance. But don't trust the duck! His green eyes look treacherous like a viper's to me, and sly like a wife forgiving her husband. I would trust the Chouans sooner than these lawyers with faces like carafes of lemonade.'

'A fig for that!' cried Merle gaily. 'With the Commandant's permission, I'll risk it! That woman has eyes like stars; it's worth risking anything for a man to see them.'

'Our friend is caught,' said Gérard. 'He's beginning to babble.'

Hulot grimaced, shrugged his shoulders and said, 'If he takes my advice he'll taste the soup before he tries swallowing it.'

'What a joy Merle is,' Gérard went on, looking back at that officer as he lagged behind as if to let the coach gradually overtake him. 'He's so gay! He's the only man in existence who can crack a joke at a comrade's death without anyone thinking he lacks feeling.'

'He's a true French soldier,' said Hulot gravely.

'Oh, look at him pulling his epaulettes over his shoulders to show that he's a captain,' cried Gérard, laughing; 'as if his rank mattered.'

The carriage towards which the officer was turning held two women, one of whom appeared to be the other's maid.

'Women like that always go in pairs,' had been Hulot's comment.

A slight pinched little man caracoled about the coach, sometimes in front of it, sometimes behind it; but although he appeared to be escorting these two privileged travellers no one had yet seen him address a word to them. His taciturnity, which might be a mark either of contempt or respect, the vast amount of baggage and boxes of the lady the Commandant called a *princess*, and indeed everything else about the party, including the costume of the attendant cavalier, had exacerbated Hulot's ill temper. The stranger was a model of the fashion of the *Incroyables* which the caricatures of the time did not exaggerate. Picture this person rigged out in a coat whose basques were so short that five or six inches of waistcoat showed below, and its tails so long that they looked like a cod's tail, in a style in fact given that name. An enormous cravat encircled his neck with so many folds that the comparatively tiny head protruding from this labyrinth of muslin almost justified Captain Merle's gastronomical fancy. The stranger wore skin-tight breeches and Suvorov boots. A huge blue and white cameo served as a shirt-pin. Two watch-chains fell from his waistband in parallel loops. His hair lay in corkscrew curls on each side of his face and almost concealed his forehead. Finally, to set off his head with the utmost elegance, his shirt collar and jacket collar rose so high that they appeared to hold it like a bouquet in a paper cornet. To the finicking accessories that swore at one another with no kind of decorative harmony add the ludicrous colour contrast of yellow breeches, red waistcoat and cinnamon jacket, and you have a faithful impression of supreme good taste as young men of fashion observed it at the beginning of the Consulate. This strikingly baroque costume seemed to have been designed to put grace through a hoop and demonstrate that there is nothing so ridiculous that fashion cannot hallow it.

The cavalier looked to be about thirty years old but was in fact barely twenty-two, and might have owed this premature ageing either to debauchery or the anxieties of the times. In spite of his charlatan mode of dress he had a certain elegance of bearing recognizably that of a well-bred man.

When the Captain was seen near the coach the dandy appeared to guess his design and favoured it by reining in his horse. Merle's sardonic glance at him met an impenetrable countenance, the mask of one of those whom the vicissitudes of the Revolution had accustomed to hiding the faintest trace of emotion. As soon as the curled-up brim of the Captain's tricorne and his epaulettes were noticed by the ladies, a voice of angelic sweetness addressed him.

'Monsieur l'Officier, would you be kind enough to tell us what part of the road this is?'

There is an inexpressible charm in a question asked by a stranger, an unknown woman travelling by herself – the simplest word seems to hold a whole romance. And if the woman asks for some helpful information, with the implication of her own need of protection and a certain ignorance of worldly things, one must admit that there is a slight tendency in every man to build an impossible castle in the air in which he sees himself in bliss. And so the words 'Monsieur l'Officier', the polite form of the request, brought a strange disturbance to the Captain's heart. He essayed to scrutinize the stranger's face and was singularly disappointed to find a veil jealously concealing her features; he could scarcely even see her eyes, which glittered through the gauzy material like two onyx jewels in the sun.

'You are now three miles from Alençon, Madame.'

'Alençon already!' And the stranger threw herself or rather let herself sink back in the coach without further remark.

'Alençon,' repeated the other woman, apparently waking. 'You'll see the country again.'

She looked at the Captain in silence. Merle, disappointed in his hope of seeing the beautiful stranger, turned his attention to her companion. She was a fair girl of about twenty-six, with a pretty figure, and the fresh skin and healthy good looks characteristic of women from Valognes, Bayeux and around Alençon. Her blue eyes did not express any great intelligence, but rather a certain steadfastness combined with tenderness. She wore a dress of ordinary stuff. Her hair, caught up under a little high muslin cap as worn by the women of Caux, quite unpretentiously, gave her face an air of charming simplicity. Her bearing, although it did not have the dignity appropriate to the fashionable world, was not without the self-respect natural in a modest girl who could look back on her past years and not find anything there to regret or blush for. Merle could see at a glance that she was a meadow flower that had survived its transplantation to Paris hothouses, with their concentrated withering blaze, and lost nothing of its pure colour and country naturalness. The girl's naïvely unwelcoming attitude and modest glance at him showed Merle that she did not wish to be overheard; and indeed when he withdrew the two strangers began a low-voiced conversation whose murmur barely reached his ears.

'You left in such a hurry', said the country girl, 'that you didn't even take time to dress properly. Here you are in a fine state! If we are going any farther than Alençon you will simply have to change your dress there . . .'

'Oh, really, Francine! . . .' protested the stranger.

'What do you mean?'

'That's the third time you have cast your fly to find out why we are making this journey and how far we are going.'

'Have I said a single thing to make you think that? . . .'

'Oh, I have noticed what you were up to. Once you were all candour and simplicity, but you have learned some guile in my school. You begin to have a horror of asking direct questions, and you are quite right, child. Of all the ways there are of trying to get hold of a secret, that's the silliest, I think.'

'Well,' answered Francine, 'I suppose one can't hide anything from you; but you'll surely agree, Marie, that your way of going on would excite a saint's curiosity. Yesterday morning you had no money and today you have handfuls. At Mortagne you are given the robbed mail-coach whose driver was killed. You are guarded by Government troops and escorted by a man who I think is your evil genius . . .'

'Who, Corentin? . . .' said the young stranger with a contemptuous accentuation of the two words and a flick of the fingers in that gentleman's direction. 'Do you remember Patriote, Francine?' she went on '– the monkey we had so much fun with, that I taught to mimic Danton?'

'Yes, Mademoiselle.'

'Well, were you afraid of him?'

'He was on a chain.'

'And Corentin is muzzled, child.'

'We used to amuse ourselves with Patriote for hours, I know,' said Francine, 'but he always played us some nasty trick in the end.'

Then with eager warmth she cast herself back in the carriage beside her mistress, took her hands and stroked them coaxingly, saying affectionately, 'But you've guessed what I want to know, Marie, and you still don't tell me. You make me feel so miserable – you don't know how miserable your fits of sadness make me feel, when you talk of killing yourself – and then within twenty-four hours you're madly light-hearted! How can you change like this? What's the cause of it? I have a right to be told something of what's in your heart. It belongs to me first, before anyone; for no one will ever love you more than I do. Tell me, Mademoiselle!'

'Well, Francine, don't you see plenty around us to make me feel gay? Just look at the coloured crests of those trees in the distance – not one like another. From far away, don't they remind you of some ancient tapestry hanging in a château? Look at those hedges – Chouans might pop up behind them at any moment. When I glance at the broom bushes I think I see gun muzzles. I love this feeling of danger springing up around us. Whenever the road looks gloomy I listen expecting to hear shots, and my heart beats hard, and I feel a strange excitement. It's not the thrill of fear nor of pleasure either: no, it's much more, it's the reaction of everything that's alive in me, it's life itself. Don't you think I have reason to be joyful at having enlivened my existence a bit?'

'Ah, how cruel you are, you tell me nothing! Holy Virgin,' Francine went on, rolling her eyes mournfully heavenward, 'who is to hear her confession if she keeps her lips sealed with me?'

'Francine,' the stranger answered gravely, 'I cannot tell you about this adventure. This time, it's dreadful.'

'Why do wrong when you know it's wrong?'

'That's how it is – I surprise myself by thinking like a woman of fifty and acting like a girl of fifteen. You have always been the voice of my better judgement, my poor child; but in this business I have to stifle my conscience. And', she went on after a pause, with a sigh, 'I'm not very successful in doing it. Now why should I make things harder by setting a confessor as strict as you after me?' And she patted Francine's hand gently.

'Oh, when have I ever reproached you for what you do?'

exclaimed Francine. 'You can even do wrong with grace. Saint Anne of Auray herself, whom I pray to so often for your salvation, would certainly grant you forgiveness for everything. Well, here I am as you see at your side on this road, not knowing where you're going!' And in an effusion of feeling she kissed Marie's hands.

'But you may leave me,' answered Marie; 'if your conscience . . .'

'Oh, come, don't say that, Mademoiselle,' Francine protested, with a vexed little grimace. 'Oh, will you not tell me? . . .'

'No, I'll tell you nothing,' said the young lady resolutely. 'Only you may be sure of this – I hate this adventure even more than I hate the man who put the plan to me with his smooth honeyed tongue. I want to be frank, so I'll tell you that I would not have let them persuade me to do what they want if I hadn't seen a thrilling mixture of terror and love combined in this shameful escapade, and been tempted. And then I didn't want to leave this world without some attempt to pluck the flowers one hopes for from it, even if I were to die for it! But remember to my credit when I'm dead that if I had been happy not even the sight of their big blade about to fall across my neck would have made me accept any part in this tragedy, for a tragedy it is. But now,' she went on, with a gesture of disgust, 'if it were called off I would immediately throw myself into the Sarthe; and that wouldn't be suicide, for I haven't lived yet.'

'Oh, Holy Virgin of Auray, forgive her!'

'What are you frightened of? You know that I don't find the tame ups and downs of domestic life satisfying or exciting. For a woman, that's unfortunate; but I've forged a finer edge for my spirit. I'm capable of being put to harder tests. I might perhaps have been a gentle creature like you. Why have I raised myself above my sex, or degraded myself beneath it? Oh, how lucky General Bonaparte's wife is! You see, I shall die young, since I've reached the point already of not being afraid of a pleasure party where there is blood to drink, as poor Danton said. But forget what I'm saying – it's the fifty-year-old woman speaking. The girl of fifteen, thank God, will soon turn up again.'

The young countrywoman shuddered. She was the only one who knew the turbulent impetuous nature of her mistress, who shared the secrets of this rich spirit with its capacity for noble enthusiasms, the only one who understood the feelings of this human being who had seen life pass as an insubstantial shadow which she vainly tried to grasp. 'We reap as we sow', but this woman had sowed generously and reaped no harvest. She had remained virtuous, unspoiled, but tormented by a host of thwarted desires. Weary of a fight without an adversary, she had come in her despair to prefer good to evil only when it presented itself as bringing joy, evil to good when it revealed some lyric quality, misery to mediocrity as something greater, the dark unknown future of death to a life starved of hope and empty even of suffering. Never was so much powder heaped up for the spark, so much riches ready to be expended in love. No daughter of Eve had ever been fashioned with so much gold in the clay. Francine, like a terrestrial angel, watched over this being in whom she saw and adored perfection. She believed that she had a sacred mission to preserve her for the choir of seraphim from which this being must have been banished in expiation of a sin of pride.

'That is Alençon spire,' their escort rode up to the carriage to tell them.

'So I see,' the lady answered curtly.

'Ah, well,' he said swallowing the snub and going off again submissively.

'Whip up the horses,' the lady said to the driver, 'Go faster. Now there's nothing to fear. Go at a fast trot or a gallop, if you can. We're on Alençon carriageway now.'

As she passed the Commandant she called to him sweetly, 'We shall meet at the inn, Commandant. Come and see me there.'

'Quite so,' said the Commandant. ' "At the inn! Come and see me!" That's the way to talk to the commanding officer of a Demi-brigade . . .' And he shook his fist at the carriage rolling rapidly ahead.

'Don't let that worry you, Commandant; she has your promotion to General up her sleeve,' said Corentin laughing, as he urged his horse to a gallop to catch up with the carriage.

'Ah, I don't intend to let myself be pushed around by those queer customers,' Hulot growled to his two friends. 'I would rather throw the General's coat into a ditch than win it in a bed. What are those dames after? Do you understand anything about it?'

'Oh, yes!' said Merle. 'I know she's the most beautiful woman I have ever seen. I think you must have misunderstood what was meant. Is she the wife of the First Consul perhaps?'

'Bah! the First Consul's wife is old and this one is young,' said Hulot. 'Besides the Minister's despatch calls her Mademoiselle de Verneuil. She's a *ci-devant*. Don't I know them! Before the Revolution they were all in that game. A man could become Commandant of a Demi-brigade in common time and six movements then – it was only a matter of saying "Dearest heart!" nicely two or three times to them.'

Chapter 8

WHILE the soldiers increased their pace, every man opening his compass legs to use the Commandant's phrase, the wretched carriage which served as mail-coach had quickly arrived at the Hôtel des Trois-Maures in the middle of Alençon main street. The jingle and clatter of the clumsy vehicle brought the innkeeper to the doorway. Its arrival was an unlikely chance that no one in Alençon could have anticipated but so many people, excited by the shocking affair at Mortagne, followed it that in order to escape the general curiosity the two women passengers made all haste to enter the inn kitchen, which is the room that is always used as an entrance chamber in inns in the West. The innkeeper, after some examination of the carriage, was about to follow them when the driver caught his arm.

'See here, Citizen Brutus,' he said, 'there's an escort of Blues and there's no guard nor despatches, so it was me brought you these citizenesses, so . . .'

'So we'll drink a glass of wine together presently, my boy,' said the innkeeper.

After one glance at the smoke-blackened kitchen and a table covered with the bloodstains of raw meat, Mademoiselle de Verneuil fled like a bird into the next room to escape from the sight and smell, as well as from the gaze of an untidy-looking chef and a small fat woman who were already studying her with absorbed interest.

'How are we going to manage, wife?' said the innkeeper. 'Who the devil could have expected so many visitors with things like they are now? That woman is going to get in a fuss before I can serve her a right meal. Upon my word, here's an idea – those are proper persons so I'll suggest they join the person we have upstairs. What about that, eh?'

When the innkeeper looked for the new arrivals he found

116

only Francine, whom he led to the back of the kitchen on the courtyard side, away from anyone who might overhear, before saying in a low voice, 'If the ladies wish to be served privately, as no doubt they do, I have a choice meal all ready for a lady and her son. I'm sure those travellers won't mind sharing their meal with you. They're quality,' he added mysteriously.

The last words were hardly out of his mouth when he felt himself lightly tapped by a whip-handle in his back. He turned abruptly and saw a small thickset man behind him, whose noiseless apparition from a neighbouring room had petrified the fat woman, the chef and his scullery boy with terror. The innkeeper turned pale as he looked back over his shoulder. The small man shook back the hair that fell over his forehead and eyes, hiding them completely, and stood on tiptoe to say in the innkeeper's ear. 'You know what a careless word or a denunciation costs, and the colour of the money we pay in, and we're not stingy neither.' And he accompanied these words with a gesture that was an appalling gloss on them.

Although the innkeeper's rotundity prevented Francine from seeing this person, she caught a few of the low-spoken words and was apparently thunderstruck by the sound of this harsh Breton voice. While everyone stood transfixed she sprang towards the small man, but he appeared to move with a wild animal's swift agility, and was already leaving by a side door giving on the courtyard. Francine thought that she might have been mistaken in her guess, for all she could see was the tawny and black skin of what looked like a medium-sized bear.

In astonishment she ran to the window. Through panes grimy with smoke she stared at the stranger slowly making his way to the stables. Before going in he raised a pair of black eyes to the first floor of the inn, and then turned them on the coach as if wishing to direct a friend's attention to some important point concerning the vehicle. At this, in spite of the goatskins, thanks to the gesture which enabled her to make out the man's face and by his enormous whip and crouching walk, agile as he might be on occasion, Francine recognized the Chouan called Marche-à-terre.

She scrutinized him as closely as she could through the obscuring dimness of the stable, where he lay down in the straw in a position from which he could observe all that might pass in the inn. Marche-à-terre was huddled in such a fashion that even from near by the most observant spy might easily have taken him for some waggoner's big dog sleeping curled up, its nose on its forepaws. The Chouan's behaviour made it clear to Francine that he had not recognized her, and in her mistress's present uncertain situation she did not know whether to congratulate herself on the fact or be annoyed. But her curiosity was excited by the mysterious connection there seemed to be between the Chouan's threatening remarks and the host's offer, quite an ordinary one for an innkeeper to make, for innkeepers are always trying to squeeze two profits from one piece of business.

She left the filthy window from which she had been staring at the shapeless dark mound in the gloom which showed where Marche-à-terre lay, and turning back towards the innkeeper saw him standing with the expression of a man who has made a serious blunder and doesn't know where to start to retrieve it. The Chouan's gesture had paralysed the poor man. No one in the West was ignorant of the cruel refinements of torture with which the Chasseurs du Roi punished people merely suspected of indiscretion, and the innkeeper thought he felt their knives already at his throat. The chef was looking in terror at the fire on the hearth, a place where they often *warmed* the feet of those who had denounced them. The round little fat woman held a kitchen knife in one hand and a half-peeled potato in the other and looked at her husband with her mouth half-open. And the scullery boy, to complete the party, was looking round for the reason, a mystery to him, for all this dumb terror. Naturally Francine's curiosity was still further stirred by this silent scene, in which the principal actor was visible to all eyes although no longer present. The girl was flattered by the Chouan's terrible power, and although the kind of malice one might find in a chambermaid was hardly an element in her unassuming character she was too closely concerned to find what was behind this mystery not to use her advantage.

'Very well, Mademoiselle accepts your suggestion,' she said gravely to the innkeeper, who awoke with a start at these words.

'What suggestion?' he asked with genuine surprise.

'What suggestion?' asked Corentin, coming in.

'What suggestion?' asked Mademoiselle de Verneuil.

'What suggestion?' asked a fourth person from the foot of the staircase, stepping lightly into the kitchen.

'Why, of lunching with your persons of quality, of course,' replied Francine impatiently.

'Quality,' repeated the caustic ironic voice of the person who had come down the stairs. 'That, my friend, strikes me as a joke only an innkeeper would think up. But if it is this young citizeness that you want to give us as table-companion, my good man, only someone out of his mind would refuse.' And he looked at Mademoiselle de Verneuil. 'In the absence of my mother, I agree,' he added, clapping the stupified innkeeper on the shoulder.

The thoughtlessness and grace of youth veiled the arrogant presumption of these words, which naturally drew the attention of all the actors in this scene to the newcomer. The innkeeper now wore the expression of Pontius Pilate trying to wash his hands of the death of Christ. He retreated a couple of steps towards his fat wife and whispered in her ear, 'You are a witness that if anything happens it's not my fault. But anyway,' he added still more softly, 'better go and tell Monsieur Marche-à-terre all about this.'

The traveller, a young man of medium height, wore a blue jacket and long black gaiters to above the knee over cloth breeches of the same blue colour. This simple uniform, without epaulettes, was that of the pupils of the École Polytechnique.* At a glance Mademoiselle de Verneuil could recognize elegance under this sober costume and the indefinable quality

* The Military Academy founded in Paris by the National Convention of 1792–5. — *Trans.*

of nobility. The young man's face looked ordinary enough at first sight, but one soon remarked in the conformation of certain features the presence of a spirit of great potentialities. His tanned skin, fair curling hair, sparkling blue eyes, delicately-cut nose, easy graceful movements, all seemed the natural endowment of a man whose life was directed by noble feeling and who had the habit of command. But the trait most characteristically his own was a chin like Bonaparte's and a lower lip which joined the upper in the graceful curve of an acanthus leaf under a Corinthian capital. Nature had made these features irresistibly attractive.

'This young man is remarkably impressive for a Republican,' said Mademoiselle de Verneuil to herself.

To perceive all this in the twinkling of an eye, light up with the wish to please, gently incline her head to one side, smile alluringly, cast one of those velvet glances that would bring to life a heart immune to love; and then to veil her long black eyes with their broad lids whose thick lashes traced a dark curve on her cheek, and employ tones of her voice that would charm birds off the trees to utter the banal phrase, 'We are much obliged to you, Sir' – this whole manoeuvre took less than the time needed to describe it. Then Mademoiselle de Verneuil asked the innkeeper for her apartment, saw the staircase, and disappeared with Francine, leaving to the stranger the problem of deciding whether this answer constituted an acceptance or refusal.

'Who is that woman?' he unceremoniously demanded of the paralysed and ever more bemused innkeeper.

'She is the Citizeness Verneuil,' Corentin replied coldly, jealously eyeing the young man, 'a *ci-devant*. What do you want of her?'

The stranger, who had begun to hum a Republican air, haughtily raised his head towards Corentin. For a moment the two young men stared at each other, like two cocks preparing to fight, and in this look undying hate sprang up between them. Corentin's green eyes signalled malice and duplicity as plainly as the École Polytechnique student's blue ones showed his candour. The latter had naturally gracious manners; the former only a way of ingratiating himself. One stood upright; the other pliantly gave way. One commanded respect; the other sought to obtain it. The word of the one was likely to be, 'Let's go in and win!'; of the other, 'Shall we go halves?'

'Is Citizen du Gua Saint-Cyr here?' asked a peasant as he entered the inn.

'What do you want of him?' the young man replied, walking forward.

The peasant bowed deeply and handed him a letter, which the young man read and then threw into the fire. He made no response but a nod, and the man left.

'You come from Paris, no doubt, Citizen?' Corentin said then, moving towards the stranger with a certain freedom of manner, a smooth and insinuating air, that Citizen du Gua seemed to find insufferable.

'Yes,' he replied shortly.

'And no doubt you have been given a commission in the Artillery?'

'No, Citizen, the Navy.'

'Ah, so you're going to Brest?' Corentin asked carelessly.

But the young naval officer turned on his heel without further ado, and without answering, and presently demonstrated that the fair hopes his appearance had aroused in Mademoiselle de Verneuil were delusive. He fussed about his lunch with a childish triviality, catechized the chef and the innkeeper's wife about their recipes, expressed amazement over provincial ways with the wonder of a Parisian torn from his silken cocoon, manifested the distastes of an affected coxcomb, and seemed all the more lacking in character because his manners and appearance had seemed to promise so much. Corentin smiled pityingly, as he watched him grimace at the taste of the best cider in Normandy.

'Pfui!' he protested. 'How on earth can you swallow such stuff? It's not a drink – you could eat it with a spoon. It's not surprising the Republic mistrusts a province where they harvest the wine by beating apple bushes and lie in wait to shoot travellers on the roads. Don't think of setting a carafe of that physic on the table, put out some good white and red Bordeaux instead. Go and make sure that there's a good fire up there. These people seem to me very primitive, very ignorant of civilized ways. Ah!' he added with a sigh, 'there's only one Paris in the world after all, and it's a great pity a man can't take it to sea with him! – What's this, spoil-sauce?' he said to the chef. 'Do you mean to say you are putting vinegar in this chicken fricassee when you have lemons here? ... As for you, mine hostess, you have given me such coarse sheets that I didn't sleep a wink last night.' Then he applied himself with puerile absorption to slashing the air with a long cane, practising the flourishes whose degree of finish and skill classed a young man as superior or inferior in the gilded ranks of the *Incroyables*.

'And is it with scented cubs like this,' Corentin said behind his hand to the innkeeper, watching his face as he spoke, 'that they're hoping to raise the level of the Republican navy?'

'This man,' the young naval officer was whispering to the innkeeper's wife, 'is a spy of Fouché's. He has police written all over him, and I'll swear that's Paris mud he hasn't washed off his chin. But let the biter beware – he may find himself bit ...'

At this moment a lady entered the inn kitchen, and the young man sprang forward with every formal mark of respect.

'My dear Mother,' he said, 'do come in. While you were away I believe I have recruited fellow-guests to share our table.'

'Fellow-guests?' she replied. 'Are you mad?'

'It is Mademoiselle de Verneuil,' he went on in a low voice.

'She perished on the scaffold after the Savenay affair. She had come to Le Mans to save her brother, the Prince de Loudon,' his mother said brusquely.

'You are mistaken, Madame,' said Corentin kindly, emphasizing the word *Madame*. 'There are two Demoiselles de Verneuil. Great families have always several branches.'

The newcomer, surprised at being thus unceremoniously addressed, drew back a few paces as if to examine the unexpected speaker. She fixed her black eyes on him, full of lively feminine shrewdness, and appeared to be wondering in whose interest he was asserting the existence of Mademoiselle de Verneuil. At the same time Corentin was covertly studying the lady and thinking that she might more appropriately claim the rewards of love than those of motherhood. A twenty-year-old son was a blessing he gallantly denied her as he admired her dazzling complexion, and the arched eyebrows and thick lashes that showed little sign of the depilation of age, and remarked how her luxuriant black hair, divided in two bands over the forehead, set off the young beauty of a fine head. Light lines on the forehead were not marks of the years but rather suggested youthful passions; and if her penetrating eyes were a little heavy one could not be sure whether that was due to the fatigue of the journey or to over-indulgence in pleasure. Corentin noticed too that the stranger was wrapped in a mantle of English stuff, and that the shape of her hat, undoubtedly foreign, was not in the least like any of the so-called Greek styles then fashionable in Paris. Corentin was a creature by nature inclined to suspect evil rather than look for good, and he at once conceived doubts about the true citizenship of the two strangers. The lady on her side had made her observations on Corentin's person with similar speed, and turned to her son with a meaning look which might be quite faithfully translated as 'Who is this odd person? Is he one of us?'

To this wordless interrogation the young naval officer replied with an attitude, a look and a wave of the hand that said, 'Faith, I know nothing about him and I like the look of him even less than you do.' Then, leaving to his mother the task of seeking enlightenment on the mystery, he turned aside to the innkeeper's wife and said to her beneath his breath, 'Try to find out who this fellow is, if he is really acting as escort to the lady, and for what purpose.'

'So you are sure, Citizen,' said Madame du Gua, looking at Corentin, 'that Mademoiselle de Verneuil exists?'

'She exists in flesh and blood as surely, *Madame*, as the Citizen du Gua Saint-Cyr.'

The reply was profoundly ironical although only the lady so understood it, and any other would have been disconcerted. Her son suddenly stared fixedly at Corentin, who coldly drew out his watch without appearing to suspect the perturbation his reply evoked. The lady, disquieted and anxious to know at once whether this remark was a treacherous shot in the dark or simply a chance form of words, continued the conversation.

'Goodness, how unsafe the roads are!' she said in the most natural way in the world. 'We were attacked beyond Mortagne by the Chouans. My son nearly lost his life there; he got two bullets through his hat, defending me.'

'Why, Madame, were you in that mail-coach that the brigands robbed in spite of its escort, the one that has just brought us here? You must know the vehicle then! They told me on my way to Mortagne that there were two thousand Chouans in the attack on the coach and that everyone had been killed, even the passengers. That's how history gets written!'

The tone of idle gossip that Corentin affected and his simpleton air made him look at this moment like some lounger in Little Provence,* disappointed to hear of the falsity of a piece of political news.

'Indeed, Madame,' he went on, 'if travellers are murdered so near Paris, just think how dangerous the roads will be in Brittany. Upon my word, I think I'll go back to Paris and not try going further.'

'Is Mademoiselle de Verneuil beautiful and young?' the lady, struck by a sudden thought, asked the innkeeper's wife.

At this point the conversation, which held a somewhat cat-and-mouse interest for the three persons involved, was interrupted by the innkeeper's announcement that lunch was served. The young naval officer offered his hand to his mother

* Little Provence was a particularly sunny corner of the Jardin des Tuileries much frequented by pensioners. – *Trans.*

with a false-seeming familiarity that confirmed Corentin's suspicions. To Corentin he said over his shoulder as he went towards the staircase, 'Citizen, if you are escorting the Citizeness Verneuil and she accepts the innkeeper's suggestion, don't stand on ceremony . . .'

Although these words were said in an offhand tone and were not at all pressing, Corentin followed. The young man grasped the lady's hand firmly, and when they were seven or eight steps ahead of the Parisian 'You see', he said in a low voice, 'what humiliating dangers your imprudent actions expose us to. If we are unmasked how can we escape? And what a part you make me play!'

The three arrived at a quite spacious room. One did not need to have travelled much in the West to realize that the innkeeper had brought out all his treasures for the benefit of his guests, and lavished quite unusual luxury on them. The table was carefully laid and furnished. The room's humidity had been fought and routed by a great fire. The condition of linen, chairs, plates and dishes was not too deplorable. It was clear to Corentin that the innkeeper had, to use a popular expression, 'split himself in four' in order to please the strangers. 'So,' he said to himself, 'these people are not what they wish to appear. This little young man has a trick or two up his sleeve. I took him for a fool, but now it seems he may be no less deep than I am myself.'

The young naval officer, his mother and Corentin, waited for Mademoiselle de Verneuil, whom the innkeeper had gone to inform that the meal was served. But the lovely stranger did not appear. The young man surmised that she must be raising objections, and went out humming the tune of *The Empire's Defence is our Trust*,* and made his way to Mademoiselle de Verneuil's room with a lively desire to overcome her scruples and bring her back with him. He may have wished to resolve his doubts concerning her, or perhaps just try out on this stranger the power that every male aspires to exercise over a pretty woman.

* A Revolutionary patriotic song, one of those played by decree at the theatre at the rise of the curtain under the Directory. – *Trans.*

'If that's a Republican,' Corentin said to himself as he watched him go, 'may I be hanged! He moves his shoulders like a courtier. And if that's his mother,' he went on, looking at Madame du Gua, 'I'm the Pope! I've got Chouans here. Shall we investigate their quality?'

Chapter 9

THE door opened presently and the young naval officer appeared with Mademoiselle de Verneuil by the hand, and led her to the table with attentive politeness and some complacency.

The hour which had elapsed meantime had not been lost for the devil. Helped by Francine, Mademoiselle de Verneuil had equipped herself with a travelling costume, a dress which may be more devastating than a ball gown. Its simplicity showed the art of a woman lovely enough to dispense with adornment who knew how to make her toilette only a pleasing setting. She wore a green dress whose close-fitting cut and spencer decorated with frogging outlined her figure in a style not designed for the young girl, and set off her supple waist, elegant bosom and graceful movements. She came in smiling with the sweetness natural in women able to display even teeth as lucent as porcelain in a rosy mouth, and two dimples as fresh as a child's in their cheeks. Without her bonnet, which had previously almost shut her off from the young officer's gaze, she could easily employ the thousand and one little artifices, apparently so artless, a woman uses to show off the charms and graces of her charming face and head. Her dress suited her appearance and her personality so well and made her look so much younger that Madame du Gua considered she might be overestimating in thinking her about twenty years old. The coquetry of the dress, obviously designed to please, was bound to raise the young man's hopes; but Mademoiselle de Verneuil thanked him by a gentle inclination of the head without looking at him and left him with a casual unconcern that was disconcerting. To the eyes of the strangers this reserve did not appear to be provocative or cautious, but due rather to indifference, real or feigned. The candid expression that their new acquaintance knew how to assume gave nothing away. No design to make a conquest was observable, and the charmingly captivating manners which had misleadingly flattered the young officer appeared to be a natural endowment. And so he returned to his seat with a certain chagrin.

Mademoiselle de Verneuil took Francine by the hand, and addressing herself to Madame du Gua said sweetly, 'Madame, would you be so kind as to permit this girl whom I think of more as a friend than a servant to dine with us? In these stormy times one can only repay devotion with affection – and indeed what else have we left now?'

Those last words were spoken in a low voice. Madame du Gua replied with a rather formal half-curtsey that gave away her discontent at encountering anyone so attractive, then turned to whisper in her son's ear.

'Oh, stormy times, devotion, Madame and the servant!' she said. 'This can't be Mademoiselle de Verneuil; it's some creature sent by Fouché.'

The party was about to sit down to table when Mademoiselle de Verneuil noticed Corentin, whose eye was still subjecting the two strangers to an acute analysis and making them feel decidedly uncomfortable.

'Citizen,' she said to him, 'naturally you are much too polite to shadow my every step. When the Republic sent my parents to the scaffold it was not magnanimous enough to give me a guardian. Although you have escorted and attended me with extraordinary chivalry whether I would or no,' and here she sighed, 'I do not intend to allow your too kind solicitude for my welfare to cause you embarrassment. I am in safe keeping here. You may leave me.'

She gave him a fixed contemptuous stare. She had made herself clear. Corentin repressed the smile that threatened to pucker the corners of his crafty lips and bowed respectfully.

'It will always be an honour to obey you, Citizeness,' he said. 'Beauty is the only queen that a true Republican may gladly serve.'

As she watched him go Mademoiselle de Verneuil's eyes

sparkled with such simple joy, she looked at Francine with a smile of such happy complicity, that Madame du Gua, in whom jealousy had sown distrust, felt inclined to abandon the suspicions Mademoiselle de Verneuil's perfect beauty had inspired.

'It is just possible she may be Mademoiselle de Verneuil,' she whispered in her son's ear.

'And what about the escort?' the young man replied, made more cautious by pique. 'Is she the Government's prisoner or protégée, friend or enemy?'

Madame du Gua's eyes narrowed, as if to say that this mystery would not remain a mystery to her. With Corentin's departure the young officer's mistrust seemed to subside however, and his face lost its stern expression. The looks he cast at Mademoiselle de Verneuil suggested an intemperate weakness for women, rather than the respectful ardour of a budding attraction. The girl's reaction was to become all the more circumspect in her behaviour and she reserved her friendliness for Madame du Gua. The young man, bitterly resentful and with no one to blame but himself, tried to affect the same insensibility. Mademoiselle de Verneuil did not appear to be aware of his tactic, and showed herself as an unpretentious person but not shy, and reserved without being prim. So this encounter of persons destined apparently for only a casual acquaintance awakened no very warm sympathy between them. There was even an inurbane stiffness, an embarrassment that destroyed all the pleasure Mademoiselle de Verneuil and the young officer had looked forward to not long before.

Women together have such an admirable sense of what is socially fitting, however, such a close common interest, or enjoy lively encounters so much, that they always know how to break the ice on such occasions. As if struck by a simultaneous thought the two beautiful table companions suddenly set about an innocent teasing of their solitary cavalier, and vied with each other in mocking him and in little attentions and solicitude for him. This unanimity set them free. Looks and words may seem significant if let slip in embarrassment, but in this playful game became of no importance. The result was that by the end of half an hour the two women who were already secret enemies seemed the best friends in the world. The young officer then surprised himself by being as vexed with Mademoiselle de Verneuil for her easy unconstraint as he had been for her reserve. He was put out to the point of regretting with smouldering anger that he had shared his table with her.

'Madame,' said Mademoiselle de Verneuil to Madame du Gua, 'is your son always so gloomy?'

'Mademoiselle,' he rejoined, 'I was asking myself what use a happiness is which will presently be gone. The keenness of my pleasure is the reason for my sadness.'

'These are madrigals,' she answered laughing, 'and they smack more of the Court than the École Polytechnique.'

'He has only expressed a very natural thought, Mademoiselle,' said Madame du Gua, who had her own reasons for wishing to keep the stranger in her place.

'Come now, laugh,' Mademoiselle de Verneuil invited him, smiling at the young man. 'How do you feel when you weep if what you are pleased to call happiness makes you so sad?'

Her smile, and the provocative look that let slip a corner of her mask of straightforward candour, gave the officer a little hope. But then, because women always have to go too far or not far enough, after a glance sparkling with invitation and rich promise in which she seemed to claim a conquest, Mademoiselle de Verneuil received his gallant phrases with a cold severe withdrawal, and alternately advanced and retreated in a feminine manoeuvre women use often enough to conceal their true feelings. For one moment, one single moment, when each expected to find the other with lowered eyelids, their true thoughts were communicated. Their hearts turned over in sudden shared illumination, and then their eyes were as quickly downcast. Ashamed at having said so much in a single glance they did not dare to look at each other again, and Mademoiselle de Verneuil, in her anxiety to disillusion the stranger, withdrew into a cold politeness and seemed to await the end of the meal even with impatience.

'You must have suffered a great deal in prison, Mademoiselle?' remarked Madame du Gua.

'Indeed, Madame, it seems to me that I am still in prison.'

'Is your escort designed to protect you, Mademoiselle, or to keep an eye on you? Does the Republic regard you as precious or suspect?'

Mademoiselle de Verneuil, whose instincts told her that she was of little interest personally to Madame du Gua, was startled by this question.

'Madame,' she replied, 'I do not know very precisely at this moment just what my relations with the Republic are.'

'Perhaps you make it tremble for its safety?' the young man said with light irony.

'Why not respect Mademoiselle's secrets?' said Madame du Gua.

'Oh, Madame, the secrets of a young person who knows nothing of life but its misfortunes are not very interesting!'

'But the First Consul', went on Madame du Gua, anxious to continue a conversation that might tell her what she wanted to know, 'seems to have the best intentions. Isn't he going to stop the enforcement of the laws against the *émigrés*, or so they say?'

'That's true, Madame,' she said, with perhaps too much emphasis; 'but in that case why are we inciting insurrection in the Vendée and Brittany? Why set France ablaze? . . .'

The warm feeling of this cry, which seemed to be laying a reproach at her own door, startled the officer. He examined her face closely but could not be sure whether she spoke in detestation of a cause or devotion to it. Her finely-textured skin and vivid colouring were a barrier to observation as effective as a mask. An irrepressible curiosity drew him unexpectedly closer to this unusual woman towards whom he was already attracted by violent desire.

'But', she went on after a pause, 'are you not going to Mayenne, Madame?'

'Yes, Mademoiselle,' the young man replied questioningly.

'Well, Madame, since your son serves the Republic . . .' Mademoiselle de Verneuil said this casually, but at the same time cast an oblique look at the two strangers of a kind peculiar to women and diplomats, '... you must be apprehensive of Chouans. An escort is not to be despised. We have become almost travelling companions, so come with us as far as Mayenne.'

Son and mother hesitated and appeared to consult each other.

'I don't know whether it is an indiscretion to tell you, Mademoiselle, that very important business requires our presence near Fougères tonight, and we have not yet found transport, but women are so kind by nature that I would be ashamed not to put my trust in you. All the same,' he added, 'before we place ourselves in your hands we must know at least whether we are likely to leave them safe and sound. Are you the queen or the captive of your Republican escort? Excuse a young serviceman's plain speaking, but I see nothing very plain in your situation ...'

'We live in times when nothing that happens is plain and natural, Monsieur; but you need not hesitate to accept, believe me. Certainly you have no treachery to fear', she added with emphasis, 'in a straightforward offer made by a person who is not concerned with political feuds.'

'A journey made in this way will not be free from danger,' he said with a keen look that gave point to the trite phrase.

'What can you fear?' she asked with a mocking smile. 'I see no peril for anyone.'

'Can that be the woman whose look showed an ardour equal to mine?' the young man said to himself. 'To speak like that, and in such a tone! She's setting some trap for me.'

At that moment the clear resonant hoot of an owl that appeared to be perched on the chimney-stack sounded like a dismal warning.

'What's that?' said Mademoiselle de Verneuil. 'It's not the luckiest of omens to begin our journey with. But how can there be owls here hooting in full daylight?' she asked with a surprised gesture.

'It does happen sometimes,' the young man said coldly. 'Mademoiselle,' he went on, 'we shall perhaps bring you ill-fortune – is that what you are thinking? Let us not travel together then.'

These words were spoken with a calmness and reserve that took Mademoiselle de Verneuil by surprise.

'Monsieur,' she said, with a quite aristocratic hauteur, 'I am far from wishing to constrain you. Let us keep such liberty as the Republic permits us. If Madame were alone I should insist . . .'

Heavy military steps were heard in the passage, and soon Commandant Hulot showed a frowning face.

'Come in, Colonel,' said Mademoiselle de Verneuil smiling, with a wave of the hand towards a chair near her. 'Let us discuss affairs of state since we have to. But don't look so serious. What's the matter? Are there Chouans here?'

The Commandant was staring dumbfounded at the young stranger, examining him with extraordinary closeness.

'Mother, will you have some more hare?' the officer was saying, attentive to his companions, and then to Francine, 'Mademoiselle, you are eating nothing.'

But Hulot's surprise and Mademoiselle de Verneuil's interest in it had a merciless intensity that it was dangerous to ignore.

'What's the matter, Commandant, do you think you know me?' demanded the young man abruptly.

'Perhaps,' the Republican replied.

'Yes, I think I may possibly have seen you at the Academy.'

'I have never been to school,' the Commandant replied brusquely. 'And from what school do you come?'

'The École Polytechnique.'

'Ah yes, the barracks where they try to create soldiers in dormitories,' commented the Commandant, who had an insuperable aversion to officers from that learned military nursery. 'But to what Corps do you belong?'

'Not the Army, the Navy.'

'Ah,' said Hulot with a malicious laugh. 'Do you know many pupils of that Academy in the Navy? It only produces Artillery officers,' he went on gravely, 'and Engineers.'

The young man was not disconcerted.

'They made an exception in my case because of the name I bear,' he explained. 'Our family has always gone into the Navy.'

'So!' answered Hulot. 'And what is your family's name, Citizen?'

'Du Gua Saint-Cyr.'

'So you were not murdered at Mortagne?'

'Ah, he very nearly was,' put in Madame du Gua vivaciously. 'My son had two bullets . . .'

'And have you papers?' said Hulot, ignoring the mother.

'Would you like to read them?' the young officer asked insolently, studying the Commandant's grim face and Mademoiselle de Verneuil's in turn with a malicious blue eye.

'A callow young puppy like you would like to push me around, would you? Here, give me your papers, or come with me!'

'Come, come, my good sir, I am not a requisitionary cage-bird. Do I have to answer your questions? Who are you?'

'The officer commanding in this Department,' rejoined Hulot.

'Oh! Then my plight may be desperate, I shall be caught with my weapons in my hand.' And he proffered a glass of claret to the Commandant.

'I am not thirsty,' said Hulot. 'Come, your papers.'

At that moment the clink of arms and tramp of soldiers outside in the road brought Hulot to the window, and Mademoiselle de Verneuil trembled at his air of satisfaction. This sign of her interest warmed the young man, whose expression had grown haughty and cold. Fumbling in the pocket of his riding-coat, he drew out an elegant pocket-book and handed papers to the Commandant which Hulot applied himself to reading slowly, comparing the passport description with the features of the suspect before him. While he was doing this the owl's hooting began again; but this time it was not difficult to recognize the intonation and performance of a human voice. The Commandant then returned the young man's papers with a mocking look.

'All that's very fine,' he said, 'but I must ask you to

accompany me to the District Post. I don't care for music, myself.'

'Why are you taking him there?' demanded Mademoiselle de Verneuil in a troubled voice.

'Little girl, that's not your business,' replied the Commandant with his usual grimace.

Stung by the old soldier's mode of expressing himself and tone, and still more by being humiliated in this way before a man who admired her, Mademoiselle de Verneuil rose with a sudden abandonment of the quiet reserved attitude she had maintained until then, with heightened colour and sparkling eyes.

'Tell me, has this young man complied with the law's requirements?' she exclaimed, quite softly but with a kind of thrill in her voice.

'Yes; at least it looks like it,' Hulot answered drily.

'Yes, well, I require you at least to *look like* leaving him alone,' she returned. 'Are you afraid he may escape you? You are going to escort him with me to Mayenne. He and his mother will be in the mail-coach. Make no comment – that is what I wish. Well, what now? . . .' she added, as she saw Hulot permitting himself to make his little grimace. 'Do you still find him suspicious?'

'A little, I'm afraid.'

'What do you want to do with him then?'

'Nothing, unless perhaps cool his brains with a bit of lead,' said the Commandant sarcastically. 'He's a hot-head.'

'You're joking, Colonel!' exclaimed Mademoiselle de Verneuil.

'Come, Comrade,' said the Commandant with a jerk of the head to the young officer. 'Come on, march!'

At this impertinence, Mademoiselle de Verneuil smiled calmly.

'Don't move,' she said to the young man, with a protective gesture full of dignity.

'Oh, what a lovely picture of defiance!' the officer murmured to his mother, making her knit her brows.

Vexation and a host of excited feelings held in check had

heightened the Parisian's beauty. Francine, Madame du Gua, her son, had all risen. Mademoiselle de Verneuil with a few quick steps placed herself between them and the smiling Commandant, rapidly undid two loops of her spencer and withdrew an open letter; and with feminine blindness to everything but her seriously threatened sense of her own importance, and also impatient or gratified to exercise her power, like a child with a new toy, imperiously presented it to the Commandant.

'Read it,' she said with a scornful smile.

She turned towards the young man, and in the intoxication of triumph looked at him with an expression in which there was love as well as malice. Both faces cleared and were coloured and animated by joy, and conflicting feelings struggled in their hearts. With one look Madame du Gua made it clear that she attributed Mademoiselle de Verneuil's kindness more to love than charity, and there was no doubt she was right. The lovely stranger at first blushed and lowered her eyelids in confusion as she realized all that this feminine look said, and then, defying the threat in its accusation, raised her head ready to face all eyes.

The Commandant, dumbfounded, returned the letter, which bore the countersignature of Ministers and enjoined on all authorities obedience to the orders of this mysterious person. But he drew his sword from the sheath, took it and broke it across his knee and threw down the pieces.

'Well, Mademoiselle, you probably know what you have to do,' he said; 'but a Republican has his own ideas and his pride. I cannot serve under the command of beautiful girls. By this evening the First Consul shall have my resignation, and other men than Hulot will obey you. When I cease to understand, I halt; especially when it is assumed that I do understand.'

There was a moment's silence, soon broken by the Parisian girl who walked up to the Commandant and held out her hand, saying 'Colonel, although your whiskers are a bit on the long side, you may salute me – you are a man whom one can truly call a man!'

'And I am pleased to be one, Mademoiselle,' he replied,

planting a rather awkward kiss on the hand this unusual girl extended to him. 'As for you, Comrade,' he added, holding up a menacing finger at the young man; 'you are lucky this time.'

'My good Commandant,' said the stranger laughing, 'it's time we put an end to this farce, and if you wish I'll go with you to the Post.'

'Accompanied by your invisible whistler, Marche-à-terre, no doubt? . . .'

'Marche-à-terre, who's that?' asked the naval officer with every appearance of genuine surprise.

'Did you not hear whistling just now?'

'Well, what has that to do with me, may I ask?' returned the young man. 'I thought the soldiers you brought here, I suppose to arrest me, were giving you notice of their arrival by the whistling.'

'Really? So that's what you thought!'

'Heavens, yes! But do drink your claret, it's delicious.'

Surprised by the young man's quite natural astonishment, the incredible frivolity of his manner, the youthfulness of his face which in its setting of carefully curled blond ringlets looked almost childish, the Commandant wavered amongst a host of suspicions. He noticed Madame du Gua who was trying to interpret her son's glances at Mademoiselle de Verneuil, and abruptly asked her, 'What age are you, Citizeness?'

'Alas, Sir, our Republic's demands are becoming very harsh! I am thirty-eight,'

'May I be shot if I believe another word. Marche-à-terre is here, he whistled, you are Chouans in disguise. God's thunder, I'll have the inn surrounded and searched!'

An erratic whistling from the yard like that previously heard cut the Commandant short. He rushed, fortunately as it happened, into the passage and did not notice the pallor that overspread Madame du Gua's face at his words. From there Hulot saw the whistler, a coachman whistling as he harnessed his horses to the mail-coach, and dismissed his suspicions, deeming it absurd to think that Chouans would risk appearing in the middle of Alençon. He returned in confusion.

'I let it pass now, but later he shall pay dearly for what he has put us through here,' the mother was saying emphatically to her son when Hulot returned to the room.

The gallant officer's embarrassed face expressed the struggle in his heart between the stringent obligations of his duty and his natural good nature. There was no alteration in his crusty air even though he now believed he had been mistaken, but he took the glass of wine and said, 'Comrade, pardon me, but your Academy sends officers to the Army so young . . .'

'The brigands take men younger still, do they?' asked the self-styled naval officer, laughing.

'Who did you suppose my son was?' Madame du Gua asked.

'The Gars, the leader sent to the Chouans and Vendéans by the Cabinet in London, the man called the Marquis de Montauran.'

The Commandant kept an alert eye on the faces of these two suspects, who with the raised eyebrows and odd succession of expressions of two ignorant and arrogant persons looked at each other in a mute dialogue, which may be translated thus:

'Do you know who that is?' 'No, do you?' 'Never heard of him.' 'What on earth is this fool babbling about?' 'He's raving.'

And then there was the insulting bantering laughter of congenital silliness when it thinks it has shown its superiority.

Mademoiselle de Verneuil's sudden change of manner and her apparent apathetic indifference when she heard the name of the royalist General went unnoticed by all but Francine, the only person to whom the subtle variations of expression in that young face were familiar. The Commandant, completely routed, picked up the two pieces of his sword, looked at Mademoiselle de Verneuil, whose warm directness had found the path to his heart, and said, 'As for you, Mademoiselle, I don't retract what I said, and tomorrow Bonaparte shall have the broken pieces of my sword, unless . . .'

'Ah, what do I care about Bonaparte, your Republic, the Chouans, the King and the Gars!' she exclaimed, barely controlling an unseemly outburst. Her face was vivid with some private mood or passion; and one could see that the whole world would count for nothing to this girl if ever the time should come when her heart singled out one person in it. But she immediately regained a wry composure, seeing herself as if she were some great actress with the eyes of all spectators fixed on her.

The Commandant rose abruptly. Disturbed and agitated, Mademoiselle de Verneuil followed him into the passage, stopped him and asked with deep concern, 'Have you very strong reasons for suspecting this young man of being the Gars?'

'God's thunder, Mademoiselle, the fellow escorting you came to warn me that the travellers by this coach and the coach-driver had been murdered by the Chouans, which I knew; but the thing I did not know was the names of the dead passengers, and they were called du Gua Saint-Cyr!'

'Oh, if Corentin had a finger in it, I'm surprised at nothing,' she exclaimed with a disgusted gesture.

The Commandant moved off, without daring to glance again at Mademoiselle de Verneuil, whose dangerous beauty was already troubling his heart.

'If I had stayed two minutes longer I would have been idiot enough to take back my sword and escort her,' he was saying to himself as he walked downstairs.

As Madame du Gua watched the young man stand with his eyes fixed on the door through which Mademoiselle de Verneuil had gone, she said in a low voice, 'Always the same! Women are the one danger you'll meet your death through. A wax doll makes you forget everything. Why did you ever allow her to share our table? What kind of Demoiselle de Verneuil can she be who accepts a meal with strangers, who is escorted by Blues and disarms them with a letter kept in reserve in her spencer like a love-note? She's one of those evil creatures Fouché is using to get hold of you, and the letter she displayed was given her to call upon the Blues' help against you.'

'Well, Madame,' the young man replied in a hostile tone

that pierced the lady's heart and made her turn pale, 'her intervention on my behalf gives the lie to your supposition. Don't forget that it is only the King's interest that brings us together, you and me. After having Charette at your feet, you find the Universe empty, don't you? It's true, isn't it, that you live only to avenge him?'

The lady stood pensively, like a man on a river bank contemplating the shipwreck of his treasures and yearning all the more passionately after his lost fortune.

Mademoiselle de Verneuil returned, and between her and the young naval officer there passed a smile and a look full of gentle mockery. The very uncertainty of their future and the ephemeral nature of any link between them made the signs that such a relation might be hoped for the more appealing. This look, although gone in a moment, could not escape Madame du Gua's experienced eye, and she at once grasped its implication. She knitted her brows slightly, unable to hide her jealous thoughts entirely.

Francine was watching this woman. She saw her eyes sparkle, her cheeks gain colour. She thought she saw a spirit from hell look out from this woman's face as she visibly underwent some terrible upheaval. This swiftly passing appearance was as startling as lightning, as decisive as death. Then Madame du Gua regained her sprightly air at once with such poise and coolness that Francine thought she must have been dreaming. Yet, recognizing a force and violence in this woman at least equal to Mademoiselle de Verneuil's, she shuddered at the thought of terrible collisions bound to occur between two spirits of such temper; and she trembled to see Mademoiselle de Verneuil go to meet the young officer with an intoxicating look of involvement with him, and taking his hands draw him to her and lead him to the light with a mischievously malicious coquetry.

'Now, confess to me,' she said, looking searchingly into his eyes, 'that you are not the Citizen du Gua Saint-Cyr.'

'Oh, but yes, Mademoiselle, I am.'

'But his mother and he were killed the day before yesterday!'

'I am desolated to hear it,' he replied laughing. 'However that may be, I am under a deep obligation to you and shall always feel grateful to you. I only wish I were in a position to prove my gratitude.'

'I thought I was rescuing an *émigré*, but you are dearer to me as a Republican.'

This was said apparently on the spur of the moment, and when she had said it she became embarrassed, blushed to the eyes, and her whole face showed a charmingly naïve feeling. She let the officer's hands fall, apparently not so much ashamed of having pressed them as impelled by a thought too momentous to bear; and she left him intoxicated with hope. She appeared suddenly vexed with herself for having behaved with a freedom perhaps justifiable in the circumstances of fellow-travellers' fleeting contacts, became formal again, bowed to her two travelling companions, and disappeared with Francine.

When they got back to their room, Francine locked her fingers together and wrung her hands as she contemplated her mistress, saying, 'Oh, Marie, what a lot in such a short time! Such things could happen to no one but you!'

In an impulsive movement Mademoiselle de Verneuil threw her arms round Francine's neck.

'Ah, that's life! I am in heaven!'

'Or perhaps in hell,' rejoined Francine.

'Oh, a fig for hell!' cried Mademoiselle de Verneuil gaily. 'Here, give me your hand. Feel how my heart beats. I am in a fever. The whole world now means so little! How often have I seen this man in my dreams. Oh, how beautiful his face is! Did you see his sparkling eyes?'

'Will he fall in love with you?' the naïve peasant girl asked helplessly, her face full of sadness.

'Do you ask me that?' replied Mademoiselle de Verneuil. 'Tell me, Francine,' and she posed before her, half-comically, half in earnest, 'do you think that would be so hard for him?'

'Ah, but will he love you always?' Francine answered with a smile.

They looked at each other for a moment as if both astonished, Francine to have shown so much worldly wisdom, Marie to envisage for the first time passion with a future of happiness before it. She stood as if leaning over a precipice, listening to hear an idly flung pebble reach bottom, anxious now to sound the depths below.

'Well, that's up to me,' she said, with the gesture of a gambler making his last throw. 'I'll never pity a deserted woman, she has only herself to blame for her desertion. I'll know how to keep, living or dead, the man whose heart has once been mine. But Francine,' she went on in surprise, after a moment's silence, 'how do you come to know so much? . . .'

'Mademoiselle,' the peasant girl said quickly, 'I hear steps in the passage.'

'Ah,' Marie said, as she listened, 'they are not *his*. But is that how you answer? I recognize the manoeuvre – I must wait till you tell me, or guess.'

Francine had some justification. Three knocks on the door put an end to their conversation. At Mademoiselle de Verneuil's invitation to enter, Captain Merle appeared.

Chapter 10

As he gave Mademoiselle de Verneuil a military salute the Captain risked a comprehensive glance at her, and quite stunned by her beauty found nothing to say but, 'Mademoiselle, I am at your service!'

'So you are now my guardian because of the resignation of the Commanding Officer of your Demi-brigade – that's what your Regiment is called, isn't it?'

'My superior officer, Adjutant Gérard, sent me.'

'Your Commandant is very much afraid of me, isn't he?'

'Pardon me, Mademoiselle, Hulot is not afraid; but women, you understand, are not in his line, and it riled him to find his General wearing a bonnet.'

'And yet it was his duty to obey his superior officers!' retorted Mademoiselle de Verneuil. 'I like people who comply with my wishes, and don't resist me, I warn you.'

'Resistance would be difficult,' replied Merle.

'Let us confer,' Mademoiselle de Verneuil went on. 'You have fresh troops here. They will escort me to Mayenne, which I can reach by this evening. Can we get fresh soldiers there in order to go straight on without stopping? The Chouans know nothing about our little expedition. Travelling by night, we would be very unlucky to meet them in sufficient number to attack us. What do you say? Do you think that is possible?'

'Yes, Mademoiselle.'

'What is the road like between Mayenne and Fougères?'

'Rough going: full of ups and downs – real squirrels' country.'

'Let's go, let's go,' she said; 'and as we've no dangers to fear on the way out of Alençon you may go ahead; we shall soon overtake you.'

'One would think she had ten years' service,' Merle said to himself as he left. 'That girl isn't one of the sort who make their living by a feather bed. And, by fire and shot, if Captain Merle ever wants promotion to Adjutant I don't advise him to mistake Saint Michael for the devil.'

While Mademoiselle de Verneuil and the Captain had been in conference, Francine had gone out to a passage window with the intention of examining a corner of the courtyard towards which irresistible curiosity had drawn her ever since her arrival at the inn. She gazed at the stable straw with absorbed attention, looking as if she were deep in prayers before an image of the Virgin. Presently she saw Madame du Gua making her way towards Marche-à-terre with the wariness of a cat unwilling to get its paws wet. The Chouan, seeing the lady, rose to his feet and stood in an attitude of the deepest respect. This strange circumstance excited Francine's curiosity, and she hurried out into the courtyard and slipped along close to the walls, careful to avoid being seen by Madame du Gua, in order to reach the stable door and hide behind it. She walked on tiptoe, held her breath, made not the slightest sound and succeeded in stationing herself quite near Marche-à-terre without being noticed.

'And if these investigations prove', the lady was saying to the Chouan, 'that it is not her name, you will shoot her without mercy as you would a mad dog.'

'All right,' replied Marche-à-terre.

The lady departed. The Chouan replaced his woollen cap on his head, and was still standing scratching his ear in an embarrassed way when he caught sight of Francine, suddenly appearing as if by magic.

'By Saint Anne of Auray!' he exclaimed. He dropped his whip, clasped his hands and stood as if in a trance of joy. A faint colour animated his heavy face and his eyes shone like diamonds lost in mud.

'Is it really Cottin's girl?' he said in a voice so deep in his chest as to be audible only to himself. And then after a pause, 'And aren't you just *godaine*!'

The strange word *godain*, feminine *godaine*, in the patois of these regions is a superlative used by lovers admiring beauty set off by a fine dress.

'I wouldn't dare touch you,' Marche-à-terre added, advancing his broad hand nevertheless as if to feel the weight of a heavy gold chain she wore twisted round her neck and falling to her waist.

'And you would be right, Pierre,' Francine replied, with the instinct that makes a woman domineer if she is not domineered over. She drew back haughtily, enjoying the Chouan's surprise, but she made up for the harshness of her words, and her use of the formal *vous* for you, by a gentle look full of kindness and came nearer to him again. 'Pierre,' she went on, 'that lady was talking to you . . .' and this time she used the intimate form of the pronoun, '. . . about my young mistress, wasn't she?'

Marche-à-terre remained dumb, and his face expressed a conflict between the forces of darkness and light like the dawn. He looked in turn at Francine, the great whip he had let fall and the gold chain, which seemed to exercise an attraction as powerful as the Breton girl's face; then as if to put an end to his disturbance, he picked up his whip, but still said nothing.

'Oh, it isn't difficult to guess that that lady ordered you to kill my mistress,' Francine continued, knowing the man's loyal unwillingness to betray a secret and anxious to overcome his scruples.

Marche-à-terre bowed his head significantly. For Cottin's girl it was an answer.

'Well then, Pierre, if the slightest harm happens to her, if even a single hair of her head is touched, this is the last time we shall ever see each other on earth and for ever more, for I'll be in paradise and you, you'll go to hell!'

If a devil were being driven out of Marche-à-terre with bell, book and candle as by the Church long ago, he could not have been more perturbed by this prophecy uttered with a faith that carried conviction. His looks which at first had expressed a rough tenderness, then been darkened by the obligations of a fanatical devotion as exacting as the devotion of love, became suddenly fierce and sullen as he remarked the imperious attitude of the guileless girl whom he had long ago innocently made 'Cottin's girl'. Francine interpreted the Chouan's silence in her own way.

'So you won't do anything for me?' she said reproachfully.

At this the Chouan turned on his sweetheart an eye as dark as a crow's wing.

'Are you free?' he asked in a growl that only Francine could have understood.

'Would I be here if I were not? . . .' she replied indignantly. 'But what are you doing here? You're still following the Chouans, running the roads like a mad beast looking for someone to bite. Oh, Pierre, if you had any sense you would come with me. This beautiful lady, who I may tell you was once a foster-child with us, has taken care of me. I have now two hundred francs a year from a good investment. Mademoiselle paid out five hundred crowns to buy me my Uncle Thomas's big house, and I have two thousand francs in savings.'

But her smile and the eager recounting of her wealth faltered before Marche-à-terre's stony expression.

'The Recteurs told us to go to war,' he said. 'Each Blue done for counts for an Indulgence.'

'But perhaps the Blues will kill you.'

By way of answer he threw out his arms as if in regret at the poorness of his offering to God and the King.

'And what will become of me?' the girl asked mournfully.

Marche-à-terre looked stupidly at Francine. His eyes seemed to grow larger and two tears rolled from them, tracing a parallel course down his hairy cheeks on to the enveloping goatskins. A low groaning came from deep in his chest.

'By Saint Anne of Auray! . . . Is that all you have to say to me, Pierre, after seven years? You have changed a lot.'

'I love you still,' said the Chouan brusquely.

'No,' she whispered, 'the King comes before me.'

'If you look at me like that,' he said, 'I'm off.'

'Well, good-bye!' she answered sadly.

'Good-bye,' repeated Marche-à-terre.

He seized Francine's hand, clasped it, kissed it, made the

sign of the Cross, and fled into the depths of the stable like a
dog that has stolen a bone.

'Pille-miche,' he said to his comrade, 'I can't see a thing.
Have you your *chinchoire* (snuff-horn) handy?'

'Oh, *cré bleu*! . . . what a fine chain,' said Pille-miche,
fumbling in a pocket sewn under his goatskin.

He held out the little ox-horn cone in which Bretons keep
the fine tobacco which they reduce to powder themselves
during the long winter evenings. The Chouan raised his thumb
to form the hollow in the wrist which disabled soldiers too
use to measure out their pinches of snuff. He vigorously shook
the *chinchoire*, whose point Pille-miche had unscrewed. An
impalpable dust sifted slowly through the small hole at the
tip of this piece of Breton equipment. Seven or eight times
Marche-à-terre silently repeated this procedure as if the powder
might possess the power to change the nature of his thoughts.
And then abruptly with a despairing gesture he threw the
horn to Pille-miche and picked up a gun hidden in the straw.

'Seven or eight *chinchées* (pinches) like that, one after the
other, that's no good,' grumbled the miserly Pille-miche.

'On our way,' said Marche-à-terre harshly. 'We have a job
to do.'

About thirty Chouans who were sleeping under the racks
and in the straw raised their heads, saw Marche-à-terre on his
feet, and quickly disappeared through a door giving on the
gardens, from which one could reach the fields.

When Francine came out of the stable she found the chaise
ready to leave. Mademoiselle de Verneuil and her two
travelling companions had already climbed in. The Breton
girl shuddered as she saw her mistress at the back of the
carriage beside the woman who had just given the order for
her death. The *suspect* sat down opposite Marie, and as soon
as Francine was seated the heavy vehicle set off at a fast trot.

The sun had dissipated the grey autumn clouds and its
rays lit up the melancholy of the fields with a certain air of
holiday and youth. Many lovers take such chance meteoro-
logical effects as omens.

Francine was surprised at the odd silence that prevailed at

first among the travellers. Mademoiselle de Verneuil had resumed her remote air, and kept her eyes lowered, her head gently bent, her hands hidden in the folds of the loose cloak in which she was wrapped. If she raised her eyes it was only to watch the landscape scenes as they whirled past and receded with the windings of the road.

Sure of being admired, she was unresponsive to admiration; but if she seemed indifferent it was certainly not because she was unaware. The touching transparency which makes the changing moods of less strong personalities consistent, and gives them a sweet harmony, was evidently not a charm that she possessed; and the intensity of her reactions seemed fated to make her experience of love a turbulent one. In the rapt delight of an intrigue's beginning the young man made no attempt yet to account for the apparent conflict between coquetry and fervent feeling in this strange girl. Her assumption of simple unconsciousness allowed him a leisurely study of a face as beautiful in repose as it had been in the agitation of the scene just before, and we rarely find fault with something that gives us pleasure.

Sitting in a carriage it is difficult for a pretty woman to withdraw from her companions' glances when their eyes naturally turn to her as if seeking some fresh distraction from the monotony of the journey. So the young man could feed his awakening passion and feast his eyes delightfully on the pure clear lines and contours of this face without the stranger's avoiding his glance or being offended by his persistence. He studied her face as if it were a painting. Sometimes the light emphasized the rose transparency of the nostrils and the double curve from upper lip to nose, sometimes a pale gleam of sunshine revealed the nuances of colouring, with nacreous reflection under the eyes and round the mouth, rose on the cheeks, and a matt surface without reflection towards the temples and on the neck. He admired the contrast of light and shade in the dark ringlets framing the face, lending an ephemeral grace. For everything is so fugitive in a woman's beauty! Today's loveliness is rarely the same as yesterday's, happily for her perhaps.

The so-called naval officer, still at an age when a man may delight in those trifles that make up love's whole, watched captivated for the repeated movement of eyelids, the seductive rise and fall of breathing. Sometimes his thoughts led him to look for a relation between the expression of the eyes and the almost imperceptible curving of the lips. Every tiny sign was a revelation of the spirit, every movement showed him some new facet of this girl. When some thought stirred her mobile features, or a sudden wave of colour or a smile brought animation, he found it infinitely delectable to try to guess this mysterious woman's thoughts.

Everything wove a web to ensnare his mind as well as his senses. Silence itself, far from raising obstacles to harmony and understanding, became a meeting-place for thoughts. When her eyes had several times encountered those of the stranger Marie de Verneuil realized that this silence would become compromising; and she then asked Madame du Gua some unimportant questions designed to lead to conversation, but she could not help including the son.

'Madame, did you not find it difficult to bring yourself to send your son to sea? Did it not mean condemning yourself to ceaseless anxiety?'

'Women are doomed, Mademoiselle, mothers I should say, to be apprehensive for their dearest treasures always.'

'Monsieur is very like you in appearance.'

'You think so, Mademoiselle?'

This innocent acceptance and *legitimation* of Madame du Gua's age as what she had claimed it to be made the young man smile and filled his so-called mother with fresh resentment. This woman's hatred grew with every passionate look her son cast at Marie. Silence, speech, whatever either of them did fanned her blazing fury, although she cloaked it with the utmost cordiality of manner.

'You are mistaken, Mademoiselle,' the stranger put in. 'Sailors are not more at risk than men in the other Services. And surely women shouldn't hate the Navy – haven't we the vast superiority over land-based forces of staying faithful to our mistresses?'

'Oh, of necessity!' replied Mademoiselle de Verneuil, laughing.

'It's still fidelity,' said Madame du Gua in an almost sombre tone.

A lively conversation followed, on subjects of interest only to the three travellers. In such circumstances people endowed with wit give platitudes fresh point; and the apparently frivolous exchanges in which these strangers entertained themselves by sounding each other was a cover for the desires, passions and hopes that stirred them. The quickness and malicious penetration shown by Marie, constantly on her guard, taught Madame du Gua that unless she used calumny and treachery she had no hope of triumphing over a rival so formidable in wit as well as beauty.

The travellers caught up with the escort, and the vehicle went more slowly. The young officer noticed a long slope to climb ahead, and proposed a walk to Mademoiselle de Verneuil. She seemed to find his perfect correctness and friendly politeness convincing, and her assent flattered his hopes.

'Madame, are you of the same mind as us?' she asked Madame du Gua. 'Will you take a walk too?'

'Hussy!' muttered the lady, as she got down from the carriage.

Marie and the stranger walked side by side but with some distance between them. The young man, already violently infatuated, was anxious to break down the barrier of reserve opposed to him, by which he was not taken in. He thought to succeed through his bantering game with Marie, by virtue of the Gallic charm, the ready wit – sometimes light-hearted, sometimes serious, always chivalrous, often mocking – which distinguished the remarkable men of the exiled aristocracy. But the laughing Parisian teased the young Republican so maliciously, and showed up and reproached him for his deliberate frivolity so disdainfully, showing her preference for the strongly-held convictions and deep feeling that in spite of him broke through what he said, that he easily guessed the way to please her.

The conversation changed therefore, and now the stranger

realized the expectations aroused by his expressive face. He found it ever harder from one moment to the next to assess the siren with whom he was falling ever deeper in love, and could only suspend judgement on a girl who made it a game to show him that his judgements were always wrong. First captivated by contemplating her beauty, he was now attracted to this unknown spirit by a curiosity that Marie took pleasure in exciting. The conversation insensibly took on an intimacy at odds with the detachment that Mademoiselle de Verneuil had endeavoured not quite successfully to give it.

Although Madame du Gua had followed the two enamoured young people, they had without noticing it increased their pace and out-distanced her presently by about fifty yards. These two charming beings strolled along the road, enjoying the childish pleasure of making the fine gravel crunch lightly under their feet in unison, happy to see themselves caught in the same spring-like burst of sunshine, and in company to breathe the scents of autumn so charged with dying leaves that they seem wafted on the breeze to feed the melancholy of budding love. Although neither appeared to see more than a passing incident in their present harmony, the skies, the region and the season lent their feelings a colour and gravity that gave them the semblance of passion. They began to speak in praise of the day, of its beauty; then of their strange meeting and how this pleasant interlude was soon to come to an end; and then of the ease with which travellers can confide in one another since they meet only to part at once. This last remark seemed tacitly to give the young man permission for soft confidences, and he ventured to make some intimate observations as a man who has had experience in such situations.

'Have you noticed, Mademoiselle,' he said, 'how feelings no longer follow their ordinary course, in the times of terror we live in? Everything around us seems to happen with inexplicable precipitation. People nowadays love or hate one another at sight. They instantly make up their minds to unite for life or part, and go to meet their death with the same celerity. Everything has quickened its pace to match the

Nation's turmoil. People surrounded by dangers come together more closely and with more intense feeling than in the ordinary course of life. In Paris lately everyone understood all that a handclasp might imply, just as though it were a battlefield.'

'One felt the need to live fast and extravagantly then,' she answered, 'because there was so little time left to live.' She cast a look at her young companion which seemed to remind him of the end of their short journey, then added maliciously, 'You are very well-informed about life for a young man who has just left the Academy.'

'What kind of man do you think I am?' he asked after a moment's silence. 'Tell me frankly how you see me.'

'So that you may acquire the right to talk to me about myself, no doubt . . .' she answered, laughing.

'You make no reply,' he went on, after a slight pause. 'Take care. Silence itself is often an answer.'

'Don't I know all you would like to have permission to say to me? Ah, good heavens, you have said too much already.'

'Oh, if we understand each other,' he returned with a laugh, 'I obtain more than I dared hope for.'

She began to smile so graciously that it seemed an acceptance of the urbane contest to which every man likes to challenge a woman. They persuaded themselves then, half-seriously, half-mockingly, that it was impossible for them ever to be anything more to each other than they were at that moment. The young man was free to abandon himself to a passion with no future, and Marie to laugh at it. Then when they had raised this make-believe barrier between them, they appeared equally anxious to take immediate advantage of the dangerous liberty they had just agreed on. Marie suddenly stumbled against a stone.

'Take my arm,' said the stranger.

'I'll have to, I think. It would make you too proud if I refused, wouldn't it? It would look as though I were afraid of you.'

'Ah, Mademoiselle!' he answered, holding her arm so

tightly that she could feel the beating of his heart. 'But you are going to make me proud by granting this favour.'

'Well, my readiness to grant it will destroy any false ideas.'

'You wish to defend me already against the danger of the emotions you rouse in me?'

'Do stop tripping me up with these boudoir fancies and word-play that belongs to literary cliques, I beg of you,' she said. 'It doesn't please me in a man of your character to meet the kind of wit any fool is capable of. Look around ... We are under a lovely sky, out in the open country; before us, above us, there is only grandeur. You wish to tell me I am beautiful, don't you? But your eyes show me that, and I know it in any case; and I am not a woman who can be flattered by compliments. Do you by any chance think of speaking to me of your *devotion*?' and she gave the word a scornful intonation. 'Can you imagine me so simple as to think such sudden sympathies strong enough to make the memory of one morning dominate a whole lifetime?'

'The memory, not of a morning,' he answered, 'but of a beautiful woman who showed herself generous.'

'You forget much greater attractions,' she retorted, laughing: 'an unknown woman in whom everything must seem odd and unusual, her name, her social position, her circumstances, the unconventionality of her speech and behaviour.'

'You are not unknown to me,' he exclaimed; 'I could perceive your quality, and would not change your perfection by a hair; except perhaps that I might wish you had a little more faith in the love you have the power of inspiring at first acquaintance.'

'Ah, poor child, seventeen years old, and talking of love already?' she said with a smile. 'Well, so be it. It's a commonplace of conversation between two people, like the rain and fine weather when paying a call, so let's talk of love. You will not find false modesty or narrow-mindedness in me. I can listen to that word without blushing; I have heard it said so many times with the lips but not the heart that it has become almost meaningless to me. It has been repeated to me in the theatre, in books, in the fashionable world, everywhere, but I have never encountered anything resembling this wonderful emotion.'

'Have you looked for it?'

'Yes.'

This was said so unreservedly that the young man made a surprised movement and stared fixedly at Marie as if he had suddenly changed his mind about her true character and circumstances.

'Mademoiselle,' he said with ill-concealed feeling, 'are you girl or woman, angel or demon?'

'I'm all of them,' she retorted, laughing. 'Isn't there always something diabolical and angelic in a girl who has not loved ever, is not in love now, and may never be in love perhaps?'

'And you think yourself happy so? . . .' he said, with a freedom of tone and manner that suggested he already felt less respect for his preserver.

'Oh, happy . . .' she answered, 'no. When it occurs to me that I am alone, ruled by social conventions that make me perforce artful and full of guile, I long for a man's privileges. But when I think of all the means nature has given us to involve and entangle you men, to hold you fast in the invisible net of a power none of you can withstand, then the part I have to play on earth wears a smiling face; and then again suddenly it seems petty, and I feel that I would despise a man who lets himself be taken in by common allurements.

'In short, sometimes I perceive the yoke we women bear and I am glad of it, and then it seems hateful and I shrug it off. At times I feel the fine impulse towards self-sacrificing devotion that makes our sex so noble, then again I experience an overwhelming desire for domination. It may be the natural tension between good and evil elements by which we all live here in this world. Angel and demon you said, and you were right. Ah, it isn't the first time I recognize how ambivalent my nature is. But we women realize our imperfection better than you do – haven't we all an instinctive apprehension of the no doubt unattainable ideal? But,' she added, looking up at the sky and sighing, 'what gives us our stature in your eyes . . .'

'That is? . . .'

'Well,' she went on, 'it's the fact that we are all struggling, more or less, to fulfil our destiny.'

'Mademoiselle, why should we part this evening?'

'Ah,' she said, smiling at the young man's ardent look. 'Let us step into our carriage again, the fresh air is not at all good for us.'

Marie turned about abruptly. The stranger followed her and grasped her arm without ceremony but in a gesture expressing both imperious desire and admiration. She walked faster; the officer guessed that she wished to avoid a perhaps unwelcome declaration, a repulse that made his ardour more insistent. He risked everything to wring a first favour from this woman, and said with a watchful look, 'Would you like me to tell you a secret?'

'Oh, yes, tell me quickly! Does it concern yourself?'

'I am not in the service of the Republic. Where are you going? I will go too.'

At this, Marie trembled violently. She withdrew her arm and covered her face with both hands to hide the colour, or perhaps the pallor, that had altered it. Then suddenly she let them fall and said in a moved voice, 'So you began as you would have ended, by deceiving me?'

'Yes,' he said.

When she heard this she turned her back on the heavy carriage towards which they were making their way, and began almost to run.

'But,' said the stranger, 'I thought the air was not good for us? . . .'

'Oh, it has changed,' she said gravely, without slackening a pace that showed the tumult of her thoughts.

'You say nothing?' said the stranger, whose heart was filling with the sweet expectancy and foretaste of pleasure.

'Oh,' she said curtly, 'the tragedy has not long delayed.'

'What tragedy are you talking about?'

She stopped and eyed the officer with a mixture of apprehension and curiosity. Then she masked her emotion with an inscrutable calm that showed that for a girl she had some experience of the world.

'Who are you?' she went on. 'But I know! When I saw you I suspected it – you are the Royalist leader known as the Gars! The former Bishop of Autun* is right when he tells us always to believe presentiments when they foretell misfortune.'

'What interest have you in knowing this person?'

'What interest could he have in hiding his identity from me, if I have already saved his life?' She began to laugh, but forcedly. 'I was wise to prevent you from telling me that you loved me. Be sure of this Monsieur, I detest you. I am Republican, you are Royalist, and I would hand you over at once if you had not my word, if I had not already saved you once, and if . . .' She stopped short.

These violent changes of feeling, these battles with herself which she no longer troubled to hide, alarmed the stranger, who tried, but vainly, to read her face.

'Let us part at once; I demand it; good-bye,' she said. She quickly turned back, took a few steps, and turned again. 'No, it is of vital concern to me to know who you are. Don't hide anything from me, tell me the truth. Who are you? For you are no more a pupil of the Academy than you are only seventeen years of age . . .'

'I am a sailor, ready to leave the sea to follow you wherever your fancy wishes to lead me. If I have the good fortune to excite your interest by some hint of mystery, I must take good care not to enlighten you. Why involve real life with its serious concerns in matters of the heart, in which we were beginning to understand each other so well?'

'We might have been able to understand each other heart and soul,' she said gravely. 'But, Monsieur, I have no right to demand that you trust me. You will never know how much you owe me. I'll say no more.'

They walked a few paces in complete silence.

'You are greatly interested in my life!' the stranger began again.

'Monsieur,' she said, 'for God's sake either tell me your

* Talleyrand. – *Trans.*

156

name or hold your tongue. You are a child,' she added, shrugging her shoulders, 'and I am sorry for you.'

His fellow-traveller's persistence in trying to learn his secret made the so-called naval officer waver between simple caution and the pursuit of his desires. A desired woman's pique can make her powerfully attractive. Her sweet reasonableness is just as demanding as her anger, and she attacks a man's heart through so many fibres that she makes it hers to do as she will. Was this attitude just another device to allure on Mademoiselle de Verneuil's part? In spite of his passion the stranger had the strength to mistrust a woman who was trying to wrest a secret of life-and-death importance from him.

'Why,' he said, taking her hand, which she absently yielded, 'why has my indiscretion, which gave this day a future, destroyed its charm?'

Mademoiselle de Verneuil, apparently painfully affected, made no answer.

'How can I have hurt you?' he went on, 'and what can I do to make amends?'

'Tell me your name.'

In his turn he walked in silence, and they went on a few paces. Suddenly Mademoiselle de Verneuil stopped as if she had taken an important decision.

'Monsieur le Marquis de Montauran,' she said with dignity, but not quite able to suppress the agitation that made a nervous tremor pass over her features, 'although I may have to pay for it, I am happy to do you a service. Here we shall part. The escort and the mail-coach are too necessary to your safety for you not to accept them both. Fear nothing from the Republicans: all these soldiers, believe me, are honest honourable men, and I mean to give orders to the Adjutant that he will carry out faithfully. For my part, I can go back to Alençon on foot with my maid; a few soldiers will accompany us. Listen to me carefully, if you value your head. If before you have reached safety you should meet the horrible dandy you saw at the inn, make your escape, for he would hand you over at once. As for me . . .' She paused. 'As for me, I return with my head high to life's sad way,' she added in a low voice, holding back tears. 'Good-bye, Monsieur. May you be happy! Good-bye.'

She beckoned to Captain Merle, who was just reaching the top of the rise; but the young man was not prepared for such an abrupt dismissal.

'Wait!' he cried in a tone of despair which sounded quite genuine.

Taken completely by surprise by this strange whim of the girl for whom he would then and there have sacrificed his life, the stranger had hit upon a deplorable deception to enable him to conceal his name and at the same time satisfy Mademoiselle de Verneuil's curiosity.

'You have guessed almost right,' he said. 'I am an *émigré*, sentenced to death, the Vicomte de Bauvan. It is love of my country that has brought me back to France, where my brother is. I hope to have my name erased from the *émigré* List through the influence of Madame de Beauharnais, now the wife of the First Consul; but if I fail then I want to die on my native soil, fighting by my friend Montauran's side. First I am going secretly with the help of a passport he sent me, to find out if any part of my estates in Brittany still belongs to me.'

While the young aristocrat was speaking Mademoiselle de Verneuil scrutinized his face searchingly. She did her best to preserve some scepticism, but she was trusting and credulous, and slowly her face regained its serenity. 'Is what you are telling me now true, Monsieur?' she exclaimed.

'Absolutely true,' declared the stranger, who in his relations with women cared little it seemed for integrity.

Mademoiselle de Verneuil gave a deep sigh, like a person returning to consciousness.

'Ah!' she exclaimed. 'I am very glad.'

'You hate my poor Montauran so much?'

'No,' she said. 'Naturally you would not understand. I could not wish *you* to be threatened with such dangers; but I shall try to protect him against them since he is your friend.'

'Who told you that Montauran was in danger?'

'Well, Monsieur, I have just come from Paris where people are talking of nothing else; and apart from that the

Commandant said enough about him at Alençon, I think.'

'Well then I shall ask you how it comes about that you will be able to protect him against every danger.'

'And suppose I do not wish to answer?' she said, with the hauteur that women can use effectively as a cloak for emotion. 'By what right do you ask to know my secrets?'

'By the right that must belong to a man who loves you.'

'So fast as that? . . .' she said. 'No, you do not love me, Monsieur. You see the object of a short-lived love-affair in me, that's all. Of course I guessed that you were an *émigré* at once. With manners as they are at present how could a person with some civilized acquaintance fail to guess the truth when she hears a cadet of the École Polytechnique express himself elegantly and hide aristocratic manners as badly as you have done under a Republican crust? And there is a trace of powder still in your hair, and a nobleman's scent which a woman of the world is bound to recognize instantly. It is because I was afraid that my guardian, who has a nose as sharp as any woman's, might realize who you were that I sent him away immediately. Monsieur, a true Republican officer from the Academy would not have thought himself in luck in meeting me and taken me for a pretty adventuress.

'Allow me, Monsieur de Bauvan, to give you some views from a woman's point of view about these matters. Are you so young that you do not know that of all the creatures of our sex the most difficult for a man to make a conquest of is the one who has her price, who is bored with pleasure? That sort of woman demands, or so they tell me, something quite remarkable in the way of charms and she follows her whim and yields when the fancy takes her. For any man to think he can seduce her is sheer fatuous folly.

'Let us leave that sort of woman out of consideration, although you are so kind as to class me as one of them, beautiful as they are all supposed to be. But you must understand that a beautiful and intelligent young gentlewoman of noble ideals (for you will grant me so much) does not sell herself, and it is not possible to win her except in one way, when she knows herself loved. Let me make myself clear! If

159

she falls in love and has a mind to commit a folly she must be justified by some quality of greatness in her lover.

'Forgive me for all this logic, a way of thinking rare enough in my sex; but for the sake of your honour . . . and mine,' she added, bowing her head, 'I would not wish us to be under any illusions about our respective merits, or that you should think Mademoiselle de Verneuil, angel or demon, girl or woman, capable of letting herself be captivated by banal gallantries.'

'Mademoiselle,' said the Marquis, in considerable though well-dissimulated surprise, and suddenly every inch an aristo-crat, 'I beg you to believe that I accept you as a very noble lady, full of sensibility and lofty sentiments, or . . . as a good girl, just as you choose!'

'I don't ask so much of you, Monsieur,' she said, laughing. 'Leave me my incognito. My mask is better adjusted than yours, besides, and it pleases me to keep it, if only to find out if the people who speak of love to me are sincere . . . So don't venture lightly too near me.

'. . . Monsieur, believe me,' she went on, grasping his arm with some intensity, 'if you were able to prove you loved me truly no human power should part us. Yes, I wish I could be linked with some great man's life, help further some vast ambition, realize some fine ideal. Noble hearts are not fickle, for constancy is one of their strengths; and so I should be for ever loved, for ever happy. But I would play my part too, for I would always be ready to make myself a stepping-stone to raise the man who had won my love, to sacrifice myself for him and endure everything from him, and love him always, even when he no longer loved me.

'I have never dared confide my heart's desires to another, nor the passionate impulses towards noble achievement that I am consumed by, but I may well say something to you about all this, since we are to part as soon as you are in safety.'

'Part? . . . Never!' he said, electrified by the eloquence of this vigorous mind as it seemed to struggle with a conception of profound significance.

'Are you free?' she returned, with a haughty and deflating look.

'Oh, free . . . yes, except for being condemned to death.'

And then she added in a voice full of bitter feeling, 'If all this were not a dream, you would have a fine life, would you not? . . . But if I have been talking nonsense, no matter, let's go no further. When I think of all you would have to be to appreciate me at my true worth, I have doubts about everything.'

'And I would have no doubts at all, if you would belong . . .'

'Hush!' she exclaimed, hearing these words spoken with the true accent of passion. 'The air is decidedly not good for us now, let us rejoin our chaperons.'

Chapter 11

THE mail-coach quickly caught up with these two people, who took their seats and travelled for some miles in complete silence. If both of them had ample matter to reflect upon, their eyes no longer feared to encounter. Both seemed to feel that it was necessary to observe the other and themselves keep some important secret guarded; but they felt the same desire draw them together, and it had now begun to take on the dimensions of passion. In their conversation each had recognized qualities in the other which made the pleasures they foresaw in their trial of strength or their union seem still more desirable.

It is possible that both of them after embarking on a life full of risks, had arrived at that strange state of mind and spirit in which, whether through lassitude or in defiance of fate, a person refuses to reflect seriously and leaves chance to decide what course to follow. It seems to him that there is no way through for him, yet he has to see the enterprise through to its necessary conclusion. Is it not true that the moral world like the surface of the globe has its gulfs and abysses into which strong-willed persons love to plunge at the risk of their lives, like a gambler delighting to stake his whole fortune?

Something like a common revelation of these ideas seemed to dawn on the aristocrat and Mademoiselle de Verneuil as a consequence of their conversation; and so they had suddenly taken a long step, for their souls' sympathy had followed the sympathy of their senses. The more they felt themselves drawn together by destiny, however, the more concerned they were to study each other, were it only in involuntary calculation to increase the sum of their future delights.

The young man, still surprised at the depth of this strange girl's thought, asked himself to begin with how she could combine so much acquired knowledge with so much freshness and youth. Then he considered the extreme touch-me-not aloofness of the attitudes she assumed, and thought he detected an exaggerated desire to appear virtuous. He suspected her of pretence, was angry with himself for his pleasure in her, and resolved to see nothing more in this stranger than a skilled comedy actress. He had some grounds for this judgement, for Mademoiselle de Verneuil was behaving as any other young woman in the world would have done – was withdrawing the more modestly the more ardour she felt. She was very naturally assuming the prudish attitude which is a woman's effective way of hiding extreme desire. All women would like to bring themselves pure and untouched to passion: and if they are not so, their dissembling of the fact is nevertheless a homage they pay to their love.

These reflections passed rapidly through the nobleman's mind and gave him considerable pleasure. In fact, for both, this mutual examination was bound to be a progress; and the lover soon arrived at the phase of passion in which a man finds in his mistress's faults reasons for loving her the more.

Mademoiselle de Verneuil remained reflective longer than the *émigré*: perhaps her imagination embraced a longer span of the future. The young man was yielding to one among hundreds of emotional impulses necessarily experienced in a man's life, and the young woman was envisaging a whole lifetime, blissfully planning its fine ordered course, filling it with happiness and great and noble aims. Happy in her dreams, as much in love with her chimeras as with reality, with the future as with the present, Marie tried to obliterate the past the better to establish her power over the stranger's young heart, and in that she was acting instinctively as all women act.

Having settled in her own mind that she would yield herself entirely, Marie wished, as it were, to dispute every inch of the way. She would have liked to take back from the past all her actions, all she had said and looked, and re-create them all to harmonize with the dignity of a woman who is loved. Her eyes, indeed, expressed something approaching horror when it occurred to her to think of the conversation she had just had, in which she had shown herself so aggressive. But study-ing the face opposite with its resolute stamp she told herself that a person so strong could not fail to be generous, and congratulated herself on having better fortune than many women in finding a man of character in her lover, a man con-demned to death, who had come of his own accord to risk his head and make war on the Republic.

The thought of being able to hold the soul of such a man unchallenged soon gave everything a different aspect. Be-tween the past when five hours before she had composed her face and voice to provoke and tease the nobleman, and the present when she could bowl him over with a look, there was the difference that divides a dead universe from a living one. Frank laughter, joyous flirtation, covered an immense passion which presented itself, as misfortune often does, with a smiling face.

In the present state of Mademoiselle de Verneuil's mind and heart the outside world took on the character of a phantas-magoria. The coach passed through villages, by valleys and mountains, of which her memory retained no impression. She arrived at Mayenne, the soldiers of the escort were changed, Merle spoke to her, she replied, traversed a whole town, and set off on the open road again; but the faces, the houses, the streets, the countryside, the men, were all whirled away like the indistinct shapes of a dream. Night fell. Marie travelled under a sky studded with diamonds, bathed in soft light, on the road to Fougères, without its occurring to her that the sky had changed its aspect, without a thought of Mayenne or Fougères, or where she was bound. That she might within a few hours leave the man of her choice, by whom she believed herself chosen, was not to her mind possible. Love is the only passion which will not suffer either past or future. Sometimes words fell from her lips to reveal her thoughts in almost incoherent phrases, but they echoed in her lover's heart like promises of joy.

Before the eyes of the two witnesses of this awakening passion it was taking on a frightening impetus. Francine knew Marie as well as the stranger knew the young man, and experience of events of the past made them silently await some terrible dénouement. Indeed they had not long to wait to see the end of the drama that Mademoiselle de Verneuil had so sadly, without truly realizing it perhaps, called a tragedy.

When the four travellers were about a league beyond Mayenne, they heard a horseman galloping very fast in their direction. When he reached the carriage he leaned over it to stare at Mademoiselle de Verneuil, and she recognized Corentin. This sinister individual boldly waved his hand and gestured knowingly with a familiarity that struck her like a searing blast, and then made off leaving her frozen by his odious implication of secret understanding. The *émigré* appeared to be disagreeably affected by the incident, and it had certainly not been missed by his so-called mother; but Marie touched him lightly, and with her eyes seemed to take refuge in his heart as the only asylum that she had on earth.

The young man's brow cleared then in his emotion at the movement with which his mistress had as if inadvertently revealed the depth of her attachment. An inexplicable dread had banished all coquetry, and love was visible for one moment undisguised. They were silent as if to prolong the sweetness of this moment. Unluckily, beside them Madame du Gua watched everything, and like a miser giving a feast seemed to count their crumbs, doling out their life.

Wrapped in their happiness, unaware of the road they travelled, the two lovers reached the part of the way that lies hidden in the Ernée valley and is the farthest of the three hollows that were the setting for the events which serve as exposition to this story. There Francine noticed and pointed out strange figures which seemed to move like shadows through the trees and among the gorse bushes surrounding the fields. As the carriage travelled on in the direction of these shadows, a volley of bullets whistling above their heads told the travellers that there was nothing ghostly about this apparition. The escort had fallen into an ambush.

This brisk fusillade gave Captain Merle poignant cause to regret his concurrence with Mademoiselle de Verneuil when she had thought that a quick nocturnal journey must be safe and let him take only sixty men. By Gérard's orders he immediately divided the little band into two columns to cover both sides of the road, and the two officers set off at a run across the fields of broom and gorse, endeavouring to deal with their assailants without pausing to count them. The Blues set themselves to beat the thick bushes to right and left of the road with rash impetuous valour, and replied to the Chouans' attack with sustained fire into the bushes from which the gunshots crackled.

Mademoiselle de Verneuil's first impulse had been to jump from the carriage and run back far enough to be out of range, but, ashamed of her fear and moved by the feeling that leads one to try increase one's stature in the eyes of a lover, she stood still and tried to observe the skirmish coolly.

The *émigré* followed her, took her hand and placed it over his heart.

'I was afraid,' she said smiling; 'but now . . .'

At this moment her scared maid cried to her, 'Marie, look out!' But as Francine was about to rush from the carriage she felt herself held by a strong hand. The weight of this huge hand drew a sharp cry from her. She turned and in silence recognized the face of Marche-à-terre.

'To your alarm I now owe the revelation of the sweetest of the heart's secrets,' the stranger was saying to Mademoiselle de Verneuil. 'Thanks to Francine I learn that you bear Mary's gracious name, Marie. Mary is the name I have called on in all my sufferings! Marie is the name I shall utter from now in joy, and I shall never be able to say it now without sacrilege, confounding religion and love. But could it be a crime to pray and love at the same time?'

At these words they held each other's hands fast and each looked into the other's face in silence, with an intensity of feeling that deprived them of all strength and power to express it.

'*It's not for you ones that there's any danger!*' said Marche-à-terre roughly to Francine, with a sinister accent of reproach in his raucous guttural voice and a heavy emphasis on each word. The innocent peasant girl was stunned. For the first time the poor girl saw ferocity in Marche-à-terre's looks.

The light of the moon seemed the fitting illumination for the figure of this half-savage Breton. Enveloped in the flood of that pale light that gives such strange appearances to forms, his cap in one hand, his heavy musket in the other, hunched like a gnome, he seemed to belong more to faery than real life. The apparition with his reproach had something of the gliding swiftness of phantoms.

He turned abruptly to Madame du Gua and exchanged some rapid words with her, but Francine who had a little forgotten her Bas-Breton patois could understand nothing of it. The lady seemed to be giving Marche-à-terre repeated orders. The short discussion ended with an imperious gesture from this woman, pointing out the two lovers to the Chouan. Before obeying, Marche-à-terre threw a final, seemingly commiserating, look at Francine as if he would have liked to speak to her; and the Breton girl knew that it was not by his own will that her lover was silent. The man's rough weather-beaten forehead furrowed painfully, his eyebrows drew angrily together. Was he resisting the order given once more to kill Mademoiselle de Verneuil? No doubt to Madame du Gua he looked more hideous than ever in this grimace, but his fiercely flashing eyes now seemed gentle to Francine for his look told her that she would be able to bend the force of this savage to her woman's will, and she hoped that she might still reign, after God, in this rude heart.

Marie's sweet communion with the aristocrat was interrupted by Madame du Gua, who came to lead her back, calling out as if in warning. Her purpose was to leave the way clear for one of the members of the Royalist Committee of Alençon, whom she recognized, to speak to the *émigré*.

'Do not trust the girl you met at the Hôtel des Trois-Maures.' After these words in the young man's ear, the Chevalier de Valois, riding a little Breton horse, disappeared again into the broom thickets from which he had just emerged.

The two sides were blazing away hotly now with astonishing noise and intensity, but had not come to grips.

'Sir, might this attack not be a feint to draw us off, kidnap our passengers and hold them to ransom?' said La-clef-des-coeurs.

'Devil fly away with me if you haven't hit the nail on the head!' Gérard answered, rushing back to the road.

The Chouan fire slackened now, for the sole purpose of the skirmish had been to allow the Chevalier to pass on the warning he had just given. Merle, who could see the Chouans retreating a few at a time across the field banks, thought it inadvisable to become involved in an unprofitable and dangerous pursuit. With a shouted command Gérard quickly brought the escort back and formed it up again on the road. It had suffered no losses and marched off once more. The Captain had the opportunity to offer his hand to assist Mademoiselle de Verneuil into the carriage, for the nobleman stood apart looking as if a thunderbolt had struck him. She was astonished, and climbed in without accepting the Republican's courtesy. When she turned her head towards her lover and saw him standing motionless she was stunned by the sudden change the horseman's mysterious communication had produced. The young *émigré* walked slowly towards the carriage, his every movement expressive of profound disillusionment.

'Didn't I tell you so?' Madame du Gua said at the young man's ear, taking his arm to lead him to the vehicle. 'There's no doubt we're in the hands of a creature who has made a bargain with them for your head; but as she's silly enough to have taken a fancy to you instead of doing her job, don't you behave like a child. Just pretend to be in love with her until we reach La Vivetière ... Once we're there! ... But how could he be in love with her already?' she said to herself as she looked at the young man sitting in his place like a man in a daze.

The carriage rolled heavily along the gravelled road. To Mademoiselle de Verneuil as she cast her first look round her everything seemed to have changed. Death was slipping into her love already. It was perhaps no more than a suggestion, an atmosphere; but to the eyes of any woman in love shadows are as clear-cut as bright colours. Francine had realized by

Marche-à-terre's look that Mademoiselle de Verneuil's fate which she had made him guardian of lay in other hands than his, and showed a pale face, unable to prevent herself from shedding tears when her mistress looked at her. The unknown lady concealed her gratified feminine spite badly with false smiles, and the sudden change that her honeyed sweetness to Mademoiselle de Verneuil introduced into her attitude, voice and face was of a nature to strike any perspicacious person with alarm.

Mademoiselle de Verneuil shuddered instinctively, even as she asked herself, 'Why should I be afraid? ... She is his mother.' She trembled in every limb, suddenly asking herself, 'Is she really his mother?' She saw a chasm open before her and another look at the *émigré* at last revealed it plainly. 'This woman loves him!' she thought. 'But why load me with kind attentions, after having been so chilly? Am I done for? Could she be afraid of me?'

As for the aristocrat, he had grown pale then flushed but preserved his calm, his downcast eyes concealing the turmoil of his emotions. His lips were compressed, destroying the gracious curve of his mouth, and his colour ebbed again as he struggled with his stormy thoughts. Mademoiselle de Verneuil could not even guess whether there remained some love mixed with his anger.

The road, lined with trees at that place, became gloomy and prevented the silent players of this scene from using their eyes to question one another. The murmur of the wind soughing through the clustering trees, the measured tramp of the escort, surrounded them with a solemn gravity that made the heart beat faster.

Searching for the cause of the change Mademoiselle de Verneuil inevitably arrived at an answer. The memory of Corentin passed like a flash of lightning, illuminating the face of her true destiny. For the first time since the morning she reflected seriously on her situation. Until this moment she had let herself drift in the happiness of loving, thinking neither of herself nor of the future. Her suffering became intolerable, and unable to endure it any longer she sought out and waited with love's gentle patience for a glance from the young man, and then implored him so urgently, her pallor and her trembling had an eloquence so searching, that he was thrown off balance; but the blighting of his hopes was only the more complete.

'Do you feel ill, Mademoiselle?' he asked.

His unfeeling voice, the question itself, the look, the gesture, all combined to convince the poor girl that the events of the day were part of a mirage, deceiving eyes and soul, and now dissolving like the half-formed clouds scattered by the wind.

'You ask if I feel ill . . .' she answered with a forced laugh. 'I was about to ask you the same question.'

'I thought there must be some sympathy between you,' said Madame du Gua with false geniality.

Neither the aristocrat nor Mademoiselle de Verneuil replied. It was another blow struck at the girl's heart to see her powerful beauty powerless. She knew she could at any moment learn what lay behind the situation, but was hesitant – a unique instance perhaps of a woman unwilling to tear the veil from a secret.

Human existence is sadly full of situations brought about by problems too deeply considered or by catastrophe, when we seem to float in a void without anchorage. Our thoughts have no form or substance, no point of departure. The present seems unconnected by any link with the past or future. Such was Mademoiselle de Verneuil's state.

She sat bowed in the back of the carriage like an uprooted shrub. Mute and suffering, she looked no more at anyone, wrapped herself in her grief, and remained so obstinately enclosed in the nebulous world where unhappiness takes refuge that she saw nothing outside it. Ravens passed croaking overhead; but, although like all free-thinkers she kept a corner in her heart for superstitions, she took no note of them.

The passengers travelled for some time in complete silence.

Chapter 12

'Parted already,' Mademoiselle de Verneuil was saying to herself. 'And yet nothing has been said. Could it have been Corentin? It is not in his interest. Who could have risen to accuse me then? Only just loved, and already comes the horror of desertion. I sow love and reap contempt. Is it always to be my destiny to see happiness only to lose it?'

She was suffering now in a fashion new to her, for she was genuinely in love and for the first time. However she had not surrendered herself so entirely as not to find armour in a young and beautiful woman's natural pride. The secret of true love is often kept in spite of torture, and she had not given hers away. She summoned her courage and, ashamed to reveal by her silent suffering how deeply she cared, tossed her head gaily, showed a smiling face or rather mask, and forced herself to disguise the alteration in her voice.

'Where are we?' she asked Captain Merle, who maintained a constant nearness to the carriage.

'Eight or nine miles from Fougères, Mademoiselle.'

'So we shall soon be there?' she said to encourage him to continue the conversation, resolving to show the young Captain that she felt a certain esteem for him.

Merle was delighted. 'It's not far as the crow flies,' he replied, 'only in this country miles are capable of going on for ever. When you have reached the crest of the slope we're climbing you'll see another valley like the one we're leaving, and on the horizon you'll then be able to see the summit of the Pellerine. Please God the Chouans don't take it into their heads to play us a return match there! Well, you understand that going up and down like this we don't go very far forward. From the Pellerine you will see another . . .'

At this name the *émigré* started, as he had done once before,

171

but so slightly that Mademoiselle de Verneuil was the only one to notice it.

'What is this Pellerine you speak of?' the girl asked with lively interest, interrupting the Captain's topographical discourse.

'It's a mountain-top,' said Merle, 'which gives its name to the valley we're about to enter which belongs to the province of Maine, and separates it from the valley of the Couësnon in Brittany, and at the far end of that Fougères lies, and it's the first town in Brittany. We had a fight there at the end of Vendémiaire with the Gars and his brigands. We were bringing in conscripts who didn't want to leave their own province and so thought they would kill us at the boundary; but Hulot is a tough customer and he gave them . . . '

'So you must have seen the Gars? What kind of man is he? . . . ' she asked.

Her piercing gaze was fixed maliciously on the false Vicomte de Bauvan's face.

'Oh, heavens, Mademoiselle,' answered Merle, interrupted yet again, 'he is so like Citizen du Gua here that if he were not wearing the École Polytechnique uniform I would swear it was the same man.'

Mademoiselle de Verneuil kept her eyes fixed on the young man who despised her, sitting cold and motionless opposite, but she saw no sign that could be interpreted as fear. A bitter smile apprised him of her discovery at this moment of the secret he had so treacherously kept. Then, her nostrils dilated in triumph, her head turned to keep both the aristocrat and Merle in view, she said to the Republican, a taunt in her tone, 'This leader gives the First Consul a great deal of anxiety, Captain. He is a bold man, so they say, but risks his neck in giddy escapades, especially chasing after women.'

'That's what we're counting on,' the Captain replied, 'to settle our reckoning with him. If we can hold him two hours we'll give him a dose of lead in the head. The Coblentz* traitor

* Coblentz was a rallying-place for the *émigrés* from 1789. The Prince de Condé went there in 1792 and under him the Princes' army was formed. – *Trans.*

would do the same for us if he happened to come across us, and send us to kingdom come, so *par pari* . . . , an eye for an eye . . . '

'Oh,' said the *émigré*, 'we have nothing to fear! Your soldiers will not get so far as the Pellerine, they are too tired, and if you agree they can make a halt quite near here. My mother is staying at La Vivetière, and there a few gunshots away you see the road leading off to it. These two ladies would probably like to rest there, they must be tired after coming from Alençon without breaking the journey – and since Mademoiselle,' he added with forced politeness, turning towards his mistress, 'has been so generous as to make our journey as safe as it has been pleasant, she will perhaps be pleased to accept an invitation to supper with my mother. At any rate, Captain,' he went on, turning to Merle, 'the times are not so bad that we can't find a cask of cider still at La Vivetière for your men. I imagine the Gars cannot have taken it all – at least my mother thinks not . . . '

'Your mother? . . . ' interrupted Mademoiselle de Verneuil incredulously, making no reply to the singular invitation extended to her.

'Can you not believe I am so old, this evening, Mademoiselle?' Madame Gua answered her. 'I had the misfortune to be married very young. I had my son at fifteen . . . '

'Are you not mistaken, Madame – should it not rather be when you were thirty?'

Madame du Gua turned pale as she swallowed this insult. She would have given anything to be able to hit back and found herself forced to smile, for she wanted to find out at all costs, at the price of even more deadly affronts, what the girl's feelings were; and so she pretended not to have understood.

'The Chouans have never had a more cruel leader than that one, if one can believe the rumours about him,' she said, including both Francine and Francine's mistress in the remark.

'Oh, as to cruel, I don't think he's that,' answered Mademoiselle de Verneuil; 'but he knows how to lie, and seems very easily led astray. The leader of an insurrection should not be anyone's toy.'

'You know him?' asked the young *émigré* coldly.

'No,' she replied, with a contemptuous glance. 'I once thought I did ... '

'Oh, Mademoiselle, he's definitely a *malin* – he's got the devil's own cunning,' said the Captain, shaking his head and throwing out his hands to point the implication the word carried then and has since lost. 'These old families sometimes throw up vigorous shoots. He's come back from the country where the *ci-devants* have had to live pretty hard, so they say, and men, you know, are like medlars, they ripen on straw. If this lad plays his cards right, he'll be able to keep us on the move after him long enough. He knows very well how to use mobile bands against our Free Companies and make all the Government's measures ineffective. If a Royalist village is burned he has two Republican villages burned in reprisal. He extends his operations over a vast area and so holds down a considerable number of our troops here at a time when we haven't too many to spare. Oh, he knows what he's about!'

'He's an assassin of his country,' Gérard interrupted vehemently.

'Well,' answered the aristocrat, 'if his death will save the country, shoot him quickly.'

Then his eyes probed Mademoiselle de Verneuil's soul, and they crossed swords silently in one of those scenes whose dramatic impact and fleeting subtle changes language can only very inadequately represent. Danger heightens tension. When death is a possibility the vilest criminal always excites some pity. Although Mademoiselle de Verneuil was by this time convinced that the lover who disdained her was the dangerous leader, she was not anxious to confirm her suspicions yet at the risk of his head. There was something quite different she was impelled to find out first. So she preferred to doubt or believe as passion swayed her and set herself to playing with fire.

With a look of mocking perfidy she triumphantly indicated the soldiers to the young leader. In thus confronting him with his evident danger she took pleasure in making him harshly realize that his life hung on just one word, and her lips seemed

174

to be already rounding themselves to utter it. She scrutinized the facial muscles of her victim at the stake as if she were a Red Indian, and brandished the tomahawk with some grace, childishly enjoying a bloodless vengeance and punishing like a mistress still in love.

'If I had a son like yours, Madame,' she said to the visibly terrified lady, 'I would wear mourning for him on the day I surrendered him to such danger.'

She received no answer. She turned her head from the officers to Madame du Gua swiftly time after time, but surprised no secret sign between her and the Gars to confirm an intimacy between them which she suspected but was still anxious to doubt. In a battle to the death when a woman holds the death-warrant she must needs prolong her hesitation.

The young General was smiling with complete coolness, and sustained the torture Mademoiselle de Verneuil was inflicting without a tremor, his attitude and facial expression those of a man unconcerned about the dangers to which he was exposed; and sometimes he seemed to be silently saying, 'This is your chance to avenge the wound to your vanity, so make the most of it! You justify my contempt for you, and I should hate to have to change my mind.'

The air of deliberately insulting offended dignity with which Mademoiselle de Verneuil set herself to scrutinize the leader from her vantage-ground of power was more than half assumed, for in her heart she admired his courage and nonchalance. She was as gratified as any woman would be to discover that her lover bore an ancient title, and pleased also to find him the champion of a cause made romantic by the odds against it, fighting with all the powers of a resolute and intelligent man against a Republic so many times victorious, and see him in the grip of danger displaying the kind of audacious bravado that wins a woman's heart. In demonstration perhaps of the feminine cat-and-mouse instinct, she set the knife to his throat a score of times.

'By what authority can you condemn a Chouan to death?' she asked Merle.

'Why, by the Decree of the 14 Fructidor last, which outlaws

the rebel Departments and sets up Courts-martial,' the Republican soldier replied.

'You favour me with your attention – I wonder why?' she asked the young leader, as he examined her closely.

'Because of a sentiment that no gallant man could express to any kind of woman,' the Marquis de Montauran said softly, leaning towards her, and then in a louder voice, 'One has to live in these times to see girls doing the headsman's work, and improving on him in their play with the axe . . .'

She stared at Montauran; and then, enchanted that this man dared insult her at the moment when she held his life in her hands, she laughed with gentle malice and whispered, 'Your head is far too troublesome for the headsman to have to do with it: I'll keep it.'

For a long moment the Marquis contemplated this un-accountable girl whose love accepted everything, even the most scathing insults, and who could take her revenge by pardoning an offence women find unpardonable. His eyes were less stern, less cold; his expression even took on a tinge of melancholy. His passion was already stronger than he himself knew. Mademoiselle de Verneuil, content with this slender pledge of the reconciliation she sought, looked at him tenderly, gave him a smile that was like a kiss; then she sat back in her place, unwilling to imperil the future of this drama of happiness further, believing she had tied the knot again securely with her smile. She was so beautiful! She knew so well how to triumph over obstacles to love! She was so accustomed to making everything a game, to trusting to chance! She delighted so much in the unpredictable and the tempests of life!

Soon, by the Marquis's order, the carriage left the main road and took the direction of La Vivetière, along a hollow road sunk between high banks planted with apple trees which made it seem less a road than a ditch. The travellers went ahead towards the mansion whose greyish roof tops appeared and disappeared behind the trees along the way, leaving the soldiers to follow slowly, for several of them were having to fight for their shoes against the sticky clay.

'This path is a fine imitation of the way that leads to eternal life!' exclaimed Beau-pied.

Thanks to the coachman's skill, it was not long before Mademoiselle de Verneuil saw the Château de la Vivetière. This mansion was situated on the high ground of a neck of land jutting out as a kind of promontory between two deep lakes, and the only access to it was along a narrow causeway. The buildings and gardens were defended at some distance behind the château by a wide moat, connecting the lakes and filled by the water flowing from them. It was to all practical purposes an almost attack-proof island, a valuable place of refuge for a leader, who could only be surprised there through treachery.

When she heard the rusty hinges of the gate creak and the carriage passed under the vaulted arch of a portal battered in the previous war, Mademoiselle de Verneuil put her head out. The scene that met her gaze was so sinisterly coloured that the sweet dreams of love and coquetry were almost wiped from her mind.

The carriage drove into a large nearly-square courtyard, bounded and enclosed by the slopes descending steeply to the lakes. These uncared-for shores washed by sheets of water stained green in wide patches were embellished only by leafless, water-loving trees, whose stunted trunks and huge hoary heads rising above reeds and brushwood had the appearance of grotesque carved figures, which seemed to come to life in their uncouth row and talk when the frogs deserted them croaking and the water-hens, roused by the sound of wheels, flew up with a splatter of feet in the water. The courtyard, surrounded by tall withering grasses and gorse and dwarfed or parasitic shrubs, banished all thought of planned order and grandeur. The château seemed to have been long abandoned. The roofs were sagging under a burden of weeds. The walls, although built of stone of the hard schistous kind common below this soil, showed many fissures to which ivy was clinging with its tenacious claw-like grip. The pile comprised two wings at right-angles united by a tall tower, facing the lake; and its decayed and hanging doors and shutters, rusted balustrades and crumbling window-frames seemed ready to fall to pieces at the first breath of a storm.

The north wind was blowing through these ruins, to which the moon's hazy light lent the character and aspect of a vast skeletal spectre. One would have to have seen it in its colours of grey-blue granite and blackish-yellow schist to appreciate the fantastically eerie suggestion of this empty and dismal shell. Its disintegrating stonework and glassless windows, the gaping crenellations of the tower and split roofs, made it look like skeleton bones, and the predatory birds that flew off screaming added one more touch to the nightmarish resemblance.

The sombre foliage of tall pine-trees planted behind the house swayed above the roof tops, and some clipped yews set to decorate the corners framed it with sad drapings like a hearse. The style of the doors, the crude ornament, the lack of harmonious plan in the building were all characteristic of the feudal manors which are the pride of Brittany, perhaps reasonably enough, for in this Celtic land they are a kind of history in stone of the times lost in mist before the establishment of the Monarchy.

Mademoiselle de Verneuil, to whose mind the word *château* was accustomed to present a castle of a more usual kind, overwhelmed by the funereal aspect of the scene, jumped lightly down from the carriage and stood alone, contemplating it with terror, thinking of the decision that she must take. Francine heard Madame du Gua heave a sigh of delighted relief at finding herself beyond the power of the Blues, and she exclaimed involuntarily when the gate was shut and she saw herself within this natural stronghold. Montauran had quickly followed Mademoiselle de Verneuil, guessing the thoughts that filled her mind.

'This château,' he said lightly, but with a sad intonation, 'has been made a ruin by the war, like the plans I built for our happiness, ruined by you.'

'How can you say that?' she said, taken aback.

'Are you indeed "a beautiful and intelligent young gentlewoman of noble ideals"?' he asked, sardonically repeating what she had said so provocatively in their roadside conversation.

'Who has said anything to the contrary?'

'Trustworthy friends who are concerned for my safety and keep their eyes open to frustrate attempts to betray me.'

'Attempts to betray you?' she said mockingly. 'Are Alençon and Hulot so far away already? You have a bad memory, a dangerous fault in a rebel leader! But if friends hold such a dominant place in your heart,' she added with a rare insulting rudeness, 'you may keep your friends. Nothing can compare with the pleasures of friendship. Good-bye. Neither I nor the soldiers of the Republic will enter here.'

She started towards the gateway with a gesture of wounded pride and disdain, but a certain nobility and despair in her bearing made the Marquis abandon all his suspicions, for it was costing him so much to give up his desires that he could not but be imprudent and credulous. He too had fallen in love already. Neither of the two lovers had any taste for prolonging a quarrel.

'Add just one word and I'll believe you,' he said imploringly.

'One word?' she retorted, compressing her lips. 'One word? Not a nod, even!'

'Even a scolding will do,' he said, trying to take her hand, which she withheld; 'that is if you dare be cross with a rebel leader who is as mistrustful and sad now as he was joyful and confident not long ago.'

As Marie looked at him without anger, he added, 'You have my secret and I have not yours.'

Marie's smooth white forehead seemed to darken as she cast an ill-humoured look at the Marquis.

'My secret?' she said, 'No. Never.'

In love every word, every glance, is eloquent in its moment, but Mademoiselle de Verneuil was not expressing anything very precise; and however adept Montauran might be he could not interpret that exclamation, although her voice had revealed some unusual emotion which could not but keenly excite his curiosity.

'You have a pretty way of dispelling suspicion,' he replied.

'So you cherish some suspicion?' she asked, measuring him with her eyes, as if saying, 'Do you imagine you hold some rights over me?'

'Mademoiselle,' the young man replied mildly but with some firmness, 'the power you exercise over the Republican troops, this escort . . .'

'Ah, that reminds me. My escort and I, your protectors, in fact, shall we be safe here?' she inquired in a lightly sarcastic tone.

'Yes, on my word and honour! Whoever you are, you and yours, you have nothing to fear under my roof.'

This solemn declaration was made with so much true and generous feeling that Mademoiselle de Verneuil was bound to feel satisfied that the Republicans' safety was secure. She was about to speak when the approach of Madame du Gua silenced her. That lady had been able to hear or guess part of the conversation between the two lovers, and with no little uneasiness saw them closely engaged, in an attitude that showed no sign of their former hostility. When the Marquis noticed her he offered his hand to Mademoiselle de Verneuil and turned quickly towards the house as if to rid himself of unwelcome company.

'I am in his way,' the stranger said to herself, standing motionless where she had been left. She watched the two reconciled lovers go slowly towards the steps, and stop to talk as soon as they had put a certain distance between themselves and her. 'Yes, yes, I stand in their way,' she went on; 'but in a little while this creature will not be in my way any more. The lake, by God, shall be her tomb! I'll keep your word and honour truly, shall I not? Once under that water what has she to fear? She'll be safe enough, won't she?'

She was staring fixedly at the calm mirror of the little lake on the right, when suddenly she heard a rustling among the brambles of the bank, and in the moonlight saw the figure of Marche-à-terre emerge against the gnarled trunk of an old willow. Only a person knowing the Chouan could have distinguished him among the group of pollard stumps of which he seemed to be one. Madame du Gua cast a cautious look about her. She saw the coachman leading his horses to a stable in the wing facing the bank where Marche-à-terre was concealed. Francine was making her way towards the two lovers, who at this moment were oblivious of the whole world. Then the lady, moving down the slope, put her finger to her lips to impose complete silence, and the Chouan understood rather than heard the question, 'How many of you are here?'

'Eighty-seven.'

'There are only sixty-five of them. I counted them.'

'Good,' said the half-savage child of nature with fierce satisfaction.

Then the Chouan, who was watching Francine's every gesture, vanished against the knotty curves of the willow bark again as he saw her turn, her eyes searching for the enemy whom she watched instinctively.

Chapter 13

SEVEN or eight people, brought out by the noise of carriage wheels, appeared at the top of the steps at the main door and shouted, 'The Gars! It's the Gars! He's here!'

At this, others ran out and their presence put an end to the conversation between the two lovers. The Marquis de Montauran hastily strode towards the noblemen, imperatively signed to them to say nothing and gestured towards the entrance to the avenue where the Republican soldiers were just appearing in the distance. At the sight of these familiar blue uniforms with red facings and the gleaming bayonets the astonished conspirators exclaimed, 'Have you come here to betray us?'

'I should not be warning you of the danger in that case,' the Marquis replied, with an acid smile. 'These Blues,' he went on after a pause, 'form the escort of this young lady, and it was her generosity that saved us by a miracle when we were in deadly danger at an inn in Alençon. We'll tell you the whole story. Mademoiselle and her escort are here because I have given my word to them, and must be received as friends.'

Madame du Gua and Francine had reached the steps. The Marquis gallantly offered his hand to Mademoiselle de Verneuil, the group of noblemen separated, forming two lines for them to pass between, and everyone peered at the stranger's face, the general lively curiosity already sharpened by the stealthy signs Madame du Gua was making behind her back.

In the first room Mademoiselle de Verneuil saw a great table, perfectly appointed and prepared for about twenty guests. This dining-room led into a vast reception room where the company soon gathered. These two rooms were in keeping with the spectacle of ruin presented by the château's exterior. The polished walnut wainscoting, of crude design and clumsy workmanship, was cracked, standing away from the walls, and seemed about to fall. Its sombre colour increased the gloom of these uncurtained glassless rooms, and the few dilapidated pieces of ancient furniture were in harmony with the general atmosphere of rack and ruin. Marie noticed some maps and plans spread out on a large table; and then, in corners of the room, piled-up swords and rifles. Everything pointed to an important conference between the Vendéan and Chouan leaders. The Marquis led Mademoiselle de Verneuil to an enormous worm-eaten armchair beside the fire, and Francine took up her position behind her mistress, leaning on the back of this antique relic.

'You will excuse me if I do my duty as host for a short time,' the Marquis said, and left the two strangers to mingle with the groups of his guests.

Francine saw all the leaders, at a few words from Montauran, hasten to hide their arms, the maps, and everything that might awaken suspicion in the Republican officers. A few took off wide leather belts holding pistols and hunting knives. The Marquis, after urging the greatest discretion, left the room, pleading the necessity of arranging for the reception of the embarrassing guests chance had brought him. Mademoiselle de Verneuil, busy holding out her feet to the blaze to warm them, let Montauran go without turning her head, which was a disappointment to the watchers, who all wanted to see her face. So Francine was the only one to witness the change the young General's departure produced in the company. The noblemen all clustered round Madame du Gua, and during the murmured conversation she held with them there was not one who did not several times look towards the two strangers.

'You know what Montauran is like,' she was saying. 'It didn't take him five seconds to lose his head over this girl; and you will understand that he was sceptical about the best of advice when it came from me. Our friends in Paris, and Monsieur de Valois and Monsieur d'Esgrignon in Alençon, all warned him that they were going to set a trap for him by throwing some creature at his head, and he gets infatuated with the first one he meets – a girl who according to my information, and I've made some inquiries, has borrowed a great name to drag it in the dust ... ' and so on, to the same effect.

This lady, in whom the reader may have recognized the woman who intervened in favour of the attack on the turgotine, will keep the name in this story which served her to avoid the dangers of her journey by Alençon. Publication of her real name could only give offence to a noble family, already deeply hurt by this lady's errant behaviour. What happened to her later, moreover, has been the subject of another Scene.

Soon the company's attitude of interested curiosity became inquisitively rude and even hostile. A few exclamations, quite offensive in tone, reached Francine's ear, and after a word to her mistress she took refuge in a window embrasure. Marie rose and looked towards the insolent group with an expression full of dignity, even of contempt. Her beauty, elegant bearing and pride immediately changed her enemies' humour, and an involuntary and flattering murmur ran round the room. Two or three men whose demeanour showed the accustomed politeness and gallantry one acquires in the more civilized atmosphere of courts moved towards Marie courteously. Her decorum inspired respect. None of them dared speak to her; and far from their arraigning her, it was she who seemed to sit in judgement on them.

The leaders of this war undertaken for God and the King were little like the fanciful portraits she had been pleased to paint. This, in fact, great cause shrank to mean proportions when she saw these representatives of the provincial gentry, all of them, except for two or three vigorous figures, woodenly lacking in expression and animation. After giving wings to her romantic imagination, Marie fell suddenly to earth. The cast of these features suggested at first sight a craving for intrigue rather than any ambition for glory. It was self-interest, in truth, that had put arms in the hands of these gentlemen, and though they may have become heroic in action, in that place they showed themselves as they were.

Her disillusionment made Mademoiselle de Verneuil unjust, and prevented her from recognizing the true devotion which made several of these men so remarkable. Most of them, indeed, showed vulgar breeding. Some faces of character stood out from the others, but they revealed the stultifying effects of aristocratic conventions and etiquette. Although Marie granted these men in general the possession of intelligence and shrewdness, she found them entirely lacking in that simplicity and that imposing quality to which the triumphs and the men of the Republic had accustomed her. This nocturnal assembly, in the old ruined baronial hall under the ill-made decoration that went with the figures well enough, made her smile; she thought she saw in it a symbolic picture of the Monarchy.

It occurred to her then with joy that at least the Marquis was playing the leading rôle among these people whose sole merit, for her, was their devotion to a lost cause. She mentally traced her lover's figure among the mass, making him stand out against it with delight, and in these slight, unnoticeable background figures saw nothing more now than the instruments of his noble purposes.

She had reached this point in her musings when the Marquis's footsteps were heard in the adjoining room. The conspirators at once split into several groups and whispering ceased. Like schoolboys plotting mischief in their master's absence, they hastened to make a display of order and silence. Montauran came in. Marie had the happiness of watching him with admiration as he walked among these people of whom he was the youngest, the most handsome, and the first. Like a king among his court he went from group to group, with a nod for one, a handshake for another, a few private words of understanding or reproach, a look, doing his job as leader of the insurgent party with a grace and poise difficult to credit in the young man she had first accused of being an irresponsible trifler.

The Marquis's presence put an end to the visible signs of the curiosity that had attached itself to Mademoiselle de Verneuil, but Madame du Gua's spiteful remarks soon produced their effect. The Baron du Guénic, nicknamed *l'Intimé*, seemed the one of all these men brought together by their important common interest whom his name and rank permitted to treat

Montauran with familiarity. He took the leader by the arm and drew him into a corner.

'See here, my dear Marquis,' he said, 'we are all concerned to see you on the point of committing an act of downright folly.'

'What do you mean?'

'Have you any idea where this girl comes from, who she really is, what her designs on you are?'

'My dear l'Intimé, between ourselves my fancy will have passed by tomorrow morning.'

'Quite so, but suppose this creature hands you over before dawn? ...'

'I'll answer that when you tell me why she hasn't done it already,' answered Montauran, affecting a fatuous playfulness.

'Yes, but if you please her she may not want to betray you until *her* fancy has passed.'

'My dear fellow, just look at that charming girl, consider her air of breeding, and can you dare to say that she is not a woman of distinction? If she cast a favouring eye on you, would you not feel in the depth of your heart some respect for her? A lady has already biased you against this person; but after what we have said to each other, if she turned out to be one of those lost creatures our friends have spoken of I would kill her ...'

'Do you believe Fouché so stupid,' Madame du Gua interrupted, 'as to send you a girl from a street-corner? He has matched the lure to the fish. But though you may be blind, your friends will have their eyes wide open for your sake.'

'Madame,' the Gars answered, shooting some angry glances at her, 'be careful not to act in any way against this person or her escort, for if you did nothing would save you from my vengeance. I wish the lady to be treated with the greatest consideration and like a relative of my own family. We are, I believe, connected with the Verneuils.'

The opposition the Marquis met had the usual effect of obstruction of this sort on young people. Although he had apparently treated Mademoiselle de Verneuil very lightly and let it be understood that his passion for her was a caprice, because his pride was involved he had just taken a long step.

He had acknowledged her as a connection, and so he found himself in honour bound to have her respected. He passed, then, from group to group, giving an assurance, as a man whom it would be dangerous to cross, that this stranger really was Mademoiselle de Verneuil. All the rumours, accordingly, died down at once.

When Montauran had established something like harmony in the hall and done everything that the circumstances required, he eagerly made his way to his mistress and said in a low voice, 'These people have stolen an hour of happiness from me.'

'I am very pleased to have you here,' she answered laughing. 'I warn you I am curious, so don't let me weary you with my questions. Tell me first who that fellow wearing a green cloth jacket is.'

'That's the famous Major Brigaut, a man from the Marais, a friend of the late Mercier, known as La-Vendée.'

'And who is the fat clergyman with the rubicund face he's talking to now about me?'

'Do you know what they're saying?'

'Do I want to know? . . . Is that what you're asking?'

'But I could not tell you without offending you.'

'If I have cause for offence and you do not exact vengeance for insults to me under your roof, then good-bye to you, Marquis! I will not stay here a minute. I already feel some qualms at deceiving these poor Republicans who are so loyal and so trusting.'

She took a few quick steps and the Marquis followed her.

'My dear Marie, listen to me. On my honour, I have silenced their ill-natured gossip, not knowing whether the damaging things they were saying were true or false. All the same, in my present situation, when I have been warned by our Paris friends in the Ministries to beware of any woman of whatever kind who should chance to cross my path, because Fouché, so I was informed, intended to use a Judith of the streets against me, my best friends may be pardoned for thinking that you are too beautiful to be virtuous . . .'

As he spoke, the Marquis looked deeply into Mademoiselle

de Verneuil's eyes. She blushed and could not help shedding a few tears.

'I have deserved these insults,' she said. 'I would only wish to see you convinced that I am some despicable creature and know that you loved me ... then I would have no further doubt of you. I believed you when you were deceiving me, yet you do not believe me when I am true. Let's leave the matter there, Monsieur.' And, knitting her brows and turning deathly pale, 'Good-bye,' she said, and rushed frantically from the room.

'Marie, my life is yours,' said the young Marquis, at her ear.

She stopped, and looked at him.

'No, no,' she said, 'I will be generous. Good-bye. I was not thinking either of my past or your future when I followed you. I was mad.'

'Can you leave me at the very moment when I am offering you my life? ...'

'You are offering it in a moment of passion, of desire.'

'Without regrets, and for always,' he said.

She turned back into the room. To cover his emotion the Marquis continued the conversation.

'That fat man you were asking about is a formidable person, the Abbé Gudin, one of those Jesuits who are stubborn enough, devoted enough perhaps, to stay on in France in spite of the edict of 1763 banishing them. He's the firebrand of the war in these parts and the propagandist of the religious society called the Sacred Heart. He's a practised user of religion as a tool, persuades his true believers that they'll come to life again and knows how to preach sermons cleverly calculated to fan their fanaticism. As you see, one has to make use of each individual's particular interests and loyalties to achieve a great end. That's the whole secret of politics.'

'And that hale old man who is so brawny and has such a repulsive face? Look, there, the man wearing a tattered lawyer's gown.'

'Lawyer? He aspires to the rank of brigadier. Have you not heard of Longuy?'

'So that's Longuy!' said Mademoiselle de Verneuil, appalled. 'And you make use of such men!'

'Hush, he may hear you. Do you see that other man, engaged in conspiratorial conversation with Madame du Gua . . .'

'The man in black who looks like a judge?'

'He's one of our negotiators, La Billardière, son of a Judge of the Breton High Court, with a name something like Flanet; but the Princes trust him.'

'And his neighbour, the one gripping his clay pipe between his teeth and leaning on the panelling with all the fingers of his right hand outspread, like a peasant,' said Mademoiselle de Verneuil, laughing.

'Quite so, you've guessed right – he's the former gamekeeper of that lady's late husband. He commands one of the companies I use against the mobile troops. He and Marche-à-terre are perhaps the most loyal and hard-working servants the King has here.'

'And who is the lady?'

'She's the last mistress Charette had,' the Marquis replied. 'She has a lot of influence over all these people.'

'Has she remained faithful to him?'

The Marquis pursed his lips dubiously by way of answer.

'And have you a high regard for her?'

'You are certainly very curious.'

'She is my enemy because she can no longer be my rival,' Mademoiselle de Verneuil said with a laugh. 'I forgive her her past errors, may she forgive me mine. And that officer with the moustaches?'

'Excuse me if I don't tell you his name. He is anxious to rid himself of the First Consul by force of arms. Whether he succeeds or not, you'll hear of him; he'll go far.'

'And you have come here to command men like these? . . .' she said, shocked. 'Such are the King's supporters! Where are the gentry and the aristocrats?'

'You'll find them in every court in Europe,' said the Marquis haughtily. 'Who else is enlisting kings, their councils and their armies in the service of the Bourbons, throwing them into the fray against this Republic which strikes the death-knell of all monarchies and threatens the entire social order with destruction? ... '

'Ah!' she said, with generous warmth of feeling. 'From now on be you my mentor, the fountain-head of these ideas I still need to learn ... I agree to that. But allow me to think that you are the only nobleman who does his duty rightly by attacking France with Frenchmen, and not calling in foreigners to help him. I am a woman, and feel that if my child struck me in anger I could forgive him, but if he looked on coldly while a stranger attacked me I should regard him as a monster.'

'You will always be a Republican,' said the Marquis, feeling a heady exhilaration as her warm tone confirmed his fondest hopes.

'Republican? No, I am not a Republican now. I should not respect you if you surrendered to the First Consul,' she answered; 'but all the same I do not want to see you commanding men who are seizing a corner of France instead of taking up arms against the whole Republic. Whom are you fighting for? What do you expect of a king set on his throne again by your hands? A woman succeeded in this supreme achievement once, and the king she set free let her be burnt alive. Such men are the anointed of God, and it's dangerous to come too close to consecrated things. Leave it to God to raise them up and cast them down and replace them on their purple stools. If you have considered your probable reward, you are ten times greater in my eyes than I thought you were; and you may trample me underfoot if you wish. I allow you. I shall be happy to let you.'

'You are enchanting! Do not try to win adherents among these gentlemen or I shall be left with no soldiers.'

'Ah, if you would let me convert you we should go a thousand leagues away from here.'

'These men you seem to despise will know how to perish in the fight,' the Marquis said more gravely, 'and their faults will be forgotten. Besides, if my efforts are crowned with some success won't triumphant laurels cover everything?'

'It seems to me that you are the only person here who is risking anything.'

'I am not the only one,' he replied with unaffected modesty. 'You see two new leaders from the Vendée over there. The first, whom you have heard called Le Grand Jacques is the Comte de Fontaine, and the other, La Billardière, I pointed out to you already.'

'And have you forgotten Quiberon,* where La Billardière played a very questionable part? ...' she said, struck by a memory.

'La Billardière assumed responsibility for a great deal, believe me. It's not all roses serving princes ...'

'Ah, you make me shudder!' exclaimed Marie, and then in a guarded tone, seeming to speak with reticence of some personal experience, 'Marquis,' she went on, 'in one moment an illusion may be destroyed and the veil torn from secrets on which the life and happiness of many people depend....' She stopped as if afraid of saying too much. 'I wish I knew the Republican soldiers were safe,' she added.

'I'll be careful,' he said, smiling to cover his emotion; 'but say nothing further about your soldiers. I have answered for them on my word and honour.'

'And after all, by what right should I seek to influence you?' she went on. 'Of us two may you always be the dominating spirit. Did I not tell you that I could not bear to rule a slave?'

'Monsieur le Marquis,' said Major Brigaut deferentially, coming to interrupt this conversation, 'are the Blues to stay here long?'

'They will leave as soon as they are rested,' exclaimed Marie.

The Marquis turned a scrutinizing gaze on the assembly, noticed some restless movement and left Mademoiselle de Verneuil, giving way to Madame du Gua who approached to take his place. That lady came up with a falsely smiling

* A small army of *émigrés* were taken prisoner by Hoche at Quiberon in 1795, and seven hundred and eleven of them shot in a meadow near Auray. – *Trans.*

mask, not at all disconcerted by the young leader's sardonic smile.

Just then Francine uttered a cry, quickly stifled. Mademoiselle de Verneuil saw with some astonishment her faithful Breton girl hurrying off towards the dining-room, and looking at Madame du Gua she was even more surprised to see how pale her enemy's face had grown. Curious and eager to learn the cause of Francine's abrupt departure, she moved to the window embrasure, where her rival followed her with the intention of lulling suspicions that some careless indiscretion might have aroused; and Madame du Gua smiled at her with inscrutable malice as, after both had cast a glance over the lakeside, they returned together to the hearth, Marie having seen nothing to explain Francine's flight, Madame du Gua satisfied that her orders had been obeyed.

The waters of the lake from whose side Marche-à-terre had appeared, as if the lady had conjured him to the courtyard, meandered in hazy sinuous loops on their way to join the moat defending the gardens, in places widening into pools and then closing in like artificially channelled park streams. The bank descended steeply to this lake at no great distance from the window. Francine had been contemplating the dark lines cast on the clear surface by the heads of some old willow trees, and casually noting how the light breeze made their branches curve all in the same direction. Suddenly she thought she saw one of these shapes seeming to stir on the mirroring water with the clipped and purposeful movements of life. The shape, however vague in outline, looked human.

At first Francine attributed this illusion to the wavering patterns cast by the moonlight shining through foliage; but soon a second head appeared, then others again beyond. The little bushes growing on the slope were bent down and sprang up again abruptly, and then Francine saw this long line of shrubs undulate like some great fabulous Indian serpent. Then here and there, among the gorse and tall thorn bushes, many bright points shone and changed their place.

Straining her eyes, Marche-à-terre's sweetheart believed she recognized the first of the dark figures moving in the depths of this shifting lakeside. His silhouette might be indistinct, but the beating of her heart told her that it was Marche-à-terre she saw, and a characteristic gesture convinced her. With breathless impatience to find out if this mysterious march portended treachery she fled towards the courtyard.

When she reached the middle of the high grass-grown expanse she scanned in turn the two wings of the building and the slopes in front of them, but found no sign of stealthy movement in the slope beyond the uninhabited wing. She strained her ears and heard a slight rustling like a wild creature moving through forest silence; and her heart throbbed, in startled surprise rather than fear.

Young and artless as she still was, curiosity promptly suggested that she should conceal herself and watch. She saw the carriage and ran to crouch inside it, raising her head only with the wariness of a hare whose ears can catch the echoes of a distant hunt.

She saw Pille-miche leave the stable. The Chouan was accompanied by two peasants, and all three carried bundles of straw which they proceeded to spread to make a long litter in front of the uninhabited wing of the building, that part facing the lakeside slope, bordered with pollard trees, where the Chouans were moving in a silence which concealed the preparation of some dreadful stratagem of war.

'You're giving them as much straw as if they were really going to sleep on it. That's plenty, Pille-miche, enough's enough,' said a deep harsh voice well-known to Francine.

'And so they are going to sleep on it, aren't they?' rejoined Pille-miche with a great guffaw. 'But aren't you afraid that the Gars will be angry?' he added in a murmur so low that Francine could not catch what he said.

'Oh, well, he'll be angry,' Marche-à-terre replied, also in an undertone, 'but the Blues will be dead all the same. There's a carriage we'll have to push under cover between us.'

Pille-miche pulled the vehicle by the pole and Marche-à-terre pushed it by one of the wheels, with such celerity that Francine found herself in the barn and about to be closed in there before she had time to think where she was. Pille-miche went off to help bring up the cask of cider that the Marquis had ordered to be broached for the escorting soldiers, and Marche-à-terre was passing the carriage on his way out to close the door when he was stopped by a hand seizing the long hair of his goatskin. He recognized eyes whose gentle sweetness held a magnetic power over him, and for an instant stood as if under a spell.

Francine jumped quickly from the vehicle and said in the stormy voice that is wonderfully alluring in a woman whose ire is roused, 'Pierre, what was the news that you brought on the road here to that lady and her son? What is being done here? Why are you hiding? I want to know everything.'

These words brought an expression to the Chouan's face that Francine had never seen there before. The Breton led his innocent mistress to the threshold; there he turned her to the whitening light of the moon and answered, staring at her with hard accusing eyes.

'Yes, by my damnation, I'll tell you, Francine! But only when you have sworn on these beads . . .' And he drew an old rosary from under his goatskin, 'on this keepsake you know, to give me a true answer to just one question.' Francine blushed as she looked at the rosary, which was no doubt a token of their love. 'It was on this', the Chouan went on with emotion, 'that you swore . . .'

He stopped. The peasant girl put her hand on her fierce lover's lips to silence him.

'Do I need to swear?' she said.

He took his mistress gently by the hand, contemplated her for a moment, and went on.

'The lady that you serve, is her name truly Mademoiselle de Verneuil?'

Francine stood there with her arms hanging, her eyelids lowered, her head bowed, pale, speechless.

'She's a whore!' said Marche-à-terre in a terrible voice.

At that word the pretty hand was placed on his lips again, but this time he violently recoiled. It was not a lover that the little Breton girl saw before her now, but a ferocious animal in all the horrifying savagery of his nature. The Chouan's eyebrows were fiercely drawn together, his lips curled back, and he showed his teeth like a dog defending his master.

'I left you a flower and come back to find you fouler than the dirt. Ah, why did I let you go? You come here to betray us, to hand over the Gars.'

These words were not said but roared in a wild animal's bellow. Although Francine was afraid, at this last reproach she dared to look at the fierce face, raised her angelic eyes to his and replied calmly, 'I swear by my salvation that's not true. Those notions are your lady's inventions.'

In his turn he bowed his head. Then she took his hand, and turned towards him appealingly.

'Pierre, what are we doing in all this?' she said. 'I don't know how you can make anything of it for I can't understand a thing! But don't forget that this lovely and high-born lady has been very kind to me, and to you too; and we live almost like two sisters. No harm ought ever to come to her while we are with her, while we're alive at least. So swear to me that it shall not! You're the only person I trust here.'

'I don't give the orders here,' the Chouan answered in a surly tone, and his face darkened. She held his large hanging ears in her hands and pulled them gently as if caressing a cat.

'Well, promise me,' she went on, as she saw his mood soften, 'to do all you can to keep our benefactress safe.'

He shook his head dubiously as if unsure whether he could do anything, and watching him the Breton girl trembled. At this critical moment the escort reached the causeway. The soldiers' tramp and the clink of their arms woke the echoes of the courtyard, and seemed to put an end to Marche-à-terre's indecision.

'I'll save her perhaps,' he said to his mistress, 'if you can make her stay inside. – And whatever happens,' he added, 'stay with her and don't make the slightest sound: if you do, well then it's no use!'

'I promise you', she said in dismay.

'Well, go in. Go in at once and don't let any one see you are afraid, not even your mistress.'

'Yes.'

She clasped the Chouan's hand, and he watched her with a fatherly air as she ran as lightly as a bird towards the steps. Then he slipped in among his bushes, like an actor making off to the wings as the curtain rises on a tragedy.

Chapter 14

'Do you know, Merle, this place looks a complete mousetrap,' said Gérard as they arrived at the mansion.

'So I see,' the Captain answered, with a worried frown.

The two officers hastened to set sentries to guard the causeway and the entrance portal, and cast some mistrustful looks at the lakeside slopes and surrounding terrain.

'Bah!' said Merle. 'We must either trust ourselves to this barracks with no doubts in our minds or not go in at all.'

'We'll go in,' answered Gérard.

The soldiers, dismissed by a word from their Captain, quickly stacked their guns in conical piles and ranged themselves in battle line before the straw litter, in the middle of which the cider cask was conspicuous. They broke into groups, and two peasants began to distribute rye-bread and butter. The Marquis came to meet the two officers and preceded them to the drawing-room. When Gérard had climbed the steps and looked about him at the two wings where the old larch trees spread their dark branches, he called Beau-pied and La-clef-des-coeurs.

'You two are to make a reconnaisance through the gardens and search the rows of bushes and undergrowth, do you hear? Then you will post a sentry in front of your line . . .'

'May we light our fire before starting off on our hunt, Sir?' asked La-clef-des-coeurs.

Gérard nodded.

'It's easy to see, La-clef-des-coeurs,' said Beau-pied, 'the Adjutant is wrong to poke his head into this hornet's nest. If it was Hulot in command of us he would never let himself be driven into a corner like this; we're just as if we were in the bottom of a stew-pot.'

'Thick in the head, aren't you?' replied La-clef-des-coeurs. 'A wily old fox like you, can't you see that this sentry-box here is the castle of the princess our ace of captains favours, and it's being alongside of her makes our blithe Merle whistle like a blackbird? And he'll marry her, that's as clear to be seen as a well-rubbed up bayonet. She'll bring honour to the Demibrigade, a woman like that.'

'True enough,' said Beau-pied. 'And you can say as well that this is good cider; but I don't relish it much in front of those wild beasts of bushes. I keep seeing Larose and Vieuxchapeau come clattering down into the ditch at the Pellerine. I'll remember the look of poor Larose's pigtail for the rest of my life; it was going like the knocker on a big door.'

'Beau-pied my friend, you have too much *imagination* for a soldier. You ought to be at the *Institut National* making up songs for them.'

'If I've too much imagination,' retorted Beau-pied, 'you haven't any worth mentioning, and it'll take *you* a long time to reach the rank of Consul.'

A general roar of laughter ended the discussion, for La-clef-des-coeurs found not a shot left in his locker to return his friend's fire.

'Are you coming to do the patrol? I'll take the right side,' said Beau-pied.

'I'll take the left, then,' his comrade answered. 'But hold on a minute, I want to drink a glass of cider first! My throat is all stuck together like the oiled silk round Hulot's best hat.'

By ill luck the left side of the gardens which La-clef-des-coeurs was in no hurry to search was the dangerous side, the slope where Francine had seen men moving. In war everything hangs on chance.

As he entered the drawing-room and bowed to the company Gérard cast a searching look at the men who composed it, and his suspicions returned with renewed force. He went directly to Mademoiselle de Verneuil and said in an undertone, 'I think you'll have to get out at once, we are not safe here.'

'How can you have any fears under the same roof as me?' she asked laughing. 'You are safer here than you would be at Mayenne.'

A woman always answers confidently for her lover. The two officers were reassured.

At this moment the company moved into the dining-room, although with some light comment about the non-arrival of an important guest who was keeping them waiting.

Under cover of the silence that prevails at the beginning of any meal Mademoiselle de Verneuil could give some attention to this gathering, strange in the circumstances of the times, to which she had given some assistance, acting with the kind of unawareness that women, accustomed to turn everything into a game, bring to the most crucial actions of their lives.

One fact suddenly impressed her. The two Republican officers dominated this assembly by the striking quality a physiognomist would have recognized. The lines of their long hair, drawn back from the temples and gathered at the nape of the neck into a huge queue, set off their young heads and revealed their foreheads with an effect of candour and nobility. Their threadbare blue uniforms emphasized their difference – the red facings worn, the epaulettes pushed out of place by wear on the march, evidence of the lack of great-coats throughout the army even for the officers. Everything about these two soldiers set them apart from the men among whom they found themselves.

'Oh, they stand for the Nation and Liberty!' she said to herself. Then, looking at the Royalists, 'And those men stand for one man, a King, and Privilege.'

She could not help admiring the figure cut by Merle – this gay soldier was so admirably typical of the French fighting man as one imagines him, whistling a tune among flying bullets and ready with some droll jest about an unlucky comrade.

Gérard commanded respect. Serious and coolly self-possessed, he looked a true Republican in mind and heart, one of those men of whom at that period there was a host in the French armies, to which the noble devotion of obscure men lent a driving force unknown until then.

'That is one of my men who take long views,' Mademoiselle de Verneuil said to herself. 'They are firmly founded on the present day and age, which they dominate, and they destroy the past, but for the sake of the future . . .'

The thought saddened her, because it had no relation to her lover; and she looked towards him to offer him a different kind of admiration, and so turn the scale against the Republic which she already detested.

She saw the Marquis surrounded by men bold and fanatical enough, with sufficient faith in their estimate of the future to attack a victorious Republic in the hope of bringing back a dead monarchy, a proscribed religion, wandering Princes and time-expired privileges.

'This man,' she said to herself, 'is not less effectively far-sighted than the other. Cast down among the débris of a ruined world, he aspires to build the future from the past.'

Her mind, full of crowding images, hovered between old and new, a past in ruins and a ruined new beginning. Her conscience cried to her that one protagonist was fighting for a man and the other for a country; but her heart led her to recognize what reason equally finds true – that King and country are one.

Hearing a man's footsteps in the drawing-room, the Marquis rose to go to meet the late-comer whom he recognized as the expected guest. This man was surprised to see the company there and about to speak when the Gars, his back to the Republicans, made a warning sign to bid him take his seat without remark at the table.

As the two Republican officers considered their hosts' faces, their earlier suspicions returned and grew. The Abbé's clerical garb and the oddness of the Chouans' dress sounded an alarm. They looked and listened with intensified alertness, and discovered absurd inconsistencies in the behaviour and conversation of their table companions. The exaggerated Republicanism manifested by some seemed as out of place as the aristocratic manners of others. Certain glances exchanged between the Marquis and his guests, certain remarks with an incautious double meaning, but above all the frill of beard adorning the necks of several guests and very ill-concealed under their cravats, finally brought the truth home to the two officers, and it struck them both at the same moment.

A look was enough to communicate their thoughts, and they could do no more than look for Madame du Gua had adroitly placed them apart. Their position was delicate and demanded careful going: they did not know whether the château was in their hands or they had been led into an ambush, whether Mademoiselle de Verneuil had had a share in bringing this extraordinary situation about or been duped. But before they could fully grasp the danger in which they stood, an unexpected happening precipitated the crisis.

The new guest was of a well-known type. He was as broad as he was long, carrying his bulk in walking with a self-important backward slant, very ruddy of complexion. Such fellows seem to take up more space and air than other mortals, and feel perfect assurance that all heads must turn to look at them and remain looking. In spite of his high degree, he had regarded life as a good joke to be used to do the best one could for oneself. He worshipped his own importance, but was as good-natured, courtly and lively in mind as any of those landowners who complete their education at court, return to their estates, and never let the idea enter their heads that the moss may have grown on them after twenty years there. He was the kind of man who makes tactless blunders with imperturbable aplomb, says something idiotic with the manner and delivery of wit, is very shrewdly suspicious of honesty and gives himself unbelievable trouble to get hold of some hook baited for him.

When he had made up for lost time, plying his fork energetically like a formidable trencherman, he raised his eyes to look at the company. His astonishment grew at the sight of the two officers, and he looked interrogatively at Madame du Gua who in reply indicated Mademoiselle de Verneuil. When he saw the siren whose beauty was having an appeasing effect on the hostility aroused at the beginning by Madame du Gua, the stout stranger began to smile, one of those impudent derisive smiles that seem to contain a whole smutty story. He leaned sideways to say a few words in his neighbour's ear, and these words – a secret so far as the officers and Marie were concerned – travelled from one ear to the next, from mouth to mouth, till they reached the man into whose heart they were destined to strike death.

The Vendéan and Chouan leaders turned their gaze upon the Marquis de Montauran with cruel curiosity. Madame du Gua's eyes went from the Marquis to the surprised Mademoiselle de Verneuil, alight with malicious joy. The uneasy officers looked questioningly at each other as they waited for the outcome of this odd scene. Then, as if at a signal, the movement of forks was arrested, silence fell throughout the room, and all eyes were fixed on the Gars. A terrible rage blazed on his passionate high-coloured face, which now grew waxen pale. The young leader turned to the guest who had sent the scurrilous squib on its way and, 'God's death, Count, is this true?' he said in a voice of doom.

'Upon my honour,' replied the Count, bowing gravely.

The Marquis lowered his eyes for a moment, and then raised them to turn them upon Marie, who had been attentive to the scene, and she received the full impact of this deadly look.

'I would give my life,' he said in a low voice, 'for immediate vengeance.'

Madame du Gua, reading his lips, smiled at the young man, as one smiles at a troubled friend knowing his despair will soon be ended. The contemptuous expressions on all the faces turned to Mademoiselle de Verneuil were the crowning insult for the two Republicans. In a flame of indignation, they rose abruptly.

'What do you want, Citizens?' asked Madame du Gua.

'Our swords, *Citizeness*,' replied Gérard, with sarcastic emphasis.

'You do not require them at table,' the Marquis said coldly.

'No, but we are about to play a game you are familiar with,' answered Gérard, returning to the room. 'We shall see each other at rather closer range here than we did on the Pellerine.'

The guests watched in stupefaction. At that moment the explosion of a volley discharged in the courtyard brought terrible news to the officers' ears. They rushed to the top of the steps. From there they saw about a hundred Chouans taking fresh aim at several soldiers who had survived the first volley, and shooting them down like rabbits. These Chouans sprang up from the lake-edge where Marche-à-terre had posted them, at the risk of their lives, for during and after the last shots and through the cries of the dying one could hear the splash of some of them falling into the water to be swallowed up like stones in the deep water.

Pille-miche took aim at Gérard. Marche-à-terre's gun was levelled at Merle.

'Captain,' the Marquis said coldly to Merle, repeating the Republican's earlier remark, '*you see, men are like medlars, they ripen on straw.*' And he waved a hand towards the entire escort of Blues lying on the bloody straw, with the Chouans despatching those still alive and stripping the dead at an incredible speed. 'I was right when I told you that your soldiers would not reach the Pellerine,' the Marquis added. 'I think too that your head is likely to be filled with lead before mine, what do you say?'

Montauran was experiencing a horrible necessity to glut his fury. His bitter words to the betrayed Republican, the ferocity, the very treachery of this military massacre, not executed by his command but which he was now taking responsibility for, satisfied his deepest urges. In his rage he would have annihilated France. The butchered Blues, the two living officers, all innocent of the crime for which he required vengeance, were nothing in his hands but the cards a despairing gambler tears across and throws from him.

'I would rather die like this than triumph in your fashion,' said Gérard. Then, seeing his soldiers naked and bloody, he cried, 'To have murdered them so basely, in cold blood!'

'As Louis XVI was murdered, Monsieur,' the Marquis replied sharply.

'Monsieur,' said Gérard haughtily, 'in the trial of a King there is a due form and ceremony that you will never understand.'

'To put the King on trial!' exclaimed the Marquis, beside himself.

'To fight against France!' answered Gérard in a contemptuous tone.

'Fiddlesticks,' said the Marquis.

'It makes you a parricide!'

'And you a regicide!'

'Well, do you have to spend your last moments wrangling?' Merle reproached him lightly.

'As you say,' said Gérard coldly, and then, turning to the Marquis, 'Monsieur, if it is your intention to kill us, at least do us the favour of shooting us at once.'

'That's just like you!' the Captain complained. 'Always in a hurry to have done! But, my dear fellow, when a man is going a long way and can't have his breakfast tomorrow, he takes his supper tonight.'

Gérard strode off without a word and with his head held high towards the wall. Pille-miche kept him covered with an eye on the motionless Marquis, then took his Chief's silence for a command, and the Adjutant fell like a tree. Marche-à-terre ran to share this new booty with Pille-miche. Like two ravenous carrion crows they wrangled and croaked over the still warm corpse.

'If you wish to finish supper, Captain, you are free to come with me,' the Marquis said to Merle, whom he wished to keep as an exchange prisoner.

As the Captain mechanically went in, he said in an undertone, as if in self-reproach, 'It's that damned tart that's the cause of this. What will Hulot say?'

'Tart!' muttered the Marquis dully. 'There seems no doubt about her being that!'

The Captain appeared to have struck a deadly blow, and the Marquis as he followed him walked uncertainly and looked wan, desolate and stricken.

Meanwhile in the dining-room another scene was taking place which in the Marquis's absence began to look so sinister that Marie, left without her protector, found the sentence of death she read in her rival's eyes only too easy to believe. At the firing of the volley all the guests had risen, except Madame du Gua.

'Sit down,' she said, 'it's nothing. It's our men killing the Blues.'

When she saw that the Marquis had gone, she rose to her feet.

'This young lady', she said dramatically, with the calm of smouldering rage, 'came to take the Gars from us! She came to try to betray him to the Republic.'

'I could have betrayed him twenty times over in the course of this day, and I saved his life,' replied Mademoiselle de Verneuil.

Madame du Gua sprang like a flash at her rival and with such blind fury that she broke the fragile loops on the girl's spencer. Her brutal hand profaned the letter's hiding-place, tearing through material, embroidery, bodice and shift. The search was made an opportunity to glut her jealousy, and she vindictively managed to make sure that she left the bleeding marks of her nails in her rival's palpitating breast, with a grim pleasure in subjecting her to such odious shame.

In the feeble resistance which was all Marie could put up against this frenzied woman's totally unexpected onslaught, her unknotted hood fell off, her hair broke from its bonds and fell around her in curling tresses; her face was bright with offended modesty and tears traced a burning path down her cheeks and burnished the fire of her eyes; her shame-stricken startled movement laid her bare and quivering to the guests' gaze. Even hardened judges would have believed in her innocence on seeing her distress.

Hate calculates its effects so badly that Madame du Gua did not even see that she had no one's attention as she triumphantly exclaimed, 'You see, gentlemen, I was not slandering this horrible creature, was I?'

'Not so horrible,' murmured the portly guest who had laid the train to disaster. 'For my part, I have a passion for such horrors.'

'This is an order,' went on the ruthless Vendéan woman, 'signed Laplace and countersigned Dubois.' A few heads were raised at these names. 'And here is what it says:

"All citizens holding military commands, district administrators, *procureurs-syndics*, etc., in the insurgent Departments, and in particular those of the regions where the *ci-devant* Marquis de Montauran, brigand leader nicknamed the Gars, may appear, are hereby required to aid and assist the Citizeness Marie Verneuil and to comply with such orders as she may give them, wherever they have authority, etc."

'An Opéra charmer takes an illustrious name and drags it in this slime!' she added.

A movement of surprise ran through the gathering.

'It's not playing fair for the Republic to employ such pretty women against us,' said the Baron du Guénic gaily.

'Especially loose women who stake nothing in the game,' retorted Madame du Gua.

'Nothing?' said the Chevalier du Vissard. 'But Mademoiselle has an estate which must bring her in high rents!'

'The Republic thinks it a good joke to send us prostitutes to represent it,' the Abbé Gudin exclaimed.

'But unfortunately the pleasures Mademoiselle courts have fatal endings,' went on Madame du Gua with a dreadful joy that looked forward to the end of these pleasantries.

'How comes it that you are still alive, Madame?' said the victim, raising her head again with her disordered dress now set to rights.

This barbed question imposed a kind of respect for a victim so proud, and silence fell on the gathering. Madame du Gua saw a smile twitch the leaders' lips and was infuriated by its sardonic comment; and then, unaware of the return of the Marquis and the Captain, 'Pille-miche,' she said to the Chouan with a gesture towards Mademoiselle de Verneuil, 'take her away. She's my share of the booty and I give her to you. Do whatever you please with her.'

At the words *whatever you please* uttered by this woman, a shudder ran through the gathering, for the hideous heads of Marche-à-terre and Pille-miche were visible beyond the Marquis, and the victim's fate was apparent in all its horror.

Francine stood with her hands clasped and her eyes full of tears as if struck by a thunderbolt. Mademoiselle de Verneuil, recovering all her spirit and presence of mind in the face of danger, cast a contemptuous look around the gathering, snatched her letter from Madame du Gua, and with her head held high, and dry and flashing eyes, made for the doorway where Merle's sword still lay.

There she met the Marquis, standing cold and motionless as a statue. There was no hint of compassion for her on the fixed stern features of that face. Stricken to the heart, she felt her life odious. The man who had shown her so much love must have heard the facetious sallies at her expense and been the icily unmoved witness of the desecration she had undergone when the beauties a woman keeps for a lover were exposed to public view. She might perhaps have forgiven Montauran for his contempt, but it shocked her to have been seen by him in such a sordidly humiliating situation. She looked at him in a daze of hatred, feeling appalling desires for vengeance rise in her heart.

Death loomed behind her, and her powerlessness choked her. A wave of madness surged through her brain; her seething blood made her see the world as if it were going up in flames. Seizing the sword, instead of killing herself, she brandished it over the Marquis, and thrust it in deep, up to the hilt. As the sword slipped between arm and side the Gars seized Marie's wrist and dragged her from the room, aided by Pille-miche, who had thrown himself upon the crazed creature at the moment when she attempted to kill the Marquis. At this spectacle, Francine uttered piercing shrieks. 'Pierre! Pierre! Pierre!' she cried in a lamentable voice, and still shrieking followed her mistress.

The spectators were left dumbfounded; and the Marquis going out closed the door on them. He reached the head of the steps, still holding this woman's wrist, gripping it convulsively. On the other side Pille-miche's muscular fingers were almost breaking her arm, but she felt only the young leader's burning hand and looking at him icily she said, 'Monsieur, you are hurting me!'

Without replying, the Marquis stared at the object of his love for a moment.

'Have you some injury to avenge too, despicably like that

woman?' she said, and then seeing the corpses stretched out on the straw, she exclaimed, shuddering, 'A nobleman's word and honour! Ha, ha, ha!' After that appalling laugh, she added, 'A glorious day!'

'Yes,' he said, 'glorious and with no morrow.'

He let go Mademoiselle de Verneuil's hand, after one last long look at the ravishing creature he could scarcely bear to renounce. Neither of these two proud spirits would give way. Perhaps the Marquis was waiting for a tear, but the girl's eyes were dry and proud. He turned on his heel, leaving Pille-miche with his victim.

'God will hear me, Marquis. I will pray to Him for a glorious day for you, with no morrow!'

Pille-miche, embarrassed by his beautiful prey, led her away with a gentleness compounded of respect and a grimacing sense of the oddity of the situation. The Marquis sighed and returned to the dining-room, where he confronted his guests with a face like that of a corpse whose eyes have not been closed.

Chapter 15

CAPTAIN MERLE'S reappearance was inexplicable to the protagonists in this tragedy. The Royalist leaders all looked at him in surprise and exchanged questioning glances. Merle noticed their astonishment and responded characteristically.

'I don't think, gentlemen, that you'll refuse a glass of wine to a man about to set out on his last march,' he said, with a wry smile.

It was just then, when the company had relaxed at these words, spoken with a very French insouciance which must have pleased the Vendéans, that Montauran came in, and his pale face and fixed eyes cast a chill over all the guests.

'You're going to see the dead man prepare the living men for action,' the Captain said.

'Ah,' said the Marquis, appearing to come to himself with a start, 'so here you are, my dear war-council!'

He held up a bottle of Graves to the Captain, as if about to pour him a glass.

'Oh, much obliged, Citizen Marquis. It might drown my sorrows, you see.'

At this quip Madame du Gua said, smiling round the table, 'Come, let us spare him the dessert.'

'You are very cruel in the vengeance you demand, Madame,' the Captain answered. 'You forget my murdered friend who is waiting for me; and I do not fail to keep my appointments.'

'Captain, you are free!' said the Marquis then, throwing him his glove, 'Take this as your safe-conduct. The Chasseurs du Roi know that one must not kill all the quarry in the forest.'

'All right, I'll take my life,' answered Merle. 'But you are making a mistake. I'll play a wary game against you, I promise you. You'll get no quarter from me. You may be very clever but you're not a match for Gérard. Your head can never make up to me for his, but I must have it, and have it I shall.'

'He was in a great hurry, however,' returned the Marquis.

'Good-bye! I might drink with my executioners, but I don't stay with my friend's assassins,' said the Captain, departing and leaving the company disconcerted.

'Well, gentlemen, what do you think of the magistrates, surgeons and lawyers who are in charge of the Republic's affairs?' the Gars asked coldly.

'Upon my soul, Marquis,' replied the Comte de Bauvan, 'they're very ill-bred, at any rate. That man, I believe, has insulted us.'

The Captain had an unspoken motive for his abrupt departure. He had been so struck by the beauty revealed in this scene by the despised and humiliated girl who perhaps was dying at this very moment, and found it so difficult to forget, that he was saying to himself as he went out, 'If she is an adventuress she is no ordinary one, and I'll certainly make her my wife . . .' He had so little doubt of his ability to save her from the hands of these barbarians that his first thought when his life was spared had been to take her from that moment under his protection.

Unhappily, when he reached the steps the Captain found the courtyard deserted. He looked round him, listening to the silence, and heard nothing but the distant boisterous laughter of the Chouans drinking in the gardens as they divided up their spoil. He ventured to turn the corner of the fatal wing where his soldiers had been shot; and from this side, by the feeble glimmer of a number of candles, he made out different groups of the Chasseurs du Roi. There was no sign of Pillemiche, Marche-à-terre or the girl. But at this moment he felt a gentle tug at his coat-tail and turned to see Francine kneeling behind him.

'Where is she?' he asked.

'I don't know. Pierre would not let me go with her, and told me not to stir from here.'

'Which way did they go?'

'That way,' she said, pointing to the causeway.

They could both make out then, as they looked in that

direction, some shadows thrown on the lake waters by the moon, and their hearts beat faster as they recognized a slender feminine form among them, in spite of its indistinctness.

'Oh, there she is!' said the Breton girl.

Mademoiselle de Verneuil appeared to be standing, still and resigned, in the middle of a group whose gestures suggested a dispute.

'There are a lot of them,' exclaimed the Captain. 'Never mind. Come on!'

'You'll be killed to no purpose,' Francine said.

'I've been killed today once already,' he answered lightly. And they started off together towards the gloomy portal beyond which the scene was taking place. Half-way there, Francine stopped.

'No, I'll not go any nearer!' she exclaimed softly. 'Pierre told me not to interfere. I know him – we'll spoil everything. Do what you like, Sir, but go away. If Pierre saw you with me, he would kill you.'

At this moment Pille-miche appeared through the gateway, calling the coachman, who had remained in the stable. He saw the Captain and exclaimed as he took aim at him, 'By Saint Anne of Auray, the Recteur of Antrain was making no mistake when he told us the Blues sign pacts with the Devil. Hold on a moment, I'll teach you to come to life again!'

'Hey! I've had my life spared,' Merle called to him, seeing his danger. 'This is your Chief's glove.'

'Yes, these are ghosts sure enough,' said the Chouan. 'I'm not going to give you life. *Ave Maria*!' And he fired.

The shot struck the Captain in the head and he fell. As Francine ran to him, she heard him say indistinctly, 'I would much rather stay with them than go back without them.'

The Chouan hurried forward to strip the Blue, saying, 'There's one good thing about these spectres, they come back to life dressed in their clothes.' When he saw the Gars's glove, that sacred safe-conduct, in the Captain's hand as Merle had held it up to show it, he was aghast. 'I'd rather not be in the shoes of my mother's son!' he ejaculated, then was gone with a bird's swiftness.

To understand how this fatal encounter had come about we must return to Mademoiselle de Verneuil, when the Marquis in despair and rage left her to Pille-miche. Francine then convulsively seized Marche-à-terre's arm, and with her eyes full of tears demanded fulfilment of the promise he had made her. A few paces from them Pille-miche was pulling his victim after him as he would have dragged some bulky package. Marie, her hair flowing round her, her head bent, turned her eyes towards the lake; but held in that grip of steel she was forced to follow the Chouan slowly. He turned several times to look at her or hurry her on, with a jubilant thought painting a horrifying smile on that face.

'Isn't she *godaine* . . . a daisy just!' he exclaimed with coarse enthusiasm.

When she heard this, Francine recovered her voice.

'Pierre?'

'Well, what?'

'He's going to kill Mademoiselle.'

'Not yet,' answered Marche-à-terre.

'But she will not yield, and if she dies I'll die too.'

'Ha! You think too much of her. Let her die!' said Marche-à-terre.

'If we are rich and happy it's because of her. But that's not what matters – you promised, didn't you, to save her whatever might happen?'

'I'll try, but stay here, don't budge.'

Marche-à-terre's arm was freed at once, and Francine, racked with torturing anxiety, waited in the courtyard. Marche-à-terre rejoined Pille-miche in the barn where he had forced his victim to climb into the carriage. Pille-miche demanded his comrade's help to pull it out through the door.

'What do you want with all that?' Marche-à-terre asked.

'Well, hasn't the big *garce* given me the woman, and all she has is mine!'

'For the carriage, that's fine, you'll make a few sous out of that; but what about the woman? – she'll fly in your face like a cat!'

Pille-miche burst into a loud guffaw and answered, 'Who

cares? I'll take the pussy to my place and tie her up.'

'All right, let's harness the horses,' said Marche-à-terre.

A few moments later, Marche-à-terre, leaving the prey to his comrade, led the horses drawing the vehicle through the gateway on to the causeway, and then Pille-miche climbed in beside Mademoiselle de Verneuil, without noticing that she was crouching to make a spring into the lake.

'Ho, Pille-miche!' shouted Marche-à-terre.

'What?'

'I'll buy all your booty.'

'You're having me on, aren't you?' the Chouan asked, holding his prisoner by the skirts as if he were a butcher restraining a recalcitrant calf.

'Let's see her. I'll quote you a price.'

The unfortunate woman was obliged to get down, and stood between the two Chouans, who each held a hand and contemplated her like the two Elders staring at Susanna bathing.

'What about ...' said Marche-à-terre, and he heaved a sigh, 'what about a solid thirty livres a year?'

'No kidding?'

'Strike the bargain,' said Marche-à-terre, holding out his hand.

'Oh, done! There's no want of Breton women and *godaine* ones too you can have for that! But what about the carriage, who's to have that?' said Pille-miche, having second thoughts.

'Me,' growled Marche-à-terre, with a daunting rumble of the ferocity that gave him the whip-hand of all his companions.

'But suppose there's gold in it?'

'Didn't you strike the bargain?'

'Yes, I struck it.'

'Well, go and get the driver, he's tied up in the stable.'

'But suppose there's gold in ...'

'Is there any?' Marche-à-terre asked Marie roughly, shaking her arm.

'I have about a hundred crowns,' she replied.

At this the two Chouans looked at each other.

'Well, mate, let's not fall out about a Blue bitch,' Pille-miche said in Marche-à-terre's ear. 'What say we shove her in the lake with a stone round her neck and split the hundred crowns?'

'I'll give you the hundred crowns from my share in d'Orgement's ransom,' cried Marche-à-terre, with a stifled groan for the sacrifice he was making.

Pille-miche uttered a raucous crow and went to find the coachman, and his delight was unlucky for the Captain, whom he met on the way.

When he heard the shot, Marche-à-terre rushed to the place where Francine was still kneeling in a state of shock beside the poor Captain, praying with her hands clasped, the appalled witness of murder.

'Run to your mistress,' the Chouan said to her brusquely; 'she is saved!'

He ran himself to get the coachman, returned at lightning speed, and passing Merle's corpse again noticed the Gars's glove still clutched in the dead man's hand.

'Oho!' he exclaimed. 'Pille-miche fired a traitor's shot here! He'll be lucky if he gets the chance of living on his means.'

He seized the glove and said to Mademoiselle de Verneuil, who with Francine was already in the carriage, 'Here, take this glove. If our men attack you on the way, shout "Ho! The Gars!" and show this safe-conduct, and no harm will come to you. Francine,' he said turning to the girl and grasping her hand with some force, 'we've paid our debt to this woman. Come with me, and let the devil fly away with her.'

'You want me to desert her at this point!' Francine answered mournfully.

Marche-à-terre scratched his ear and rubbed his forehead. Then he raised his head, showing eyes shuttered with ferocity.

'Right,' he said. 'I'll let you stay with her for eight days. After that, if you do not come with me . . .' He did not finish, but slapped the muzzle of his gun violently with the flat of his hand. Then after sketching the gesture of aiming at his mistress he went off without waiting for a reply.

As soon as the Chouan had gone, a voice which seemed to issue from the lake called stealthily, 'Madame, Madame.'

The driver and the two women shuddered in horror, for several corpses had floated to the spot. A Blue hiding behind a tree showed himself.

'Let me get up behind your wagon or I'm a dead man. That cursed glass of cider that La-clef-des-coeurs had to drink has cost more than one pint of blood. If he had done what I did and made his round, the poor comrades would not be there, floating about like galliots.'

While these events were taking place outside, the envoys from the Vendée and the Chouan leaders were deliberating, glass in hand, presided over by the Marquis de Montauran. Copious draughts of claret enlivened the discussion, which considered serious and important questions at the end of the meal. At dessert, the common plan for military operations having been agreed, the Royalists drank a toast to the Bourbons. Into this scene the crack of Pille-miche's shot came like an echo of the disastrous war these merry and high-born conspirators were engaged in planning against the Republic. Madame du Gua started, and seeing her thrill with pleasure in knowing herself rid of her rival, the guests looked at one another in silence. The Marquis rose from the table and went out.

'So he loved her in spite of all!' said Madame du Gua sarcastically. 'Do go and keep him company, Monsieur de Fontaine. He'll be as tiresome as a bear with a sore head if he's left to brood.'

She went to the window giving on the court to try to see Marie's corpse. From there she could make out by the last glimmer of the setting moon the carriage moving along the avenue of apple trees at unbelievable speed, with Mademoiselle de Verneuil's veil floating from the vehicle in the wind. At this spectacle, Madame du Gua left the room in a fury.

The Marquis was leaning on the balustrade above the steps plunged in sombre meditation, contemplating about a hundred and fifty Chouans, who after dealing with their division of the booty in the gardens had returned to finish off the cask of cider and bread provided for the Blues. Various groups of these soldiers of a new kind on whom the Monarchy's hopes were based stood about drinking, while seven or eight were busy by the lakeside opposite the steps tying stones to the Blues' bodies and throwing them into the water. Monsieur de Fontaine, who in the Vendéan bands had been shown a certain discipline and idealism, was struck by this spectacle. He had found these independent and barbarous *gars* in their various pursuits with their bizarre dress and fierce expressions so strange and novel that he seized the opportunity to say to the Marquis de Montauran, 'What do you hope to achieve with savages like these?'

'Not much: is that what you are thinking, dear Count?' the Gars answered.

'Will they ever be able to manoeuvre in face of the Republican troops?'

'Never.'

'Are they even capable of understanding and carrying out your commands?'

'No.'

'How can they be of use to you then?'

'They can plunge my sword into the Republic's belly,' said the Marquis in a ringing voice, 'give me Fougères in three days and the whole of Brittany in ten!' And then more gently, 'Come, Monsieur,' he said, 'go back to the Vendée. Let Autichamp, Suzannet and the Abbé Bernier only march as swiftly as I shall, and not treat with the First Consul as I've been led to fear they may (here he gripped the Vendéan leader's hand), and we shall be thirty leagues from Paris within twenty days.'

'But the Republic is sending sixty thousand men and General Brune against us.'

'Sixty thousand men, forsooth!' returned the Marquis with a mocking laugh. 'And what would Bonaparte use for the Italian campaign? As for General Brune, he'll not come; Bonaparte has sent him against the English in Holland, and General Hédouville, the friend of our friend Barras, is to replace him here. You follow me?'

Hearing him speak in these terms, Monsieur de Fontaine looked at the Marquis with a sly and knowing air as if accusing him of not following himself the implications of the strange things he was saying. The two noblemen understood each other perfectly, but the young leader answered with a smile difficult to describe the thoughts their eyes expressed.

'Monsieur de Fontaine, do you know my arms? My device is *Persist until Death*.'

The Comte de Fontaine took Montauran's hand and clasped it, saying, 'I was left for dead on the field at Quatre-Chemins, so you need not doubt me; but believe what my experience tells me: times have changed.'

'Oh, yes, indeed!' said La Billardière coming up to them. 'You are young, Marquis. Listen to me. Your lands have not all been sold . . .'

'Ah, can you imagine devotion without sacrifice?' said Montauran.

'Do you know the King well?' asked La Billardière.

'Yes!'

'I admire you.'

'The King,' answered the young leader, 'is the priest, and I am fighting for the Faith!'

They went their ways, the Vendéan convinced of the necessity of going with the tide, submitting to events while keeping faith in his heart, La Billardière to return to England, Montauran to fight on desperately, hoping by the triumphs he dreamed of to force the Vendéans to cooperate in his undertaking.

Chapter 16

AFTER the emotional havoc wreaked by these events, Mademoiselle de Verneuil lay prostrated, like a dead woman, at the back of the carriage, after giving the order to drive to Fougères. Francine took her cue from her mistress and was as silent as she. The coachman, fearing some fresh misadventure, made all speed to reach the main road, and soon reached the summit of the Pellerine.

In the thick whitish morning mist Marie de Verneuil traversed the beautiful wide valley of the Couësnon where this story began, and from the Pellerine heights barely caught a glimpse through the haze of the schistous crag on which the town of Fougères is built. About two leagues still separated the three travellers from it. Benumbed with cold herself, Mademoiselle de Verneuil thought of the poor infantryman perched behind the carriage and insisted in spite of his protests that he should get in beside Francine. The sight of Fougères drew her for a moment from her reflections. She was, besides, obliged to show her letter signed by the Ministers to the guard stationed at the Saint-Leonard Gate before they would let these strangers enter the town. Once there she realized that she was safe from hostile action, although for the moment the town was defended only by the inhabitants. The coachman found no better shelter for her than the Auberge de la Poste, the post staging-inn.

'Madame,' said the Blue whom she had rescued, 'if you ever need to sabre some fellow, my life is yours. You can count on me. They call me Beau-pied, otherwise Jean Falcon, Sergeant in Hulot's First Company, Seventy-second Demi-brigade, known as *La Mayençaise*. Pardon my forwardness and high-flown ideas; but I can only offer you a sergeant's devotion, that's all I have for the moment, at your service.'

He turned on his heel and went off whistling.

'The lower one goes in the social scale,' said Marie bitterly, 'the more likely one is to find an unassuming generous sense of gratitude. A Marquis gives me death in return for his life, and a Sergeant ... Well, let it go.'

When the beautiful Parisian lay in a warmed bed, her faithful Francine waited vainly for the affectionate word she was accustomed to; and seeing her standing there uneasily her mistress made a gesture full of sadness.

'That's what is called a day, Francine,' she said. 'I am ten years older.'

Next morning when Marie had got up Corentin presented himself, and was allowed to come in.

'I must be badly off indeed, Francine,' she said; 'the thought of meeting Corentin is positively not unwelcome.'

All the same, when she saw this man again, she experienced for the thousandth time an instinctive aversion that two years of acquaintance had not succeeded in lessening.

'Well,' he said smiling, 'I thought you had succeeded. Was the man you held not he?'

'Corentin,' she replied, with the slow utterance of suffering, 'don't speak of this affair to me until I can speak about it myself.'

He strolled about the room, with sidelong glances now and then at Mademoiselle de Verneuil, trying to guess the secret thoughts of this strange girl whose eye could be sufficiently penetrating at times to disconcert the most devious and evasive of men.

'I foresaw this setback,' he began again after a short silence. 'I have been making inquiries in case you might wish to set up your headquarters in this town. We are in the centre of the Chouan country here. Do you wish to stay?'

She answered with a nod; and Corentin felt that he could make a shrewd guess, not far off the mark, about what had happened the evening before.

'I have rented a house for you, nationalized property not sold yet. They're pretty backward in this part of the world. Nobody has dared buy this heap because it belongs to an *émigré* they think a brute. It is situated near the Église Saint-

Léonard; and 'pon my soul it has a ravishing view. One could make something of the dump, it's tolerably inhabitable. Would you like to go there?'

'This very moment,' she exclaimed.

'But it needs a few more hours spent on it to set it in proper order, if you're to find everything as you would wish it.'

'What does it matter?' she said. 'I shouldn't care if I lived in a convent or a prison. But do make it possible for me to be completely alone there to rest, by this evening. Go away now, leave me. I can't bear you here. I want to be alone with Francine; I'll be better off with her company than with my own, perhaps ... Good-bye. Now, go, go!'

This outpouring of words, at first with strong emotion and then coquettishly domineering and peremptory, showed her to be completely mistress of herself. Sleep had no doubt gradually imposed order on the previous day's impressions; and reflection had urged her on to vengeance. A sombre expression passing from time to time across her face was only an indication that she was one of those women capable of keeping their most ardent feelings buried in the depths of their hearts and plotting the destruction of their victims with a gracious smile on their faces. Her mind was wholly occupied with consideration of the means by which she might bring the Marquis into her hands alive. For the first time this woman had known life as she had longed for it, but from this life nothing survived, no feeling but the passion for revenge, a revenge unlimited and complete. It was her only thought, her sole desire.

Francine's remarks and her attentions found no response, and were met with complete silence; she seemed asleep with her eyes open; and the long day passed without a word or gesture to suggest the nature of her thoughts. She lay on a sofa that she had contrived with chairs and pillows. Only towards evening did she let these words fall, looking at Francine.

'I understood yesterday, child, what it was to live only for love, and today I understand that a person can die to be avenged. Yes, I would give my life to go and find him where-ever he may be, encounter him again, seduce him and make him mine. And if I do not have this man who has despised me at my feet within a few days, if I do not make him my humbled slave, my foot-stool, then I'll have sunk to the lowest depths, I'll not be a woman any more, I'll not be me! . . .'

The house that Corentin had suggested to Mademoiselle de Verneuil held sufficient resources for him to satisfy this girl's taste and innate feeling for elegance and luxury. He collected all that he knew should please her with a lover's assiduous care for his mistress's enjoyment, or more exactly with the false homage of a man in a position of power doing his best to court some inferior whom he needs. He came next day to suggest to Mademoiselle de Verneuil that she should now go to this hastily arranged residence.

Although she did no more than move from her makeshift ottoman to an antique sofa that Corentin had been able to find for her, this extraordinary Parisian took possession of the house as if it were her own. It was a royal taking for granted of everything she saw in it, an immediate sympathy with the least pieces, that she accepted as hers without hesitation as if she had long been familiar with them. These are trivial details, but not without value in depicting an exceptional personality such as hers. It seemed as though she were already familiar in dreams with this dwelling where she existed on her hate as she might have lived there by her love.

'At least I haven't his insulting deadly pity to bear,' she was saying to herself; 'I don't owe my life to him. O my first, my only and my last love, that it should come to this!'

She sprang impetuously at the alarmed Francine.

'Are you in love? Oh, yes, you're in love, I remember. Ah, I'm very lucky to have a woman with me who understands me! Well, my poor little Francine, don't you see man as a monstrous creature? Look, he said he loved me, and he could not stand up to the slightest test. And yet if the whole world had rejected him my soul would have been a refuge for him; if the universe had accused him I would have defended him. Before, I saw the world as filled with beings who came and went, they meant nothing at all to me. The world was a sad place, but not horrifying. But now what is the world without him? Is he to go on living when I'm not near him, not seeing him, talking to him, feeling his nearness, holding him, clasping him? ... Ah! I'll cut his throat myself, in his sleep, rather than that.'

Francine looked at her for a moment in silent dismay.

'Kill a man one loves? ...' she said gently.

'Ah, of course! When he no longer loves me.'

But after these dreadful words she hid her face in her hands, sat down again and fell silent.

Next day, a man presented himself brusquely without being announced. His face was stern. It was Hulot. She raised her eyes and trembled.

'You have come,' she said, 'to ask me what has happened to your friends? They are dead.'

'I know,' he answered; 'and not in the service of the Republic.'

'For me and because of me,' she said. 'You are going to speak of their country! Does their country restore to life again those who die for her, does she even avenge them? But I, I'll avenge them!'

The grisly scenes of the catastrophe which had overwhelmed her suddenly unfolded again before her, and this gracious being who prized reserve as first among the weapons in a woman's armoury had a moment of madness, and with a sudden abrupt movement confronted the disconcerted Commandant.

'For the sake of some slaughtered soldiers I'll bring a head worth a thousand heads to your guillotine blade,' she said. 'Women rarely make war, but you may learn some useful stratagems in my school, old soldier though you are. I'll hand a whole family over to your bayonets: him and his ancestors, his future and his past. The more kind and true I have been to him, the more treacherous and false I'll be. Yes, Commandant, I mean to bring this paltry aristocrat to my bed and he shall leave it to walk to his death. That's how it must be. I'll never have a rival. ... This miserable wretch pronounced his own death-sentence: *a day with no morrow*! Your Republic and I shall be avenged. The Republic!' she repeated, and Hulot was startled by the strangeness of her voice. 'And so the rebel dies for taking up arms against his country? And so France robs me of my revenge! Ah, what a slight thing life is, death expiates but one crime! But if this gentleman has only one head to give, I shall have a night to convince him that he is losing more than a life. Commandant, you who will kill him' (a sigh escaped her) 'must arrange things above all so that nothing betrays my treachery and that he dies sure of my fidelity. That's all I ask of you. Let him see only me, me and my caresses!'

At that she fell silent, and in her flushed face Hulot and Corentin could see that anger and fever did not entirely stifle modest shame. Marie shuddered violently as she uttered these last words. She listened to their echo as if she hardly believed she had said them, and involuntarily made the naïve gesture of a woman clutching an escaping veil to her.

'But you had him in your hands,' said Corentin.

'Probably so,' she agreed, with bitterness.

'Why stop me when I held him?' pursued Hulot.

'Ah, Commandant, we did not know that it was *he*.'

And then this agitated woman, feverishly moving about the room and casting burning glances at the two spectators of the storm, suddenly grew calm.

'I don't know what I'm doing,' she said in a deep and resolute voice. 'Why talk? I must go and find him.'

'Go and find him?' said Hulot. 'But, my dear child, beware! We do not hold the country districts, and if you ventured outside the town you would be captured or killed within a hundred paces.'

'There are no dangers ever for those determined on vengeance,' she answered with a disdainful gesture, and dismissed these two men from her presence whom it shamed her to see.

'What a woman!' exclaimed Hulot as he moved off with Corentin. 'What a notion that was they had in Paris, those police folk! But she will never hand him over to us,' he added, shaking his head.

'Oh yes, she will!' answered Corentin.

'Don't you see, she's in love with him?'

'Precisely for that reason. Besides,' Corentin said, looking at the surprised Commandant, 'I'm here to prevent her from doing anything she might regret; for in my view, comrade, there's no love worth three hundred thousand francs.'

As this spy acting against his fellow citizens went off, the soldier followed him with his eyes until the sound of his footsteps had died away, and then, heaving a sigh, he said to himself, 'So it may sometimes be a good thing to be only a blunt honest fellow like myself! By God's thunder, if I come across the Gars we'll fight hand to hand or my name isn't Hulot! If that fox were to make me pass sentence on him, now that they've created Courts-martial, I would feel my conscience as filthy as a young soldier's shirt-tail when he hears his first gunfire.'

It was the massacre at La Vivetière and the urge to avenge his two friends that had brought Hulot back to command his Demi-brigade, as much as the official answer from a new Minister, Berthier, which stated that his resignation could not be accepted in the present situation. A confidential letter was enclosed with the official one, in which the Minister, without giving him any information about Mademoiselle de Verneuil's mission, told him that the incident, which was quite outside the military field of action, must not interfere with the prosecution of the war. The military leaders, he said, must confine their participation in this matter to assisting *this honourable citizeness if they had occasion to do so*.

Learning from his sources of information that the Chouans' movements revealed a concentration of their forces towards Fougères, Hulot had secretly brought two battalions of his Demi-brigade to this vital point by a forced march. The country's danger, his detestation of the aristocrats whose partisans threatened a considerable tract of country, the claims of friendship, had all contributed to restore youth's fiery spirit to the veteran soldier.

'This is how I wanted to live,' Mademoiselle de Verneuil said when she was alone with Francine. 'However swiftly the hours pass, they are centuries filled with thoughts for me.'

She suddenly took Francine's hand, and in a voice like the notes of the first robin after a storm slowly let fall these words, 'No matter what I do, child, I can't help seeing his charming mouth and rounded full chin and his eyes sparkling with fire, and I still hear the coachman's shout to his horses. I'm dreaming, of course ... and why so much hate then when I wake up?'

She heaved a long sigh, and rose. Then for the first time she looked around her at the country handed over to civil war by this ruthless aristocrat whom she was setting herself to strike at single-handed. Beguiled by the prospect, she went out to breathe more freely under the sky; and though she may have chosen her path at random, she was certainly led towards the town's *Promenade* by that strange compulsion, as if a spell were laid on us, which makes us look for hope where hope is an absurdity. Daydreams conceived under that enchantment often come true, and then we call them prescience and attribute our prevision to the operation of a real though inexplicable force, a force that the passions always find ready to favour them, like a flatterer who among all his lies sometimes tells the truth.

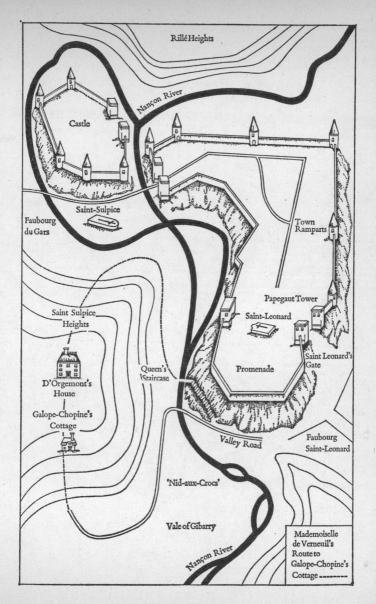

Rillé Heights

Nançon River

Castle

Saint-Sulpice

Faubourg du Gars

Town Ramparts

Saint Sulpice Heights

Papegaut Tower

Saint-Leonard

D'Orgemont's House

Queen's Staircase

Galope-Chopine's Cottage

Saint Leonard's Gate

Promenade

Valley Road

Faubourg Saint-Leonard

'Nid-aux-Crocs'

Vale of Gibarry

Nançon River

Mademoiselle de Verneuil's Route to Galope-Chopine's Cottage --------

Plan of Fougères

PART THREE – A DAY WITH NO MORROW

Chapter 17

As the concluding events of this story were affected by the terrain where they took place, in the town and its surroundings, a detailed description is indispensable at this point; otherwise the unwinding of the plot would be difficult to follow.

The town of Fougères is built partly on a schistous crag which looks as if it had fallen from the mountains which close in the great valley of the Couësnon to the west, and are given different names according to their situation. On that side the town is separated from the mountains by a gorge, at the bottom of which flows a little river called the Nançon. The part of the rock looking east has the same view of the countryside that one enjoys from the summit of the Pellerine, and that facing west looks down only on the winding valley of the Nançon; but there is a place from which one can look out over part of the circle of the great valley and at the same time see the picturesque meanderings of the little one which winds its way into it. This place, where the citizens have chosen to make their Promenade, and towards which Mademoiselle de Verneuil was making her way, was the theatre where the drama begun at La Vivetière was to achieve its final solution. And so, picturesque as the other parts of Fougères may be, we are bound to concentrate our attention on the features we see from its height.

The rock of Fougères seen from this side presents a picture

rather like one of those enormous saracenic towers, on all sides of which the architects have placed wide balconies, one above the other, linked by spiral staircases. The rock is crowned by a Gothic church whose little spires, bell tower and buttresses complete its almost perfect sugarloaf shape. In front of this church, dedicated to Saint Leonard, there lies an irregular-shaped little *Place* terraced by a wall rising to form an ornamental parapet, and leading by a ramp to the Promenade.

A few fathoms below the Place Saint-Leonard on a second rocky ledge the Promenade winds about the height, opening out into a wide expanse planted with trees, built at its lower end on the ramparts of the town.

Then, some sixty feet below the walls and rock supporting this esplanade, which owes its existence to geological accident and patient hard work, there is a spiral way called the *Queen's Staircase* cut out of the rock, leading to a bridge built across the Nançon by Anne of Brittany.

Finally, below this way which forms a third cliff balcony, gardens fall from terrace to terrace, in tiers filled with flowers, down to the river.

Parallel to the Promenade, across the river, a high plateau extends which falls in gentle slopes to the great valley and makes an abrupt turn northwards. Its barren vertical cliffs, called by the name of the outlying part of the town they look down on, the Saint-Sulpice Heights, seem to loom sombrely over the rocky Promenade, in certain places within gunshot range of it. They shelter from the north winds a narrow valley more than six hundred feet below, where the Nançon divides into three arms which water meadowland, with scattered buildings, delightfully set with verdure.

Towards the south, where the town proper ends and the Faubourg Saint-Léonard begins, the rocky promontory of Fougères folds back upon itself, becomes less steep, diminishes in height and turns into the great valley, following the river which it here confines against the Saint-Sulpice Heights, forming a bottleneck, from which the river escapes in two streams to meet the Couësnon into which it pours itself. This picturesque group of rocky hills is called the *Nid-aux-Crocs*, the valley which they shape is the *Val de Gibarry*, and its fat pastures supply most of the butter known to gourmets as *Prée-Valaye* butter.

At the place where the Promenade leads on to the ramparts of the town there rises a tower, a square-built structure called the *Papegaut Tower*, above which the house that was Mademoiselle de Verneuil's lodging stands.

From there the ramparts descend, held sometimes by a high retaining wall, sometimes by the living rock where it falls vertically; and the part of the town set on this high impregnable foundation describes a vast crescent, at the lower end of which the rocks tilt and are hollowed out to allow passage to the Nançon. At that point the gateway is placed which leads to the Faubourg de Saint-Sulpice and bears the same name, the Porte Saint-Sulpice.

Below, on a mamelon of granite, dominating three valleys along which several roads converge, there rise the ancient battlements and medieval towers of the Castle of Fougères, one of the most impressive and massive strongholds built by the Dukes of Brittany, with walls ninety feet high and fifteen feet thick. It is defended on the east by a moat through which a deviation of the Nançon flows, pouring along its fosses and turning mill-wheels between the Porte Saint-Sulpice and the castle drawbridge, and on the west by the steep face of the granite on which it stands.

So, from the Promenade to this superb relic of the Middle Ages, clothed in ivy, crowned with its square and round towers each one capable of harbouring a regiment, the castle, the town and its rock, defended by walls with vertical faces or sheer escarpments, form a vast precipitous horseshoe, down the sides of which the Bretons with the help of time have traced some narrow paths. Masses of stone jut out here and there like architectural ornament. In places water trickles down breaks in the rock from which spring stunted trees, and beyond goats are attracted to tufts of grass clinging to the less steep granite slabs. There is heather everywhere, springing from every damp crack and hanging grim dark crannies with its pink garlands. Below, at the bottom of this enormous funnel-shaped panorama of hill and hollow, the little river winds through ever-fresh green meadow, softly spread like a carpet.

At the Castle foot the church dedicated to Saint Sulpice rises among several granite masses and gives its name to some groups of houses beyond the river, the Faubourg Saint-Sulpice. This Faubourg, which looks as if it had been cast down into an abyss, with its church whose slender steeple does not reach the top of the rocks apparently poised to fall on it and the cottages round it, is picturesquely washed by streams of the Nançon, embowered in trees and adorned with gardens. It breaks capriciously into the crescent formed by the Promenade, the town and the Castle, and with its varied detail produces effects of naïve contrast to the solemn grimness of the amphitheatre it faces.

Finally, the complete mass of Fougères, its Faubourgs and its Churches, even the Saint-Sulpice Heights, are framed by the Heights of Rillé which form part of the circle of mountains enclosing the great valley of the Couësnon.

These are the most striking features of this place, naturally wild and austere, but relieved by gay ornament and the addition of the most impressive works of human hands to the grand accidents of the upflung rock, in odd juxtaposition, with astonishing unexpected contrasts that take the breath away.

Nowhere in France does the traveller meet with such imposing contrasts as those presented by the great valley of the Couësnon and the little valleys hidden between the rock masses of Fougères and the Heights of Rillé. It is a changing variable beauty, owing its effects to chance and the completeness of the harmonies of nature. Clear limpid streams flow everywhere; mountains rise clad with the luxuriant trees and flowers of these regions; there are grim cliffs and elegant structures, ramparts built by nature and granite towers by man; with all the effects of light and shade, all the contrast in colour and form of different foliage that artists prize so much; groups of houses filled with the life of an active population and deserted places where the granite will not suffer even the stone-clinging white lichen to grow – in sum, all the inspiration one asks of a landscape: grace and frowning grimness, a poem of ever-renewed enchantment, scenes of sublime drama and delightful pastoral charm. Brittany flowers there!

The tower called the Papegaut Tower above which rises the house occupied by Mademoiselle de Verneuil has its base at the very foot of the precipice and rises as high as the esplanade carved out on the cliff ledge before Saint-Leonard's church. From that house, isolated on three sides, one can see at the same time the great horseshoe which begins at the Tower itself, the winding valley of the Nançon and the Place Saint-Léonard. It is one of a group of timber-framed dwellings, three centuries old, parallel to the north side of the church and forming a cul-de-sac whose exit leads to a road sloping down past the church to the Saint-Leonard Gate. It was naturally in this direction that Mademoiselle de Verneuil walked, turning aside from the Place de l'Église which lay above her and walking towards the Promenade.

When she had passed through the little green-painted gate in front of the guard-house then placed in the tower of the Saint-Leonard Gate, the magnificence of the spectacle for a moment made her passions fall silent. She marvelled at the vast section of the great valley of the Couësnon that her view embraced, from the top of the Pellerine to the plateau along which the road passes to Vitré. Then her eyes rested on Nid-aux-Crocs and the windings of the Vale of Gibarry, its crests bathed in hazy light from the setting sun. She was almost frightened by the depth of the valley of the Nançon, whose tallest poplars barely rose to the walls of the gardens below the Queen's Staircase. She walked on from surprise to surprise to the point from which she could see both the great valley beyond the Vale of Gibarry and the enchanting landscape framed by the town's horse-shoe, the Saint-Sulpice cliffs and the Heights of Rillé.

At this evening hour, smoke from the houses of the Faubourg and the valleys formed a vaporous cloud through which objects appeared veiled in a blue canopy. The too vivid colours of day were beginning to fade and the firmament to take on a pearly grey, while the moon cast its veils of light over the lovely depths below. Everything combined to plunge the mind into reverie and lead it to evoke the presence of those dear.

Suddenly neither the shingled roofs of the Faubourg Saint-Sulpice nor its church whose soaring spire is lost in the depth of the valley, nor the age-old mantle of ivy and traveller's joy clothing the walls of the ancient fortress beyond which the Nançon gushes past the mill wheels, nor any feature of the landscape held further interest for her. The setting sun cast its golden dust and flakes of fiery light unnoticed over the gracious dwellings scattered among the heights, into the waters below and over the meadows. She stood motionless facing the Saint-Sulpice cliffs. The insane hope which had led her to the Promenade was miraculously fulfilled.

Beyond the gorse and broom of the crests opposite it seemed to her that she recognized several of the guests of La Vivetière, in spite of their disguising goatskins, and among them the Gars stood out, his slightest gestures clear in the softened light of the setting sun. A few paces behind the principal group she saw her formidable enemy, Madame du Gua.

For a moment Mademoiselle de Verneuil might think that she was dreaming, but her rival's hatred soon provided proof that there was nothing unreal about this dream. The concentration of her attention upon the Marquis's every movement prevented her from noticing Madame du Gua taking careful aim with a long-barrelled gun. But presently a shot awoke the mountain echoes and made her aware that her rival had marked her.

'She sends me her visiting card!' she said to herself with a wry smile.

Immediately a shout of *Who goes there?* rang out from sentry to sentry from the castle to the Saint-Leonard Gate, and showed the Chouans that the Fougères garrison were leaving nothing to chance since the least vulnerable of their ramparts was so well guarded.

'So she's there, and so is he!' said Marie.

To go in quest of him, follow him, track him down, was a resolve conceived in a flash.

'But I have no arms!' she exclaimed.

It occurred to her then that when she was leaving Paris she had thrown a beautiful dagger once worn by a sultana into one of her boxes, with the idea of equipping herself for a theatre of war, like those absurd people who provide themselves with albums on a journey for the thoughts they expect to have; but she had been less captivated then by the prospect of shedding blood than by the pleasure of wearing an elegant *kandjar*, or Eastern poniard, set with jewels, and playing with this blade as direct as a look. Three days before she had acutely regretted having left the weapon with her baggage when to kill herself seemed her way of escape from the hideous fate her rival was reserving for her.

She turned back quickly to her lodging, found the dagger and fastened it at her waist, threw a large all-enveloping shawl round her shoulders, wrapped her hair in a black lace scarf and covered her head with a wide-brimmed Chouan hat belonging to a servant of the household, and with the presence of mind strong emotion sometimes finds took the Marquis's glove Marche-à-terre had given as a safe-conduct. Then, after replying to the alarmed Francine, 'I'm going where I must, to find *him* I would go to hell!' she returned to the Promenade.

The Gars was still in the same place, but alone. He seemed to be examining the approaches to the town with a soldier's searching concentration, turning his telescope on the different ways across the Nançon, the Queen's Staircase, and the road which leads from the Porte Saint-Sulpice, winds past the church and goes to meet the main roads under the guns of the castle.

Mademoiselle de Verneuil hurried along the little paths made by goats and their goatherds down and across the escarpment below the Promenade, reached the Queen's Staircase and the foot of the cliff, crossed the Nançon and passed through the Faubourg. Like a bird in the desert she divined her way among the dangerous precipitous slopes of the Saint-Sulpice cliffs, presently reached a slippery path over granite slabs and set herself to climb through the broom, spiked gorse and sharp-edged pebbles that beset the way, with an intensity of energy that is perhaps unknown to men but is lent to women temporarily by strong feeling.

Marie was surprised by nightfall at the point when on reaching the plateau she was trying to make out by the pale light of the moon the way the Marquis must have taken. Her determined search met with no success, and the pervading silence made it clear that the Chouans and their Chief had retreated. Her passionate impulse died with the hope that had inspired it. Finding herself alone, by night, in unknown country, exposed to the risks of war, she began to reflect, and the thought of Hulot's injunction, Madame du Gua's shot, made her shiver fearfully. The quiet of the night, so profound on the mountains, made even a falling leaf audible at a great distance, and such slight sounds disturbed the air as if to give a mournful measure of the solitude and silence. There was a strong wind in the higher regions of the sky, driving the clouds tempestuously, with changing effects of shadow and light which increased her terror by giving a fantastic and sinister appearance to the most harmless objects.

She turned her eyes towards the houses of Fougères, whose homely lights twinkled like so many terrestrial stars, and suddenly saw distinctly the Papegaut Tower. Only a short distance separated her from her dwelling, but this distance was across a chasm. She retained a sufficiently vivid impression of the gulfs that yawned beside the narrow path by which she had come to know that she would run more risks in returning to Fougères than in pursuing her enterprise. It occurred to her that the Marquis's glove would shield her from all the perils of her nocturnal walk if the Chouans held this part of the country. Only Madame du Gua was to be feared.

At this thought Marie clasped her dagger, and did her best to make her way towards a house whose roofs she had glimpsed when she reached the plateau; but she walked slowly, only then aware of the sombre majesty weighing upon a person alone at night in a wild place with high mountains inclining their heads on every side like giants in conclave.

The rustling of her dress, clutched by the bushes, made her tremble more than once, and she more than once hurried on only to pause again, thinking her last hour had come. But soon her circumstances in fact became such as might have daunted the most intrepid man, and plunged Mademoiselle de Verneui l into a state of terror of that kind that acts acutely on the nervous system, producing extremes of either resistance or collapse. It becomes possible at such times for the most feeble persons to perform acts of supernatural strength, and the strongest may go out of their minds with fear.

Marie heard strange noises not far away. They were distinct yet vague, like the light of the now overcast now luminous night, speaking of confusion and tumult so that the ear strained to make them out. They came from under the ground, which seemed to be shaken by the tramp of a vast multitude of marching men. In a momentary brightening a long line of hideous figures was revealed a few paces from Mademoiselle de Verneuil, undulating like blades of grain in a field and gliding like ghosts; but she caught barely a glimpse of them before darkness fell again like a black curtain and hid this fearful spectacle with its host of gleaming dark eyes from her. She turned back instantly, and ran to the top of a bank to escape three of the horrible figures that were approaching her.

'Did you see it?' one asked.

'I felt a cold wind from it when it passed near me,' a hoarse voice answered.

'And I felt a breath of damp air and a graveyard smell,' said the third.

'How white it looks!' the first speaker exclaimed.

'Why did only it *come back*,' said the second, 'of all the ones that died on the Pellerine?'

'Ah, you may well ask why!' answered the third. 'Why are those who belong to the *Sacred Heart* favoured more than the others? Anyway I would rather die unconfessed than wander like him, with no food or drink, no blood in your veins or flesh on your bones.'

'Ah! . . .'

That exclamation, or rather terrible cry, rose from the groups as one of the three Chouans pointed to the slight figure and pale face of Mademoiselle de Verneuil, who was fleeing at a frightening speed without making the slightest sound that they could hear.

'There it is!' – 'Here!' – 'Where is it?' – 'There!' – 'Here!' – 'It's gone!' – 'No.' – 'Yes' – 'Can you see it?'

The exclamations sounded like the monotonous crash of waves on the beach.

Mademoiselle de Verneuil walked on resolutely in the direction of the house, and saw the indistinct figures of a host of men who fled at her approach with all the signs of panic terror. She seemed to be carried onward by some unknown power, like a straw before the wind. The lightness of her body, which was inexplicable to her, became a new source of fear. The hollow cries of these figures which rose in crowds at her approach, seemingly from underground, had nothing human in their sound.

At last, with considerable difficulty, she reached a ruined garden with broken-down hedges and gates. Stopped by a sentry, she displayed the glove. As the moon shone on her form, the gun already aimed fell from the Chouan's hands and his raucous cry repeated those of which the air was full. She saw large buildings with several lights showing inhabited rooms, and approached the walls without meeting further obstacles.

By the first window she looked through she saw Madame du Gua with the leaders who had been assembled at La Vivetière. Stunned by this sight and by the sense of her danger she recoiled violently against a little opening protected by heavy iron bars, and inside in a long vaulted hall perceived the Marquis sitting sad and alone two paces away. The flames of the fire before his heavy chair cast a reddish flickering light over his face and gave the semblance of a vision to this scene. Not daring to move and trembling, the poor girl clung to the bars, and hoped, in the prevailing deep silence, to hear his voice if he spoke. As she saw him downcast, dejected and pale, it pleased her to think that she was one of the causes of his sadness. Then her anger turned to pity, and from pity to tenderness, and she suddenly felt that it was not only revenge that had brought her to that place.

The Marquis rose and turned his head, and stood thunder-struck, seeing the hazy apparition of Mademoiselle de Verneuil's face. He made an impatient and contemptuous gesture and exclaimed, 'Am I to see this she-devil every-where, even when I'm awake!'

The deep contempt expressed for her drew a frenzied laugh from the poor girl which made the young leader shudder, and he rushed to the casement. Mademoiselle de Verneuil fled.

She heard a man's tread behind her that she thought was Montauran's, and, fleeing him, there was no obstacle that could stop her. She would have passed through walls and flown through the air, she would have taken the road to hell rather than read the words again in strokes of flame *He despises you!* as they had been plain to see on the face of this man, as they were still shrilling in her brain with a trumpet's voice.

On she went, not knowing where, until she was stopped by a penetrating dampness of the air. Alarmed at the sound of several people approaching and driven by fear, she walked down steps which brought her to a cellar. At the bottom step she strained her ears to hear the direction her pursuers were taking. To her increasing horror, the quite loud confused noise outside did not cover the sound near at hand of the mournful groaning of a human voice.

A flash of light from the top of the steps made her fear that her refuge was known to her persecutors, and to escape them she gathered new strength. A few moments later when she had come to herself again she found it hard to understand by what means she could have climbed up the little wall on top of which she was hidden. She did not even notice at first the dis-comfort of her cramped position; but it shortly became in-tolerable, for she was forced in under an arch below the roof like a crouching Venus an art patron had placed in a niche too small for it.

This quite thick granite wall divided the well of a stairway from a small cellar from which the groans were coming. She presently saw a man dressed in goatskins walk down the steps and turn in under the arch below her, with nothing in his movements to suggest a person making an eager search. Impatient to know if she had a chance of preserving her safety, Mademoiselle de Verneuil waited anxiously for the man's torch to light the cellar, in which she could make out a shapeless but living bundle lying on the ground, and making efforts to reach a certain part of the wall by violent contortions like the flapping of a carp on a river bank.

Chapter 18

A LITTLE resin torch now threw its wavering bluish light into the cellar. Mademoiselle de Verneuil, whose imagination had been caught by the sombre romance of this place whose vaulted roof reverberated the voice of a mournful prayer, was forced to recognize that she was in an underground kitchen, long derelict. In the light the shapeless bundle became a very fat little man whose arms and legs had been secured with great care, but who had then apparently been thrown on the damp flags by those who had seized him, without further concern.

When he saw the newcomer with the torch in one hand and a bundle of firewood in the other, the captive uttered a deep groan which so affected Mademoiselle de Verneuil's sensibilities that she forgot her own terror, her despair, and the acute pain in her cramped and now benumbed limbs; but she did her best to refrain from moving.

The Chouan threw his faggot down on the hearth, after testing the strength of an old pot-hook dangling in front of a tall cast-iron fireback, and set fire to it with his torch. With some alarm Mademoiselle de Verneuil then recognized the wily Pille-miche to whom she had been handed over by her rival, looking in the flicker from the flames like one of the grotesque boxwood gnomes they carve in Germany. The prisoner's lamentation made a vast silent laugh spread over that furrowed weather-beaten countenance.

'You see,' he said, 'we Christians don't break our word; we're not like you. This fire's going to take the stiffness out of your legs and tongue and your fists . . . Oh, tch! tch! there doesn't seem to be any basting pan to place under your feet – they're so plump the fat might put out the fire. Is this house so badly fitted out that the master can't have all he needs when he wants to warm himself?'

The victim uttered a piercing shriek, as if he were trying to make himself heard beyond the vault and bring a deliverer.

'Oh, you can sing your head off, Monsieur d'Orgemont! They're all asleep up there, and Marche-à-terre's following me here and he'll shut the cellar door.'

While he was speaking Pille-miche was using the butt of his gun to tap the chimney-breast, the flagstones of the kitchen floor, the walls and the ovens, trying to find the hiding-place where the miser had hoarded his gold. He did this so knowingly that d'Orgemont was silent as if fearing that he might have been betrayed by some frightened servant; for although he had not told his secrets to anyone, his habits might have led someone to draw correct conclusions. Pille-miche sometimes turned round sharply to stare at his victim, as if he were playing the children's game when they try to guess whether they are getting near a hidden object by the naïvely revealing expression of the child who has hidden it. D'Orgemont feigned terror when he saw the Chouan tapping the ovens, which had a hollow sound, and seemed to be casting a bait for Pille-miche's greedy credulity with the hope of keeping him busy for some time. But now three more Chouans rushed down the steps and appeared precipitately in the cellar. At the sight of Marche-à-terre Pille-miche abandoned his search, with a ferocious look at d'Orgemont, inflamed by all the fury of disappointed avarice.

'Marie Lambrequin has risen from the dead,' said Marche-à-terre, and his demeanour showed that all interests paled before such important news.

'That doesn't surprise me,' replied Pille-miche. 'He was always having Holy Communion! God seemed to belong to only him.'

'Ah, but that was just about as much use to him as shoes to a dead man,' Mène-à-bien pointed out. 'There he was, not having had absolution before that scrap on the Pellerine. He got that daughter of Goguelu's into trouble, and there he was, in mortal sin. So the Abbé Gudin says that like that he has to stay two months as a ghost before resurrecting completely! We saw him, all of us three, pass in front of us – he's pale and cold, and he floats in the air and he smells of the graveyard!'

'And His Reverence said too that if the ghost could seize hold of anyone he would make a companion for himself out of him,' the fourth Chouan added.

The sight of this last speaker's grotesque countenance roused Marche-à-terre from the pious reverie prompted by the working of a miracle which, according to the Abbé Gudin, every devout defender of religion and the King might work again for himself by his own fervour.

'You see, Galope-chopine,' he said to that neophyte, with a certain solemnity, 'what the least failure in the duties of our sacred religion brings us to. It's a warning Saint Anne of Auray is giving us to come down upon each other without mercy for the slightest faults. Your cousin Pille-miche has asked for you to have the post of *look-out man* for Fougères. The Gars is willing to trust you with it, and you'll be well paid; but you know what kind of flour we use for kneading traitors' bread with, eh?'

'Yes, Monsieur Marche-à-terre.'

'You know why I say that? Some people say that you've a weakness for cider and a fistful of sous; but you can't let anything stick to your fingers in this job, you have to be all for us and only us.'

'His Reverence said, Monsieur Marche-à-terre, cider and sous is two good things and doesn't stand in the way of salvation.'

'If the cousin does something stupid,' said Pille-miche, 'it will only be because he doesn't know.'

'If things go wrong, no matter how,' cried Marche-à-terre in a voice that shook the cellar roof, 'I'll deal with him, never fear! – You'll answer to me for him,' he added, turning to Pille-miche, 'and if he's found wanting I'll go for the one inside your goatskin.'

'But, saving your presence, Monsieur Marche-à-terre,' Galope-chopine pursued, 'hasn't it not often happened to you to think *Counter-Chuins* was *chuins*?'

'My lad, see that that never happens to you again,' answered Marche-à-terre sharply, 'or I'll cleave you in two like a

243

turnip. As for messengers from the Gars, they'll have his glove. But since the affair at La Vivetière the *Big Garce* sticks a green ribbon on it.'

Pille-miche urgently nudged his comrade with a nod towards d'Orgemont, who was pretending to be asleep; but Marche-à-terre and Pille-miche knew from experience that no one ever dozed off by their fireside, and thinking that the last words to Galope-chopine might have been understood by the prisoner, although they had been said in a low voice, the four Chouans all looked at him for a moment, but probably came to the conclusion that fear had bereft him of his senses.

Suddenly, at a nod from Marche-à-terre, Pille-miche pulled d'Orgemont's shoes and stockings off, Marche-à-terre and Galope-chopine seized him round the body and pulled him to the hearth; then Marche-à-terre took one of the cords from the bundle of firewood and tied the miser's feet to the pot-hook. This concerted action carried out at incredible speed drew cries from the victim, which turned to shrieks when Pille-miche heaped embers under his legs.

'Friends, good friends,' cried d'Orgemont, 'you'll hurt me. I'm a Christian like yourselves!'

'You're lying in your throat,' answered Marche-à-terre. 'Your brother abjured Christ, and as for you, you bought the Monastery in Juvigny. The Abbé Gudin says that anyone may roast apostates without a pang of conscience.'

'Brothers in God, but I'm not refusing to pay you!'

'We allowed you a fortnight, and two months have gone by, and here's Galope-chopine who hasn't been given a sou.'

'Haven't you been given anything, Galope-chopine?' the miser asked despairingly.

'Naught, Monsieur d'Orgemont!' answered Galope-chopine in a fright.

The miser's cries, that had become a low continuous groan like a death-rattle, rose again with incredible vehemence. The four Chouans, as used to this spectacle as they were to see their dogs run about unshod, coolly contemplated the writhing and howling d'Orgemont, like travellers waiting before an inn hearth until the joint roasting on the spit is ready for eating.

'I'm dying! I'm dying!' shrieked the victim. '. . . And then you won't get my money.'

In spite of the violence of this outcry, Pille-miche noticed that the flame was not yet scorching the skin, so the embers were very artistically poked to make them blaze a little. D'Orgemont then said in a defeated voice, 'Friends, untie me. What do you want? A hundred crowns, a thousand, ten thousand, a hundred thousand? I'll give you two hundred crowns . . .'

His voice was so lamentable that Mademoiselle de Verneuil forgot her own danger, and uttered an exclamation.

'Who was that?' asked Marche-à-terre.

The Chouans cast scared looks about them. These men who could face the cannon's murderous throat so bravely could not stand firm before a *ghost*. Only Pille-miche was listening undistracted to the confession increasing pain was drawing from the victim.

'Five hundred crowns, yes, I'll give you that,' the miser was saying.

'Bah! Where are they then?' Pille-miche calmly answered.

'Oh! They are under the first apple tree . . . Holy Virgin! . . . at the bottom of the garden, to the left . . . You are brigands – thieves . . . Ah, I'm dying! . . . There are ten thousand francs there.'

'I don't want francs,' retorted Pille-miche. 'We need livres. Your Republican crowns have heathen faces on them, and they'll never pass for real money.'

'It is in livres, good gold louis. But untie me, untie me . . . You know where my life is . . . my treasure.'

The four Chouans looked at one another, considering which one of them they could trust sufficiently to send him to dig up the money.

At this point Mademoiselle de Verneuil's horror at their cannibal cruelty reached such a pitch that without knowing whether the rôle that her pale face had assigned to her would still preserve her from all danger, she bravely called out in a deep solemn voice, 'Do you not fear the wrath of God? Untie him, barbarous men!'

The Chouans looked up, then saw suspended in the air two eyes that shone like stars, and fled aghast. Mademoiselle de Verneuil jumped down into the kitchen, ran to d'Orgemont and drew him with such force from the fire that the cords tying him to the pot-hook gave way; then with the edge of her dagger she cut the ropes with which they had bound him. When the miser was free and on his feet his face screwed first into a painful but sardonic laugh.

'Run, run to the appletree, brigands!' he said. 'Oho, that makes twice I've foxed them; and they won't catch me a third time!'

A woman's voice was heard outside.

'"*A ghost*! *A ghost*!"' cried Madame du Gua. 'Idiots, it was *that woman*. A thousand crowns to the man who brings me that whore's head!'

Mademoiselle de Verneuil turned pale; but the miser smiled, took her hand and drew her under the chimney hood, carefully leading her round the little fire so that they did not disturb it or leave traces to show they had gone that way. He pressed a spring, the cast-iron fire-back opened; and when their common enemies re-entered the cellar the heavy door of the hiding-place had already fallen noiselessly back into place. The Parisian understood then the object of the carp-like flappings she had seen the unhappy banker make.

'You see, Madame!' exclaimed Marche-à-terre. 'The ghost has taken the Blue for its companion!'

Their fear must have been great, for the words were followed by a deep silence and presently d'Orgemont and his companion could hear the Chouans repeating in a murmur, '*Ave Sancta Anna Auriaca gratia plena, Dominus tecum* . . .'

'They're praying, the imbeciles,' said d'Orgemont.

'Are you not afraid,' Mademoiselle de Verneuil interrupted him, 'of showing them where . . .'

The old miser with a laugh dispelled her fears.

'The plate is set in a granite block ten inches thick. We hear them, but they cannot hear us.'

Then he gently took his liberator's hand and placed it against a fissure from which there were wafts of fresh air, and she guessed that this opening had been cut out in the chimney flue.

'Oh! Oh! Devil take it!' d'Orgemont exclaimed. 'My legs are smarting a bit! That *Charette's Mare*, as they call her in Nantes, is not so stupid as to go against the faithful; she well knows that if they weren't such simpletons they wouldn't fight against their own interests. There she is, praying too. She must be a sight to see, saying her *Ave* to Saint Anne of Auray. She would do better to rob some stage-coach and pay me back the four thousand francs she owes me. With the interest and expenses that amounts to quite four thousand seven hundred and eighty francs and some centimes . . .'

When the prayer was finished, the Chouans rose and left. Old d'Orgemont gripped Mademoiselle de Verneuil's hand as if to warn her that the danger was not yet at an end.

'No, Madame,' exclaimed Pille-miche after some minutes of silence, 'you might stay here ten years but they won't come back.'

'But she didn't go out, she must be here,' said *Charette's Mare* stubbornly.

'No, Madame, no, they've flown off through the walls. Haven't we seen the devil fly off with a priest who took the Oath, with our own eyes?'

'Can't you see, Pille-miche, you a miser like him yourself, that the old skinflint could easily have spent a few thousand livres to close off a corner in the foundations of this cellar with a secret entrance released by a spring?'

The miser and the girl heard Pille-miche give a great guffaw.

'True enough,' he said.

'Stay here,' said Madame du Gua. 'Wait for them at the exit. For one single gunshot I'll give you all you find in our usurer's treasure. If you want me to forgive you for having sold this girl when I told you to kill her, you had better obey me.'

'Usurer!' said old d'Orgemont. 'And I let her have money

at only nine per cent. It's true I hold a mortgage as security. But see how grateful she is! It's clear, Madame, if God punishes us for wrong-doing the devil is there to punish us for doing good, and a man placed between the two without knowing anything of the future always makes me think of a rule-of-three sum with the X undiscoverable.'*

He heaved his characteristic hollow sigh in which the air passing through his larynx seemed to encounter and battle its way through two slack old vocal cords.

The noise that Pille-miche and Madame du Gua made in tapping the walls again, and the arches of the roof and the flagstones, seemed to reassure him and he seized his deliverer's hand to help her to climb a narrow spiral staircase in the thickness of a granite wall. When they had climbed about twenty steps, a faint lamp-light shone on their heads. The miser stopped, turned towards his companion and examined her face as he might look at and handle a bill of exchange he was doubtful about discounting, and turn it over and over again. Then he heaved his terrible sigh.

'By bringing you here,' he said, after a moment's silence, 'I have repaid in full the service you did me; so I don't see why I should give you . . .'

'Monsieur, don't trouble about me, I'm not asking anything of you,' she said.

Her concluding words, and perhaps the disdain expressed on that beautiful face, reassured the little old man, for he went on, not without a sigh, 'Ah, by bringing you here I did too much not to continue . . .'

He politely helped Marie up some very awkwardly placed steps and reluctantly, but with the best grace he could muster, showed her into a little room, four feet square, lit by a lamp hanging from the arched roof. It was easy to see that the miser had made every preparation to spend some days in

* *Rob Roy* Chap. 2. William Osbaldistone's head clerk says: ' "Mr Francis seems to understand the fundamental principle of all moral accounting, the great ethic rule of three. Let A do to B as he would have him do to him: the product will give the rule of conduct required." ' – *Trans.*

this retreat, if the events of the civil war should make a pro-
longed retirement necessary.

'Don't go near the wall – the white plaster might rub off on
you,' d'Orgemont said suddenly. And he hastily placed his
hand between the girl's shawl and the wall, which appeared to
have been freshly replastered.

The old miser's gesture produced a quite contrary effect to
that he had intended. Mademoiselle de Verneuil looked
quickly in front of her, and in a corner saw an oddly-shaped
form that drew a cry of terror from her, for she guessed that a
human being had been coated with mortar and placed standing
there. D'Orgemont made a repressive sign to silence her and
his little china-blue eyes showed as much fright as his
companion's.

'Dolt, do you think I killed him? . . . It's my brother,' he
said, giving a lugubrious variant of his usual sigh. 'He was the
first Recteur to take the Oath. This was the only refuge where
he could be safe from the fury of the Chouans and fellow priests.
Imagine harrying a worthy man who was so law-abiding!
He was my elder brother, the only person with the patience
to teach me decimal reckoning. Oh, he was a good priest! He
was thrifty and knew how to salt money away. It's four years
since he died, I don't know of what illness; but you know
priests are accustomed to kneeling from time to time to pray,
and perhaps he wasn't able to get used to standing up here like
me. I put him over there, anywhere else *they* would have dug
him up. One day I'll be able to bury him in consecrated
ground, as the poor man talked of. It was only because he was
afraid he took the Oath . . .'

A tear appeared in the little old man's sharp eyes, and even
his rusty wig seemed less repulsive to the girl and she turned
her eyes away in silent respect for his grief; but this emotion
did not prevent his saying to her again, 'Don't go near the wall,
you might . . .' And he kept his eyes fixed on Mademoiselle
de Verneuil's, hoping thus to prevent her closer examination
of the walls of this oppressive little room where the air was too
devoid of oxygen for the lungs to breathe. Marie, however,
succeeded in snatching a glance away from her Argus, and

guessed by the odd bulging of the walls that the miser had built them himself of bags of silver or gold.

In the past moments d'Orgemont had been experiencing a grotesque mixture of emotions. The pain of his scorched legs and his terror at seeing a human being in the midst of his treasures could be read in every wrinkle of his face; but at the same time an unaccustomed fire in his arid eyes expressed the emotion aroused by his deliverer's dangerous proximity. The roses in her cheeks were made for kisses, and her dark velvety glance sent the blood coursing so hotly through his heart that he no longer knew whether it was a sign of new life or of death.

'Are you married?' he asked in a trembling voice.

'No,' she said, smiling.

'I have a little,' he went on, heaving his sigh; 'although I'm not so rich as they all say. A girl like you must be fond of diamonds, jewels, carriages ... gold,' he added casting a scared glance around. 'I have all that to give, after my death. Hey! if you wished ...'

The old man's eye betrayed so much calculation, even in this momentary impulse of love, that as she shook her head. Mademoiselle de Verneuil could not help thinking that the miser's only idea in wanting to marry her was to bury his secret in her heart by making her a second version of himself.

'Money,' she said, with a quizzical look at d'Orgemont that made him feel both relieved and angry, 'money means nothing to me. You would be three times as rich as you are if you had all the gold I have refused here ...'

'Don't go near the w ...'

'And yet all that was asked of me was a look,' she added, with superb pride.

'You were wrong, that was an excellent speculation. Consider ...'

'Consider,' returned Mademoiselle de Verneuil, 'that I have just heard a voice every single note of which is worth more to me than all your riches.'

'You don't know my riches ...'

Before the miser could stop her, Marie touched a little

coloured print of Louis XV on horseback with her finger, saw it move, and suddenly there below her saw the Marquis, engaged in loading a blunderbuss. The aperture hidden by the little panel on which the print was stuck apparently corresponded with some ornament in the ceiling of the room below, which was no doubt where the Royalist leader slept. D'Orgemont cautiously pushed back the old print, careful to make no sound, and looked at the girl severely.

'Don't say a word if you value your life,' he said. And then after a pause, 'That's no small craft you've got your grappling hook aboard,' he went on in a whisper. 'Do you know that the Marquis has a hundred thousand livres in income from leased lands which haven't been sold yet? And now a Decree by the Consuls I read about in *Le Primidi de l'Ille-et-Vilaine* has just put a stop to the sequestration of property. Aha! you find that *gars* a more attractive man now, don't you? Your eyes are shining like two mint-new gold louis.'

The sound of a well-known voice had indeed given fire to Mademoiselle de Verneuil's eyes. Since she had come to stand there in the hidden room, as if buried in a silver mine, her spirit, crushed by the recent events, had regained its resilience. In her mind, a grim course of action seemed to have been resolved on and the means of carrying it out envisaged.

'One does not forgive contempt like that,' she was saying to herself. 'And if he is not to love me any more I'll kill him: no woman shall have him.'

'No, Abbé, no!' exclaimed the voice of the young leader from below. 'It must be this way.'

'Monsieur le Marquis,' returned the Abbé Gudin haughtily, 'you will scandalize the whole of Brittany if you give this ball at Saint-James. It's preaching not dancing that will rouse our villages. Give them guns, not violins.'

'Abbé, you don't need me to tell you that it's only in a general gathering of all our supporters that I'll be able to see how much I can expect of them and do with them. It seems to me easier to examine their faces and learn their intentions at a dinner than try any possible form of espionage, which I detest in any case. We'll make them talk with a glass in their hands.'

Marie trembled as she heard this, conceiving the plan of going to the ball and there avenging herself.

'Do you take me for a fool with your sermon about dancing?' Montauran went on. 'Would you yourselves not take part in a *chaconne* with a good grace for the sake of finding yourselves re-established under your new name of Fathers of the Faith? ... Don't you know that after Mass Bretons go dancing? Are you unaware that five days ago Messieurs Hyde de Neuville and d'Andigné had a meeting with the First Consul on the question of the restoration of His Majesty Louis XVIII? If I'm preparing at this moment to risk such a foolhardy surprise attack it's only to add the weight of our hobnailed shoes to our negotiating power. Are you aware that all the leaders from the Vendée, including even Fontaine, are talking of surrendering? Ah, Monsieur, the Princes have evidently been misled about the state of France. The devotion they've heard so much about is a devotion to appointments. Abbé, I may have dipped my foot in blood, but I don't propose to wade in it up to the waist without knowing what I'm doing. I have dedicated myself to the King's service, not to four hot-heads, men over head and ears in debt like Rifoël, and braggarts and ... '

'You may as well say at once, Monsieur, Abbés who collect contributions on the highway to carry on the war!' interrupted the Abbé Gudin.

'Why should I not say it?' the Marquis replied tartly. 'I'll say more, the heroic days of the Vendée are over ...'

'Monsieur le Marquis, we'll be able to work miracles without you.'

'Yes, miracles like Marie Lambrequin's,' said the Marquis with a laugh. 'Come, no hard feelings, Abbé. I know that you risk your own skin and fire at a Blue as readily as you say "Let us pray". God willing, I hope to have you officiating with a mitre on your head at the King's coronation.'

This last remark evidently produced a magical effect on the Abbé, for the clink of a gun was heard and his exclamation, 'I have fifty cartridges in my pockets, Monsieur le Marquis, and my life is the King's!'

'That's another of my debtors,' the miser said to Mademoiselle de Verneuil. 'And I'm not talking of the paltry five or six hundred crowns he borrowed from me, but of a debt of blood that I have every hope will be repaid. He can never have so much ill-fortune as I wish him, the damned Jesuit. He swore to have my brother's life and raised the country against him. And why? Because the poor man was afraid of the new laws!'

He applied his ear to a certain spot in his hiding place.

'There, they're making off, all those brigands,' he added. 'They're going to work another miracle maybe! Let's hope they don't try to say good-bye, like last time, by setting fire to the house!'

After about half an hour, which Mademoiselle de Verneuil and d'Orgemont spent looking at each other as if each was looking at a picture, Galope-chopine's harsh raucous voice called in an undertone, 'There's no danger now, Monsieur d'Orgemont. But I had to work hard for my thirty crowns this time.'

'Child,' said the miser, 'swear to keep your eyes closed.'

Mademoiselle de Verneuil placed a hand over her eyes and as an additional precaution the old man blew out the lamp. He took his deliverer by the hand and helped her down seven or eight awkward steps. After a few minutes he gently pulled away her hand, and she found herself in the room which the Marquis de Montauran had just left, which was the miser's own room.

'My dear child,' said the old man, 'you can go now. Don't look round you like that. I suppose you have no money? Here, here are ten crowns; some of them are clipped, but they'll pass. When you leave the garden you'll find a path leading to the town, or as they call it now the *District*. But the Chouans are at Fougères, it's not likely you can go back so soon, and so you may need a safe retreat. Remember what I'm going to tell you but only make use of it if you're hard pressed. You will see a farm-house where Grand-Cibot lives, the man they call Galope-chopine, on the road leading to Nid-aux-Crocs by the Vale of Gibarry. Go in and say to his wife, "Good day, Bécanière!" and Barbette will hide you. If Galope-chopine should discover you he will either take you for a ghost if it's dark or ten crowns will make a friend of him if it's daylight. Good-bye! Our account is settled. ... If you wished,' he added, waving his hand at the fields round his house, 'all that would be yours.'

Mademoiselle de Verneuil thanked this odd being with a look which drew his sigh with some very unusual variations from him.

'You will no doubt repay my ten crowns; notice I say nothing about interest. Lodge them to my credit with Maître Patrat, the notary, who if you liked would draw up our marriage contract, lovely treasure. ... Good-bye!'

'Good-bye,' she said smiling, with a friendly wave of the hand.

'If you need money,' he called after her, 'I'll let you have it at five per cent! Yes, only five ... Did I say five?'

She was gone.

'That looks to me a good girl,' d'Orgemont said to himself. 'All the same, I'll change the secret spring for the entrance to my chimney.'

Then he took a twelve-pound loaf and a ham and returned to his hiding place.

When Mademoiselle de Verneuil walked out into the open country she felt reborn. The coolness of the morning was fresh against her face which for hours had burned in a stifling atmosphere. She tried to find the path the miser had told her about; but it was so dark since the moon had set that she was forced to go on blindly. Presently a heart-stopping fear of falling over a cliff overcame her, and saved her life. She suddenly came to a standstill with a feeling that there was no ground before her feet. A colder wind caressing her hair, the murmur of water, an instinctive feeling, together made her realize that she was at the edge of the Saint-Sulpice cliffs. She rested with her arms about a tree and waited anxiously for the dawn, alarmed by a clinking of arms and sound of horses and human voices and thankful for the darkness which preserved her from falling into the hands of the Chouans, if, as the miser had said, they were surrounding Fougères.

Chapter 19

ABOVE, like night fires lighted to herald liberty, some glimmers tinged with crimson were appearing above the crests of the mountains whose bases remained dark blue, in solid contrast with the cloudy vapour floating among the hollows. Soon a ruby disk rose slowly on the horizon and the skies acknowledged it. The heights and hollows of the countryside, Saint-Leonard's tower, the cliffs, the meadows wrapped in shadow, gradually reappeared, and the trees on the summits were sketched against its growing fire.

The sun leapt up and gracefully threw off its enveloping scarfs of flame, ochre and sapphire. Its intense light flowed in level rays from hill-top to hill-top and flooded into hollow after hollow. The shadows were scattered; day took possession of the world. A sharp breeze shivered through the air, the birds sang, life everywhere awoke. But the girl scarcely had time to look down over the masses of this surprising countryside before, as often happens in these cool regions, swirls of vapour spread into sheets, filled the valleys and rose to the highest hills, shrouding the rich basin in a snowy mantle. Soon it seemed to Mademoiselle de Verneuil that she was looking out over an Alpine sea of ice. Then this cloudy air heaved up waves like the ocean, raised opaque billows which softly swayed, eddied, violently swirled, took on tints of bright pink in the sun's rays, with transparent openings here and there apparently revealing a fluid silver lake. The north wind blew suddenly on the phantasmagoria, dissipating the mist, which precipitated a fertilizing dew over the meadows.

Mademoiselle de Verneuil could then see a great brown mass disposed about the Fougères heights. Seven or eight hundred armed Chouans were swarming around the Faubourg Saint-Sulpice like ants in an anthill. The outworks of the Castle were being furiously attacked by three thousand men, sprung up as if by magic. The sleeping town, in spite of its grassy ramparts and old grey towers, would have fallen if Hulot had not been vigilant. A battery hidden on an eminence within the bowl formed by the ramparts replied instantly to the first shots, raking the Chouans with an oblique fire on the road south of the castle. The grapeshot swept the road and cleared it. Then a company sallied from the Saint-Sulpice Gate, taking advantage of the Chouans' disarray, took up a battle position along the road and opened fire with devastating effect. The Chouans did not attempt to fight back, seeing the castle ramparts fill with soldiers as though a theatrical scene-shifter had brought on their blue-clad lines, and the Republican sally-party protected by the castle guns.

Other Chouans, however, held the little Nançon valley. They had scaled the Rock from gallery to gallery and reached the Promenade and were now climbing on to it, so that it was covered with goatskins, giving it the appearance of a thatched roof darkened by time. At the same moment violent detonations were heard in the part of the town looking out on the Couësnon Valley. Evidently Fougères was being attacked on all sides and completely surrounded. Flames bursting out to the east side of the Rock showed that the Chouans were even setting fire to the outskirts of the town. The sparks and fiery flakes rising from broom and shingle roofs, however, soon ceased and columns of black smoke showed that the blaze was under control. Clouds of white and brown smoke concealed the scene again from Mademoiselle de Verneuil's gaze, but the wind soon carried this powder smoke away.

Almost before the Republican Commandant from his high observation point above the Promenade had seen his first instructions admirably carried out, he had redirected the battery fire to sweep one after the other the Nançon Valley, the Queen's Staircase and the Rock. Two cannon from their emplacement at the Saint-Leonard Gate guard-post cut through the swarm of Chouans who had seized that position, while the Fougères National Guard who had rushed to the Place in front of the church completed the enemy's rout.

This battle did not last half an hour and did not cost the Blues a hundred men. Already the crushed and defeated Chouans were withdrawing in all directions, obeying the Gars's urgent orders. His daring attempted coup had failed, although he did not know it, as a result of the affair at La Vivetière, which had brought Hulot back in such secrecy. The ordnance had only arrived that night; for just the rumour of an artillery-train would have sufficed to make Montauran abandon the enterprise, which could not hope to succeed if there was wind of it. Hulot was as anxious, in fact, to give the Gars a sharp lesson as the Gars could be to succeed in his attempt to bring some weight to bear on the First Consul's decisions. At the first thunder of cannon, therefore, the Marquis had understood that it would be madness to follow up through pride an attempted surprise that had come off badly. So to avoid the useless slaughter of his Chouans he had made haste to send seven or eight messengers with orders for a general retreat at all points forthwith.

The Commandant, having observed his adversary on the Saint-Sulpice Heights, surrounded by a large council of war among whom was Madame du Gua, let fly at them with a volley; but the place had been too well chosen for the young leader to be exposed to that kind of danger. Hulot changed his tactics now, and from undergoing attack suddenly became the aggressor. At the first movements that indicated the Marquis's intentions, the Company positioned under the castle walls set themselves to cut off the Chouans' retreat by taking possession of the higher exits from the Nançon Valley.

In spite of her hatred Mademoiselle de Verneuil had backed the cause of the men her lover commanded, and turned anxiously to see if the other way out were open. But she observed Blues, no doubt victorious on the other side of Fougères, returning from the Couësnon Valley by the Vale of Gibarry to secure Nid-aux-Crocs and that part of the Saint-Sulpice Heights in which the lower exits from the Nançon Valley lay. The Chouans, shut off in the narrow plain of that gorge, must perish, it seemed, to the last man – the veteran

Republican Commandant had so exactly foreseen what would happen and so well calculated his counter-measures.

But at those two places the cannon that had served Hulot so well could not be used, and fierce close-range fighting developed there. With no further attack being made on the town of Fougères, the engagement became the kind of fighting the Chouans were accustomed to.

Mademoiselle de Verneuil now understood the reasons for the presence of the large numbers of men she had seen outside Fougères, the gathering of the leaders at d'Orgemont's house, and all the events of that night; and marvelled at her escape among so many dangers. She was so intensely interested in the fortunes of this raid, a last throw dictated by despair, that she stood there watching the changing animated scenes before her.

Soon the battle being fought at the foot of the Saint-Sulpice Heights had an added interest. Seeing that the Blues were pressing the Chouans hard, the Marquis and his friends rushed down into the Nançon Valley in support. The lower part of the cliffs was covered with a multitude of fiercely fighting groups, fighting to the death on terrain and with arms that favoured the Goatskins. Little by little this moving battlefield extended its area. The Chouans, practising their usual fighting withdrawal, swarmed up the cliffs, making use of the bushes growing here and there. Mademoiselle de Verneuil felt a rather belated thrill of apprehension as she saw her enemies on the cliff-tops, furiously defending the dangerous upward paths. With all the ways between the plateau and Fougères held by the two sides, she was afraid of finding herself surrounded, and thinking that she might now profit by the advice the old miser had given her, she left the big tree she had sheltered behind and fled.

When she had run for some time towards that part of the plateau overlooking the Couësnon Valley she saw a stable in the distance that might belong to Galope-chopine's house. His wife must have been left alone during the battle, so she felt encouraged to hope that she might be made welcome in this dwelling and spend a few hours there until it was possible to return to Fougères without danger. By all appearances

Hulot was about to carry the day. The Chouans were withdrawing so rapidly that she heard shots all round her, and fear made her hurry to reach the cottage whose chimney marked her goal.

The path that she had followed ended at a kind of outhouse, with a broom-thatched roof supported by four large tree-trunks still bearing their bark. A mud wall formed the back of this shed, which sheltered a cider-press, a threshing-floor for buckwheat and some farm implements. She came to a halt by one of the posts, unable to make up her mind to cross the dirty swamp which was the yard of this dwelling which from a distance, like a true Parisian, she had taken to be a stable.

The cabin was protected from the north winds by the hill which rose above its roof and against which it was built. It did not lack picturesqueness, for elm shoots, heather and the wild flowers of rocky places spread their garlands above it. A flight of rustic steps cut out between the shed and the house allowed the occupants to climb the crag for a breath of fresh air at the top. To the left of the cabin the height fell away abruptly, revealing a series of fields of which the first no doubt belonged to this holding. Graceful groups of trees rose among the fields, which were separated by high banks planted with hedgerow trees. The nearest bank closed in the yard on the other side.

The path leading to the fields was blocked by a heavy tree-trunk, half-decayed, a Breton form of barrier with a name which must be the subject of a digression later in order to complete the description of this country.

Between the steps hollowed out of the stone and the path closed by the large tree, facing the swamp and under the overhanging rock, a number of roughly squared granite blocks were built up to make the four corners of the cabin and hold the wretched cob, boards and stones of which the walls were made. The roof was partly thatched with broom and partly shingled with the kind of stave-wood coopers use cut into the shape of slats, a division which indicated that there were two rooms; and in fact one part, closed by a rickety hurdle, served as a stable and the owners lived in the other.

The nature of this cabin, which indeed owed certain amenities to its nearness to the town not found in others two leagues further away, throws some light on the instability of the serf's existence under the feudal system. The wars and usages of feudal life made the villein's individual manner of existence of so little consequence that to this day many peasants in these regions give the name of *house* only to the château inhabited by their lords.

As she examined this place with understandable surprise, Mademoiselle de Verneuil presently noticed pieces of broken granite placed here and there in the farmyard dirt as stepping stones to make a hazardous causeway to the cottage; and hearing the rattle of gun-fire appreciably closer she went on to ask for shelter, jumping from stone to stone as if crossing a stream.

The house door was of the kind divided horizontally into two separate halves, the lower of ordinary solid wood, the upper a kind of shutter, serving as window when open. This type of door is to be seen in many shops in certain small towns in France, but much more elaborately finished and with a little bell on the lower part to warn of customers' entry. This one had a primitive wooden latch worthy of the golden age, and the upper part was evidently closed only at night as the opening was the only source of light. There was indeed a roughly made window, but its panes were like bottle bottoms and the lead holding them took up so much space that it seemed to intercept the light rather than let it in.

When Mademoiselle de Verneuil pushed the door open on its creaking hinges she was met by gusts of noisome ammoniac vapours from within, and saw that the animals had kicked the interior wall that separated them from the room to pieces. So the interior of the farmhouse, for it was a farmhouse, did not belie the exterior.

Mademoiselle de Verneuil was asking herself if it were possible for human beings to be living in such filthy conditions when a little ragged boy of about eight or nine suddenly appeared and held up his fresh rosy face to her, with round plump cheeks, bright eyes, ivory teeth and flaxen hair falling in silky locks on his half-naked shoulders. His limbs were robust, and with his childish charm of round-eyed wonder and artless surprise he was enchanting in his beauty.

'Where is your mother?' Marie asked gently, stooping to kiss his eyes.

After the kiss the child slipped away like an eel and disappeared behind a dunghill set on the ridge between the path and the house. It was Galope-chopine's habit to pile his manure on high ground as many Breton farmers do, practising a method of husbandry entirely their own, so that when they come to make use of it the rain has leached it of all its fertilizing power.

Left alone in the dwelling meanwhile, Marie had soon taken stock of its contents. The room where she was waiting for Barbette was the only one in the house. The most striking and pretentious feature of it was a vast fire-place whose *mantel*-shelf was a slab of blue granite. The meaning and derivation of the word was underlined by a strip of green serge with a scallop-edging of pale green ribbon mantling this shelf, and in the middle stood a statuette of the Virgin of coloured plaster. On the base Marie read two lines of a sacred poem very popular in the region:

> I am the Mother of God,
> Protectress of this place.

Behind the Virgin a deplorable picture, stained with red and blue blotches rather than painted, represented Saint Labre. A green serge-draped box bed of the kind known as a *tomb*, a crudely-made child's crib, a spinning wheel, clumsy chairs, a carved dresser with some household utensils, made up almost the whole of Galope-chopine's furnishings. In front of the window stood a long chestnut table with two benches of the same wood, to which the opaque glass lent the sombre hue of old mahogany. An enormous cask of cider was proof that Galope-chopine's Chouan nickname, which means *Pint-sinker*, was no misnomer, and Mademoiselle de Verneuil noticed that a damp yellowish mud beneath its bung was eating away the hard floor of granite chips bound with a reddish clay.

Mademoiselle de Verneuil raised her eyes and looked up, away from this spectacle, and then it seemed to her that she was looking at all the bats on earth, there were so many spiders' webs hanging thickly from the rafters. On the long table there were two enormous *pichés*, full of cider. A *piché* is a kind of brown earthenware jar found in a similar design in several parts of France, and a Parisian can picture it for himself if he imagines the pot in which gourmets serve Breton butter with a rounder belly, glazed in patches here and there, and with splotches of brown and fawn like some kinds of shellfish. This vessel is topped with what looks like the throat and head of a frog sticking out of the water taking the air. Marie's gaze rested finally on these two *pichés*; and then the noise of the fighting becoming all at once more distinct made her think she must look for somewhere to hide without waiting for Barbette, when that woman suddenly appeared.

'Good day, Bécanière,' she said to her, suppressing an involuntary smile at the sight of a face very like the heads architects place above transept arches.

'Ah, so you come from d'Orgemont,' answered Barbette, with no great enthusiasm.

'Where are you going to put me? For the Chouans are here ...'

'There,' said Barbette, bewildered by the strange attire as well as the beauty of a being she hardly dared consider a woman like herself, 'there, in the priest's hiding-place.'

She led her to the bed-head, to the space between bed and wall, but they were distracted by the noise of a stranger apparently floundering through the swamp. Barbette had barely time to pull a curtain from the bed and wrap it round Marie before she found herself face to face with a Chouan fugitive.

'Where is there a place to hide here, old woman? I am the Comte de Bauvan.'

Mademoiselle de Verneuil shuddered as she recognized the voice of the guest who had spoken a few words, still a mystery to her, that had precipitated the catastrophe at La Vivetière.

'I'm sorry, as you can see, Monseigneur, there's *naught* here!

What's the best thing I can do is go out and watch, and if the Blues come, I'll warn you. If I stayed and they found me with you they'd burn my house.'

And Barbette went out, for she was not so clever as to find a way of reconciling the interests of two enemies with equal rights to the hiding-place by virtue of her husband's double rôle.

'I have two bullets left,' the Comte said despondently, 'but the Blues are all round and in front already. Bah! I should be very unlucky if they returned this way and took it into their heads to look under the bed.'

He set his gun down carelessly close to the bed-post where Marie was standing wrapped in the green serge, and bent down to make sure that there was room for him under the bed. He was assuredly about to catch sight of the feet of the other fugitive, and in this desperate moment she seized the gun, jumped quickly out into the room and threatened the Comte with it. He burst out laughing as he recognized her, for in order to hide Marie had taken off her wide Chouan hat and her hair was cascading in heavy tresses from under a kind of lace cap.

'It's no joke for you, Comte; you are my prisoner. Just make a movement and you shall see what an insulted woman is capable of.'

The Comte and Marie were looking at each other with very mixed emotions when confused voices shouted from the rocks, 'Look out, the Gars!' 'Scatter! Scatter!' 'Run, the Gars, run!'

Barbette's voice rose above the tumult outside and was heard by the two enemies in the cottage with very different feelings; she was speaking less to her little boy than to them.

'Don't you see the Blues?' Barbette cried sharply. 'Come here, you naughty codlin, or I'll go after you! Do you want to get shot? Come on, run away quick!'

As these incidents followed one another in rapid succession, a Blue jumped into the swamp.

'Beau-pied,' called Mademoiselle de Verneuil.

At the sound of this voice Beau-pied came running into the cottage, and took a rather surer aim at the Comte than his former rescuer.

'*Aristo*,' said the soldier, who was enjoying himself, 'don't move, or I'll blow you up like the Bastille in double quick time.'

'Monsieur Beau-pied,' said Mademoiselle de Verneuil, cooing like a dove, 'you will answer to me for this prisoner. Do what you like with him, but you must hand him over to me safe and sound at Fougères.'

'Right, Madame.'

'Is the road to Fougères clear now?'

'Unless the Chouans resurrect themselves, it's safe.'

Mademoiselle de Verneuil armed herself gleefully with the light sporting gun and mockingly smiled as she said to the prisoner, 'Good-bye, Monsieur le Comte, *au revoir*!', and departed along the path after resuming her wide hat.

'I learn a little too late,' said the Comte de Bauvan sarcastically, 'that one should never make jokes about the honour of ladies who no longer possess it.'

'*Aristo*,' Beau-pied threatened him roughly, 'if you don't want to be sent to your *ci-devant* heaven don't say a word against that beautiful lady.'

Mademoiselle de Verneuil returned to Fougères by the paths leading down from the Saint-Sulpice Heights to the Nid-aux-Crocs hills. Then when she had reached them, as she hastened along the tortuous road cut out across the slope of the rugged granite, she looked down from this lower level, wondering at the serenity of the pretty little valley of the Nançon, in such tumult only a short time before. Seen from this angle the vale was a wide avenue paved with verdant sward. She came in by the Saint-Leonard Gate to which the little road leads. The towns people, still uneasy about the outcome of the battle, which according to the gunshots heard in the distance seemed as if it must last the whole day, were waiting there for the return of the National Guard, anxious to learn how many men they had lost.

The sight of this girl in her bizarre assortment of garments, her hair in disorder, a gun in her hand, her shawl and dress the worse for being rubbed against walls, soiled by mud and damp with dew, excited a lively curiosity, all the more intense because the power in the hands of this Parisian, her beauty and strangeness, were already the talk of the town.

Chapter 20

FRANCINE had waited for her mistress all night in the most dreadful anxiety; but when she saw her again her attempt to speak was silenced by a kind friendly gesture.

'I am not dead, child,' said Marie, and then after a pause; 'Ah, was I looking for excitement when I left Paris? . . . Well, I have found it.'

Francine was about to go out to order a meal, saying that her mistress must be badly in need of one.

'Oh, a bath, a bath!' said Mademoiselle de Verneuil. 'That's what I need first of all.'

Francine was not a little surprised to hear her mistress call for the most elegant of the fashionable dresses she had brought from Paris. After breakfasting, Marie dressed – a task to which she devoted all the care and attention to detail of a woman engaged in the important business of preparing for a ball where she is to meet the gaze of someone dear. Her mistress's mocking gaiety perplexed Francine. It was not an expression of the joy of love – a woman is never at a loss to understand that – it was a voicing of concentrated malice, and boded no good.

Marie draped the curtains by the window with its arresting view over the panorama below with her own hands. Then she pulled the sofa near the fire, placed it in a flattering light and sent Francine to fetch flowers to give the room a festive air, and when Francine returned showed her where to place the flowers to the best effect. After a last satisfied look round the room she told Francine to send someone to claim her prisoner from the Commandant.

She stretched herself luxuriously on the sofa, not only because she needed rest but in order to pose in the attitude of graceful helplessness that in some women is irresistibly attractive. A languid softness, the provocative placing of her feet with the points of her slippers just peeping from the folds of the dress, her relaxed ease, the curve of her neck, everything was harmoniously arranged to produce a seductive effect, to the angle of her tapering fingers as her hand drooped from a cushion like the florets of a cluster of jasmine, and the sidelong glance from her eyes. She had burnt essences to fill the air with the sweet perfume that has such a softening effect on men's fibres and often paves the way to the triumphs that women wish to achieve without apparently seeking them. A few moments later the old soldier's heavy tread was audible from the drawing-room, with which her room communicated.

'Well, Commandant, where is my captive?'

'I have just detailed a dozen men to shoot him as taken with his weapon in his hand.'

'You have disposed of my prisoner!' she said. 'Listen, Commandant. A man's death, after the battle, cannot be very pleasing to you, if I read the cast of your features aright. Well, return my Chouan to me, give him a stay of execution and I'll be responsible for him! I declare to you that this aristocrat has become quite essential to me, and he'll cooperate in carrying out our plans. Besides, it would be absurd to shoot this amateur Chouan, like taking a gun to burst a balloon instead of a pin. For God's sake leave the cruel deeds to the aristocrats. Republics should be generous. If you had had the power would you not have pardoned the victims of Quiberon, and so many others? Come, send your dozen men to do a patrol and dine with me and bring my prisoner too. There's only another hour of daylight; and don't you see,' she added, smiling, 'if you delay, my toilette will lose all its effect.'

'But, Mademoiselle . . .' said the Commandant in some surprise.

'Well, what then? I understand your feelings, but you know the Comte is not likely to escape you. Sooner or later that overgrown butterfly will flutter again before your firing-squad.'

The Commandant slightly shrugged his shoulders, like a man obliged in spite of himself to do what a pretty woman wishes. And he returned half an hour later followed by the Comte de Bauvan.

Mademoiselle de Verneuil feigned to be taken by surprise by her two guests, and seemed embarrassed to be seen by the Comte so unceremoniously relaxing. Once she had read in the nobleman's eyes, however, that the first effect had been produced, she rose and gave them her attention with poised grace and courtesy. There was nothing studied or constrained in her bearing, smile, attitude or voice to give away her premeditation or her plans. Her behaviour was consistent, and nothing exaggerated allowed the thought that she might be affecting the manners of a world she had not lived in.

When the Royalist and the Republican were seated, she looked severely at the Comte. That nobleman knew women well enough to be aware that the offence he had committed against this one carried a death sentence. This suspicion notwithstanding, without being either merry or sad, he looked like a man who was not expecting such an abrupt termination. Within a short time it seemed ridiculous to him to fear death in a pretty woman's company. Soon Marie's air of severity began to give him *ideas*.

'Who knows,' he thought, 'whether the winning of a Comte's coronet might not please her better than the Marquis's coronet she has lost? Montauran is a dry stick, while I . . .' And he looked at himself with satisfaction. 'The least I can achieve is to save my head.'

These diplomatic reflections did not avail him much. The desire which the Comte promised himself he would feign for Mademoiselle de Verneuil became a violent flame that that dangerous lady had much pleasure in fanning.

'Monsieur le Comte,' she said, 'you are my prisoner and I have the right to dispose of you. Your execution will not take place without my consent, and I have too much curiosity to let you be shot now.'

'And if I were so obstinate as to refuse to talk?' he answered cheerfully.

'With someone respectable, you might perhaps refuse, but with a creature! Come now, Monsieur le Comte, that's impossible.'

These bitterly sarcastic words were *hissed with a forked*

tongue, to use Sully's phrase when speaking of the Duchesse de Beaufort, so venomously that the astonished nobleman could only stare at his malicious antagonist.

'Well,' she went on mockingly, 'not to belie your opinion, I'll be like those creatures, a *kind girl*. First of all, here's your gun.' And with a lightly derisive gesture she presented him with it.

'Upon my word and honour, Mademoiselle, you deal . . .'

'Ah!' she interrupted him. 'I have had enough of the word and honour of noblemen. It was upon that word that I entered La Vivetière. Your leader had sworn to me that I and my men should be safe there.'

'Vile treachery!' exclaimed Hulot, knitting his brows.

'The blame belongs to Monsieur le Comte,' she answered Hulot, with a wave of her hand towards the nobleman. 'There is no doubt the Gars had every wish to keep his word; but Monsieur le Comte spread some slanderous tale about me which confirmed all it had pleased the *Charette Mare* to suppose . . .'

'Mademoiselle,' said the Comte, in some distress, 'with my head on the block I would swear that I said no more than the truth . . .'

'When you said what?'

'That you had been the . . .'

'Say it, the mistress . . .'

'Of the Marquis de Lenoncourt, now the Duke, one of my friends,' finished the Comte.

'Now I might let you go to the firing-squad,' she said, apparently unmoved by the Comte's factual accusation, while he was dumbfounded by her seeming indifference, real or assumed, to this slur. 'But you may dismiss for ever the sinister picture of those bits of lead,' she went on, with a laugh; 'for you have no more offended my modesty than that friend did whom you would have me the . . . Oh, shame! Listen, Monsieur le Comte, did you visit my father, the Duc de Verneuil? Well? . . .'

Judging no doubt that it was unnecessary to let Hulot share the important confidence she was about to make, Mademoiselle de Verneuil beckoned the Comte nearer to her and whispered a few words in his ear. Monsieur de Bauvan uttered a confused exclamation of surprise and looked dazedly at her; and she quickly completed the picture she had just evoked in his memory by leaning against the chimney-piece in a child's artless innocent attitude. The Comte went down on one knee.

'Mademoiselle,' he exclaimed, 'I implore your pardon, though indeed my offence is unpardonable!'

'I have no need to pardon,' she said. 'Your repentance is as uncalled for now as your insolent supposition was at La Vivetière. But such matters are perhaps beyond your understanding. Only rest assured, Monsieur le Comte,' she went on gravely, 'that the daughter of the Duc de Verneuil is too magnanimous not to be keenly concerned about you.'

'Even after an insult,' said the Comte, with a tinge of regret.

'Some persons are too highly placed for insult to touch them, is that not so? I am such a person, Monsieur le Comte.'

This was said with an aristocratic hauteur that impressed the prisoner and made this intrigue much less clear to Hulot. The Commandant put a hand to his moustache as if to brush it up the wrong way and cast an uneasy look at Mademoiselle de Verneuil, and she glanced at him understandingly as if to assure him that this was all part of her plot.

'Now, let's talk,' she went on after a pause. 'Francine, give us some lights, my girl.'

She smoothly brought the conversation round to discussion of the times which had in such a few years become the *ancien régime*, and carried the Comte back completely to those days by the liveliness of her comments and descriptions. She gave him numerous opportunities to display his wit, slyly contriving openings for brilliant repartee. And in the end the Comte came to believe that he was a more charming fellow than he had ever thought before, and with the fresh youth that notion gave him he tried to make this seductive person share his good opinion of himself.

The girl amused herself maliciously by trying out all the devices of her coquetry on the Comte, and found it the easier to show off her skill since it was nothing but a game to her.

Sometimes she let him believe that he was making rapid progress, and sometimes, as if astonished at the keenness of her own feelings, she showed a coldness that charmed the Comte and insensibly increased this instant passion. She was exactly like an angler who raises his line from time to time to see if the fish is biting. The poor Comte let himself be hooked by the innocent way his preserver accepted two or three not badly turned compliments. The Royalist *émigrés*, the Republic, Brittany and the Chouans were a thousand leagues from his thoughts.

Hulot sat stiffly, motionless and silent as the god Terminus. His lack of education made him quite useless at this kind of conversation. He had some inkling, certainly, that the two conversationalists were being very witty; but all he could do was try to understand enough to be sure that they were not covertly weaving plots against the Republic.

'Montauran, Mademoiselle,' the Comte was saying, 'has blue blood, he's well brought up, a handsome boy; but he knows nothing whatever about gallantry. He is too young to have seen Versailles. His education has been neglected, and he's readier with a sword-thrust than a damaging aspersion. He's capable of falling violently in love, but he'll never have that fine flower of gallant manners that distinguished Lauzun, Adhémar, Coigny, and so many others! . . . He has no notion of the pleasant art of flattering women with pretty nothings, which suit them much better after all than gusts of passion, which they soon find wearying. Yes, although he's a man women fall easily in love with, he just doesn't possess the ease or grace for love affairs.'

'Yes, I noticed that,' Marie answered.

'Ah!' the Comte said to himself. 'There was an inflection in her voice there, and a look, signs that I'll not have to wait long to be on the *best possible terms* with her; and upon my word, if she only lets me be hers I'll believe anything she wants me to believe.'

He offered her his hand, for dinner was served. Mademoiselle de Verneuil did the honours of the repast with a polished courtesy and tact that could only have been acquired by

271

education and within the elegant conventional life of the Court.

'You go off,' she said to Hulot as they left the table. 'You will frighten him; while if I'm alone with him I shall soon know all I need to. He has reached the point where a man tells me all his thoughts and looks at things only through my eyes.'

'And afterwards?' asked the Commandant, with the air of claiming his prisoner again.

'Oh, free!' she answered. 'He shall be free as the air.'

'All the same, he was taken with his weapon in his hand.'

'No,' she said, with the kind of mocking sophistry that women enjoy opposing to peremptory right, 'I had disarmed him.'

As she entered the next room, 'I have just obtained your freedom, Comte,' she said to the nobleman. 'But nothing for nothing,' she added, smiling and putting her head on one side questioningly.

'Ask anything of me, even to my name and honour!' he exclaimed rapturously. 'I lay everything at your feet.'

And he strode forward to seize her hand in an attempt to make her accept his passionate desire as passionate gratitude; but Mademoiselle de Verneuil was not a person likely to make such a mistake. 'Would you make me regret my trust?' she said, smiling in a way that gave some hope to this new admirer, but moving back a few paces.

'A girl's imagination runs faster than a married woman's,' he answered with a laugh.

'A girl has more to lose.'

'That's true. One must be mistrustful when one bears a treasure.'

'Enough of this,' she said; 'let's talk seriously. You are giving a ball at Saint-James. I hear that you have established your magazines and arsenal there, and your centre of government. When is the ball?'

'Tomorrow evening.'

'It will not surprise you, Monsieur, that a slandered woman should show a feminine obstinacy in demanding public acknowledgement of the wrong done her in the presence of those who heard her insulted. So I shall go to your ball. I ask you to give me your protection from the moment I appear there to the moment I leave . . . I don't want fine words,' she said, seeing him place his hand on his heart. 'I detest oaths, they imply too much doubt. Simply say to me that you pledge yourself to protect me from any criminal or outrageous attempt against my person. Promise me to do something to atone for the wrong you did me, proclaim that I am certainly the Duc de Verneuil's daughter and keep quiet about all the misfortunes I suffered through lack of a father's protection. Then we shall be quits. Ha! Two hours' protection for a woman at a ball – that's not asking a lot for your ransom, is it? Well, you're not worth a stiver more! . . .' And with a smile she effaced all the bitterness of her words.

'What do you ask for returning my gun?' the Comte asked laughing.

'Oh, a higher price than for you.'

'What price?'

'Secrecy. Believe me, Bauvan, only a woman can read another woman's mind. I am certain that if you say a word I am likely to perish on the way. I was warned by bullets yesterday of the dangers I may expect on the road. Oh, that lady is capable of shooting me as efficiently as she undressed me. I have never had a maid disrobe me so quickly. Ah, for mercy's sake arrange matters so that I have nothing of that kind to fear at the ball! . . .'

'You will be there under my protection,' answered the Comte self-importantly. 'But will you be coming to Saint-James for Montauran's sake?' he went on, in a rather crest-fallen way.

'You want to know more than I do myself,' she said laughing. 'Now you must go,' she added after a pause. 'I'll escort you out of the town myself, for it's a cannibal war you are waging here.'

'So you are a little concerned about me?' said the Comte triumphantly. 'Ah, Mademoiselle, allow me to hope that you will not be indifferent to my friendship; for I suppose I must be content with friendship, mustn't I?' he added fatuously.

'Ah, that is for you to guess!' she said, with the joyous lightness of a woman appearing to make an admission, but at no cost to her dignity or private feelings.

Then she put on a pelisse and accompanied the Comte as far as Nid-aux-Crocs. At the end of the path, she said to him, 'Monsieur, be absolutely discreet, even with the Marquis.' And she put a finger to her lips.

The Comte, made bold by Mademoiselle de Verneuil's air of kindness, took her hand, and, when she permitted this as a great favour, kissed it tenderly.

'Oh, Mademoiselle, count on me for life or death!' he exclaimed, seeing himself now beyond risk of danger. 'The debt I owe you for my life is almost equal to the debt I owe my mother, but it will be very difficult for me to feel only filial respect . . .'

He set off along the path. When she saw him reach the Saint-Sulpice Heights Marie nodded in a satisfied way and murmured to herself, 'That fat gentleman has given me something worth a lot more than his life in exchange for his life. I could make him my creature at little cost! A creature or a creator, that's all the difference there is between one man and another.'

She did not complete her thought but cast a despairing look at the sky, and slowly returned to the Saint-Leonard Gate, where Hulot and Corentin were awaiting her.

'Two more days,' she exclaimed, 'and . . .' she stopped, seeing that Hulot was not alone, ' . . . and your guns will lay him low,' she said in Hulot's ear.

The Commandant stepped back a pace and looked in a quizzical way, difficult to describe, at this girl whose bearing and face showed no trace of compunction. There is this to be said for women, that they never consider the rights or wrongs of their most reprehensible actions: they are governed by feeling. Even in their double-dealing there is a natural straightforwardness of impulse, and it is only in women that one will find crime without baseness. Most of the time, women *just don't know how their action happened.*

'I'm going to Saint-James, to the ball the Chouans are giving and . . .'

'But that's five leagues from here,' Corentin interrupted. 'Would you like me to escort you?'

'You are much concerned,' she said to him, 'with something I never think of – yourself.'

Marie's evident scorn for Corentin was oddly pleasing to Hulot, and he screwed up his face in his usual grimace as he watched her disappear in the direction of Saint-Leonard's Church. Corentin too followed her with his eyes, his face openly showing his inner certainty of holding this charming creature ineluctably in his power, convinced as he was that he could turn her passions to his own uses and find her his in the end.

On her return home the first thing Mademoiselle de Verneuil did was to consider her ball dresses. Francine, by now accustomed to obeying her mistress without ever understanding her ultimate intentions, ransacked the boxes and suggested a Greek toilette. Fashion at that time showed Greek influence in everything. The dress Marie decided on could be packed in an easily-carried band-box.

'I'm going on a rough journey across country, Francine,' she said. 'You can stay here, child, or come with me, as you please.'

'Stay here?' exclaimed Francine. 'And who's to dress you if I did?'

'Where did you put the glove I gave you this morning?'

'Here it is.'

'Sew a green ribbon to the glove, and don't forget to bring money.' Then, seeing Francine holding some new-minted coins, 'That's all we need to get ourselves murdered,' she exclaimed. 'Send Jérémie to waken Corentin. No, the wretched man would follow us! Send to the Commandant instead and ask him to let me have some old-currency six-franc crowns.'

With the feminine foresight that covers the smallest details, she thought of everything. While Francine was completing the preparations for this unimaginable sallying forth, she set herself to practise mimicking the owl's hoot and achieved a passable imitation of Marche-à-terre's signal. At midnight she left by the Saint-Leonard Gate, reached the little path to Nid-aux-Crocs, and ventured, followed by Francine, across the Vale of Gibarry, walking steadily, sustained by the resolute will that in some unknown fashion gives firmness to the step and powerfully increases the stamina. Just how to avoid catching cold as they leave a ball is a matter women usually think worth serious consideration, but let them have a passion in their heart and their bodies are made of steel. It would have taken a bold man a long time to make up his mind to such an enterprise as this one; but it had scarcely occurred to her imagination before its dangers became so many attractions.

'You are leaving without commending yourself to God's care,' said Francine, who had turned to contemplate Saint-Leonard's tower.

The devout Breton girl stopped, clasped her hands, and repeated an *ave* to Saint Anne of Auray, imploring her to give a happy outcome to this journey; while her mistress stood by plunged in thought, looking in turn at the artless pose of her fervently praying maid and the effect of the hazy light of the moon as it sailed behind the church's pierced openings, giving the granite the lightness of filigree.

Chapter 21

THE two travellers soon reached Galope-chopine's cottage. The light sound of their footsteps was loud enough to awaken one of those great dogs to whose faithful guardianship the Bretons entrust the simple wooden latch that secures their doors. The dog rushed towards the two strangers, and his barking became so menacing that they were forced to call for help and retreat a little way; but nothing stirred. Mademoiselle de Verneuil uttered the owl's cry. Immediately the rusty hinges of the cottage door squeaked sharply and Galope-chopine, hastily risen from bed, showed his sinister face.

'I must go at once to Saint-James,' said Marie, presenting the Marquis de Montauran's glove to the Chouan official look-out man for Fougères. 'Monsieur le Comte de Bauvan told me that you were the person who would guide me there and act as guard. So, my good Galope-chopine, get us two riding asses and prepare to escort us. Time is precious, because if we don't arrive at Saint-James before tomorrow evening, we'll see neither the Gars nor the ball.'

Galope-chopine, gaping with amazement, took the glove, turned it over and looked at every side. He lit a resin candle, about as thick as a little finger and the colour of gingerbread. The use of this commodity, imported into Brittany from Northern Europe, argues complete ignorance of even the most elementary principles of commerce, as does everything else that meets one's eye in this odd country.

When he had seen the green ribbon and looked at Mademoiselle de Verneuil, scratched his ear and drunk a *piché* of cider after offering a glass to the fine lady, Galope-chopine left her sitting on the polished chestnut bench before the table and went to find two asses.

The violet glimmer thrown by the exotic candle was too feeble to outshine the intermittent gleams of moonlight that set bright points along the floor and furniture, deepening their dark tones in the smoke-blackened cabin. The little boy had raised his sweet surprised head, and above his silky hair the pink muzzles and large lustrous eyes of two cows were visible through the holes in the stable wall. The great dog, whose physiognomy was not the least intelligent in the family, seemed to be examining the two strangers with the same curiosity as the child. It was a night-piece that would have held a painter for long; but as she saw Barbette sit up suddenly like a spectre and open round astonished eyes at recognizing her, Marie, far from anxious to start a conversation, escaped outside from the pestilent air and the questions La Bécanière would ask.

She lightly climbed the steps up the crag sheltering Galope-chopine's cabin, and stood looking out over the wide countryside with its immense variety of detail, where every step in any direction from mountain heights to the depths of valleys unfolds a different prospect. The moonlight was filling the Couësnon Valley with a luminous haze. No woman with a scorned love in her heart could fail to linger savouring the melancholy this gentle light awakens in the soul, with the fantastic appearance it gives unbroken masses and the nuances of light and shadow reflected on the water.

Soon, however, the silence was disturbed by the braying of the asses. Marie climbed down quickly to the Chouan's cabin and they left at once. Galope-chopine, armed with a double-barrelled shotgun, was wearing a long goatskin that made him look like Robinson Crusoe. His seamed and grog-blossomed face was barely visible under the wide hat that the peasants still preserve as a heritage from the past, proud after their years of servitude of having achieved the ancient adornment of seignorial heads. This nocturnal caravan, led by a guide whose attire, bearing and figure suggested patriarchal protection, was reminiscent of the painting of the Flight into Egypt that we owe to Rembrandt's sombre brush. Galope-chopine carefully avoided the main road and led the two strangers into the vast labyrinth of Breton cross-paths.

Mademoiselle de Verneuil then began to understand the

kind of war the Chouans were waging. Moving along these roads she could appreciate better the nature of the country which had appeared so entrancing to her viewed from above – only by walking through it was it possible to form a conception of its dangers and inescapable obstacles. Around every field and from time immemorial the peasants have built up banks of earth, six feet high, triangular in section, from the ridge of which grow chestnuts, oaks or beech trees. This earth wall, so planted, is called a *haie* (the Norman *haie* or hedge); and the trees that surmount it, almost always throwing out branches in long arms across the roads, weave above the roads an unending arbour roof. The roads themselves, so gloomily boxed in by walls of clayey soil, are like the moats round strongholds; and unless the granite, usually very near the surface in these regions, makes a kind of rough paving they become almost impassable, so that even the smallest cart can only negotiate them with the help of two pairs of oxen and two of the native horses, which are small but generally sturdy. The roads are normally so swampy that custom has perforce established a path for pedestrians in the field along the *haie*, called a *rote*, and this begins and ends with each successive unit of land. To pass from one field to another, then, one has to climb the *haie* by means of several steps often made slippery by rain.

The travellers had many other obstacles to get round along these tortuous ways. Each piece of land, thus fortified, has its entrance, about ten feet wide, closed by a kind of gate called in the West an *échalier*. The *échalier* is a tree-trunk or heavy branch one of whose ends has a hole bored through so that it fits on another piece of unshaped wood which serves as pivot. The end of the tree-trunk extends a little beyond this pivot to carry a heavy weight by way of counterpoise, so that a child can manoeuvre this peculiar rustic barrier, the other end of which rests in a hole made inside the *haie*. Sometimes the peasants economize on the counterpoise stone by letting the heavy end of the tree-trunk or branch project. The exact nature of the gate varies according to the invention of each landowner. It often consists of a single branch with ends sealed into the *haie* with earth. It often looks like a piece of lattice with several thin branches at equal distances like the rungs of a ladder laid on its side. That kind of gate pivots like an *échalier* and rolls to the other side on a little solid wheel.

The *haies* and *échaliers* covering the land make it look like a vast chess-board, of which each square is a field completely isolated from the others, sealed off like a fortress with rampart-like defences. The gate, easy to defend, gives assailants a most dangerous obstacle to storm.

The Breton peasant imagines that he is enriching his fallow land by encouraging the growth of giant furze, a shrub so well treated here that it rapidly attains a man's height. Thanks to this idea, worthy of people who deposit their manure-heap at the highest point in their yard, forests of furze bushes are raised in the fields, in one field out of four; and a thousand ambushes can be set up in their shelter. There is hardly a field, too, without a few old cider-apple trees extending their low drooping branches over the ground and smothering all growth. Add the small area of the fields, all supporting huge trees in their *haies* with greedy roots using a quarter of the ground, and you will have some idea of the cultivation and character of the land Mademoiselle de Verneuil was travelling through.

It is uncertain whether it is the need to discourage dispute or the slothful custom of putting animals to graze without guarding them that has made it advisable to construct these formidable enclosures, which form permanent obstacles making the country impregnable and military manoeuvre impossible. When one has investigated the terrain step by step it is clear that regular soldiers must inevitably fail against guerrilla partisans, for five hundred men can defy the troops of a whole kingdom. That was the whole secret of the Chouans' warfare.

Mademoiselle de Verneuil now understood the Republic's necessity to make what use it could of police agents and diplomacy to end the strife rather than deploy military force ineffectively. What could be done in fact against people so crafty as to care little about holding the towns but make sure of holding the countryside with indestructible fortifications? How could one fail to negotiate when the whole strength of these blindfolded peasants lay in a clever and daring leader? She marvelled at the genius of the Minister who saw while closed up in a study where peace must be looked for. It seemed to her that she caught a glimpse of the considerations that sway men strong enough to embrace a whole empire in their survey, and whose actions, criminal in the crowd's eyes, are only moves in the working out of a vast design. In the awe-inspiring achievements of such formidable men one does not know what part is due to fate or destiny, what mysterious prescience gives them signs that suddenly raise them above their fellows. The crowd looks for them one moment among its numbers, lifts its eyes, and sees them soaring far above. Such thoughts seemed in some sense a justification of Mademoiselle de Verneuil's desires for vengeance, and even made them appear noble; and then her heart-searching and her hopes infused her with sufficient vigour to bear the extraordinary fatigues of her journey.

At the boundary of each farmer's land Galope-chopine had to make the two travellers dismount and help them over the difficult crossing; and then again when the pathways in the fields came to an end they were obliged to take to their saddles and venture into the miry roads, which bore the marks of winter's approach. The large trees, sunken roads and heavy barriers together held a dampness in the low ground that often enveloped the travellers like an icy cloak. At sunrise, after toil and wearying struggle, they reached the Marignay forest. The journey became less arduous along the wide forest path. The arching branches above their heads, the close tracery of the trees, sheltered the travellers from the weather's inclemency; and the many and varied difficulties they had had to deal with previously were seen no more.

They had made scarcely a league through the forest when they heard a confused murmur of voices in the distance and the sound of a little bell whose silvery note was not the monotonous tinkle of the bells of moving cattle. As they went, Galope-chopine listened to the sound with close attention.

Soon a gust of wind brought some intoned words and this chant seemed to affect him strongly. He led the weary asses into a path which must take the travellers away from the road to Saint-James and turned a deaf ear to Mademoiselle de Verneuil's remonstrances. Her apprehensions were increased by the gloomy aspect of the place.

To the right and left enormous granite boulders rose, heaped one upon another in bizarre disorder. Among these blocks great roots wormed their way like huge snakes, searching for nourishment for a number of ancient beech trees at a considerable distance. The heaped rocks on both sides of the road gave it the appearance of some subterranean grotto renowned for its stalactites. Huge tumbled piles of stone stained with the green or whitish growth of mosses and interlaced with heather and dark-foliaged holly masked chasms and the entrances to several deep caverns. The three travellers had gone a short way along a narrow path when a most astonishing sight burst suddenly upon Mademoiselle de Verneuil's gaze, and she understood then the reason for Galope-chopine's stubbornness.

A semi-circular bowl of granite slabs in broken tiers, with tall dark ranks of pine trees and autumn-tinted chestnuts rising one above the other among their irregular steps, composed a vast natural amphitheatre. Into it the wintry sun was pouring pale colour rather than diffusing light, and autumn had spread its tawny carpet of dead leaves over all. At the centre of this chamber, which appeared to have had the Flood for architect, rose three enormous Druidic stones, a vast altar above which was fixed a banner taken from a church. About a hundred men were kneeling bare-headed and praying fervently in this arena and a priest assisted by two other clergy was saying Mass.

The austerity of the priestly vestments, the priest's feeble voice which sounded like a murmur in space, these conviction-filled men united by the same strong feeling kneeling before an altar without trappings, the bareness of the Cross, the wild rural genius of the natural temple, the hour, the place, all combined to lend this scene the naïve quality of simple self-forgetful devotion that marked the earliest era of the Christian faith.

Mademoiselle de Verneuil remained gazing, struck with wonder. This Mass celebrated in the depths of the forest, religion driven back to its source by persecution, the romance of earlier ages boldly set in a freakish upheaval of nature, these Chouans armed yet defenceless, cruel yet at prayer, men who were children too, resembled nothing she had ever before seen or imagined.

She well remembered having admired in her childhood the pomps and splendours of the Roman Church which are so flattering to the senses, but she had never yet known God alone, his Cross set on the altar, his altar on the ground; instead of the carved foliage and Gothic arches of cathedrals the autumn trees sustaining the sky's vault, instead of the myriad colours thrown by stained glass the sun's red-tinged rays and subdued gleams barely touching altar, priest and congregation. Men were there sharing an affirmation, not a doctrinal system, a prayer rather than a religion. But the human passions momentarily suppressed to leave the harmonies of this mystery undisturbed were presently to make their appearance on the scene and animate it dramatically.

When Mademoiselle de Verneuil arrived the Gospel reading was nearing an end. In the officiating priest she recognized the Abbé Gudin, not without some alarm, and she hastily withdrew beyond his line of vision behind an enormous broken granite boulder and drew Francine quickly after her; but it was impossible to tear Galope-chopine from the place he had chosen for his participation in the blessings of this service. She saw with relief that there was a way of escape among the confusion of slabs that would allow her to be off and away from her dangerous position before the rest of the congregation. Through a wide fissure in the rock she saw the Abbé Gudin mount a granite block serving as pulpit, and begin with the invocation: '*In nomine Patris et Filii, et Spiritus Sancti*'.

At these words all devoutly crossed themselves.

'My dear brethren,' the Abbé then addressed his hearers in a strong and resonant voice, 'we shall pray first for the dead:

Jean Cochegrue, Nicholas Laferté, Joseph Brouet, François Parquoi, Sulpice Coupiau, all of this parish and all dead of wounds received in the battle of the Pellerine and the besieging of Fougères. *De profundis*, etc. . . .'

This psalm was recited, according to custom, by priests and congregation alternately, the verses being repeated with a fervour that augured well for the response to the homily. After the psalm for the dead, the Abbé Gudin continued in an increasingly thunderous tone, for the former Jesuit was not unaware that the vehemence of the delivery was the most powerful of arguments to sway his barely civilized hearers.

'These defenders of God, Christians, have set you an example in duty,' he said. 'Are you not ashamed of what may be said of you in Heaven? If it were not for these blessed men who must have been welcomed with open arms by all the Saints, Our Lord might well believe that your parish has a population of heathen Moslemites! . . . Do you know what they are saying about you in Brittany and among the King's companions, my lads? . . . You don't know, do you? Well, I'll tell you. "Can you believe it!" they are saying. "The Blues have overturned the altars, killed the Recteurs, murdered the King and Queen; they want to take all the true believers of Brittany to make Blues of them like themselves and send them out of their parishes to fight in far away places where they run the risk of dying without confession and so going to hell for all eternity – and the *gars* of Marignay whose church they have burnt stand there with their arms hanging and do nothing! Shame upon them! This Republic of damned souls has sold God's land by public auction and the lands of the seigneurs, and divided the money among the Blues. And now as if it were not enough for it to gorge on our blood it is going to gorge on our money too. It has passed a decree taking three francs from every six-franc crown piece, just as it wants to take away three men out of every six. And the *gars* of Marignay have not taken up their guns to drive the Blues out of Brittany! What can they be thinking of? . . . Heaven will be closed to them, and they will never be able to find salvation!"

'That's what they are saying about you. It's your salvation that is at stake, Christians! It is your souls that you will save fighting for religion and the King. Saint Anne of Auray herself appeared to me the day before yesterday at half-past two. This is what she said to me just as I'm saying it to you. "You are a priest of Marignay?" "Yes, Madame, ready to serve you." "Well, I am Saint Anne of Auray, God's cousin, once removed. I am still at Auray although I'm here as well; and I have come so that you may tell the *gars* of Marignay that there is no salvation for them to hope for if they do not take up arms. So you are to refuse them absolution unless they serve God. You shall bless their guns, and *gars* who are free from sin cannot fail to shoot the Blues because their guns will be sanctified! . . ."

'And then she disappeared, leaving an odour of incense under the oak tree at Patte-d'oie. I marked the place. A fine wooden Virgin has been placed there by Monsieur le Recteur of Saint-James. The mother of Pierre Leroi, known as Marche-à-terre, went there to pray in the evening and was cured because of what her son has done. There she is among you, and you will see her with your own eyes walking by herself. It is a miracle shown you, like the resurrection of the blessed Marie Lambrequin, to prove to you that God will never forsake the Bretons' cause when they fight for His servants and the King. So, my dear brethren, if you wish to find salvation and show yourselves defenders of the King, our Seigneur, you must do whatever you are commanded to by the man the King has sent whom we call the Gars. Then you will not be like heathen Moslemites any more, and you will find yourself with all the *gars* of the whole of Brittany, under God's banner.

'You will be able to repay yourselves out of the Blues' pockets for the money they'll have stolen from you, for if your fields are left unsown while you are at war Our Lord and the King will give you what his dead enemies leave. Christians, do you want to have it said that the *gars* of Marignay lag behind the *gars* of Morbihan and the *gars* of Saint-Georges, and those of Vitré and Antrain, who are all serving God and the King? Will you let them take everything? Will you stand there like heretics with your arms crossed when so many Bretons are working out their salvation and saving their King?

' "You shall give up all for My sake!" So says the Gospel. We priests have already given up our tithes, haven't we? Give up everything then to fight this holy war! You will be like the Maccabees who freed Judaea. Everything will be forgiven you. The Recteurs and their Curés will be with you and you will triumph!

'Note this well, Christians,' he said in conclusion; 'it is only today we have the power to bless your guns. Those who do not take advantage of this act of grace will not find the Saint of Auray so compassionate again, she will not lend her ear to them in the same way as she did in the last war.'

This homily forcibly delivered in an emphatic voice with vigorous repeated gestures that made the preacher sweat seemingly produced little effect. The motionless peasants, their eyes fixed on the speaker, stood like statues; but it was soon clear to Mademoiselle de Verneuil that the Abbé had cast a spell over the crowd. Like a great actor, he had made his hearers respond as one man, speaking directly to their self-interest and passions. He had granted absolution in advance for their excesses and removed the only restraints that held these rough men to the observance of religious and social precepts. He had prostituted the ministry of the Church to serve political ends. In these Revolutionary times, indeed, every man turned what he had to a weapon for the benefit of his faction, and Christ's peace-bringing Cross became an instrument of war no less readily than the peacefully productive ploughshare.

Seeing no single being there with whom communication was possible, Mademoiselle de Verneuil turned to look at Francine and was not a little surprised to see her sharing the general fervour, devoutly telling her beads on a rosary that no doubt Galope-chopine had let her have during the sermon.

'Francine,' she whispered, 'you're surely not afraid of being a heathen Moslemite, are you?'

'Oh, Mademoiselle!' the Breton girl answered. 'Do you see Pierre's mother down there, walking? . . .'

The profound belief expressed in Francine's attitude was illuminating for Marie: the power of the sermon was brought home to her, the influence the clergy exerted throughout the rural districts, and the prodigious effectiveness of the scene which was just beginning. The peasants nearest the altar advanced one by one and kneeling held out their guns to the preacher, who placed them on the altar. Galope-chopine hurried forward to bring his old fowling-piece. The three priests intoned the *Veni Creator*, while the celebrant enveloped these instruments of death in a bluish cloud of incense, his gestures weaving interlacing patterns about them. When the breeze had blown the incense fumes away, the guns were distributed in order. Each man received his own gun kneeling from the hands of the priests who as they gave them intoned a prayer in Latin. When the armed men returned to their places the profound emotion of the congregation, silent until then, burst forth in a formidable but moving way.

'*Domine, salvum fac regem*! . . .' (God save the King!)

That was the prayer the preacher broke into thunderously, and it was twice passionately repeated. These shouts held something wild and warlike. The two syllables of the word *regem*, easily translated by these peasants, were declaimed with so much vehemence that Mademoiselle de Verneuil could not prevent her thoughts from turning back with sad emotion to the exiled Bourbons. These thoughts were linked with recollections of her own past life. Her memory recreated the festivities of the now scattered Court where she had shone. The figure of the Marquis was evoked in that setting. Then with a woman's natural volatility she forgot the scene before her eyes and returned to her plans for vengeance, on which her life was staked, but which a single look might bring to nothing. Thinking of how she might appear beautiful in the most decisive moment of her life, it occurred to her that she had no ornament for her hair for the ball, and was attracted by the idea of using some of the holly whose cockled leaves and scarlet berries caught her eye.

'Aha! If I fire at birds with this gun I may miss, but if it's Blues . . . never!' said Galope-chopine, nodding his head in satisfaction.

Marie studied her guide's face more closely, and found in him the type of all those that she had just seen. The old Chouan showed no sign of having even so much power of thought as a child. It was a simple delight that puckered his cheeks and forehead when he looked at his gun; but at the same time religious bigotry coloured his joy with a fanaticism that for a moment allowed this rude face to express civilized vices.

They soon reached a village, a group of four or five dwellings like Galope-chopine's, where the newly recruited Chouans gathered while Mademoiselle de Verneuil was finishing a frugal meal of bread and butter with milk and cheese. This band of irregulars was led by the Recteur, who held a crude crucifix now become a standard and was followed by a *gars* very proudly carrying the parish banner. Mademoiselle de Verneuil found herself perforce a member of this party, going like her to Saint-James. They quite naturally became her protectors against any kind of danger as soon as Galope-chopine had told the leader of the band, indiscreetly but as it turned out not unfortunately, that the beautiful *garce* for whom he was acting as guide was the Gars's good friend.

Chapter 22

TOWARDS sunset the three travellers arrived at Saint-James, a little town which owes its name to the English by whom it was built in the fourteenth century when they held sway over Brittany. Just outside it Mademoiselle de Verneuil saw a strange scene of war but paid it little attention, for the fear that she might be recognized by some of her enemies made her hurry on. Between five and six thousand peasants were encamped in a field. Their dress, rather like that of the requisitioned men on the Pellerine, was singularly unmilitary. This clamorous gathering of men was like a great fair. One needed to look closely to discover that these Bretons were even armed, for their very variously fashioned goatskins almost concealed their guns, and the weapon most in evidence was the scythe which some of them had taken up as a substitute for the gun that they had not yet received. Some were drinking and eating, others fighting or loudly disputing; but most were sleeping stretched out on the ground. There was no appearance of order or discipline. An officer in a red uniform caught Mademoiselle de Verneuil's eye; she supposed he must be in the English service. A little distance away two other officers seemed to be trying to teach some of the more intelligent Chouans how to fire two pieces of ordnance, which evidently formed the whole artillery of the future Royalist army. A welcoming roar greeted the *gars* from Marignay who were recognized by their banner. Thanks to the commotion set up in the camp by the arrival of these new recruits and the Recteurs, Mademoiselle de Verneuil was able to get by safely and entered the town.

She came to an unpretentious inn not very far from the house where the ball was to take place. The town was swarming with so many strangers that it was only with the greatest difficulty that she obtained a shabby little room. When she

289

was settled in it and Galope-chopine had handed over the boxes that contained her mistress's toilette to Francine, he still stood waiting in an indescribably irresolute attitude. At any other time it would have entertained Mademoiselle de Verneuil to see what a Breton peasant away from his own parish is like; but now she broke the spell by taking four six-franc crowns from her purse and presenting them to him.

'Take these,' she said to Galope-chopine; 'and oblige me by going straight to Fougères, without going through the camp or sampling the cider.'

The Chouan, astonished at such liberality, still stood looking from his four crowns to Mademoiselle de Verneuil and back again until she made a dismissive gesture, and he vanished.

'How can you send him away, Mademoiselle?' Francine protested. 'Didn't you see how the town is surrounded? How shall we leave it, and who is to protect you here? . . .'

'Haven't you your protector?' said Mademoiselle de Verneuil, and she mockingly gave a low owl's hoot like Marche-à-terre, and tried to mimic his crouch.

Francine blushed, and smiled sadly at her mistress's gaiety.

'But where is yours?' she said.

Mademoiselle de Verneuil abruptly drew her dagger and showed it to the frightened Breton girl who collapsed on a chair, clasping her hands.

'What are you trying to find by coming here, Marie?' she exclaimed imploringly, in a voice that required no answer.

Mademoiselle de Verneuil was busy twining together the sprigs of holly she had gathered.

'I don't know if this holly will look well in my hair,' she said. 'But perhaps a colouring as vivid as mine can carry off such a sombre hair ornament, what do you say, Francine?'

Several observations of the sort showed this strange girl in possession of complete freedom of mind and detachment while she was preparing for the ball. Anyone hearing her could hardly have credited the seriousness of this moment when her life was at stake.

A dress of Indian muslin, rather short and clinging as if it had been damped, did not conceal her delicately rounded lines. Over it she wore a red tunic, finely pleated, whose fullness fell in many soft folds, longer at the sides, in the graceful curve of Greek tunics. This voluptuous garment of the kind once worn by pagan priestesses veiled her figure slightly, and made the dress that the permissive mode of that period allowed women to wear less revealing. To mask its fashionable indecorum further, Marie covered her white shoulders, that the tunic left bare much too low, with a fine gauze scarf. She twisted her long hair into a Grecian knot, the flattened softened cone behind the head which by prolonging the line of the head gives so much grace to a woman's pose in many ancient statues; and some curls were set above the forehead, and fell on each side of her face in long shining ringlets. With this dress and hairstyle she perfectly resembled the Greek sculptors' supreme conception of a goddess.

Her smile approved this arrangement of her hair, which set off the beauty of her face from all points of view, and then she tried on the holly circlet she had made, with its numerous red berries which by a happy chance reflected the colour of the tunic in her hair. She twisted a few leaves to point a different way in casual contrast with the others, and looked in her glass to judge her toilette's general effect.

'I look dreadful this evening,' she said, as if she were surrounded by flatterers. 'I look like a statue of Liberty.'

She carefully placed her dagger in the centre of her corsage so as to let the jewelled hilt be seen, with its eye-catching rubies drawing the glance downward to the treasures that her rival had so shamefully laid bare.

Francine could not make up her mind to leave her mistress. When she saw her ready to go, she was able to find plenty of reasons for accompanying her, in all the difficulties a woman has to cope with going to a ball in a little town in the confines of Brittany. Francine would be needed, there was no question, to help Mademoiselle de Verneuil off with her cloak and the double foot covering which the mud and filth of the road had obliged her to put on, in spite of the dressing of gravel that had been laid on it, and Francine would have to remove the chiffon veil she was wearing over her head for concealment from the eyes of the Chouans. Curiosity had brought such a throng of Chouans to the house where the festivity was taking place that they were walking between two lines of them. Francine no longer tried to hold her mistress back, but when she had put the necessary finishing touches to a toilette that owed its effect to superlative freshness she remained in the courtyard, so that she might not abandon her mistress to the chances of her fate without being near enough to fly to her aid, for the poor Breton girl foresaw only disaster.

While Marie de Verneuil was on her way to the ball, a very strange scene was taking place in Montauran's apartment. The young Marquis had nearly finished dressing and was putting on the broad red ribbon which was to mark him as the most eminent personage of this gathering when the Abbé Gudin came in, looking anxious.

'Monsieur le Marquis, come quickly,' he said. 'There's uproar among the leaders and you're the only one who can pacify them. I don't know what it's about. They're talking of leaving the King's service. I think it's that accursed Rifoël that's at the bottom of the commotion. That sort of quarrel is always started by some piece of nonsense. Madame du Gua accused him of arriving for the ball not well enough dressed, so I was told.'

'That woman must be mad,' exclaimed the Marquis, 'to want . . .'

'The Chevalier du Vissard,' the Abbé interrupted him, 'answered that if you had given him the money promised in the King's name . . .'

'That's quite enough, Monsieur l'Abbé. I understand it all now. That was a pre-arranged scene, wasn't it, and you are their envoy . . .'

'I, Monsieur le Marquis?' the Abbé interrupted again. 'I am going to suppport you vigorously! And you will do me the justice, I hope, of believing that the re-establishment of our religion in France and the King's re-establishment on the throne of his ancestors are much more powerful inducements for me to exert my humble efforts than that Archbishopric of Rennes that you . . .'

The Abbé dared not go on, for at these words the Marquis had begun to smile sarcastically. But the young leader immediately suppressed his bitter reflections, and with a grim face followed the Abbé into a hall that rang with tumult and shouting.

'I recognize the authority of no one here!' Rifoël was exclaiming, casting blazing glances at all the men round him, with his hand on the hilt of his sword.

'Do you recognize that of common sense?' the Marquis asked him coldly.

The young Chevalier du Vissard, better known by his surname Rifoël, was silent before the General in command of the Catholic Armies.

'What is the matter, gentlemen?' the young leader said, scrutinizing the faces about him.

'What's the matter, Monsieur le Marquis?' returned a well-known smuggler, embarrassed like any man of the people in the presence of a high-born aristocrat. Such men are inhibited at first by traditional ideas, but as soon as they have crossed the barrier between them see only a man like themselves and recognize no distinctions at all. 'What's the matter is,' he said, 'that you don't come any too soon. I don't know how to use smooth words so I'll just speak straight out. I commanded five hundred men all through the last war. When we took up arms again I was able to find a thousand heads as hard as my own to serve the King. That makes seven years now that I've been risking my life for the good cause. I'm not blaming you, but the labourer is worthy of his hire. Now, to begin with, I want to be called Monsieur de Cottereau. I want my rank as Colonel confirmed, and if it isn't I'll negotiate terms for my surrender with the First Consul. My men and me, you see Monsieur le Marquis, have a devilish pressing creditor who keeps dunning us! . . . And that's this!' he added, slapping his stomach.

'Are the violins here?' the Marquis asked Madame du Gua in a lightly mocking tone.

But the smuggler had bluntly broached a subject too important to all his hearers, men both calculating and ambitious who had been for too long in suspense about what they might hope for from the King, for the young leader's disdainful lack of comment to end this scene. The impetuous young Chevalier du Vissard moved forward quickly to confront Montauran and took his hand urgently to oblige him to stay.

'I warn you, Monsieur le Marquis,' he said to him, 'that you are too casual in your treatment of men who have some right to the gratitude of the person you represent here. We know that His Majesty has given you complete authority to recognize our services, and they have to find their reward in this world or the next for the scaffold is set up for us every day. For my own part, I know that the rank of Brigadier . . .'

'You mean Colonel . . .'

'No, Monsieur le Marquis, Charette appointed me Colonel; and since the rank I speak of is incontestably mine I'm not pleading at all at this moment for myself, but for all my gallant brothers in arms whose services need to be acknowledged. Your signature and promise will be enough for them for the present. And I must say,' he added under his breath, 'that they let themselves be very easily satisfied. But,' and now he raised his voice, 'when the Sun rises at Versailles to shed its light on the glad days of the Monarchy, will the loyal subjects who have aided the King in France to conquer France easily obtain advancement for their families, pensions for widows, and the restitution of property seized so unwarrantably from them? I very much doubt it. And so, Monsieur le Marquis, documents attesting the services rendered will not be without their uses then. I don't doubt the King and never shall, but I have a great deal of distrust of those cormorants of Ministers and courtiers who will clamour considerations of public interest in his ears, and the honour of France, and what is best for the Crown, and stuff and nonsense of a thousand kinds. Then a loyal Vendéan or a brave Chouan will be a subject for derision because he'll be old, and the sword he has drawn in the Cause will be knocking against shanks withered by the hardships he's endured . . . So, can you think we're wrong?'

'You speak eloquently, Monsieur du Vissard, but a little too early in the day,' the Marquis answered.

'Listen, Marquis,' said the Comte de Bauvan in an undertone; 'upon my word, Rifoël has spoken very sensibly. You're always sure of having the King's ear; but what about us? We're only going to see the man at the top of the tree from farther and farther off; and I must say that if you don't give me your assurance on your word and honour that at the proper time and place you'll see that I obtain the office of Warden of the Woods and Forests of France, the devil fly away with me if I'd be right to risk my neck. To conquer Normandy for the King is no light task, so I've some grounds for hoping to be given the Order ... However,' he added, reddening, 'there's time enough to think of that. God forbid I should pester you like these poor devils. You'll mention my name to the King, and that'll do.'

Every one of the leaders found a more or less tactful way of letting the Marquis know the very high price he put on his services and the reward he expected. One modestly asked to be made Governor of Brittany, another wanted a Barony, some demanded promotion to high rank in the Army, others a certain Command, all wanted pensions.

'Well, Baron,' the Marquis said to Monsieur du Guénic, 'don't you want anything?'

Faith, Marquis, these gentlemen leave me nothing to ask for but the Crown of France, but I could make do with that ...'

'Gentlemen,' thundered the Abbé Gudin,' can't you see that if you are in such a hurry to claim your due, you'll ruin everything on the day of victory? Don't you know that the King will be obliged to make concessions to the Revolutionaries?'

'To the Jacobins!' exclaimed the smuggler. 'Ah, the King may let me deal with them. I'll guarantee to use my thousand men to hang them, and they'll soon be out of our way.'

'Monsieur *de* Cottereau,' said the Marquis, 'I see some of the guests we have invited coming in. We must use all our efforts and vie with one another in fervour and zeal in order to persuade them to cooperate in our sacred Cause. You will understand that it is not the appropriate moment to attend to your demands, however just.'

As he spoke the Marquis was moving towards the door as if going to meet several noblemen whose lands lay within reach of the town whom he had noticed arriving; but the bold smuggler respectfully and deferentially barred his way.

'No, no, Monsieur le Marquis. Pardon me; but the Jacobins taught us only too well in 1793 that it is not always those who cut the corn who eat the bread. Sign this bit of paper for me and tomorrow I'll bring you fifteen hundred stout fellows; otherwise I treat with the First Consul.'

A haughty look about him made it clear to the Marquis that the old partisan's boldness and blunt determination were not displeasing to any of those concerned in this discussion. One man sitting in a corner seemed to take no part in the scene and was busy filling a clay pipe. His air of despising the speakers, his unassuming attitude, and the commiseration the Marquis saw in his eyes made him look more closely at this undemanding servant of the King, in whom he recognized Major Brigaut. The leader turned to him abruptly.

'And you,' he said, 'what do you want?'

'Oh, if the King returns, Monsieur le Marquis, that's enough.'

'But for yourself?'

'A reward for me? . . . Monseigneur is joking.'

The Marquis gripped the Breton's horny hand, and then, moving off, said to Madame du Gua nearby, 'I may perish in this business, Madame, before I've had time to send the King a faithful report on the Catholic Armies of Brittany. If you see the Restoration, don't forget this gallant man nor the Baron du Guénic. There's much more true devotion in them than in all these people.'

And he gestured towards the chiefs who were waiting with a certain impatience for the young Marquis to allow their claims. They were all holding papers open in their hands, in which no doubt their services had been attested by the liberal Royalists of the previous wars, and they were all beginning to murmur. In their midst the Abbé Gudin, the Comte de Bauvan and the Baron du Guénic were debating how they could help the Marquis to repudiate these excessive claims, for they thought the young leader's position very delicate.

Suddenly the Marquis let his blue eyes, sparkling with unspoken sarcastic comment, wander over this assembly, and said in his clear voice, 'Gentlemen, I do not know if the powers the King has graciously entrusted to me are wide enough to allow me to satisfy your demands. He perhaps did not foresee such zeal and such devotion. You shall judge for yourselves what it is incumbent on me to do, and perhaps I shall be able to fulfil my obligations.'

He vanished, and returned at once with a document open in his hand bearing the royal seal and signature.

'These are the letters patent in virtue of which you are required to obey me,' he said. 'They authorize me to govern the provinces of Brittany, Normandy, Maine and Anjou, in the King's name, and to recognize the services of the officers who distinguish themselves in the Armies.'

A movement of lively satisfaction ran through the assembly. The Chouans moved nearer the Marquis and formed a respectful circle about him. All eyes were fixed on the King's signature. The young leader, standing before the fireplace, threw the document into the fire, where it was consumed in an instant.

'From now on I wish to command only men who see a King in the King, and not booty to be divided!' the young man cried. 'You are free, gentlemen, to desert me . . .'

Madame du Gua, the Abbé Gudin, Major Brigaut, the Chevalier du Vissard, Baron du Guénic, Comte de Bauvan enthusiastically raised the shout 'Long Live the King!' If at first the other leaders hesitated to take the cry up, they soon, carried away by the Marquis's noble gesture, begged him to forget what had just occurred and assured him that, letters patent or no, he should always be their chief.

'Let's go and dance,' cried the Comte de Bauvan, 'and let come what may! After all, my friends, it's better to make application to God than to his Saints,' he added gaily. 'Let's fight first and see what happens afterwards.'

'Ah, that's as it should be. With respect, Monsieur le Baron,' said Brigaut to the loyal Baron du Guénic under his breath, 'I have never before seen the day's wages asked for before the day was out.'

The assembly dispersed through the rooms, where a number of guests had already gathered. The Marquis tried ineffectually to shake off the sombre shadow that made his face look drawn. It was easy for the leaders to see the painful impression that this scene had made on a man in whom devotion was still linked with the idealistic dreams of youth; and they were ashamed.

A joyous exhilaration spread through this assembly of members of the Royalist party of the highest rank. Living as they did in the depth of an insurrectionary province, they had never been able to appreciate the facts of Revolutionary events, and were bound to regard as reasonable assumptions what were really hopes founded on nothing. The bold operations Montauran had begun, his name, his success, his ability, fired everyone's ardour and aroused that political intoxication which is the most dangerous kind of all because it is only quenched by torrents of blood almost **invariably** shed to no purpose.

For all the persons present the Revolution was just a passing disturbance, and nothing had changed in the Kingdom of France. This countryside still belonged to the Bourbons. The Royalists were so completely masters here that four years previously Hoche had not so much made peace as achieved an armistice.

The nobles, then, took the Revolutionaries very lightly; for them Bonaparte was only a Marceau who had been luckier than his predecessor. The women too were gay and in the mood for dancing. Only some of the leaders who had fought against the Blues were aware of the seriousness of the present crisis, and knowing that they would not be understood if they discussed the First Consul and his power with these fellow-countrymen who were quite behind the times, they talked among themselves and looked at the women with no interest at all.

The women in their turn gave vent to their feelings by criticizing each other. Madame du Gua, who seemed to be doing the honours of the ball, tried to appease the impatient would-be dancers by paying each in turn the usual flattering compliments. The discordant tuning of the violins filled the air when Madame du Gua caught sight of the Marquis, whose face still looked sad, and went directly to him.

'I do hope that you're not letting the affair with those clod-hoppers depress you,' she said. 'There's nothing extraordinary in a scene like that.'

She obtained no response. The Marquis was lost in reverie, thinking of Marie's prophetic voice and the reasons she had given him at La Vivetière, surrounded by these same leaders, for urging him to abandon the struggle of kings against peoples. But this young man was too high-minded, had too much pride, too much conviction perhaps, to abandon the task he had set his hand to, and in that moment he was making up his mind to go resolutely on in spite of the difficulties, and he raised his head in proud determination. Then he realized that Madame du Gua was speaking to him.

'Your mind is in Fougères, I suppose,' she was saying, with a bitter recognition of the futility of her efforts to draw the Marquis from his thoughts. 'Ah, Monsieur, I would willingly shed my blood if I could put *her* in your hands and see you happy with her!'

'Was that why you were so quick to fire at her?'

'I wanted her either dead or in your arms. Yes, Monsieur, it was possible for me to love the Marquis de Montauran when I believed I saw a hero in him. Now all I feel for him is regret-ful friendship; I see him barred from glory by the fickle heart of an Opéra woman.'

'You speak of love,' returned the Marquis, with an ironic note in his voice, 'but you are not at all a good judge of my feelings! If I loved that girl, Madame, I should have less desire for her ... and if you had not reminded me I should perhaps not have had another thought about her.'

'There she is!' said Madame du Gua abruptly.

The precipitate sharpness with which the Marquis turned

his head to look behind was bitterly wounding to this poor woman. But when he turned his face again towards her, smiling at this feminine piece of trickery, in the clear candle-light that illumined the slightest change in the expression of the man she loved so vehemently, she thought she discovered new reason to hope.

'What is the joke?' asked Comte de Bauvan.

'A bubble bursting!' answered Madame du Gua gaily. 'The Marquis, if we are to believe him, is astonished now that he ever felt his heart beat faster even for a moment for that creature who called herself Mademoiselle de Verneuil. You know whom I mean?'

'That creature? . . .' said the Comte, reproach in his tone. 'Madame, it is for the man who has done wrong to make amends, and I give you my word of honour that she is indeed and certainly the daughter of the Duc de Verneuil.'

'Monsieur le Comte,' said the Marquis in a noticeably strained voice, 'which of your two words of honour are we to believe, the one given at La Vivetière or the one at Saint-James?'

A stentorian voice announced Mademoiselle de Verneuil. The Comte hastened towards the door, offered his hand to the beautiful stranger with every mark of the deepest respect and led her through the curious throng towards the Marquis and Madame du Gua.

'Only believe the word I give today,' he answered the thunderstruck young leader.

Madame du Gua turned pale at the sight of this ill-omened girl, who stood there for a moment glancing haughtily at the gathering, looking for guests who had been present at La Vivetière. She waited for her rival's conventional greeting, and without looking at the Marquis let the Comte conduct her to a seat of honour near Madame du Gua, to whom she made a slight patronizing answering bow. That lady, however, with an instinctive feminine reaction, showed no sign of anger and at once adopted a smiling friendly air.

Mademoiselle de Verneuil's extraordinary toilette and her beauty sent a momentary stir and murmur through the crowd.

When the Marquis and Madame du Gua turned their eyes to the guests who had met at La Vivetière they found them looking at her in an attitude of respect which appeared to be quite sincere: they all seemed to be racking their brains to find a way of re-establishing themselves in the good graces of the misjudged young Parisian.

The enemies were now face to face.

Chapter 23

'But are you a sorceress, Mademoiselle? There's no one in the world like you for taking people by surprise! Did you really come here all alone?' said Madame du Gua.

'All alone,' Mademoiselle de Verneuil repeated her last words; 'and so, Madame, you will have no one but me to kill this evening.'

'Do be forbearing,' Madame du Gua returned. 'I cannot tell you how pleased I am to see you again. Truly I was overwhelmed by the memory of how badly I had behaved towards you, and was looking for an opportunity that would allow me to make amends.'

'As for your behaviour, Madame, I can easily pardon your behaviour to me; but I have on my mind the death of the Blues that you murdered. I might also complain perhaps of the severity of the missives you send me . . . Well, never mind that, I excuse it all because of the service you have done me.'

Madame du Gua changed countenance as she found her hand pressed by her lovely rival, who smiled at her with insulting graciousness. The Marquis had been standing motionless, but at this moment he gripped the Comte's arm with some force.

'You have tricked me shamefully,' he said, 'and cast a slur on my honour. I am not a kind of Géronte of comedy,* and I'll have your life for this, or you'll have mine.'

'Marquis,' returned the Comte haughtily, 'I am ready to give you all the satisfaction you require.'

And they moved off to the next room. Even the spectators who knew least about what lay behind the scene were beginning to realize its interest, and were so absorbed that when the violins struck up for the dance no one moved.

'What service have I done you, Mademoiselle,' said Madame

* Géronte, a stock comedy character – a credulous weak old man.

du Gua, her lips pinched with rage, 'so important as to deserve . . .'

'Have you not enlightened me, Madame, about the true character of the Marquis de Montauran? With no more feeling than that monster showed when he allowed me to go to my death I give him up to you, with pleasure.'

'Then what have you come here to look for?' retorted Madame du Gua sharply.

'The regard and respect that you stripped me of at La Vivetière, Madame. As for anything else, set your mind at rest. Even if the Marquis were to return to me, you ought to know that a return is never the same thing as love.'

Madame du Gua took Mademoiselle de Verneuil's hand with the affectionate sweetness that it pleases women to show one another, especially when men are present.

'Well, my poor child, I am delighted to find you so reasonable. If the service I rendered you was a rather rough one at first, at least I can make it complete,' she said, pressing the soft delicately-boned hand she held although her fingers were itching to scratch it. 'You may be sure I know what the Gars is like,' she went on with a treacherous smile. 'Well, he must have deceived you, he neither wishes to nor can he marry anyone.'

'Ah! . . .'

'Yes, Mademoiselle, he accepted his dangerous commission only in order to win the hand of Mademoiselle d'Uxelles, an alliance for which the King has promised his support.'

'Really? . . .'

Mademoiselle de Verneuil added not another word to that scoffing exclamation. The handsome young Chevalier du Vissard, anxious to be forgiven for the pleasantry which had been the first of the insults at La Vivetière, came up and deferentially asked her to dance. She accepted his hand and hastened to take her place in the quadrille in which Madame du Gua was also a dancer. The toilettes of the other women were all reminiscent of the style of the exiled Court, with curled or powdered hair. Mademoiselle de Verneuil's dress in the permissive mode of the times, elegant and rich in effect in spite of its simplicity, as she stood beside them instantly made theirs appear absurd. The other women found the style shocking, so they said, but *in petto*, in their secret hearts, were enviously admiring. The men constantly turned to look with surprised pleasure at natural hair, and the details of a dress whose grace was all in the graceful proportions of the figure it revealed.

The Marquis and the Comte returned to the ballroom just then, and came to a halt behind Mademoiselle de Verneuil, who did not turn her head. If a glass opposite had not apprised her of the Marquis's presence she would have guessed it by Madame du Gua's face, for under her front of indifference Madame du Gua was finding it difficult to conceal the impatience with which she was waiting for the confrontation of the two lovers and the passage of arms which must sooner or later take place. Although the Marquis was talking with the Comte and two others he could hear the remarks of the ladies and their partners as they moved according to the figures of the dance and stood for a few moments in turn in Mademoiselle de Verneuil's and her neighbour's places.

'Oh, yes indeed, Madame, she came here by herself,' said one young man.

'It takes a bold face to do that,' his partner answered.

'But if I were dressed like that, I would think I had no clothes on at all,' said another lady.

'Oh, it's not a very modest dress,' her partner replied; 'but she is so lovely and it becomes her so well!'

'You know, I feel embarrassed for her because she dances so faultlessly. She's just like an Opéra girl, don't you think?' said the jealous lady.

'Can she possibly be here to negotiate on the First Consul's behalf?' a third lady wondered.

'What a joke if she were,' her partner said.

'She'll hardly wear white at her wedding,' commented the lady with a laugh.

The Gars turned brusquely to see the woman who allowed herself this innuendo; and then Madame du Gua gave him a look that said clearly, 'You see what they think of her!'

'It's only the ladies, Madame,' said the Comte, laughing, to Marie's assailant, 'who have so far deprived her of maiden-hood . . .'

For this reply the Marquis in his heart forgave the Comte all his sins. When he ventured to glance at his mistress, whose charms were enhanced, like those of nearly all the ladies, by the soft candlelight, she turned her back as she was led to her place and talked to her partner, allowing the Marquis to catch the sweet caressing tones of her voice.

'The First Consul sends us very dangerous ambassadors,' her partner was saying.

'That has been said already, Monsieur,' she returned; 'at La Vivetière.'

'You have a memory as long as the King's,' the gentleman retorted, put out by his tactlessness.

'One has to remember injuries if one is to forgive them,' she swiftly answered, and her smile relieved his embarrass-ment.

'Are we all included in this amnesty?' the Marquis asked her.

But she swung away into the dance with a youthful ex-hilaration, leaving him unanswered and without words. He watched her with a chilled melancholy; and when she noticed this she inclined her head sweetly towards her partner in a pose made effective by her graceful neck, and in every change of movement she lost no chance of showing off her figure's rare perfection. Marie was as inviting as hope, as elusive as a memory. To see her thus was to desire to possess her at all costs. She knew it, and her awareness of her beauty shone in her face with inexpressible charm. She awoke a tempest of love, rage and madness in the Marquis's heart. He gripped the Comte's hand and left him.

'Oh, has he gone?' said Mademoiselle de Verneuil, return-ing to her place.

The Comte strode off to the next room and returned, with a conspiratorial glance for his protégée, escorting the Gars.

'He's mine,' she said to herself, as in a glass she watched

the Marquis approaching, his face full of tender feeling and radiant with hope.

She received the young leader unwelcomingly and without a word, but left him, as she danced, smiling. She saw him as so far above the others that she felt proud of her power to impose her will, and wished him to pay dearly for a few kind words so that he should appreciate them at their full value, with a feminine instinct all women obey more or less.

When the quadrille came to an end, all the guests who had been present at La Vivetière crowded round Marie, and each in turn begged forgiveness for his error with more or less well-turned compliments. But the one she would have wished to see at her feet held aloof and did not join the group where she held sway.

'He thinks himself still loved,' she said to herself. 'He does not want to be one of a crowd who don't matter.'

She refused the next dance. Then as if this ball had been given for her, she went from one group of dancers to another on the Comte de Bauvan's arm, taking pleasure in showing him some friendliness. The events at La Vivetière were by now known to the whole assembly in complete detail, thanks to Madame du Gua, who was hoping by exposing Mademoiselle de Verneuil and the Marquis together to public gossip to put one more obstacle in the way of their reconciliation; and so general attention was focused on the estranged lovers. Montauran dared not move towards his mistress, for his consciousness of the wrongs he had committed and the violence of his reawakened desires combined to make her almost terrifyingly unapproachable; and on her side the girl watched his face with its mask of assumed composure while appearing to be watching the dancing.

'It's desperately hot in here,' she said to her escort. 'I see Monsieur de Montauran's forehead quite damp with heat. Take me over there for a breath of air, I'm stifling.'

And she turned her head towards the next room, where there were some people playing cards. The Marquis, reading her lips, followed her there. He dared to hope that she had left the crowd only for the purpose of seeing him again, and this apparent mark of favour roused his passion to new heights; for his love had grown by all the resistance he had thought himself bound to oppose to it in the past few days. Mademoiselle de Verneuil was delighted to keep the young leader on the rack. Her eyes, so soft and velvety for the Comte, turned cold and sombre when they chanced to encounter the Marquis's gaze. With what was visibly a painful effort, the Marquis said in a strained voice, 'Will you not forgive me then?'

'Love,' she replied coldly, 'either forgives nothing or forgives all. But it needs to be love,' she added as she saw him make a movement of joy.

She had taken the Comte's arm again, and moved quickly off into a small room like a boudoir opening out of the cardroom. The Marquis followed.

'You shall give me a hearing!' he exclaimed.

'You would make one think, Monsieur,' she answered, 'that it was for your sake I came here and not for the sake of my own self-respect. If you do not stop this odious pursuit, I'll leave.'

'Well,' he said, remembering one of the craziest escapades of the last Duke of Lorraine, 'allow me to talk to you only so long as I can hold this ember in my hand.'

Stooping down to the fireplace, he seized a burning fragment and violently closed his fist on it. Mademoiselle de Verneuil changed colour, impulsively took her arm from the Comte's and stared at the Marquis in amazement. The Comte quietly withdrew, leaving the two lovers alone. The recklessness of the action had shaken Marie's heart, for in love there is nothing more persuasive than a piece of daring folly.

'What you are proving to me by this,' she said, trying to make him throw down the burning wood, 'is that you would be willing to subject me to the most cruel tortures. You go to extremes in everything. On the word of a fool and because of a woman's slanders you suspected the person who had just saved your life of being capable of selling you.'

'Yes,' he said smiling, 'I have treated you cruelly, and even if you forget it, I never shall. You must believe me. It is true

I was shamefully deceived, but so many circumstances on that fatal day were loaded against you.'

'And those circumstances were enough to put an end to your love?'

He hesitated. With a contemptuous gesture, she rose.

'Oh, Marie, you are the only one I believe now! . . .'

'Oh, throw that down! You're mad. Open your hand. I say you must!'

He made a show of resistance to his mistress's use of gentle force, delighting to prolong the painful pleasure he experienced as her tender delicate fingers did their best to force his apart; but she succeeded at last in opening the hand that she could have wished to have the right to kiss. Blood had extinguished the ember.

'Well, what good has that done you? . . .' she said.

She crumpled her handkerchief for lint and laid it on the scorched skin, and the Marquis quickly covered it with his glove. Madame du Gua appeared on tiptoe in the card-room to spy furtively on the two lovers, evading their observation by dodging adroitly out of sight whenever they made a movement. But it was by no means easy for her to make out what they were saying by what she saw them do.

'If all they said of me were true, you must acknowledge that I should be well avenged at this moment,' said Marie, with an ill-will that made the Marquis turn pale.

'And what feeling brought you here?'

'My dear boy, you're a conceited coxcomb. Do you really think you can despise a woman like me with impunity? . . . I came here with a purpose for both you and myself,' she went on after a pause, putting her hand to the cluster of rubies at her breast and displaying the blade of her dagger.

'What can all that mean?' Madame du Gua was asking herself.

'But you still love me!' she went on. 'Or at least you desire me; and that mad thing you did', and she took his hand 'gave me proof of it. Now I'm what I wanted to be again and I go away content. We can always forgive a person who loves us. Now I am loved, I have regained the esteem of the man who represents the whole world in my eyes; now I can die.'

'You still love me then?' said the Marquis.

'Did I say that?' she answered mockingly, taking pleasure in watching the screw turn and the increasing pain of the torture she had been applying to the Marquis since her arrival. 'I have had to make some peace-offerings in order to come here. I saved Monsieur de Bauvan from death, and because he at least is a grateful man, he has offered me his name and fortune as some return for my protection. That is a thought you never had.'

The Marquis, stunned by these last words and thinking that the Comte had made a fool of him, was fighting the most violent access of rage that he had ever experienced, and did not reply.

'Ha . . . that demands consideration!' she said with a bitter smile.

'Mademoiselle,' the young man returned, 'your doubt of me is justification for mine of you.'

'Monsieur, let's leave this place,' exclaimed Mademoiselle de Verneuil, catching a flicker of Madame du Gua's dress and rising as she spoke. The strong desire to strike despair into her rival's heart, however, made her pause.

'Do you want to cast me down into hell?' said the Marquis, taking her hand and holding it fast.

'Isn't that where you cast me five days ago? Are you not leaving me at this very moment in the most cruel uncertainty about the sincerity of your love?'

'What certainty have I that instead of killing me you may not carry your desire for revenge so far as to take possession of my whole life in order to drag it through the mud? . . .'

'Ah, you do not love me, you're thinking of yourself, not me!' she said fiercely, shedding tears. The coquette knew well enough the efficacy of her eyes when drowned in tears.

'Take my life then,' he said, beside himself, 'but don't cry.'

'Oh, my love,' she said, in a voice choked with emotion, 'this is what I was waiting for: these are the words and the accent and look which let me put your happiness before my own! But,' she went on, 'I ask a final proof of your affection that you declare to be so great, Monsieur. I do not want to stay a moment longer here than I need to make it clear that you are mine. I would not take even a glass of water in the house where a woman lives who has twice tried to kill me, and who is still perhaps plotting some new treachery against us, and who is listening to us at this very moment!' And she pointed out to the Marquis the floating folds of Madame du Gua's gown.

Then she dried her tears and leaned towards the young leader, who trembled as he felt the soft warmth of her breath at his ear.

'Get everything ready for us to leave,' she whispered. 'You must escort me back to Fougères, and that is where you will really know if I love you! For the second time I trust myself to you. Will you trust yourself a second time to me?'

'Ah, Marie, you have wrought my feelings to such a pitch that I don't know what I'm doing. Everything you say intoxicates me, and your looks, all that is you, I mean, and I'm ready to do whatever you say.'

'Well, then, make me very happy for just a short time. Allow me to enjoy the only triumph I have wished for. I want to breathe in the open air, living the life I dreamed of, and rejoice in my illusions before they are blown away. Now come and dance with me.'

They returned together to the ballroom. Mademoiselle de Verneuil had now been as thoroughly flattered in her heart and vanity as any woman could be, but the secret of her thoughts was guarded by the impenetrable softness of her eyes, her subtly smiling lips, the flying movements of a lively dance, as the sea guards the secret of the criminal who entrusts a heavy corpse to its keeping. However that might be, a murmur of admiration ran through the assembly as she turned in the arms of her love in the voluptuous embrace of the waltz. Closely entwined, her eyes turned up to his, they felt with dimming eyes and heavy head a distracted revelation of the delight they might enjoy in a more intimate union.

'Comte,' said Madame du Gua to Monsieur de Bauvan, 'go and find out if Pille-miche is in the camp, and bring him to me.

For this small service you may be assured of obtaining all you may ask from me, even my hand. – My vengeance will cost me dear,' she said, as she watched him go off; 'but this time I shall not miss.'

A few minutes after this scene, Mademoiselle de Verneuil and the Marquis were seated in a travelling-coach drawn by four strong horses. Francine, surprised to see the two declared enemies holding hands in such perfect concord, was silent, not daring to wonder whether on her mistress's side this was perfidy or love.

The silence and obscurity of the night prevented the Marquis from observing Mademoiselle de Verneuil's increasing agitation as she approached Fougères. The faint dawn light revealed Saint-Leonard's spire in the distance, and then Marie said to herself, 'I am going to die'.

At the first hill, the two lovers simultaneously had the same thought: they got down from the coach and climbed the slope on foot as if in memory of their first meeting. Marie took the Marquis's arm and after a few steps thanked him with a smile for respecting her silence. Then when they reached the point on the plateau from which Fougères was visible, she woke from her reverie.

'Don't go further,' she said. 'My power would not save you from the Blues again now.'

Montauran showed some surprise. She smiled sadly, pointed to a boulder as if requiring him to sit there, and herself remained standing in a melancholy pose. She was too torn with emotion now to make use of the wiles she had lavishly employed before. At this moment she might have kneeled on glowing charcoal and felt it no more than the Marquis had felt the ember he had grasped to attest the violence of his passion. It was after a long look at her lover of the deepest grief that she said these terrible words.

'All you have suspected me of is true!'

The Marquis made an involuntary gesture.

'Ah, for pity's sake,' she said, clasping her hands, 'listen to me without interrupting.

'I am truly,' she went on, her voice faltering, 'the Duc de

311

Verneuil's daughter, but his natural daughter. My mother, Demoiselle de Casteran, entered a convent to escape the suffering her family had in store for her, made expiation of her sin by fifteen years of penitence and tears, and died at Séez. It was only on her deathbed that this dear Abbess implored the help of the man who had deserted her, for my sake, for she knew me to be without friends, fortune or future. . . . That man, who was always remembered under the roof of Francine's mother, to whose care I had been committed, had forgotten his child.

'The Duc received me, all the same, with pleasure and acknowledged me because I was beautiful, and perhaps too because he saw his own youth in me. He was one of those great noblemen who in the previous reign gloried in demonstrating that they possessed the grace that could commit crimes and be forgiven them. I'll add nothing to that – he was my father! But let me explain how my stay in Paris inevitably harmed me morally.

'The society the Duc de Verneuil moved in, and into which he introduced me, was enchanted by the derisively cynical philosophy which was being acclaimed in France, because of the wit with which it was expounded everywhere. I listened, fascinated, to brilliant conversationalists whose intellectual grasp and subtlety won acceptance for a wittily expressed contempt for every moral belief. Those men could satirize fine feelings and transfix them with their shafts all the more shrewdly because they had never known them. Their epigrams were insidiously persuasive, and so was the gay geniality with which they could sum up a whole experience in a *bon mot*. Their failing, though, often was too much wit, and they wearied the women by making love an art rather than a matter that concerned the heart.

'I did not try to swim against that current very hard. Yet my temperament, if you will forgive my thinking this to my credit, was too passionate for me not to feel that wit had desiccated all those hearts; and the result of the life I lived then was to set up a perpetual conflict between my natural feelings and the wrong habits of thought I had contracted.

Several people of distinction enjoyed encouraging my freedom of thought and contempt for public opinion, an attitude of mind that strips a woman of a certain intellectual modesty without which she loses charm. Sadly, misfortune had no power to correct the faults luxury created . . .

'My father,' she went on, after a sigh, 'the Duc de Verneuil, died after acknowledging me as his daughter and leaving me an inheritance which considerably diminished the fortune of my brother, his legitimate son. I found myself one morning without home or guardian. My brother disputed the Will which had made me rich.

'Three years spent with a wealthy family had encouraged my vanity. My father had gratified all my whims and given me a taste for luxuries and luxurious ways of living, and in my still young and simple heart there was no realization of how demanding such tastes are or their dangers. A friend of my father's, Marshal the Duc de Lenoncourt, seventy years old, offered me his services as guardian and I accepted. I found myself once more, a few days after the beginning of that horrible lawsuit, in a brilliant household where I enjoyed all the advantages that a brother's cruelty had deprived me of when our father lay in his coffin.

'Every evening the old Marshal came to spend a few hours with me, and I never heard anything from that old man but words of kindness and consolation. His white hair and all the touching proofs he gave me of fatherly tenderness made me bound to credit his heart with the feelings of mine, and I was pleased to think of myself as his daughter. I accepted the ornaments he offered me and I made no secret to him of any of my whims, seeing him so pleased to gratify them. One evening I learned that the whole of Paris believed me to be the mistress of that poor old man.

'It was demonstrated to me that it was beyond my power to regain an innocence that everyone was gratuitously divesting me of. The man who had taken advantage of my inexperience could not be a lover and did not wish to be my husband. Within a week of the day when I made this appalling discovery, on the eve of the day fixed for my marriage with the man whose name I could demand as the sole reparation he might make me, he left for Coblenz. I was shamefully driven from the little house in which the Marshal had settled me, which did not belong to him.

'All I have told you is the truth, as if I were standing before God; but as for what happened afterwards do not ask an ill-fated woman for the whole tale of the sufferings buried in her memory. One day, Monsieur, I found myself married to Danton. A few days later the hurricane toppled the huge oak I had clasped my arms about. When I saw myself once more plunged into the depths of misery, I resolved that this time I would die.

'I do not know whether it was love of life that unconsciously influenced me and the hope of tiring out misfortune and finding the happiness that constantly escaped me in the depths of this seemingly endless hell, or whether I was persuaded by the arguments of a young man from Vendôme who two years ago attached himself to me like a serpent to a tree, in the belief no doubt that extreme misfortune might deliver me up to him. Indeed I do not know exactly how I came to accept the odious mission of going, for a fee of three hundred thousand francs, to captivate a stranger whom I was to betray.

'I saw you, Monsieur, and recognized you at once by one of those intuitive feelings that never deceive us. However, I was only too pleased to hold doubts, for the more I loved you the more appalling certainty became. In saving you from the hands of Commandant Hulot then, I renounced my rôle and I resolved to outwit the executioners instead of their victim. I was wrong to play with men in this way, with their lives and their political convictions and with myself, with the recklessness of a girl who sees nothing but emotions in the world. I believed I was loved and yielded to the hope of beginning my life anew; but everything, even to my very self perhaps, betrayed the irregularities of my past life, for you were bound to feel distrust of a woman so passionate as me.

'Is there anyone who would not find both my love and my deceit excusable? Indeed, Monsieur, it seemed to me that I had had a distressing nightmare, and wakened to find myself sixteen years old again. Here I was in Alençon where the pure untarnished memories of childhood were mine again. I had the crazy simplicity to think that love would give me a baptism of innocence. For a moment I thought that I was a young girl since I had never yet loved. But yesterday evening it seemed true to me that your passion was sincere and a voice cried in my ears "Why do you deceive him?"

'So take note, Monsieur le Marquis,' she went on in a deep hollow tone that expressed a proud acceptance of reprobation, 'take good note that I am only a dishonoured creature, unworthy of you. From this moment I take up my rôle of lost soul again, tired as I am of playing the part of the woman whose heart you had recalled to all its sacred obligations. Virtue weighs heavy on me. I should despise you if you were so weak as to marry me. That's a folly a Comte de Bauvan may commit; but you, Monsieur, must be worthy of your future and leave me without regret.

'The courtesan, you must know, would be too exacting. She would love in a quite different fashion from the simple young naïve child who cherished the delightful hope in her heart for a moment that she could be your companion, make you happy always, be someone you would take a pride in and become a great and honourable wife. It was this child who drew the courage from her feeling for you to bring the vice and infamy of her old evil nature to life again, in order to set an eternal barrier between herself and you.

'I sacrifice honour and fortune for you, and I am proud to do so. That pride will sustain me in my wretchedness; and now destiny may do as it wishes with my life. I will never betray you. I am returning to Paris. There your name shall be cherished by me as my own, and the splendid honour you will achieve for it will console me for all my sorrows. As for you, you are a man, you will forget me. Good-bye.'

She hurried off in the direction of the Saint-Sulpice valleys, and was gone before the Marquis could rise to prevent her. But she returned secretly on her steps, using the cavities of a hollowed rock for cover, raised her head stealthily and watched the Marquis with a mixture of anxious concern and doubt, and saw him walking blindly not knowing where he was going, like a man overwhelmed. 'Can he be irresolute? . . .' she said to herself when he had disappeared and she felt that she had lost him. 'Will he understand me?' And she shuddered. Then abruptly she set off alone towards Fougères, hurrying along as if she were afraid of being followed by the Marquis into this town where he would have met death.

'Well, Francine, what did he say to you? . . .' she asked the faithful Breton girl when they were together again.

'Oh, Marie, I was sorry for him. You great ladies, you use your tongues as if they were daggers to stab a man.'

'How did he look when he came up with you?'

'I don't think he even saw me. Oh, Marie, he loves you!'

'Oh, he loves me or he does not love me!' she answered. 'Two statements which to me mean the difference between heaven and hell. Between that height and depth there isn't a ledge for me to plant my foot on.'

Now that she had fulfilled her terrible destiny, Marie could give herself up to all her grief. The beauty of her face, that through so many changing emotions had maintained its bloom, rapidly altered. At the end of one day spent in endless see-saw between presentiments of happiness and despair, she had lost her radiant beauty, and the freshness that comes only from the absence of all passion or the intoxication of felicity.

Hulot and Corentin, anxious to know the outcome of her rash adventure, had come to see her shortly after her arrival. She received them smilingly.

'Well,' she said to the Commandant, whose face wore a worried and very questioning expression, 'now the fox returns within range of your guns, and it will not be long until you win a very glorious victory.'

'So what happened?' Corentin asked carelessly, with the oblique glance at Mademoiselle de Verneuil this kind of police agent uses to spy on thought.

'Ah!' she answered, 'the Gars is more enamoured of me than ever, and I compelled him to escort us to the gates of Fougères.'

'Your power of compulsion seems to have stopped there,'

returned Corentin. 'The *ci-devant*'s fear is evidently greater than the love you inspire in him.'

Mademoiselle de Verneuil threw Corentin a disdainful glance.

'You judge him by yourself,' she answered.

'Well, why,' he asked impassively, 'did you not bring him to your doorstep?'

'If he truly loved me, Commandant,' she said to Hulot, with a slily mischievous look, 'would you be very angry with me if I took him out of France and saved him?'

The old soldier moved quickly towards her and raised her hand to his lips impulsively; then he looked at her with a set gaze and said sombrely, 'You forget my two friends and my sixty-three men.'

'Ah, Commandant, it was not his fault,' she said with all the naïveté of passion; 'he was tricked by a wicked woman, Charette's mistress, who is capable, I believe, of drinking the Blues' blood . . .'

'Come, Marie,' Corentin broke in, 'don't play games with the Commandant, he's not accustomed to your pranks.'

'I don't ask for your comment,' she answered. 'One day you may go too far and offend me a bit too much, and there's no future in that for you.'

'I see, Mademoiselle, that I must prepare for battle,' said Hulot mildly.

'The odds are not in your favour, dear Colonel. I saw more than six thousand of their men at Saint-James, with Regular Army troops, artillery and English officers. But what could those people do without him? I agree with Fouché, his head means everything.'

'Well, shall we have it?' asked Corentin impatiently.

'I don't know,' she replied with indifference.

'Englishmen! . . .' cried Hulot in a rage. 'That's all he needed to make him a complete brigand! Englishmen indeed! I'll give him Englishmen! . . .'

Chapter 24

'So you keep on letting that girl win a victory over you, Citizen police spy, it seems,' Hulot said to Corentin when they were a short distance from the house.

'It's quite natural, Citizen Commandant,' Corentin replied reflectively, 'that you should have seen nothing in all she said to us but fire and shot. You warriors don't know that there are many ways of making war. But to manipulate the strings of men's and women's passions skilfully to make them serve the State, set the cogs in their place in the great machine that we call government, play the fascinating game of holding the most ungovernable emotions under control, and directing them as a motive force . . . that's a kind of creation, making oneself the centre of the universe, like God, don't you see?'

'You will allow me to prefer my profession to yours,' replied the soldier drily. 'And you may do what you please with your cogs, but I recognize no superior but the War Minister. I have my orders, and I intend to take the field with fellows who are ready and willing. I'll meet the enemy face to face, not take it in the rear like you.'

'Oh, you may prepare to march,' returned Corentin. 'According to what I could guess from what that girl let me understand, however unfathomable she may seem to you, you are in for a skirmish, and I promise you the pleasure of a tête-à-tête with the leader of these brigands before long.'

'How can you do that?' Hulot demanded, stepping back a pace the better to stare at this strange individual.

'Mademoiselle de Verneuil is in love with the Gars,' Corentin resumed, with an undercurrent of feeling, 'and perhaps she is loved by him! A Marquis with the Order of Saint Louis! Young, idealistic, and, who knows, he may even be rich still! So many temptations! She would be very silly not to work for her own interests and try to marry him instead of handing him over to us. She's trying to keep us happy, but I can read some duplicity in that girl's eyes. It's most likely the two lovers will arrange a trysting-place, and perhaps it's arranged already. Well, tomorrow I'll hold my man by the ears! Until now he was only an enemy of the Republic to me, but some minutes ago he became my enemy too. They're all dead men, however, dead on the scaffold, those who took it into their heads to come between that girl and me in the past.'

Corentin returned to his reflections after saying this, and did not see the profound distaste expressed on the loyal soldier's face when he discovered the depth of this plot and the methods of Fouché's tools. On the spot Hulot resolved to thwart Corentin in any way not essentially prejudicial to the Government's undertakings or contrary to its wishes, and that he would give the Republic's enemy a chance of dying honourably, arms in hand, and not let him be the prey of the headsman to whom this myrmidon of the higher police was the declared purveyor.

'If the First Consul listened to me,' he said to himself, turning his back on Corentin, 'he would leave these foxes to fight the noblemen – they're fit opponents for one another – and use the soldiers for quite a different kind of job.'

Corentin looked coldly at the soldier, whose thoughts were clear in his face, and then his eyes regained the sardonic expression that showed this junior Machiavelli's consciousness of his own superiority.

'Just give these dolts three yards of blue cloth and a length of metal to hang at their side,' he said to himself, 'and they imagine that there's only one way to use to kill men in the political game.'

He walked slowly on for several minutes, then said to himself suddenly, 'Yes, now is the moment – so this woman is to be mine! For five years the circle I've drawn round her has been gradually closing in. She's in my hands now, and with her I'll rise as high as Fouché in the Government. – Yes, if she loses the only man she has ever loved, grief will give her to me body and soul. To surprise her secret now is only a matter of watching her day and night.'

Shortly after, an observer might have caught a glimpse of this man's pale face at the window of a house from which he could see everyone who entered the blind alley formed by the row of houses parallel to Saint-Leonard's Church.

Next morning Corentin was there again, watching with the patience of a cat at a mousehole, alert for the slightest sound, and subjecting every passer-by to a close examination. It was the morning of a market day. Although in those disturbed times peasants were reluctant to venture into town, Corentin saw a sinister-looking little man, wearing a goatskin and carrying a little round flat basket on his arm, making his way towards Mademoiselle de Verneuil's house, after some fairly casual glances about him.

Corentin went down to the street with the intention of waiting for the peasant to come out; but it suddenly occurred to him that if he could turn up unexpectedly in Mademoiselle de Verneuil's house a single glance might perhaps surprise the secrets hidden in this emissary's basket. Besides he knew from hearsay that it was almost impossible to extract an intelligible answer from the close-mouthed Bretons and Normans.

'Galope-chopine!' exclaimed Mademoiselle de Verneuil, when Francine led the Chouan in. 'Does he truly love me then?' she whispered to herself. A sudden hope brought the most vivid colour to her cheeks and joy to her heart. Galope-chopine looked from the mistress of the house to Francine with mistrust in his eyes, but Mademoiselle de Verneuil reassured him with a gesture.

'Madame,' he said, '*he* will be at my house about two o'clock, and will wait for you there.'

Emotion made Mademoiselle de Verneuil incapable of reply, but a Mongolian from beyond Siberia would have understood her nod. Corentin's footsteps were audible at this moment in the drawing-room. Galope-chopine was not in the least perturbed when Mademoiselle de Verneuil's look and start warned him of danger, and as soon as the spy showed his crafty face the Chouan raised his voice in an ear-splitting bawl.

'Ah! Ah!' he said to Francine. 'But there's Breton butter and Breton butter! You want Gibarry butter and only offer eleven sous a pound? You shouldn't have bothered to send for me! That there's good butter,' and he uncovered his basket to display two little pats of butter Barbette had made. 'Fair's fair, good lady, make it another sou.'

His hoarse gruff voice showed no emotion, and his green eyes overhung by heavy greying eyebrows sustained Corentin's piercing stare without flinching.

'Come, that's enough, my man. You didn't come here to sell butter – your business is with a woman who never haggled over anything in her life. The occupation you follow, my friend, will shorten you by a head one day.' And, tapping him amicably on the shoulder, 'It's not possible to be the Chouans' man and the Blues' at the same time for very long,' Corentin added.

Galope-chopine had need of all his presence of mind to swallow his rage and not raise his voice against this accusation, which indeed his greed for money had made only too well-founded. He contented himself with replying, 'Monsieur's making game of me!'

Corentin had turned his back on the Chouan, but while he greeted Mademoiselle de Verneuil, whose heart stood still, he could easily watch him in the glass. Thinking himself unobserved by the spy, Galope-chopine directed a questioning glance at Francine. She nodded towards the door saying, 'Come with me, my man, we'll soon settle the price.'

Corentin had missed nothing. Mademoiselle de Verneuil's shaken look, ill-covered by her smile, and her colour and changed expression had not escaped him, nor had the Chouan's uneasiness, nor Francine's gesture. Convinced that Galope-chopine was a messenger from the Marquis, he stopped him by the long hair of his goatskin as he was about to go out, pulled him round to face him and fixed him with his eye, saying, 'Where do you live, my friend? I need some butter...'

'Don't you know, Monsieur?' answered the Chouan. 'Why, everyone in Fougères knows where I live. I come, as you might say, from...'

'Corentin!' exclaimed Mademoiselle de Verneuil, cutting off Galope-chopine's answer. 'It's very impudent of you to come here at this hour and break in on me like this. I've scarcely finished dressing. . . . Leave this peasant alone, he doesn't understand what trick you're up to any more than I do what you suspect him of. Go on, my good man!'

Galope-chopine hesitated for a moment. The indecision, real or feigned, of a poor devil not knowing whom to obey was indeed having some effect on Corentin when the Chouan, in obedience to the girl's imperative gesture, tramped off heavily.

Now Mademoiselle de Verneuil and Corentin contemplated each other in silence. This time Marie's limpid eyes could not sustain the brilliant cold flame of this man's gaze. The air of determination with which the spy had walked into the room, an expression on his face that Marie had never seen before, his thin high-pitched voice, his attitude, all filled her with alarm. She understood that a dark struggle was beginning between them and that he was bringing all the forces of his sinister power to bear against her. She had a clear complete picture at that moment of the abyss into which she was hurling herself, but still found strength in her love to shake off the icy chill of her forebodings.

'I hope you are going to let me dress now, Corentin,' she said, almost gaily.

'Marie, yes, allow me to call you that,' he began, 'you don't know me yet! Believe me, a man much less perspicacious than I would have discovered your love for the Marquis de Montauran before now. I have several times offered you my heart and hand. You don't think me worthy of you; and perhaps you are right. But if you consider yourself too highly placed, too beautiful or too great for me, I know very well how to bring you down to my level.

'You think little of me because of my ambition and the scale of values I live by: and frankly you are wrong. I value men at what they're worth, no more, and that's not much. I am bound to reach a high position, and the honour due to it will please you. Who could love you better, let you rule him more completely, than the man who has loved you for the past five years?'

'I risk making you suspect my motives, for you don't understand that great love may make a man give up the person he idolizes, but however that may be I'm going to let you see how disinterested my adoration is. Don't shake your pretty head.

'If the Marquis loves you, marry him; but first make very sure that he is sincere. I could not bear it if I learned that you had been deceived, because your happiness is more important to me than my own. My giving you up may surprise you, but put it down to the common sense of a man who is not so stupid as to wish to possess a woman against her will. It's not you I blame but myself for my lack of success. I hoped to win you by yielding to your wishes and devoted service. As you know, for a long time I have tried to make you happy according to my lights. But you have not been willing to give me any reward at all.'

'I have allowed you to stay with me,' she said, with cold dignity.

'Add that you regret it . . .'

'Am I to thank you for involving me in this abominable adventure? . . .'

'When I suggested an adventure that timorous souls would find reprehensible, it was only your interests I was considering,' he said with bare-faced mendacity. 'Whether I succeed or fail is immaterial to me for whatever happens now I can use it to further my plans. Suppose you marry the Marquis? Then I'll be delighted to serve the Bourbon cause, and can do so to some effect in Paris – I'm a member of the Clichy Club.*

'It only needs some occurrence that would put me in touch with the Princes to make me decide to stop working for a Republic that is moving to its downfall. General Bonaparte is far too clever not to realize that he can't be everywhere at once – he's needed in Germany, Italy and here, where the Revolution is practically finished. He no doubt fixed the events of the 18 Brumaire to back his hand in negotiating with the Bourbons for the future of France, for he's a very astute fellow and not without political grasp; but the politicians are

* A club frequented by anti-Revolutionaries and Royalists. –*Trans.*

bound to get the better of him in the path he's beginning to tread now.

'Qualms of conscience about betraying France are the kind of nonsense that people with minds of their own like us leave to fools. I don't mind telling you that I have authority to open negotiations with the Chouan leaders, or alternatively to have them executed. Fouché, my patron, is a cunning man, difficult to fathom; he has always played a double game. During the Terror he worked for both Robespierre and Danton.'

'Danton, whom you cravenly deserted,' she said.

'Nonsense,' answered Corentin; 'he is dead, forget him. Come, talk to me frankly, as I am doing to you. This Demi-brigade Commandant is wilier than he appears, and if you want to give him the slip I can be of some help to you. Remember that the valleys are swarming with his Counter-Chouans, and he would soon catch you at any meeting-place! If you stay here under his nose you are at the mercy of his spies. You see how quickly he found out that this Chouan was here. Don't you realize that he's a crafty old soldier and doesn't need telling that if the Marquis loves you, every movement you make will give him a clue to what the Marquis is doing?'

Mademoiselle de Verneuil had never heard such a gentle affectionate voice. Corentin was all good faith, and seemingly full of trust. The poor girl's heart so readily accepted and responded to kindness that she was on the point of yielding up her secret to the boa-constrictor whose coils were wrapping themselves about her. It struck her, however, that there was nothing to prove the sincerity of this change of tone, which was out of character, and she did not scruple to deceive her self-constituted guardian.

'Well,' she answered, 'you have guessed right, Corentin. Yes, I love the Marquis; but he is not in love with me – at least I'm afraid he isn't. So it seems to me that the assignation he has given me may be a trap of some sort.'

'But you told us yesterday,' Corentin took her up, 'that he escorted you as far as Fougères ... If he had wanted to use violence against you, you would not be here.'

'You have an unfeeling heart, Corentin. You can work out

clever calculations from the events of a human life but not from the vagaries of a passion. Perhaps that is the reason for the aversion I can't help still feeling for you. Try to understand, since you are so shrewd, how a man whom I parted from in anger the day before yesterday will be waiting impatiently for me today, on the Mayenne road, in a house in Florigny, towards evening . . .'

At this impetuous admission, which seemed to fall quite naturally from the lips of this candid and passionate creature, Corentin changed colour, for he was still young; but at the same time he stealthily cast a piercing soul-searching look at her. Mademoiselle de Verneuil's naïveté was so well acted that the spy was deceived, and he replied with false geniality, 'Would you like me to accompany you at a distance? I would bring soldiers in disguise, and we would be there under your orders if you needed us.'

'Very well,' she said; 'but promise me on your honour . . . Oh, no! I don't believe in that . . . by your salvation – but you don't believe in God! . . . by your soul, but perhaps you haven't one . . . Is there any assurance you can give me of your secrecy and loyalty? And yet I do trust you, and give more than my life or love or revenge into your keeping.'

The slight smile apparent on Corentin's sallow face was evidence to Mademoiselle de Verneuil of the trap she had just avoided. The agent, whose nostrils grew pinched instead of expanding, took his victim's hand and raised it to his lips with every sign of the deepest respect, and then left her with a bow not without grace.

Three hours after this scene, Mademoiselle de Verneuil, who was afraid that Corentin might return, slipped stealthily out by the Saint-Leonard Gate and reached the little path by Nid-aux-Crocs into the Nançon valley. She thought herself safe as she walked without anyone to see her along the maze-like paths to Galope-chopine's cabin, and she went gaily, led on by the hope of at last finding happiness and the urgent wish to rescue her lover from the danger threatening him.

Meanwhile Corentin had gone to look for the Commandant. He had difficulty in recognizing Hulot when he found him on a cramped parade-ground, busy with certain military preparations. The bold veteran, indeed, had made a sacrifice it would be difficult to over estimate. His queue and moustaches had been cut off and his hair dressed in clerical fashion, with a sprinkling of powder. He wore heavy nailed shoes, and with his old blue uniform exchanged for a goatskin and pistols in his belt and a heavy musket instead of his sword, he was inspecting two hundred Fougères citizens whose dress would have passed the sharp eye of the most knowing Chouan.

The scene, which was no novelty to these townsmen, demonstrated the bellicose spirit of this little town and of the Breton character. Among the men were mothers and sisters bringing a flask of brandy or forgotten pistols to their sons and brothers. Several old men were counting and inspecting the condition of the cartridges for these National Guardsmen disguised as Counter-Chouans, whose high spirits suggested a hunting party rather than a dangerous expedition. For them these Chouan skirmishes in which Bretons from the towns fought country Bretons seemed a modern substitute for the tournaments of Chivalry. Their patriotic enthusiasm had perhaps originated in the acquisition of some confiscated land. Nevertheless the benefits of the Revolution, which were better appreciated in the towns, partisan spirit and a certain national love of a fight had a great deal to do with it.

Hulot, marvelling, passed from group to group with Gudin by his side to answer his questions about them, for Gudin was now regarded by the old soldier with all the comradely friendship once given to Merle and Gérard. A large number of the town's inhabitants watching the preparations appreciated the contrast between their noisy fellow-townsmen and a nearby battalion of Hulot's Demi-brigade. Motionless, drawn up in silent ranks before their officers, the Blues were awaiting the Commandant's orders, and only their eyes moved as they followed his progress among the groups of National Guards.

Corentin could not help smiling at the change in Hulot's appearance when he reached the Commandant. He looked like a portrait painted long ago and no longer a likeness of its original.

'What's in the wind?' Corentin asked him.

'Come and carry a gun with us and you'll soon learn,' the Commandant replied.

'Oh, I'm not a Fougères man!' answered Corentin.

'That's not hard to see, Citizen,' said Gudin.

There were some guffaws from all the groups within hearing.

'Do you imagine,' Corentin demanded, 'that only men with bayonets can serve France? . . .'

Then he turned his back on the mocking laughter to ask a woman the object of this expedition and where it was bound for.

'It's a terrible thing, young fellow, the Chouans have reached Florigny already! They say there's more than three thousand of them and they're on their way here to take Fougères.'

'Florigny!' exclaimed Corentin, turning pale. 'So that can't be where they are meeting! You mean Florigny on the Mayenne road?'

'There isn't two Florignys,' the woman answered, pointing to the road leading to the top of the Pellerine.

'Is it the Marquis de Montauran you're in quest of?' Corentin asked the Commandant.

'Partly,' Hulot answered shortly.

'He's not at Florigny,' said Corentin. 'Send your battalion and National Guards there, but keep some of your Counter-Chouans with you and wait for me.'

'He can't be crazy – he's too crafty,' exclaimed the Commandant. 'He must know something. There's no doubt he's a master spy!'

Then Hulot gave the command to the battalion to set off. The Republican soldiers marched without drum-beat silently through the houses that close in on the narrow way to the Mayenne road, winding in a long blue and red line among trees and houses. The disguised National Guards followed them. But Hulot stayed where he was with Gudin and twenty or so of the brightest young fellows of the town, and waited with a lively curiosity to learn the reason for Corentin's air of mystery.

Francine herself told this astute spy about Mademoiselle de Verneuil's departure and changed all his doubts into certainties as he set out at once to find out what he could about this extremely suspicious-looking flight. Learning from the soldiers on guard at the Saint-Leonard Gate that the beautiful foreigner had gone by Nid-aux-Crocs, Corentin ran to the Promenade and reached it in time, by bad luck, to watch everything Marie did. Although she had put on a green dress and hooded cloak to make herself less conspicuous, her impetuous almost headlong course, visible through the leafless frost-silvered hedges, revealed the goal she was making for.

'Aha!' he exclaimed. 'So your route to Florigny goes by way of the Vale of Gibarry, does it? I'm an idiot, she fooled me properly. But just wait. You don't catch me napping. I keep my lamp trimmed by day as well as night!'

Guessing then correctly enough where the two lovers were to meet, Corentin hurried to the parade-ground and reached it just as Hulot was about to leave to rejoin his troops.

'Stop, General!' he called, and the Commandant turned round.

Corentin quickly told him of the happenings like threads in a plot although the whole web could not be seen, and Hulot, struck by the agent's perspicacity, eagerly gripped his arm.

'Thunder and lightning! You are quite right, Citizen spy. Those brigands yonder are making a feint attack! The two mobile detachments I sent to take a look at the country between the Antrain and Vitré roads have not returned yet so we'll find reinforcements on our way, which we shall find a use for no doubt, for the Gars is not such a fool as to risk his neck without his accursed owls.

'Gudin,' he said to the young Fougères man, 'go quickly and tell Captain Lebrun that he can give the brigands at Florigny a drubbing without my help, and be back here again quicker than *that*. You know the paths, and I'll be waiting to go a-hunting for the *ci-devant* to exact vengeance for the men murdered at La Vivetière. . . . . God's thunder! How he can run!' he exclaimed watching Gudin vanish as if by magic. 'How Gérard would have liked that boy!'

On his return Gudin found Hulot's little band augmented by several soldiers taken from the different guard-posts of the town. The Commandant told the young man to choose about a dozen of his fellow-townsman best suited to the difficult craft of Counter-Chouan, and lead them out by the Saint-Leonard Gate to skirt the further side of the Saint-Sulpice Heights overlooking the Couësnon Valley, where Galope-chopine's cabin stood. Then he himself at the head of the rest of his band left by the Saint-Sulpice Gate to cover the higher level of the plateau. There, according to his calculations, he should meet Beau-pied's men whom he proposed to use to reinforce a cordon posted to guard the cliffs from the Faubourg Saint-Sulpice to Nid-aux-Crocs.

Corentin, sure that he had placed the fate of the Chouan General in the hands of his most implacable enemies, hastened to the Promenade from where he could best follow Hulot's military dispositions. It was not long until he saw Gudin's little band leaving the Nançon Valley and skirting the hills on the side overlooking the Couësnon Valley, while Hulot, coming into sight as he and his men moved round the south side of the Château, was climbing the dangerous path that led to the top of the Saint-Sulpice Heights. Thus the two groups were deployed on parallel lines. The many trees and bushes, decorated by the frost with rich arabesques, reflected a pale light over the countryside against which the advancing grey lines of the two little forces could be plainly seen.

When he reached the plateau Hulot detached all the soldiers in uniform from his squad, and Corentin saw them in obedience to his commands set up a moving cordon, in which each soldier was in touch with the next though with a space between, and the first, closing the gap, proceeding parallel to Gudin, and the last to Hulot. In this way the wily Commandant was ensuring that no bush should escape the bayonets of the three advancing lines which were to track down the Gars across mountain and field.

'He's a crafty old war-dog, the old boy!' exclaimed Corentin as the last flashing gun-tip was lost to view in the gorse. 'The Gars is done for. Now if only Marie had handed that damned Marquis over, we should be accomplices in treachery with the strongest of bonds to unite us. . . . But I'll have her, there's no doubt about that! . . .'

Chapter 25

THE twelve young men from Fougères led by Sublieutenant Gudin soon reached the side of the Saint-Sulpice Heights where they decline by gentle hills into the Vale of Gibarry. Gudin himself left the road and nimbly jumped the *échalier* closing the first field of gorse he came to, and was followed by six of his fellow townsmen; the other six, by his orders, took to the fields on the right, so that the roads might be searched on both sides. Gudin pushed his way energetically towards an apple tree growing in the middle of the gorse.

As they heard the rustling of the six Counter-Chouans following him through this wilderness of gorse and broom and trying not to shake the frost-covered clumps, seven or eight men with Beau-pied at their head hid behind a number of chestnut trees growing on the top of the high bank surrounding the field. In spite of the white reflections lighting up their surroundings, and their experienced eyes, the Fougères men did not at first notice these adversaries, who were using the trees for cover and as a kind of stockade.

'Hush, here they come,' said Beau-pied, the first to raise his head. 'A fine dance this lot have led us and run us off our legs, and now that we have them at our gun-muzzles' ends we mustn't miss, or by the sacred name of my pipe we'll not be fit to make Pope's soldiers!'

Gudin's keen eyes, however, had at length descried the guns covering his little squad. In the same moment there were eight bitterly derisive shouts of '*Who goes there?*' and simultaneously eight shots were fired. The bullets whistled round the Counter-Chouans' ears. One of them was struck in the arm and another fell. The other five, unhurt, quickly riposted with a volley and the shout '*Friends!*' Then they advanced rapidly upon their assailants in order to be upon them before they could reload.

'We spoke only too truly!' exclaimed the young Sub-lieutenant, recognizing the uniforms and old hats of his own Demi-brigade. 'We've certainly acted like true Bretons – fought first and left explanations till afterwards!'

The eight soldiers were aghast as they recognized Gudin.

'Cross my heart, Sir! The devil himself wouldn't have taken you for anything but brigands under those goatskins!' cried Beau-pied in a grief-stricken wail.

'It's an unlucky accident and we're none of us to blame as you weren't warned about our Counter-Chouan game. But what are you doing?' Gudin asked.

'Sir, we're hunting a dozen Chouans who are amusing themselves making us run. We run like poisoned rats. But after all the ups and downs over these *échaliers* and banks – may lightning blast them! – our compass legs got rust in the works and we were taking a rest. I think the brigands must be somewhere near that big hut from which you see smoke coming.'

'Good,' said Gudin. 'You will now fall back on the Saint-Sulpice Heights, across the fields, to join the cordon the Commandant has set up there,' he told the eight soldiers and Beau-pied. 'We must not be seen in your company because of your uniforms. By flame and shot! We want to get hold of those dogs and put an end to them; the Gars is with them! The boys will tell you more about this business. Slip away there on the right, and don't go shooting six of our men wearing goatskins whom you may meet. You can recognize our Counter-Chouans by their neckcloths with the ends twisted together instead of being knotted.'

Gudin left the two wounded men under the apple tree and went on towards Galope-chopine's house, which Beau-pied had just pointed out, guided by the smoke.

While the young officer was being put on the trail of the Chouans by an encounter of a kind not uncommon in this war and one that might have had even more lethal consequences, the little detachment commanded by Hulot advancing along its line of operation had reached a point parallel to Gudin on his. The old soldier, at the head of his Counter-Chouans, slipped noiselessly along the banks with all a young man's ardour. He jumped the *échaliers* limberly enough still, with a wary eye searching every height, and an ear like a hunter's alert for the slightest sound.

In his third field he found a woman of about thirty bent over a hoe, busy scraping the soil with dogged perseverance, while a little boy of seven or eight armed with a bill-hook was shaking the frost from clumps of thorn-broom that had grown up here and there, cutting them and piling them in a heap. As Hulot landed heavily from the other side of the *échalier*, the little boy and his mother raised their heads.

Hulot pardonably mistook this young Breton woman for an old one. Her forehead and the skin of her neck were prematurely lined and wrinkled, and she was so grotesquely wrapped in a worn goatskin that if it had not been for her distinguishing skirt of dirty discoloured cloth Hulot would not have known which sex she belonged to, for her long locks of black hair were concealed in a red woollen cap. The little boy's skin gleamed through the rags that barely covered him.

'Ho, old woman!' Hulot called in a low voice as he approached. 'Where is the Gars?'

As he was speaking the twenty Counter-Chouans following him climbed into the field in their turn.

'Ah, if it's Gars you want to go to you'll have to go back the way you came,' the woman answered, with a suspicious look at the party.

'Do you think I'm asking you the way to the Faubourg du Gars in Fougères, old bag of bones?' Hulot replied roughly. 'By Saint Anne of Auray, have you seen the Gars go by?'

'I don't know what you mean,' the woman said, stooping over her hoe again.

'Curse you, woman, do you want us to be gobbled by the Blues on our heels?' cried Hulot.

At this the woman raised her head again and again eyed the Counter-Chouans distrustfully as she said, 'How in the Blues be after you? I just saw seven or eight of them off back to Fougères by the lower road.'

'Anyone would think by her suspicious loo at she was

going to bite us!' Hulot said. 'Look over there, nanny goat-skin.'

And the Commandant pointed to three or four soldiers of his cordon visible about fifty paces in his rear and easily recognizable with their hats, uniforms and guns.

'You don't care if our men have their throats cut when the bands from Fougères are out to take the Gars and we've been sent by Marche-à-terre to help him!' he went on angrily.

'Ah, I'm sorry,' the woman answered, 'but it's so easy to get taken in! What parish do you come from then?'

'We're from Saint-Georges,' shouted two or three Foug-ères men, in the Low Breton dialect, 'and we're dying of hunger.'

'Well, see here,' she said, 'do you see that smoke down there? That's my house. If you follow the paths on the right you'll come on it from above. You'll perhaps meet my man on the way. Galope-chopine is to be on the look-out for the Gars, because as you know he's coming to our house today,' she finished proudly.

'Thank you, my good woman,' said Hulot, and then to his men, 'Forward, you men. God's thunder! We have him!'

The detachment followed the Commandant at a quick march along the paths pointed out to them.

When she heard the so-called Chouan's oath, very unlikely from a Catholic tongue, Galope-chopine's wife turned pale. She looked at the young men's leggings and goatskins, sat down on the ground and clasped her child in her arms as she said, 'May the Holy Virgin of Auray and the blessed Saint Labre have pity on us! I don't believe those are our fellows, there's no nails on their shoes. Run by the lower road and warn your father. He could lose his head,' she said to the little boy, who vanished like a deer among the broom and gorse.

Mademoiselle de Verneuil had not met along her way any of the parties of Blues and Chouans which were chasing one another among the labyrinth of fields about Galope-chopine's cabin. When she saw a column of bluish smoke rising from the broken chimney of this dilapidated dwelling, her heart quickened and thudded so fast and loudly that she felt its roar and surge in her very throat. She stopped, leaning a hand on the branch of a tree, and contemplated this smoke that was to serve as beacon to both the young leader's friends and his enemies. She had never before felt such overwhelming emotion.

'Oh, I love him too much!' she said to herself, with something approaching desperation. 'Today I may perhaps not be able to go on controlling my feelings ...'

On a sudden impulse she crossed the ground towards the cottage and entered the yard, where the frost had congealed the dirt underfoot. The huge dog rushed out barking, but a word from Galope-chopine made him stop short and wag his tail. As she entered the cottage, Marie cast a comprehensive look around her. The Marquis was not there, and she breathed more freely. She noticed with some pleasure that the Chouan had made an attempt to restore a degree of cleanliness to the dirty single room of his lair. Galope-chopine seized his fowling-piece, silently nodded to his guest and went off with his dog.

She followed him to the door and watched him take the path to the right of his cabin closed off by a broken-down *échalier* in the form of a giant rotting tree-trunk. From there her view was of a succession of fields, their *échaliers* presenting themselves to the eye in perspective in a long line of barriers, for the bareness of the trees and hedges showed up all the surface detail of the landscape.

When Galope-chopine's broad-brimmed hat had passed quite out of sight, she turned her head to the left towards Fougères to look for the Church, but the shed completely blocked all view of it. She looked out over the Couësnon Valley which lay before her in what looked like a vast spread of muslin, whose whiteness further darkened the grey snow-laden sky. It was one of those days when nature seems silenced and sounds are absorbed by the atmosphere. The Blues and their Counter-Chouans were marching across country on three lines, closing in to form a triangle about the cabin as they approached, yet the silence was profound; and Mademoiselle de Verneuil felt herself affected by conditions that added a sort of sadness of nature to her emotional anguish. There was misfortune in the air.

Eventually, in the distance, where a little screen of trees closed the perspective of *échaliers*, she saw a young man flicking over the barriers like a squirrel and running towards her at a surprising speed. 'It's the Gars,' she said to herself. Dressed like any Chouan, and carrying his blunderbuss slung across his back over his goatskin, he was recognizable only by the grace of his bodily movement.

Marie retired precipitately into the cabin, in an instinctive impulse as inexplicable as fear; but soon the young leader was at her side in front of the hearth, where a brisk fire was burning brightly. Both found themselves incapable of speech, unable to meet the other's eyes or make a movement. The same hope was in their minds, the same misgiving separated them; it was both anguish and ecstasy.

'Monsieur,' said Mademoiselle de Verneuil at last, in a faltering voice, 'it is concern for your safety that has brought me here.'

'My safety!' he said with some acerbity.

'Yes,' she answered. 'So long as I stay in Fougères your life is endangered, and because I care for you too much to endanger it I must leave this evening; so don't look for me there again.'

'Leave then, darling! I'll follow you.'

'Follow me! Can you think of that? But what about the Blues?'

'Dearest Marie, what have the Blues to do with our love?'

'It would be difficult for you to stay in France with me, it seems to me, and still more difficult to leave it.'

'Is anything impossible to a person who truly loves?'

'Ah, yes, you are right – I think everything is possible. For your sake haven't I had the courage to give you up!'

'Are you telling me that you could give yourself to a dreadful creature you do not love, and are not willing to make a man who adores you happy, a man whose life you would fill, who swears to be yours and only yours for ever? Listen to me, Marie, do you love me?'

'Yes,' she said.

'Well, then, be mine!'

'Have you forgotten that I am playing a courtesan's shameful rôle, and that it is your rôle to succumb to me? If I am trying to escape you it is to prevent your risking the contempt that I am likely to encounter. If I were not afraid of that, perhaps . . .'

'But if I have no fears . . .'

'And how can I feel confident of that? I have misgivings. In my situation who would not have? . . . If our love is destined not to last, at least it must be complete, able to make us bear the world's injustice joyfully. What have you done for me? . . . You desire me. Do you think that places you in a different category from everyone who has seen me before you? Have you risked your Chouans for an hour of pleasure without troubling more about them than I worried about the murdered Blues when everything was lost for me? And suppose I commanded you to give up all your plans, your hopes, your King who stands in my light and who will perhaps laugh at you when you have died for him while I could die for you, reverencing you! Suppose I wanted you to surrender to the First Consul so that you could follow me to Paris? Suppose I demanded that we should go to America to live far from a world where all is vanity, so that then I might know if you truly love me for myself as I love you at this moment! To say all I mean in one question, suppose I wished that instead of raising me to your level you fell to mine, what would you do?'

'That's enough, Marie. You mustn't try to prove yourself worse than you are. Poor child, I have guessed what is troubling you! There, there, if my first desire for you grew into passion, my passion has now become love. Dear soul of my soul, I know that you are as worthy of worship as your name implies, and as noble as you are beautiful.

'I can be magnanimous too, and believe I am strong enough to make the world accept you. I don't know why it is so: it may be because I foresee a future of unending unimaginable rapture with you. . . . Or is it because in you I meet the rare qualities of soul that keep a man for ever in love with the same woman? Whatever the reason, my love is as wide as the ocean and without reservation and I feel that I can't do without you now. Yes, it's true; my life would be loathsome if you were not part of it always . . .'

'Part of it – how?'

'Oh, Marie! Can't you understand me? . . . your own Alphonse!'

'Ah, you think I should feel flattered if you offer me your name and hand?' she said, with apparent disdain, but with her eyes fixed on the Marquis so that no slightest thought should escape her. 'And do you know whether you will still love me six months from now, and what my fate would be if you didn't? . . .

'No, no, only a mistress can be sure that the feeling a man shows her is whole-hearted, because there is no question of duty, the law, society, the interests of children bolstering it with dreary obligation. And if her power is enduring, she finds a homage in it and a happiness that make the greatest possible sorrows bearable.

'How could I be your wife and face the possibility of one day being a drag on you! . . . I prefer a fleeting love but a true one to that risk, even if death and misery be the end of it. I could indeed be a virtuous mother and devoted wife, better than anyone; but if such affections are to be fostered in a woman's heart a man should not marry her in an explosion of passion. Besides, do I know myself whether you will please me tomorrow?

'No, I do not choose to bring you unhappiness. I'll leave Brittany,' she said, noticing some hesitation in his looks. 'I'll go back now to Fougères, and you must not follow me there . . .'

'Well, then, if you see smoke rising from the Saint-Sulpice Heights in the morning of the day after tomorrow, I'll be with you in the evening as your lover and husband, whatever you wish me to be. I'll have shown you that I defy all risk!'

'You really do love me, Alphonse,' she said in rapture, 'to risk your life before it belongs to me! . . .'

He made no answer but looked at her and she lowered her eyes; but he read on his mistress's ardent face a fever that equalled his own and held out his arms to her. Marie was swept by a wave of madness and about to fall defencelessly into the Marquis's embrace, ready to give herself to him and let this be the summit of happiness, to hazard her whole future which she would make more secure if she came victoriously through this final test.

But scarcely had she laid her head on her lover's shoulder when a slight noise was heard outside. She tore herself from his arms as if suddenly awakened and rushed out of the cottage. She was able then to recover some of her self-possession and consider her situation.

'He would have accepted me and then snapped his fingers at me perhaps,' she said to herself. 'Ah, if I believed that I would kill him! – Ah, not yet though!' she added as she caught sight of Beau-pied. She gestured to him to go away, and the soldier understood and obeyed. The poor boy turned abruptly on his heel, pretending to have seen nothing. Mademoiselle de Verneuil returned at once to the room, her finger to her lips in warning to the young leader not to make the slightest sound.

'They are there,' she said, in the deadened voice of terror.

'Who?'

'The Blues.'

'Ah! I don't intend to die without . . .'

'Yes . . .'

He embraced her, cold and unresisting, and took from her lips a kiss in which joy was mingled with horror, for it might be the last as well as the first. Then they went together to the door and looked out cautiously so as to see all round without being seen. The Marquis caught sight of Gudin at the head of a dozen men cutting off the Couësnon Valley below. He turned towards the line of *échaliers*: the great decaying tree-trunk was guarded by seven soldiers. He stepped on to the order to cider cask and broke in part of the shingle roof tily with-climb out on the rising ground behind; but blot held the drew his head from the hole he had made. at his mistress height and cut the road to Fougères. He and she uttered a despairing cry. She heard the tramp of the three detachments surrounding the house.

'Go out first,' he said, 'and you will preserve me.'

At these words, which to her seemed sublime, she stationed herself gladly at the door while the Marquis loaded his blunderbuss. He first measured with his eye the distance to the great tree-trunk, then threw himself at the seven Blues, riddled them with shot and made a passage through them. All the soldiers rushed towards the *échalier*, which the Gars had jumped, and saw him by that time running across the field at an incredible speed.

'Fire, fire, in the name of ten thousand devils! You're not Frenchmen, you bastards! Fire, damn you, can't you!' thundered Hulot.

As he shouted from the top of the rise, his men and Gudin's fired a ragged volley, fortunately wide of the mark. The Marquis was already nearing the *échalier* at the end of the first field; but as he passed into the second he was almost overtaken by Gudin following hard at his heels. Hearing this formidable enemy a few yards behind him the Gars increased his speed, but the two men reached the next *échalier* almost simultaneously. The Marquis threw his blunderbuss at Gudin's head so adroitly that he struck him and almost brought him to a halt. The anxiety with which Marie watched this scene and Hulot and his soldiers held their breath is indescribable, and involuntarily their gestures as their eyes followed the runners repeated their movements.

The Gars and Gudin arrived together at the screen, white with frost, of the little wood, and then the officer stepped aside suddenly and vanished behind an apple tree. A score of Chouans who had not fired for fear of killing their chief ·ppeared and riddled the tree with bullets. All Hulot's little ba⌐ rushed headlong to save Gudin, who finding himself ⌐d retreated from apple tree to apple tree, seizing his ⌐gun while the Chasseurs du Roi were reloading. His ⌐t last long. The mixed band of Counter-Chouans Hulot at their head ran to the young officer's

340

aid, and reached the place where the Marquis had thrown his blunderbuss.

Just then Gudin caught sight of his exhausted foe sitting under one of the trees of the little wood. He left his comrades exchanging shots with the Chouans entrenched behind a bank enclosing the field, moved round them and picked his way towards the Marquis with a wild creature's speed and wariness. Catching sight of this manoeuvre, the Chasseurs du Roi uttered ear-splitting yells to warn their chief. They fired at the Counter-Chouans with poachers' luck and attempted to hold their ground against them, but the Counter-Chouans courageously climbed the bank which was their enemies' rampart and took a bloody revenge.

The Chouans then retreated to the road beyond the field within which this action had taken place, and took possession of the high ground which Hulot had made the mistake of abandoning. Before the Blues had time to see where they stood, the Chouans had entrenched themselves in the hollows among the rocky ridges, from whose shelter they could fire without risk to themselves if Hulot's soldiers made any show of following to attack them in this stronghold.

While Hulot with a few soldiers went slowly towards the little wood to search for Gudin, the men from Fougères stayed to strip the dead Chouans and despatch those still living. In this dreadful war neither side took prisoners. With the Marquis safe, the Chouans and the Blues mutually recognized the strength of their opponents' position and the futility of further fighting, and both now thought only of retreat.

'If I lose that young man,' Hulot exclaimed, as he sanned the wood, 'may I never make another friend!' *the dead.*

'Aha!' said one of the young men busy stripp *ld coins that* 'Here's a bird with yellow feathers.' *man dressed in*

And he showed his comrades a purse ful *ing a breviary* he had just found in the pocket of a p *ulling a breviary* black.

'But what's he got here?' said a from the dead man's coat.

'Serves him right, he's a priest!' he exclaimed, throwing the breviary on the ground.

'This one's a fraud, he's robbing us,' observed a third young man, finding only two six-franc crowns in the pockets of the Chouan he was stripping.

'Yes, but he has a first-rate pair of shoes,' remarked a soldier, preparing to take them for himself.

'You'll have them if they fall to your share,' one of the Fougères men told him, pulling them off the dead man's feet and throwing them on the heap of clothes and possessions.

A fourth Counter-Chouan was collecting the money found in order to share it equitably when all the members of the expedition should be together.

When Hulot returned with the young officer, whose final bid to get at the Gars had proved as vain as it was dangerous, he found about a score of his soldiers and thirty Counter-Chouans with the booty from eleven dead enemies, whose bodies had been thrown into the ditch at the foot of the bank.

'Soldiers,' Hulot exclaimed sternly, 'I forbid you to take those rags. Form up in line, and quicker than *that*!'

'That's all right for the money, Sir,' protested a soldier, showing Hulot ten bare toes protruding from his shoes; 'but what about these?' And with the butt-end of his gun he pushed out the pair of hobnailed shoes. 'These shoes, Sir, would suit me to a T.'

'Would you put English shoes on your feet?' Hulot answered him.

'Commandant,' one of the Fougères men said respectfully, 'since the beginning of the war we have always shared out the booty'

'I'm not preventing you men from following your customs,' Hulot interrupted him harshly.

'Look here, here's a purse with three louis in it. You deserve it, you did more than anyone. Your commandant won't make that officer's difficulty about your taking it,' said one of Hulot's comrades.

Hulot looked murderously at Gudin, and saw him turn pale.

'It's my uncle's purse!' the young man exclaimed.

Faint with fatigue as he was, he stumbled to the heap of corpses, and the first body that met his eyes was his uncle's. He barely looked at the rubicund face marked with bluish streaks, the stiffened arms and the bullet wound, but after one stifled cry exclaimed, 'Let's go, Sir.'

The band of Blues went on their way. Hulot gave his young friend the support of his arm. 'God's thunder, you'll get over that,' the old soldier told him.

'But he's dead,' answered Gudin, 'dead! He was my only relative and in spite of cursing me he loved me. If the King had returned and the whole country been after my head, the good fellow would have hidden me under his cassock.'

'Isn't he a fool!' the National Guardsmen were saying as they shared out the spoils in the field. 'The old fellow's rich and that way he didn't have time to make a will disinheriting him.'

When the distribution was completed, the Counter-Chouans set off to join the little band of Blues, and followed them at a distance.

Chapter 26

AT nightfall a dreadful uneasiness crept into Galope-chopine's cottage, where life until then had been so artlessly carefree. Barbette, carrying her heavy load of thorn-broom on her back, and her little boy with a supply of grass for the cattle, returned at the family's supper-hour. As they came in, mother and son looked vainly to see Galope-chopine, and never had this wretched room seemed so large to them, its emptiness was so pervasive. The fireless hearth, the gloom, the silence, all spoke to them of impending misfortune.

When it was quite dark, Barbette bestirred herself to light a bright fire and two *oribus*, which is the name given to resin candles inland from the coastal belt to the Upper Loire, and on the northern side of Amboise in the country round Vendôme. She moved about her preparations with the slowness of a person overwhelmed by deep feeling. She was listening for the slightest sound; and often, misled by the gusts of wind that whistled about the house, went to the door of her wretched dwelling and returned sadly again. She washed two *pichés*, filled them with cider and placed them on the long walnut table. Several times she looked at her son who was watching the cooking buckwheat cakes, but was unable to speak to him. At one point the little boy's eyes rested on the two nails that served as support for his father's fowling-piece, and Barbette shivered as she noted like him that the place was empty. The silence was broken only by the lowing of the cows or by drops of cider falling periodically from the bunghole of the cider-cask. The poor woman sighed as she prepared and filled three earthenware bowls with a kind of soup made of milk, broken pieces of buckwheat cake and boiled chestnuts.

'They were fighting in the field belonging to the Béraudière farm,' the little boy volunteered.

'Run and look,' said his mother.

The boy ran to the field, and saw the heap of corpses in the moonlight, but no sign of his father, and returned joyously whistling; he had picked up a few hundred-sou pieces that the triumphant Counter-Chouans had trampled underfoot and left forgotten in the mud. He found his mother sitting on a stool by the fireside spinning hemp, and shook his head; but Barbette did not dare accept good tidings thankfully. Then when it chimed ten o'clock from Saint-Leonard's tower, the little boy went to bed after murmuring a prayer to the Holy Virgin of Auray.

At daybreak, the sleepless Barbette uttered a cry of joy, hearing the sounds of heavy nailed shoes that she recognized approaching, and Galope-chopine soon showed his sinister face.

'The Gars is safe, thanks be to Saint Labre! I've promised a fine candle to him. Don't forget we owe the Saint three candles now.'

Galope-chopine seized a *piché* and swallowed the contents at a draught. When his wife had served his soup and taken his gun from him, he said as he pulled the walnut bench up to the fire and sat down. 'How did it happen that the Blues and Counter-Chouans came here? It was at Florigny they were fighting. Who the devil could have told them that the Gars was at our house? His *garce* and him and us were the only ones who knew.'

His wife turned pale.

'The Counter-Chouans made me believe they were lads from Saint-Georges,' she answered, trembling, 'and I told them where the Gars was.'

Galope-chopine in his turn changed colour, and laid his bowl down on the table edge.

'I sent our boy to warn you,' Barbette went on, in dismay, 'but he didn't find you.'

The Chouan rose and struck his wife so violently that she stumbled to the bed, where she lay as pale as death.

'Damn you, you cursed *garce*, you've killed me,' he said. And then, suddenly scared, he took his wife in his arms and cried, 'Barbette? Barbette? Holy Virgin, I hit her too hard!'

'Do you think,' she said, opening her eyes, 'Marche-à-terre knows yet?'

'The Gars said to find out how he had been betrayed,' the Chouan answered.

'Did he say it to Marche-à-terre?'

'Pille-miche and Marche-à-terre were at Florigny.'

Barbette breathed more freely.

'If they touch a hair of your head, I'll rinse their glasses with vinegar,' she said.

'Ah! I've lost my appetite,' exclaimed Galope-chopine sadly.

His wife pushed the second full *piché* in front of him, but he did not even glance at it. Two great tears traced a path down Barbette's cheeks and glistened in the wrinkles of her faded face.

'Listen, wife, tomorrow morning you're to pile a heap of faggots on the Saint-Sulpice Heights right opposite Saint-Leonard's and set fire to them. It's the signal arranged between the Gars and the old Recteur of Saint-Georges who's to come to say mass.'

'Is he going in to Fougères, then?'

'Yes, to his fine *garce*. I'm to be kept running tomorrow because of it! I think he's going to marry her and carry her off, for he told me to go and hire horses and relay them on the road to Saint-Malo.'

And thereupon Galope-chopine lay down exhausted and slept for a few hours before setting off again.

He returned the following morning, after having carefully carried out the commissions the Marquis had entrusted to him. When he learned that Marche-à-terre and Pille-miche had not appeared, he made light of his wife's fears and she left, almost reassured, for the Saint-Sulpice Heights, where the evening before she had prepared a pile of frost-covered faggots on a mound facing Saint-Leonard's. She led her little boy by the hand, and he carried some live embers in a broken sabot.

His wife and son had barely disappeared beyond the outhouse roof when Galope-chopine heard two men jumping the nearest of the *échaliers* one after the other, and saw craggy forms gradually take shape as indistinct shadows on the thick mist.

'It's Pille-miche and Marche-à-terre,' he said in his mind, and he shuddered.

The two Chouans appeared in the little yard, looking with their dark faces and well-worn wide hats like the figures engravers place in their landscapes.

'Good day, Galope-chopine,' said Marche-à-terre gravely.

'Good day, Monsieur Marche-à-terre,' humbly replied Barbette's husband. 'Will you come in and drink a few *pichés*? I have cold buckwheat cake and fresh-made butter.'

'That's not to be turned down, Cousin,' said Pille-miche.

The two Chouans entered the house. There was nothing in this first approach to alarm the master of the house; and he hastened to his big cask to fill three *pichés*, while Marche-à-terre and Pille-miche, sitting on each side of the long table on the gleaming benches, cut buckwheat cakes for themselves and spread them with rich yellow butter oozing droplets of milk under the knife. Galope-chopine placed the *pichés* of foaming cider before his guests and the three Chouans began their meal. But the host cast a sidelong look at Marche-à-terre from time to time as he busied himself satisfying his guests' thirst.

'Give me your snuff-horn,' Marche-à-terre said to Pille-miche.

And when he had vigorously shaken several pinches into the palm of his hand, the Breton sniffed his tobacco like a man preparing for serious business.

'It's cold,' said Pille-miche, rising and going to close the upper leaf of the door.

The mist-darkened daylight now entered the room only through the little window, and shed a very dim light on the table and two benches, but the surfaces gleamed with red reflections from the fire. Galope-chopine finished replenishing his guests' *pichés* for the second time and set them before them; but they refused to drink, threw aside their wide-brimmed hats, and suddenly adopted a solemn air. Their movements and the look they exchanged as though consulting each other made Galope-chopine quake, and he thought he saw blood under the red woollen caps they were wearing.

'Bring us your chopper,' said Marche-à-terre.

'But, Monsieur Marche-à-terre, what do you want with that?'

'Come, Cousin, you know very well,' said Pille-miche, putting away the snuff-horn that Marche-à-terre returned to him. 'You're sentenced.'

The two Chouans rose simultaneously, seizing their guns.

'Monsieur Marche-à-terre, I said *naught* about the Gars . . .'

'I told you to fetch your chopper,' the Chouan answered.

The unhappy Galope-chopine stumbled against his son's clumsy wooden crib, and three hundred-sou coins rolled out on the floor. Pille-miche picked them up.

'Oho! So the Blues gave you new coins,' exclaimed Marche-à-terre.

'As true as that's Saint Labre up there, I said *naught*,' protested Galope-chopine. 'Barbette took the Counter-Chouans for *gars* from Saint-Georges, that's all.'

'Why do you talk to your wife about business?' Marche-à-terre said sternly.

'Besides, Cousin, we're not asking for excuses, only your chopper. You're sentenced.'

At a sign from Marche-à-terre, the two men seized their victim. Finding himself in the Chouans' hands, Galope-chopine lost all power of resistance, fell on his knees and held out despairing hands towards his executioners.

'Good friends, Cousin, what would become of my little boy?' he said.

'I'll take care of him,' said Marche-à-terre.

'Dear comrades,' said Galope-chopine, ghastly pale, 'I'm not in a fit state to die. Would you let me go without confession? You have the right to take my life, but not to make me lose the eternal blessedness.'

'That's true,' said Marche-à-terre, looking at Pille-miche.

The two Chouans stood there for a moment greatly embarrassed, unable to find a way of resolving this problem of conscience. Galope-chopine listened to the faintest sounds caused by the wind as if he still retained some hope. The noise of the drop of cider falling at regular intervals made him throw a mechanical look at it and sigh sadly. Suddenly Pille-miche pulled the condemned man by one arm into a corner and said, 'Confess all your sins to me. I'll repeat them to a priest of the true Church and he'll give me absolution; and if there's penance to do, I'll do it for you.'

Galope-chopine's circumstantial account of his sins gained him some respite; but numerous and fully detailed though they were, he came to the end of his recital at last.

'Wrong it may be, Cousin,' he said in conclusion, 'but after all, as I'm talking to you like it was my confessor, I tell you by God's holy name that I've nothing much to blame myself for, except for having a few pickings here and there and buttering my bread a bit too freely, and I call Saint Labre above the chimney-place there to vouch for me that I said *naught* about the Gars. No, good friends, I'm no traitor.'

'Come, that's all right, Cousin, get up. You can settle with God about that, all in good time.'

'But let me have a moment to say a word of good-bye to Barbe . . .'

'Come on,' answered Marche-à-terre; 'if you don't want to be blamed more than you have to be, behave like a Breton and make a proper end.'

The two Chouans took hold of Galope-chopine again and laid him along the bench, where he made no more sign of resistance now than the convulsive movements of animal instinct. Finally he uttered one or two mindless howls, ended abruptly at the heavy thud of the cleaver. The head was struck off at one blow.

Marche-à-terre lifted the head by a lock of hair and went outside the cottage. He searched in the roughly-made doorposts for a large nail, and when he had found one twisted the fistful of hair he held round it and left the bloody head to hang there, not even closing the eyes.

The two Chouans washed their hands unhurriedly in a large basin filled with water, took their hats and guns again, and crossed the *échalier*, whistling the air of *The Captain's*

Ballad. At the far end of the field Pille-miche in a hoarse voice struck up some verses from that simple song as they came into his mind, and the rustic cadences were carried on the wind.

> At the first town, her lover
> Dresses her in satin,
> All in fine white silk.
>
> At the next town her lover
> Decks her out in silver,
> In silver and gold.
>
> There she was, so lovely,
> Bridal veils were proffered
> By the whole regiment.

The tune gradually died away as the two Chouans went further off; but the stillness of the countryside was so deep that a snatch reached Barbette's ear as she returned to the house with her little boy by the hand. A peasant girl never hears this song which is so popular in the West of France without being moved to join in, and Barbette involuntarily began the first verses of the ballad.

> Time to go, my lovely,
> Come, my pretty sweeting,
> Time to go to war.
>
> Bold and gallant Captain,
> Don't let it dismay you,
> My girl is not for you.
>
> She'll not be yours by land,
> She'll not be yours by sea,
> But only by treachery.
>
> The father takes his daughter,
> Strips her of her garment,
> Throws her in the sea.
>
> Captain he knows better,

Throws himself in after,
Brings her safe ashore.

Time to go, my lovely,
Come, my pretty sweeting,
Time to go to war.

At the first town, her lover . . . etc.

As Barbette came to the refrain of the ballad, that Pille-miche had begun with, she reached her yard. Her tongue froze, she stood stock-still, and a great cry, immediately cut short, broke from her gaping mouth.

'What's the matter, Mother dear?' the child asked.

'Walk by yourself!' exclaimed Barbette hollowly, pulling her hand away and pushing him from her with extraordinary roughness. 'You have no father nor mother now.'

The child yelled, rubbing his shoulder, but in mid yell caught sight of the suspended head and was struck silent, while his fresh face remained screwed up in the distortion of tears. He opened his eyes wide and stared at his father's head with an apparently stupid lack of emotion; then on his face made doltish by ignorance a primitive curiosity gradually dawned.

Suddenly Barbette took her son's hand, clasped it vehemently and pulled him with her into the house. While Pille-miche and Marche-à-terre were laying Galope-chopine on the bench one of his shoes had fallen under his neck, so that it became filled with blood, and this was the first thing his widow saw.

'Take off your sabot,' the mother said. 'Put your foot in that. That's right. Never forget your father's shoe,' she exclaimed sombrely, 'and never put a shoe on your foot without remembering the shoe filled with blood the *Chuins* shed, and kill the *Chuins*!'

As she spoke she shook her head convulsively so that her black hair fell in elf-locks over her neck, giving her face a witch-like look.

'I take Saint Labre to witness,' she went on, 'that I promise you solemnly to the Blues. You'll be a soldier to avenge your father. Kill, kill the *Chuins*, and do as I do. They've taken the head of my man – I'll give the Gars's head to the Blues!'

She leapt at one bound to the bed, seized a little bag of money from a hiding-place, took her astonished son's hand again and pulled him violently after her without giving him time to put on his sabot; and they walked rapidly away together towards Fougères, without a backward look from either of them at the cottage they were forsaking.

When they reached the top of the Saint-Sulpice cliffs, Barbette stirred up the smouldering pile of faggots and her son helped her to cover them with green frost-covered gorse to make the smoke denser.

'That will last longer than your father, me and the Gars,' Barbette said grimly to her son, pointing to the fire.

Chapter 27

WHILE Galope-chopine's widow and his son with the blood-stained foot were watching the smoke swirl up, with a sombrely vengeful expression on one face and curiosity on the other, Mademoiselle de Verneuil was gazing fixedly towards the same rock and vainly trying to make out the signal the Marquis had spoken of. The fog had gradually thickened, and enshrouded the whole district in a grey veil that obliterated the landscape masses even near the town. She looked with a tender anxiety in turn towards the cliffs, the Castle and the buildings that loomed through the fog like darker patches of fog. Near her window some trees were dimly visible against the bluish background like branching coral apprehended in the depths of a calm sea. The sun lent the sky the dull tones of tarnished silver, and the almost bare branches of the trees where a few last leaves still hung were touched with vague reddish colour by its gleams.

But Marie's soul was too full of sweet emotion for her to see evil omens in this scene, which was out of harmony with her intimations of happiness. In the past two days her outlook on life had been strikingly modified. The distressing acuteness of her passionate feelings, their uncontrolled violence, had slowly yielded to the tranquil equable climate a true love provides. The certainty of being loved, which she had sought through so many dangers, had created the desire to return to the social fold, and a happiness socially approved, which only despair had ever made her turn away from. To love only for a time seemed to her to show an inability to love at all.

She pictured herself transported at once from the social depths into which she had fallen through misfortune to the high position her father had briefly given her. The cruel ups and downs of a passion now happy now despised had put a check on vanity, which now awoke to paint all the pleasures of high social rank. For a Duke's daughter, marrying Montauran surely meant living and moving in her proper sphere?

Having known the hazards of an adventurous life, she could appreciate better than any woman the importance of the emotional bonds that create a family. Marriage, children and the cares they bring did not mean a burden to her, but rest and relaxation. She loved the calm conjugal life she caught a glimpse of through this latest storm, as a woman tired of domesticity may cast an envious glance at an illicit passion. Virtue was for her a new form of seduction.

'Perhaps I treated him too much like a coquette?' she said, turning away from the window without seeing the fire on the Heights. 'But then I didn't know how much he loves me. . . . Francine, it's not a dream now! This evening I'll be the Marquise de Montauran. What have I done to deserve such utter happiness? Oh, I love him, and love can be requited only by love! It's true God must want to recompense me for having preserved a feeling heart in spite of so much wretchedness, and to make me forget my sufferings; for you know, child, I have suffered a great deal.'

'Marquise de Montauran, you, this evening, Marie? Ah, until it actually happens I'll believe I'm dreaming! Who told him that you truly should be that?'

'Dear child, he's not only handsome, he has a soul! If you had seen him surrounded by danger, as I did! Oh, he must know how to love, he is so brave!'

'But if you love him so much, why do you allow him to come to Fougères?'

'We didn't have time to exchange a word before we were surprised. Besides, isn't it a proof of love? And can one ever have too many? Meantime, do my hair.'

But she disturbed the becoming arrangement of her hair over and over again by quick movements as if she were charged with electricity. Her thoughts were still troubled, even while she paid careful attention to her toilette. As she curled a ringlet into shape or smoothed her shining locks, doubt still had a place in her mind; and she would ask herself whether the Marquis might perhaps be deceiving her, and then realize how impossible to understand such duplicity would be, since he was boldly exposing himself to immediate vengeance in coming to seek her at Fougères. As she tried the charming effect in her looking-glass of a sidelong glance, a smile, a slight frown, a pose of anger, love or disdain, she considered what feminine ruse she could find to probe the young leader's heart to the very last moment.

'You are right, Francine!' she said. 'Like you, I wish this marriage was made. Today is the last of my unsettled days; it's big with my death or our happiness. The fog is hateful!' she added, looking again towards the Saint-Sulpice peaks, which were still wrapped in mist.

She set herself to drape the silk and muslin curtains at the window with her own hands, and took pleasure in veiling the daylight to produce a voluptuous contrast of light and shade.

'Francine,' she said, 'take away all those knick-knacks littering the chimney-piece. Leave only the clock and the two Dresden vases – I'll arrange the winter flowers Corentin found for me in them myself. . . . Take out all the chairs, I want only the sofa and an armchair here. When you've finished, child, brush the tapestry to bring up the colours, and then put candles in the fireside sconces and the candlesticks . . .'

Marie studied the old tapestry with which the walls of this room were hung, with concentration and for some time. Her innate taste enabled her to find the shades among the brilliant colours of the design that would marry this ancient hanging to the furnishings and accessories of the boudoir, by harmonizing with it or by the charm of contrast. With the same thought in mind she arranged the flowers and filled the convoluted vases that decorated the room. The sofa was placed near the fire. On two little gilt tables on each side of the bed by the wall opposite the fire-place she placed great Dresden vases with foliage and flowers that filled the room with a sweet scent.

She trembled more than once as she arranged the flowing folds of green silk damask hanging above the bed and considered the sweep of the flower-embroidered covering. Such preparations always hold an inexpressible secret happiness, an excitement so delightful that often as she makes ready for love a woman may forget all her doubts, as Mademoiselle de Verneuil then forgot all hers. There seems an almost religious devotion in this multiplicity of pains taken for the sake of a loved person not there to see and requite, but whose smiling understanding will later be recompense enough for such graceful attentions.

Women, one may say, give themselves up to love before the event; and there is not one who does not say to herself, like Mademoiselle de Verneuil then in her thoughts, 'This evening I shall be in heaven!' Even the most innocent of them writes this sweet hope into the smooth folds of the silk or muslin. Then little by little the harmony which she establishes round her imparts an atmosphere of love to everything. The objects about her, contained in her voluptuous dream, become living witnesses; she makes them sharers in all her coming joys. With every movement, every thought, she takes fresh encouragement to plunder the future. Soon she becomes unable to wait, to hope, but accuses the silence and requires an omen from the slightest sound. Finally doubt comes to lay its clutching fingers on her heart. She cannot rest, she is on fire in the grip of an idea in the mind which seizes her like a purely physical force. At first glorying in her love, she then suffers torture which she could not bear without the hope of joy to come.

A score of times Mademoiselle de Verneuil had pulled the curtains aside in the hope of seeing a pillar of smoke rise above the cliffs; but the fog seemed from moment to moment to take on a deeper grey, and in its darkening her imagination came in the end to show her sinister presages. Finally she let the curtain fall impatiently, vowing not to go near it again. She looked gloomily around the room to which she had given a soul and a voice and asked herself if it were all to be in vain. The thought roused her to consider additional things to be done.

'Child, tidy that,' she said to Francine, drawing her into a dressing-room next door, which was lit by an *oeil-de-boeuf* window giving on the the dark corner where the town ramparts joined the rocky heights of the Promenade; 'and put everything in order. As for the drawing-room, you may leave that as untidy as you like,' she added, with the smile that women reserve for their moments of intimacy with one other, that has a mischievous slyness that men know nothing about.

'Oh, you look lovely!' exclaimed the little Breton girl.

'Ah, silly creatures that we women all are – it's only a lover who can make us look our best!'

Francine left her lying relaxedly on the sofa and gently withdrew, convinced that whether she were loved or not her mistress would never hand over Montauran to his enemies.

Chapter 28

'Are you sure of the truth of this tale you're telling me, old woman?' Hulot was saying to Barbette, who had recognized him as she came into Fougères.

'Have you got eyes in your head? Here, look at the Saint-Sulpice rocks there, my lad, right opposite Saint-Leonard.'

Corentin turned to gaze at the top of the cliffs, to where Barbette was pointing, and as the fog began to thin could see the pillar of whitish smoke Galope-chopine's wife had spoken of, quite clearly.

'But when will he come, hey, can you tell me that, old dame? Will it be this evening or tonight?'

'My good lad, I know nothing about *that*,' returned Barbette.

'Why are you betraying your party?' Hulot asked searchingly, drawing the woman a few paces away from Corentin.

'Ah, Monseigneur le Général, just look at my boy's foot! Eh, well, it's been dipped in my man's blood, killed by the *Chuins* like a calf, saving your presence, to punish him for the three words you dragged out of me the day before yesterday when I was working in the field. Take my boy, since you've bereaved him of his father and mother, but make him a real Blue, my good lad, so that he can kill a lot of *Chuins*. Here, take this, two hundred crowns, and keep them for him. If he spends them carefully he'll go far with that, since it took his father twelve years to save them.'

Hulot stared in astonishment at this pale wrinkled peasant-woman, who was quite dry-eyed.

'But what about you,' he said, 'you, his mother? What are you going to do? It would be better if you kept this money.'

'Oh, me, I don't need nothing now,' she answered, shaking her head sadly. 'If you locked me up safe and sure in the very bottom of the innermost part of the Mélusine Tower yonder,' and she nodded towards the castle, 'the *Chuins* would soon find the way to come and kill me!'

She kissed her son in sombre grief, looked at him and shed a couple of tears, looked at him again, and vanished.

'Commandant,' said Corentin, 'two good heads are better than one if we're to make the best use of an opportunity like this. We know the whole thing and we know nothing. If we had Mademoiselle de Verneuil's house surrounded now at once, we would set her against us. We're not strong enough, you, I, your Counter-Chouans and your two Battalions, to fight against that girl if she takes it into her head to save her *ci-devant*. This lad is a courtier, and so he's wily; he's a young man and a man of mettle. We'll never be able to catch him coming into Fougères. Perhaps he's already here. Can we search the houses? Ridiculous! We learn nothing, give the alarm, and annoy the householders.'

'I'm off,' said Hulot impatiently, 'to give the sentry at the Saint-Leonard guard-post orders to set his beat forward three paces, and he'll then be facing Mademoiselle de Verneuil's house. I'll agree a signal with each sentry. I'll stay with the force on guard, and when the signal is given that any young man whatever has come in, I'll take a corporal and four men and ...'

'And,' Corentin interrupted the impetuous soldier, 'if the young man is not the Marquis, if the Marquis does not come in by way of a Gate, if he is already with Mademoiselle de Verneuil, if, if ...'

Thereupon Corentin looked at the Commandant with an air of superiority that held something so insulting that the old soldier exclaimed, 'God send me a thousand thunderbolts! Take yourself off, citizen of hell, and mind your own devilish business. What has all that got to do with me? If that hot-head comes and falls into one of my guard-posts it will certainly be my job to shoot him; and if I hear that he's in a house I'll have to see that he's surrounded, taken and shot! But devil take me if I'm going to rack my brains to find a way of dirtying my hands and dishonouring my uniform.'

'The letter signed by three Ministers orders you to obey Mademoiselle de Verneuil, Commandant.'

'Let her come herself, Citizen, and I'll see then what I have to do.'

'Very well, Citizen,' Corentin replied haughtily, 'she will not be slow to do so. She will tell you herself the hour and the minute when the *ci-devant* will be here. It may even be that she won't rest until she has seen you posting the sentries and surrounding her house.'

'He's the devil in human shape,' the old Demi-brigade Commandant said dolefully to himself, as he watched Corentin striding away from him up the Queen's Staircase to reach the Saint-Leonard Gate. 'He'll hand Citizen Montauran over to me bound hand and foot, and I'll find myself with a plaguy annoying court-martial to conduct. — But after all,' he concluded, shrugging his shoulders, 'the Gars is an enemy of the Republic, he killed my poor Gérard, and it will always be one nobleman fewer. To hell with it!'

He turned briskly on his booted heel and went to make the rounds of all the guard-posts of the town, whistling the Marseillaise.

Chapter 29

MADEMOISELLE DE VERNEUIL was absorbed in reflection of the kind whose sources lie deep in the heart, where warring emotions have often proved to unfortunate victims that life may be burned out in storm and passion within the four walls of a room without even leaving a sofa. This girl had now reached the dénouement of the drama which she had come to this province in search of, and she was living again its scenes of love and anger that had filled her life so tumultuously in the ten days since her first meeting with the Marquis.

The sound of a man's step in the drawing-room adjoining her boudoir made her tremble. The door opened. She turned her head quickly, and saw Corentin.

'What a little cheat you are!' said the senior police spy, laughing. 'Are you still anxious to trick me? Ah, Marie! Marie! It's a very dangerous game you're playing if I'm not enlisted on your side and you decide on your strokes without consulting me. If the Marquis has escaped his fate. . .'

'It's not your fault, is it?' Mademoiselle de Verneuil finished scathingly. 'Monsieur,' she gravely went on, 'by what right do you come back to my house?'

'Your house?' he commented bitterly.

'You do well to remind me,' she answered with dignity; 'this house is not mine. The choice of it is perhaps calculated to further your schemes for committing murder. I'll leave it. I would go into a wilderness if it would deliver me from the sight of . . .'

'Spies, I suppose you mean,' returned Corentin. 'But this house is neither yours nor mine, it belongs to the Government; and as for leaving, you mean to do nothing of the sort . . .' and he cast a look of diabolical understanding at her.

Mademoiselle de Verneuil rose indignantly and took several steps, but suddenly stopped as she saw Corentin raise the curtain at the window and begin to smile as he motioned her to join him there.

'Do you see that rising smoke?' he said, with his pallid face as imperturbably calm as it always was however deeply involved his emotions might be.

'What possible connection can there be between my leaving and a bonfire of weeds?' she asked.

'Why do you speak so falteringly?' Corentin retorted. 'Poor child,' he added gently. 'I know everything. The Marquis is coming to Fougères today; and it's not with the intention of handing him over to us that you have arranged this boudoir so voluptuously with these flowers and candles.'

Mademoiselle de Verneuil turned pale as she saw the Marquis's death written in the eyes of this ferocious tiger in human form, and felt her passion for her lover take on an aspect of delirium. Each individual hair of her head seemed to stab her with unbearable atrocious pain, and she fell on the sofa. Corentin stood, his arms crossed on his chest, for a moment, half gratified by the sight of a torture that avenged all the sarcasms and disdain this woman had heaped on him, half grieved to see a creature suffer whose slave he still was however heavy her yoke.

'She loves him,' he muttered to himself.

'Love him!' she exclaimed. 'Oh, what does that word mean? Corentin, he is my life, my soul, the breath I breathe!' She threw herself at the man's feet, appalled at his unmoved composure. 'Vile, earthbound soul,' she said, 'I would rather humble myself to gain his life than stoop so low to take it. I mean to save him, whatever the cost in my blood may be. Tell me what you want.'

A tremor passed through Corentin.

'I came to take your orders, Marie,' he said with great gentleness, raising her to her feet with graceful politeness. 'Yes, your insults will not prevent me from being entirely yours to command, provided you stop trying to pull wool over my eyes. You know, Marie, that I can never be duped with impunity.'

'Ah, if you want me to love you, Corentin, help me to save him!'

'Well, what time is the Marquis coming at?' he said, forcing himself to put this question calmly.

'I can't tell you. I don't know anything about that.'

They looked at each other in silence.

'I'm done for,' Mademoiselle de Verneuil was saying to herself.

'She's lying,' Corentin was thinking. 'Marie, I have two maxims,' he said. 'The first is never to believe a word a woman says – in that way one doesn't get taken in. The other is always to look for the motive a woman may have to do the opposite of what she has said she'll do, and when she kindly takes us into her confidence about her plans to expect her to adopt a quite contrary course. I believe we understand each other.'

'Perfectly,' answered Mademoiselle de Verneuil. 'You want proofs of my good faith; but I'm reserving them until you have given me proof of yours.'

'Good-bye, Mademoiselle,' said Corentin stiffly.

'Come,' the girl said, smiling, 'sit down, over there, and don't sulk, or else I can do very well without your help in saving the Marquis. As for the three hundred thousand francs that are always glittering in front of your eyes, I can give you the money there, spread out on that chimney-piece, in gold, the moment the Marquis is in safety.'

Corentin rose, drew back several paces and stared at Mademoiselle de Verneuil.

'You've got rich very suddenly,' he said, ill-disguised bitterness in his tone.

'Montauran will be able to offer you far more himself for his ransom,' Marie said, smiling pityingly. 'So give me proof that you have the means to keep him quite clear of danger and . . .'

'Can you not see that he makes his escape the moment he comes?' Corentin cried suddenly. 'Since Hulot doesn't know the time and . . .' He stopped as if blaming himself for saying too much. '– But you don't need to ask me for a clever way out,' he went on, smiling in the most natural way in the world. 'See here, Marie, I am sure I can trust you. Promise me to compensate me for all I'm losing in helping you, and I'll lead this dolt of a Commandant astray so thoroughly that the Marquis will be as free in Fougères as he was in Saint-James.'

'I promise,' the girl said with solemn earnestness.

'No, not like that,' he said. 'Swear it by your mother.'

Mademoiselle de Verneuil shuddered, and raising a trembling hand she swore as he had demanded. There had been a sudden change in the man's manner and attitude.

'I'm at your service,' he said. 'Don't deceive me, and this evening you'll bless me.'

'I believe you, Corentin,' cried Mademoiselle de Verneuil, feeling touched. She inclined her head sweetly in dismissal, and smiled with a kindness mingled with surprise as she saw an expression of melancholy tenderness on his face.

'What a ravishing creature!' exclaimed Corentin as he went off. 'Will the day never come when she'll be mine to enjoy, and through her I can achieve my ambitions too? To think of her, her, at my feet! ... Oh, the Marquis will die all right! And if I can only have this woman by plunging her in trouble, that's what I'll have to do. – At least she does not distrust me now, I imagine,' he told himself as he reached the Place, where his feet had brought him without his conscious volition. 'A hundred thousand crowns, cash down! She thinks I'm a miser. There's some catch in it, there must be, or else she's married to him.'

Corentin meditated irresolutely, unable to decide on any plan. The fog, dispelled by the sun in the middle of the day, had gradually closed down again as thick as ever and was now so impenetrable that he could not even see the trees a short distance away. 'Here's a new piece of bad luck,' he reflected, slowly making his way home. 'One can't see anything six paces away. The weather protects our lovers. How can one keep a house under observation when it has a fog like this to guard it? – Who's there?' he exclaimed, seizing the arm of some person unknown who seemed to have climbed dangerously up to the Promenade by way of the cliff-face over the boulders.

'It's me,' a childish voice said artlessly.

'Ah, the little boy with the red foot. So you want to avenge your father?' Corentin demanded.

'Yes!' said the child.

'Good. Do you know the Gars?'

'Yes.'

'Better still. Well, stay with me. Do exactly what I tell you. You will put the finishing hand to your mother's work and you'll earn big money. Do you like big money?'

'Yes.'

'You like big money and you want to kill the Gars. I'll take good care of you. – Well,' Corentin said to himself after a pause, 'you shall betray him to us yourself, Marie! She is too impetuous to pause to consider coolly the blow I'm going to strike her; besides passion never reflects. She doesn't know the Marquis's handwriting, so now is the moment to lay the snare and her own temperament will make her rush headlong into it. But I need Hulot to make sure my ruse succeeds. I'll go at once and see him.'

Meanwhile Mademoiselle de Verneuil and Francine were deliberating how the Marquis might be preserved from Corentin's suspect benevolence and Hulot's bayonets.

'I'll go and warn him,' cried the little Breton girl.

'Do you know where he is, silly? Even I, with all my heart's instinct to guide me, might search for ever and not find him.'

They thought of and proposed to each other plenty of the wild plans that seem to people plotting by the fireside so easy to carry out; and at last Mademoiselle de Verneuil exclaimed, 'When I see him his danger will give me inspiration.'

Like all ardent spirits she found something appealing in leaving her line of action undecided to the last moment, trusting to her star or the opportunist instinct that rarely lets women down. Perhaps never before had she suffered such acute emotional stress. At times she stayed motionless, as if in a daze, her eyes fixed; and then at the slightest sound she would vibrate like some almost uprooted tree that the foresters violently tug and jerk by a rope to hasten its fall.

Suddenly a dozen shots were heard loudly in the distance. Mademoiselle de Verneuil turned pale, grasped Francine's hand and said, 'This is my death-blow – they have killed him.'

A soldier's heavy tread was heard in the drawing-room. Francine in terror opened the door to a corporal. The Republican soldier saluted Mademoiselle de Verneuil and held out letters whose paper was slightly soiled. There was no response from the girl, and he withdrew after saying, 'Madame, the Commandant sent these.'

With a feeling of deep foreboding, Mademoiselle de Verneuil read a letter from Hulot, written evidently in haste.

'Mademoiselle, my Counter-Chouans have just intercepted one of the Gars's messengers, who was shot. Among the letters he was carrying was the one herewith which may be of some use to you, etc.'

'Thank God, he's not the man they have just killed!' she exclaimed, throwing this letter into the fire.

She breathed more freely, and avidly turned to the note that had been passed on to her. It was from the Marquis and seemed to be addressed to Madame du Gua.

'No, my dear, I shall not be going to La Vivetière this evening. This evening you will lose your bet with the Comte and I shall triumph over the Republic in the person of that luscious girl, who is certainly worth a night, you must admit. It will be my only actual profit from this campaign, for the Vendée is surrendering. There's nothing one can do now in France, and we may leave for England again, I suppose, together. But serious business may wait till tomorrow.'

The note fell from her hands, she closed her eyes and remained deeply silent, leaning back, her head on a cushion. After a long pause she raised her eyes to the clock, which indicated four in the afternoon.

'And Monsieur keeps us waiting,' she said, with harsh sarcasm.

'Oh, if only he wouldn't come!' said Francine.

'If he did not come,' Marie said hollowly, 'I would go out

to meet him! But no, he cannot be long now. Francine, do I look really beautiful?'

'You look very pale!'

'You see this scented room, the flowers, the candles, the intoxicating perfume – everything might make the man I wished to taste the sweetness of love tonight think he was in heaven.'

'Why, Mademoiselle, what's the matter?'

'I am betrayed, deceived, deluded, tricked, cast away, destroyed, and I mean to kill him, rend him! Oh, yes, there was always a contempt in his manner that he could not hide and that I closed my eyes to! Oh, I can't go on living! – Oh, fool that I am,' and she laughed, 'he is coming. I have the night to teach him that a man who has once possessed me, married to him or not, can never forsake me. I'll mete out a vengeance to him equal to his offence and he shall die in torment. I imagined he had some greatness of soul, but he can be nothing but some lackey's son! He certainly deluded me very cleverly, for I can scarcely believe even yet that this man, although he was capable of handing me over mercilessly to Pille-miche, can stoop to tricks worthy of *Scapin*.* It is so easy to trick a loving woman that there's no baser meanness. That he should kill me, well and good; but to lie, the man I thought so great! To the scaffold with him! The scaffold! Ah, how I wish I could see him guillotined! Am I so cruel, then? He shall die lapped in caresses, with kisses worth twenty years of his life . . .'

'Marie,' Francine answered her with an angel's sweetness, 'be your lover's victim, like so many others, but don't make yourself either his mistress or his executioner. Keep his image in the depths of your heart and don't make it an instrument of torture to yourself. If there were no joy in a hopeless love, what would become of us poor women? That God whom you never spare a thought to, Marie, will reward us for having done what it is our vocation to do on earth – to love and to endure!'

'Dear child,' said Mademoiselle de Verneuil, patting

* The knavish valet in Molière's famous comedy. – *Trans.*

Francine's hand, 'your voice is very sweet and very persuasive!
Right and reason are very attractive with your face! I wish I
could do as you tell me . . .'

'You will forgive him and not hand him over!'

'Don't say another word, don't speak to me about that
man. Compared to him, Corentin is a noble creature. Do you
understand?'

She rose, her face desperately calm, not revealing either her
bewilderment in a disordered world or her burning thirst for
revenge. Her slow measured step seemed the outward expression of some irrevocable decision. Tortured by her
thoughts, but swallowing the insult to her pride and haughtily
refusing to show a trace of the torment she was suffering, she
went to the guard-post at the Saint-Leonard Gate to ask
where the Commandant was staying. She had scarcely left the
house when Corentin came in.

'Oh, Monsieur Corentin,' exclaimed Francine, 'if you're
concerned about this young man, save him! Mademoiselle is
going to hand him over. This dreadful paper has destroyed
everything!'

Corentin carelessly took the letter, asking, 'And where has
she gone?'

'I don't know.'

'I'll hurry and save her from herself and her despair,' he
said.

He vanished, taking the letter with him, strode quickly
through the house and said to the little boy playing before the
door, 'Which way did the lady go who has just gone out?'

Galope-chopine's son, answering the cry for vengeance his
mother had breathed into his heart, walked a little way with
Corentin to point out the path leading down to the Saint-
Leonard Gate.

'That way,' he said, without hesitation.

At that moment four men in disguise entered Mademoiselle
de Verneuil's house, unseen by either the boy or Corentin.

'Go back to your post,' said the spy. 'Pretend to be playing
at clicking the shutter latches, but keep your eyes open, look
everywhere – not forgetting the roof-tops.'

Chapter 30

CORENTIN, hurrying in the direction the little boy had indicated, thought he recognized Mademoiselle de Verneuil through the fog, and did in fact overtake her just as she reached the Saint-Leonard guard-post.

'Where are you going?' he asked her, offering his arm. 'You are pale – what has happened? Do you think it proper for you to go out all alone like this? Take my arm.'

'Where is the Commandant?' she asked.

She had scarcely finished speaking when she heard the bustle of a military reconnaissance party beyond the Saint-Leonard Gate, and soon distinguished Hulot's deep voice in the midst of the hubbub.

'God's thunder! I've never had such thick conditions to make the rounds in,' he was declaring. 'This *ci-devant* has ordered the weather to suit himself.'

'Why should you grumble?' Mademoiselle de Verneuil answered him, gripping his arm. 'This fog can hide vengeance as well as treachery!' Then she added, in a low voice. 'Commandant, there are measures that must be taken in concert with me so that the Gars may have no chance of escaping today.'

'Is he in your house?' he asked in a voice that showed his astonishment.

'No,' she answered, 'but give me a man you can depend on and I'll send him to warn you when this Marquis comes.'

'Think what you're doing, Marie,' Corentin said emphatically. 'A soldier in your house would scare him off, but a child, and I'll find you one, will not cause suspicion . . .'

'Commandant, thanks to this fog you're cursing, you can surround my house at once,' Mademoiselle de Verneuil went on. 'Post soldiers everywhere. Place a guard-post by the Church to cover the level space on which my drawing-room windows give. Station men on the Promenade – the windows of my bedroom may be twenty feet from the ground but desperation can give strength to leap from more dangerous heights. And this is very important – I'll probably send this gentleman out by my house-door, so let it be a brave man who is entrusted with watching it; because one can't deny him courage,' and she heaved a sigh, ' and he will defend himself!'

'Gudin!' cried the Commandant.

The young Fougères citizen detached himself smartly from the band who had returned with Hulot, and who had remained drawn up a short distance away.

'Listen carefully, my boy,' the old soldier said to him in an undertone. 'This thunderbolt of a girl is handing over the Gars to us. I don't know why, but it doesn't matter, it's not our business. You will take ten men and take up your position guarding the entrance to the cul-de-sac where this girl's house is; but make sure that neither you nor your men can be seen.'

'Yes, Sir, I know the ground.'

'Well, boy,' Hulot went on, 'I'll send Beau-pied to warn you when it's time to start the gun-play. Try to reach the Marquis yourself; and if you can kill him and save me from having to have him shot judicially, you'll be a Lieutenant within a fortnight or my name isn't Hulot. – Here, Mademoiselle, here's a fellow who won't shrink from action,' he said to the girl, indicating Gudin. 'He'll keep a close watch over your house, and if the *ci-devant* leaves or tries to get in, he'll not miss.'

Gudin went off with a file of soldiers.

'You realize what you're doing?' Corentin said in a low voice.

She did not answer, and watched with a kind of assuagement the men under the Sublieutenant go to take up their position on the Promenade, and the others that following Hulot's instructions posted themselves along the dark sides of Saint-Leonard.

'There are houses adjoining mine,' she said to the Commandant. 'Surround them too. Don't let us neglect a single precaution we might have cause to regret omitting later.'

'She's out of her mind,' thought Hulot.

'What did I tell you?' Corentin said, at his ear. 'As for the child I mean to put in her house, it's the little boy with the bloody foot, so . . .'

He left the sentence unfinished. Mademoiselle de Verneuil had gone like an arrow towards her house, and he followed her whistling like a happy man. When he caught up with her she had already reached her door, where Corentin found Galope-chopine's son.

'Mademoiselle,' he said, 'take this little fellow with you. He's the quickest and most innocent messenger you can have. – When you see the Gars inside the house, whatever anyone may say to you, dash off. Come and find me at the guard-post and I'll give you enough to keep you in buckwheat cake for the rest of your life.'

At these words, breathed in the little boy's ear rather than spoken, Corentin felt his hand vehemently pressed by the young Breton, who then followed Mademoiselle de Verneuil.

'Now, my good friends, you can explain it all to each other when you like!' exclaimed Corentin when the door had shut. 'If you make love now, little Marquis, it'll be on your winding-sheet.'

But Corentin could not make up his mind to let this fateful house out of his sight, and walked to the Promenade where he found the Commandant busy issuing orders. Soon night fell. Two hours elapsed, without the sentries stationed from point to point being given any reason to suspect that the Marquis might have crossed the triple line of watchful hidden men cordoning the three sides by which the Papegaut Tower was accessible. Corentin had gone twenty times from the Promenade to the Guard-room, and twenty times his hopes had been disappointed: his young messenger had not come to find him.

Deep in his thoughts the spy walked slowly along the Promenade, a prey to the devastating torture of three conflicting passions: love, avarice, ambition. Eight o'clock rang out from all the clock-towers. The moon was late in rising; so mist and darkness wrapped the theatre in grim shadow where the drama plotted by this man was to be played out.

Fouché's trusted agent had the power to hold his passions on a tight rein. He crossed his arms finally across his chest, and stared steadily at the window rising like a luminous phantasm above the Tower. Whenever his pacing brought him to the side looking down from the precipitous height on the valleys, he automatically listened and looked through the fog pierced by the pale glimmer of a few lights in the houses here and there in the town or the Faubourgs, above and below the ramparts. The profound silence was broken only by the murmur of the Nançon, by the lugubrious periodical strokes from the belfry, the heavy tread of sentries or the sound of arms when the posts were relieved hour by hour. A deep solemnity had fallen on man and Nature.

'It's as dark as the inside of a wolf's throat,' Pille-miche said.

'Keep going,' answered Marche-à-terre, 'and don't have any more to say than a dead dog.'

'I hardly dare to breathe,' retorted the Chouan.

'If the man who has just sent a stone rolling wants to find a sheath for my knife in his heart he has only to do it again,' muttered Marche-à-terre, in a voice so low that it mingled with the soft continuous murmur of the Nançon streams.

'But it was me,' said Pille-miche.

'Well, slide on your belly, old leather-pouch,' the chief said, 'like a snake in the hedge. Otherwise we'll leave our carcases here sooner than we count on.'

'Hey, Marche-à-terre,' the incorrigible Pille-miche continued, pulling himself forward on his belly till he reached his comrade's level, and speaking in such a muted tone in his ear that the Chouans following did not catch a syllable. 'Hey, Marche-à-terre, if what our Big Garce says is true there's fine pickings up there. What about you and me going halves, fifty-fifty?'

'Look here, Pille-miche!' said Marche-à-terre, stopping and resting flat on his face.

The whole Chouan band followed his example, exhausted by the arduous struggle up the face of the cliff.

'I know', Marche-à-terre went on, 'that you're one of those Johnny-take-alls who would as soon give blows as take them only if that's all there is to take. But we're not here to look for dead men's shoes, we're devils fighting devils and bad luck to the ones with short claws. The Big Garce sent us here to save the Gars. He's there, look! Lift your dog's nose and look at that window above the Tower.'

At that moment, midnight struck. The moon shone out, making the fog look like white smoke. Pille-miche violently gripped Marche-à-terre's arm, silently indicating the triangular points of several bayonets gleaming ten feet above their heads.

'The Blues are there already,' he said; 'we'll not be fit to match them.'

'Take it easy,' answered Marche-à-terre. 'If I saw it right this morning we ought to find a little place at the bottom of the Papegaut Tower between the ramparts and Promenade where they always pile rubbish, and we can let ourselves drop on it just like on a bed.'

'If Saint Labre wanted to change all the blood that'll be let into good cider,' said Pille-miche, 'the Fougères folk wouldn't go thirsty tomorrow.'

Marche-à-terre put his broad hand over his friend's mouth, then sent a muttered word from man to man till it reached the last of the Chouans hanging in the air on the heather of the schist cliffs. Corentin's professionally keen ear of course had not missed the rustle of bushes the Chouans had brushed or the rattle of light stones sent rolling down the steep face, and he was at the edge of the esplanade. Marche-à-terre, who appeared to possess the power of seeing in the dark or whose constantly exercised senses must have acquired a savage's acuteness, had caught sight of Corentin – perhaps he had scented him like a well-trained dog. It was in vain the police spy listened to the silence and stared at the natural wall of stone: he could distinguish nothing. If the fog's uncertain glimmer did let him see Chouans he took them for boulders, these human bodies so readily took on the likeness of inert nature.

The band's danger was not of long duration. Corentin was drawn away by a very distinct sound from the other extremity of the Promenade, from the point where the sustaining wall ended and the steep cliff slope began. A path among the rocks leading from the Queen's Staircase ended just there. As Corentin reached the place he saw a figure rise as if by magic. He stretched out his hand to grasp this ghostly or real being, whom he did not credit with any good intentions, and encountered the rounded softness of a woman.

'Devil take you, good woman!' he muttered below his breath. 'If it hadn't been me you knocked into you might have had a bullet through your head. . . . But where are you coming from and where are you off to at this hour? Have you lost your tongue? – It's certainly a woman, all the same,' he said to himself.

The silence was becoming suspicious, when the stranger answered in a voice that showed that she was very frightened.

'Eh, my good man, I were coming back from watching a sick-bed.'

'It's the Marquis's so-called mother,' Corentin said to himself. 'Let's see what she's up to.'

'Well, go that way, old woman,' he said aloud, pretending not to recognize her. 'To the left, there, if you don't want to be shot!'

He stayed where he was; but when he had watched Madame du Gua make her way towards the Papegaut Tower, he followed at a distance, shadowing her unseen with a devil's skill.

Meanwhile during this fateful encounter the Chouans had taken up their position with craft and skill on the rubbish heap Marche-à-terre had guided them to.

'That's the Big Garce!' Marche-à-terre muttered to himself, rearing himself up on his toes and climbing up the Tower as a bear might have done.

'We're here,' he said to the lady.

'Good!' answered Madame du Gua. 'If you can find a ladder down there in that house with the garden ending six feet below the refuse-heap, the Gars will be saved. Do you see that bull's-eye window up there? It gives on a dressing-room adjoining the bedroom: that's where you have to get to. This corner of the Tower above you is the only part not surrounded. The horses are ready, and if you have kept the way across the Nançon clear we can have him out of danger in a quarter of an hour in spite of his folly. But if that whore tries to follow him, stick your dagger through her.'

Corentin, descrying through the darkness the stealthy movement of several of the indistinct shapes that he had taken for rocks, went immediately to the Saint-Leonard Gate guard-room, where he found the Commandant sleeping fully-dressed on the camp-bed.

'Leave him be,' said Beau-pied roughly to Corentin. 'He's only just laid down there.'

'The Chouans are here,' cried Corentin in Hulot's ear.

'Impossible, but so much the better!' exclaimed the Commandant, still more than half asleep. 'At least we'll get fighting them.'

When Hulot reached the Promenade, Corentin pointed out the odd position the Chouans were holding.

'They must have slipped through the sentries I posted between the Queen's Staircase and the castle, or strangled them!' exclaimed Hulot. 'Ah, what a thundering pest of a fog! But never mind. I'll send fifty men to the foot of the rock under a lieutenant. We mustn't attack them where they are, for these animals are so tough that they could let themselves roll down the cliff like stones without breaking a limb.'

The cracked bell was striking two o'clock from the bell-tower when the Commandant returned to the Promenade, after giving orders for the most stringent military precautions to prevent the Chouans commanded by Marche-à-terre from escaping. With the numbers at the posts doubled, Mademoiselle de Verneuil's house was now the centre of a small army. The Commandant found Corentin absorbed in contemplation of the window above the Papegaut Tower.

'Citizen,' said Hulot, 'I think the *ci-devant* is playing a game with us. Nothing has moved yet.'

375

'He's there,' Corentin exclaimed, pointing to the window. 'I saw a man's shadow on the curtains . . . I don't understand what's become of my little boy. They must have killed or bribed him. Look, Commandant, do you see? There's a man there! Let's move in!'

'I'm not going to take him in bed, God's thunder! He'll come out if he's gone in. Gudin will not miss him,' exclaimed Hulot, who had his reasons for waiting.

'Come on, Commandant, I call upon you in the name of the Law to take action at once against that house.'

'You have a brazen neck to think you can order me about!'

Corentin, quite unmoved by the Commandant's wrath, said coldly, 'You'll obey me! Here is an order in proper form signed by the Minister of War which obliges you to,' and he drew a paper from his pocket. 'Do you imagine we are so simple as to let that girl do as she thinks fit? It's a civil war we are putting down, and the importance of the end justifies the pettiness of the means.'

'I take the liberty, Citizen, of sending you to . . . your order— You understand me? Enough said. Leave me to mind my own business. Take yourself off, and quicker than *that*!'

'Read it,' said Corentin.

'Take your official importance out of it and don't *bother* me!' exclaimed Hulot, indignant at being given orders by a being he found so contemptible.

At this moment Galope-chopine's son appeared in their midst like a rat risen out of the ground.

'The Gars is away!' he cried.

'Which way? . . .'

'The Rue Saint-Leonard.'

'Beau-pied,' Hulot said in an undertone to the Corporal at his side, 'run to warn your Lieutenant to advance upon the house and strike up a good burst of fire ahead, you hear? — Left wheel, you men, forward upon the Tower!'

Chapter 31

To understand the dénouement fully we must return to Mademoiselle de Verneuil's house with her.

The modest escape from reality produced by alcohol or drugs is nothing compared with the bursting from its bonds of the mind when catastrophe overtakes the passions. The lucidity with which ideas present themselves to the mind then, and the rarefied keenness with which the senses react, produce the strangest and most unexpected effects. Certain obsessed minds see some things clearly that are by no means obvious and the plain palpable things of everyday life are as if they did not exist. Mademoiselle de Verneuil after reading the Marquis's letter was in this state approaching alienation, and like someone walking in her sleep she had hurried to take all possible measures to ensure that he should not escape her vengeance, as single-mindedly as she had previously prepared for the first celebration of her love.

But when she saw her house carefully surrounded by a three-fold barrier of bayonets by her orders, a sudden illumination shone in her mind. She looked at her own behaviour and was filled with horror at the thought of the crime she had just committed. In a first alarmed impulse she rushed towards her front door, and then stood a moment motionless, trying to consider and unable to achieve a logical sequence of thought.

She was so incredulous of what she had just done that she wondered why she was standing in the lobby of her house holding a strange child by the hand. Myriads of flashes of light seemed to move in the air before her like tongues of flame. She walked through the house, trying to shake off the horrible torpor that enveloped her, but like a sleep-walker saw no object in its proper form or colours. She grasped the little boy's hand with extraordinary force in a way quite unlike her and pulled him along so fast that she seemed possessed of the strength and energy of insanity.

She saw nothing and no one in the drawing-room when she walked through it, although there were three men there who bowed to her and stood aside to let her pass.

'Here she is,' one of them said.

'She is very beautiful,' the priest exclaimed.

'Yes,' answered the first man; 'but how pale and agitated she looks . . .'

'And absent in mind,' the third man added. 'She doesn't see us.'

At the door of her room Mademoiselle de Verneuil noticed Francine's kind happy face; and the girl whispered. 'He is here, Marie!'

Mademoiselle de Verneuil started awake and her brain began to function. She looked at the child she held by the hand, recognized him and said to Francine, 'Lock up this little boy and don't let him escape if you care for my life.'

As she slowly uttered these words she raised her eyes to the door of her room, and they remained fixed in a terrifying stare as if she saw her victim through the thickness of the wood. She gently pushed the door open and closed it behind her without looking back, for she saw the Marquis standing before the fireplace. Without being too studied, the nobleman's dress had a certain air of rejoicing and celebration, which added to the glamour all women find in their lovers.

At sight of him Mademoiselle de Verneuil recovered all her self-possession. Her parted lips were strained and tense and showed her white teeth in a set smile more frightening than inviting. She walked slowly towards the young man and pointed to the clock.

'A man worth loving is worth waiting for,' she said with an attempt at gaiety. But then, overcome by the violence of her feelings, she sank down on the sofa near the hearth.

'Dearest Marie, you are enchanting when you are angry,' said the Marquis, sitting down beside her, taking her hand which she let him hold, and imploring a glance which she refused. 'I hope,' he went on tenderly and caressingly, 'that

378

Marie will be very sorry in a moment that she denies the favour of her countenance to her happy husband.'

When she heard this, she turned abruptly and looked him in the eyes.

'What does this terrible look mean?' he asked laughing. 'But your hand is burning! My darling, what's wrong?'

'My darling!' she repeated in a strange hollow voice.

'Yes,' he said, falling on his knees, and taking both her hands and covering them with kisses. 'Yes, my darling, I am yours for my whole life.'

She pushed him violently away and rose, her features distorted. She laughed like a person distraught and said, 'You don't mean a word of it, you're a double-dealer falser than the vilest cheat!'

She rushed to the dagger, which was lying by a vase of flowers, and flashed it inches from the chest of the astonished young man.

'Bah!' she said, throwing down the blade. 'I don't respect you enough to kill you! Your blood is even too vile for soldiers to shed, and I see nothing for you but the headsman.'

The words were uttered painfully, in a low voice, and she stamped her foot like an impatient spoilt child. The Marquis followed her, trying to clasp her.

'Don't touch me!' she exclaimed, recoiling in horror.

'She's mad,' the Marquis said desperately.

'Yes, mad,' she repeated, 'but not mad enough to be your toy. There's nothing I wouldn't have forgiven to passion; but to want to possess me without love, and to write to that . . .'

'Whom did I write to?' he asked, with an astonishment which was obviously not feigned.

'To that pure woman who tried to kill me.'

At this the Marquis turned pale, gripped the back of the chair he was holding as if he would break it, and exclaimed, 'If Madame du Gua is responsible for some vile slander . . .'

Mademoiselle de Verneuil looked for the letter but could not find it. She called Francine and when the girl came demanded, 'Where is that letter?'

'Monsieur Corentin took it.'

'Corentin! Ah, I understand it all! He wrote the letter, and tricked me like the devil he is, with his own horrible devilish skill!'

She uttered a piercing cry and tottered towards the sofa, falling on it in a flood of tears. Certainty of the truth was as appalling as her suspicion. The Marquis threw himself at his lady's feet, held her to his heart, repeating over and over again the only words he could utter, 'Why are you crying, my angel? What does it matter? Your angry words are full of love. Don't cry now; I love you! I'll always love you.'

Suddenly she clasped him with extraordinary vehemence, and still sobbing she said. 'You still love me? . . .'

'Do you have any doubt of it?' he answered with an almost melancholy ruefulness.

She freed herself abruptly from his arms and stood two steps away, looking frightened and confused.

'Suppose I do doubt it? . . .' she exclaimed.

She saw the Marquis smile with such tender mocking gentleness that the words died on her lips. She let him take her by the hand and lead her to the threshold of the next room. There Marie saw, at the far end of the drawing-room, an altar hastily set up in her absence. The priest was now wearing his canonical dress. Lighted candles cast a radiance as soft as hope towards the ceiling. She recognized two men who had bowed to her: the Comte de Bauvan and the Baron du Guénic, the witnesses chosen by Montauran.

'Will you still refuse me?' the Marquis whispered.

At this she quickly stepped back into her room, fell on her knees, held out her hands towards the Marquis and said imploringly, 'Oh, forgive me! Forgive, forgive me!'

Her voice failed, her head fell back, her eyes closed, and she lay in the arms of the Marquis and Francine as if she were dead. When she opened her eyes again it was to meet the eyes of the young leader, a look full of kindness and love.

'Marie, have patience! This storm is the last,' he said.

'The last!' she repeated.

Francine and the Marquis looked at each other wonderingly, but she imposed silence with a gesture.

'Call the priest,' she said, 'and leave me alone with him.' They left her.

'Father,' she said to the priest, who appeared at once; 'in my childhood, Father, a venerable old man like you often used to tell me that with earnest and living faith there was nothing one might not ask God for and hope to obtain. Is that true?'

'It is true,' the priest answered. 'Everything is possible to the Creator of all.'

Mademoiselle de Verneuil fell on her knees and prayed with intense fervour and exaltation. 'O God,' she cried ardently, 'my faith in You is as great as my love for him! Inspire me! Grant a miracle here; or take my life.'

'Your prayer will be heard,' said the priest.

Mademoiselle de Verneuil went into the next room, the cynosure of all eyes, leaning on the arm of this old white-haired priest. A profound mysterious emotion made her loveliness more radiant than ever in the past as she went to her lover, with an arresting serenity like that of the martyrs as painters like to depict them. She held out her hand to the Marquis, and they moved hand in hand to the altar and kneeled before it.

In this marriage about to be celebrated a few paces from the nuptial bed, and in the touching and strange scene, with the hastily raised altar, the crucifix, vessels and communion-cup brought by the priest in secret, the smoke of incense rising under ceilings familiar only with the smoke of meals, the candles lit in a drawing-room, the priest wearing only a stole over his cassock – in them the portrait is complete of those times of sad memory when civil discord overturned the most hallowed institutions.

The religious rites of those days were full of the grace of the earliest mysteries. Infants were baptized in the bedrooms where their mothers still groaned. The Saviour went as once long ago, simple and poor, to comfort the dying. Young girls received the Eucharist for the first time in the room where they had been playing the evening before. The union of the

Marquis and Mademoiselle de Verneuil was about to be solemnized, like so many other unions, in a ceremony in contravention of the new laws. Later, indeed, such marriage ceremonies, usually performed under the oak trees in the forest, were all to be scrupulously recognized.

The priest who was thus maintaining the ancient rites so long as it was possible was one of those who remained true to their principles while the storm raged. Through the tempest his voice rose clear, speaking only words of peace. He had not compromised with the Republic by taking the required oath. Unlike the Abbé Gudin, he had not fanned the flames of the conflagration. Like many others he had devoted himself to the hazardous work of executing the functions of the priesthood for those souls that had remained Catholic. To carry on his dangerous ministry successfully he employed all the means made necessary by persecution; and the Marquis had managed to reach him only by way of one of those underground hiding-places which are still called *priest-holes*.

The sight of this pale ascetic face so readily evoked reverence and prayer that it alone gave this mundane room the atmosphere of a holy place. The instrument of union for joy or sorrow was prepared. Before beginning the ceremony, amid profound silence, the priest asked the bride's names.

'Marie-Nathalie, daughter of Mademoiselle Blanche de Castéran, late Abbess of Notre-Dame de Séez, and of Victor-Amédée, Duc de Verneuil.'

'Born at –?'

'La Chasterie, near Alençon.'

'I didn't think Montauran would be such a fool as to marry her,' the Baron said in an undertone to the Comte. 'A Duke's natural daughter! Shame on him!'

'If she were the King's it would pass,' said Comte de Bauvan smiling. 'I'm not one to blame him. I find the other one attractive, and it's that *Charette's Mare* I'll lay siege to now. She's no cooing dove, that lady! . . .'

The Marquis's names had already been filled in. The two lovers signed, and after them the witnesses. The ceremony began. Marie was the only one to hear at this moment the clink of muskets and the heavy regular tramp of soldiers, no doubt coming to relieve the guard of Blues that she had had posted by the Church. She trembled and raised her eyes to the crucifix on the altar.

'Look at the saint,' said Francine softly.

'Let them give me saints like that, and I'll be devilish pious,' the Comte added under his breath.

When the priest put the customary question to Mademoiselle de Verneuil, she answered 'I will' with a deep sigh. She leaned to her husband's ear and said, 'You will soon know why I have broken my vow never to marry you.'

When after the ceremony the company had passed into a room where dinner was served, as the guests were sitting down, Jérémie arrived looking terrified. The poor bride rose abruptly and went to meet him, followed by Francine. Offering one of the pretexts women so easily find, she begged the Marquis to do the honours of the meal alone for a moment, and bore the servant away before he could commit an indiscretion which might be fatal.

'Ah, Francine, to feel oneself die and not be able to say "I am dying"! . . .' exclaimed Mademoiselle de Verneuil.

She did not appear at the table again; her absence could find its excuse in the ceremony that had just taken place.

At the end of the meal, when the Marquis's uneasiness had become acute, Marie returned in the splendour of bridal dress. Her face was happy and serene, while Francine's beside her expressed such desperate terror in every feature that the guests seemed to be seeing some bizarre picture from Salvator Rosa's extravagant brush, representing life hand in hand with death.

'Gentlemen,' she said to the priest, the Baron and the Comte, 'you shall be my guests tonight for it would be too dangerous for you to leave Fougères. This good girl has my instructions and will take you all to your rooms.

'Please don't protest,' she said to the priest, who was about to speak. 'I hope you won't disobey a woman on her wedding-day.'

An hour later she was alone with her lover in the voluptuous room she had arranged with such graceful art. They reached that fateful bed at last, in which as in a tomb so many hopes are broken, where the awakening to a rewarding life is so uncertain, where love may die or be born, according to the calibre of the characters that can only be tested there. Marie looked at the clock and said to herself, 'Six hours to live'.

'So I could fall asleep!' she exclaimed towards morning, waking with the sudden start of those who have made a pact with themselves the evening before to wake at a certain hour. 'Yes, I must have slept,' she repeated, seeing the hands of the clock in the candlelight almost at two o'clock. She turned and contemplated the Marquis, sleeping with one hand under his head as children do, the other clasping his wife's, and a half-smile on his parted lips as if he had fallen asleep on a kiss.

'Ah, he is sleeping like a child,' she said softly to herself. 'But how should he distrust me, the person who owes ineffable happiness to him?'

She shook him gently, he woke and smiled completely. He kissed the hand he held and looked at this unhappy woman with such sparkling eyes that she was unable to bear their fire and slowly let her broad lids fall as if to shield herself from such dangerous contemplation. This gesture, veiling her own flame, excited desire in appearing to offer resistance, so that if she had not had such deep fears to conceal her husband might with some justification have accused her of unreasonable coquetry. They raised their charming heads together and exchanged a grateful kiss full of the pleasures they had tasted. But with a rapid scrutiny of his wife's lovely face the Marquis noted the shadow on Marie's brow, and guessing at a lingering melancholy, gently asked, 'Why are you sad, my darling?'

'Poor Alphonse, into what path do you think I have led you?' she said, trembling.

'The path of happiness.'

'The path of death.'

Shuddering in horror, she leaped from the bed. The Marquis followed in astonishment, and was led by his wife to the window. With an irrepressibly frantic gesture Marie raised the curtains and pointed.

There were twenty soldiers outside on the Place. The

moon, having dispersed the mist, shed its pale light on the uniforms, the guns, the expressionless Corentin who was prowling like a jackal waiting for its prey, and the Commandant with his arms folded, motionless, his nose in the air, his lips drawn back, watchful and troubled.

'Oh, don't let's think of them, Marie! Come back here.'

'Don't laugh, Alphonse. *I* placed them there.'

'You're dreaming, aren't you?'

'No!'

They looked at each other for a moment. The Marquis guessed the whole story, and clasping her in his arms he said, 'Never mind! I love you still.'

'All is not lost then!' exclaimed Marie. And then after a pause, 'Alphonse, there is a hope,' she said.

At that moment they heard the low hoot of an owl sounding distinctly, and Francine rushed from the dressing-room.

'Pierre is here!' she said, with a joy that was almost delirious.

Chapter 32

The Marquise and Francine hastily clad Montauran in Chouan dress with the swift readiness and the surprising presence of mind that are feminine traits. When the Marquise saw her husband busy loading the arms that Francine brought, she slipped away unobtrusively with a meaning glance at the faithful Breton girl. Francine then led the Marquis into the adjoining dressing-room. There the young leader had evidence in the shape of a large number of sheets strongly knotted together of the girl's active concern that he should foil the soldiers' vigilance.

'I'll never be able to get through that,' the Marquis said, examining the narrow oval of the *oeil de boeuf* window.

A large swarthy face at this moment entirely filled the opening, and a harsh voice well-known to Francine called in an undertone, 'Hurry up, General, these Blue toads are stirring.'

'Oh, one more kiss!' said a soft trembling voice.

The Marquis, his feet groping for the ladder that led to freedom but with half his body still inside the room, felt himself clasped in a despairing embrace. He uttered an exclamation as he realized that his wife was dressed in his clothes. He tried to hold her, but she tore herself from his arms and he found himself forced to go on downwards. A fragment of cloth remained in his grasp, and the suddenly brightening moonlight showed him threads that must have come from the waistcoat he had worn the evening before.

'Halt! Company, fire!'

This command from Hulot, breaking a silence filled with menace, shattered the spell that had seemed to lie over men and place. A hail of bullets directed at the foot of the Tower from below in the valley followed the volleys from the Blues posted on the Promenade. The Republican fire was without intermission, incessant, merciless. The victims did not utter a cry. Between the volleys the silence was appalling.

Corentin, nevertheless, had heard one of the persons he had told Hulot of high above the Tower drop from the ladder, and suspected a trick.

'Not a squeak from any of those brutes!' he said to Hulot. 'Our two lovers are quite capable of keeping us happy here by some feint while they're perhaps escaping by a different way . . .'

Impatient for light on the mystery, the spy sent Galope-chopine's son to fetch torches. Corentin's thought was clear enough to Hulot, and the old soldier, listening to the noise of very heavy action before the Saint-Leonard guard-post, exclaimed, 'True, there can't be two of them.' And he rushed off to the guard-post.

'We've given him a good whiff of lead, Sir,' Beau-pied said, coming to meet him; 'but he killed Gudin and wounded two others. Oh, he was desperate! He broke through three lines of our fellows, and he would have reached the fields if it had not been for the sentry at the Saint-Leonard Gate who spitted him with his bayonet.'

At this the Commandant rushed into the guard-room, and on the camp-bed saw a blood-stained body that had just been placed there. He went up to the supposed Marquis, removed the hat that covered the face and fell into a chair.

'I was afraid of this,' he exclaimed, crossing his arms in a violent gesture; 'by God's thunder, she had kept him there too long.'

The soldiers all stood motionless. The Commandant had let fall a woman's long dark hair. The silence was broken suddenly by the noise of an armed multitude. Corentin entered the room at the head of four soldiers who on their guns crossed to form a kind of litter were carrying Montauran, his thighs and arms shattered by bullets.

The Marquis was laid on the camp-bed beside his wife. He saw her, and with a convulsive effort managed to touch her hand. The dying woman painfully turned her head, and recognized her husband. She shuddered with a shock distressing to see and murmured in an almost inaudible voice, 'A day with no morrow! ... God has heard me only too well.'

'Commandant,' said the Marquis, still holding Marie's hand, and gathering all his strength, 'I rely on you as an honourable man to announce my death to my young brother in London. Write to him that my last wish for him is that he should not bear arms against France, although I hope that he will never cease to serve the King.'

'That shall be done,' Hulot answered, grasping the dying man's hand.

'Take them over to the hospital,' cried Corentin.

Hulot took the spy by the arm, leaving the mark of his nails in the flesh, and said, 'Your job is done, so get out of here. Take a good look at Commandant Hulot's face; and make sure you never find yourself in his path again if you don't want him to sheathe his sword in your belly.' And the old soldier's hand was already on his sword-hilt.

'Well, there goes another of those honest folk that are never likely to make their fortunes,' Corentin commented when he had put the guard-post behind him.

The Marquis was still able to thank his adversary with a nod that expressed a soldier's regard for an honourable enemy.

In 1827, an old man accompanied by his wife was selling cattle at the Fougères market unremarked and unmolested, although he was the killer of more than one hundred persons; indeed, no one even remembered his nickname of Marche-à-terre. The person to whom a debt is due for valuable information about all those who have figured in this Scene watched him driving a cow, going about his business with the kind of straightforward simplicity that calls forth the observation, 'There's a fine honest fellow!'

As for Cibot, otherwise Pille-miche, we know what end he came to. It is possible that Marche-à-terre tried to help his friend escape from the guillotine in vain; and that he was there in the Place in Alençon when the riot and uproar took place which marked the famous Rifoël, Bryond and La Chanterie trial.

Fougères,
August 1827

MORE ABOUT PENGUINS, PELICANS
AND PUFFINS

For further information about books available from Penguins please write to Dept EP, Penguin Books Ltd, Harmondsworth, Middlesex UB7 0DA.

In the U.S.A.: For a complete list of books available from Penguins in the United States write to Dept DG, Penguin Books, 299 Murray Hill Parkway, East Rutherford, New Jersey 07073.

In Canada: For a complete list of books available from Penguins in Canada write to Penguin Books Canada Ltd, 2801 John Street, Markham, Ontario L3R 1B4.

In Australia: For a complete list of books available from Penguins in Australia write to the Marketing Department, Penguin Books Australia Ltd, P.O. Box 257, Ringwood, Victoria 3134.

In New Zealand: For a complete list of books available from Penguins in New Zealand write to the Marketing Department, Penguin Books (N.Z.) Ltd, P.O. Box 4019, Auckland 10.

In India: For a complete list of books available from Penguins in India write to Penguin Overseas Ltd, 706 Eros Apartments, 56 Nehru Place, New Delhi 110019.

THE PENGUIN CLASSICS

A selection